Roots of His Evil

by Emersyn Park

Root of His Evil is a companion novel to
He Loves Me, She Loves Me Not.

Other novels by Emersyn Park:

Puppet's Shadow

Secrets Maple Keeps

God gave you one mouth and two ears
so you should listen twice as much as you talk.

Prologue

You assumed my silence meant compliance, that I agreed with your twisted version of the truth. Unfortunately, you were wrong. In the shadows, I watched and waited until the perfect opportunity presented itself.

Punch after punch, kick after kick, lie after lie, I remained silent, allowing your words and actions to influence opinions, causing people to turn their backs on me. With my lips sealed shut, their judgment caused guilt to build up inside of me and made me question my self-worth. Mutual friends voiced their viewpoints on our relationship. Yet, out of respect for you and our shared past, I took the unnecessary abuse and quietly backed down from the conflict. I thought it didn't matter, and I was doing the right, respectful thing by keeping my mouth shut and locking the truth inside. Beaten by the judgment, my lips were sealed.

However, my patience has expired. Green, fuzzy mold has grown in the deep crevices of the dark, cool basement of my heart, creating a putrid smell. The silence that rings in my ears is almost deafening. I can't take it anymore. The truth crawls out of my mouth like an alien breaking from its human vessel.

Gut-wrenching, uncontrollable vomiting. Word vomit. The secrets, the lies, and the cover-ups churn in my stomach, creating acid bubbles that are fighting their way to the surface. My side of the story forces its way out. I can't stop it. I don't want to stop it anymore.

Tick tock. Tick tock.

The time is up. It's my turn. It's the *truth's* turn.

You can run, but you can't hide.

Chapter 1

Lisa - 1978

When I laid eyes on Tony Shade for the first time, I was stretched out on the college campus's front lawn. The end-of-the-semester hustle and bustle aroused every corner of the campus. Students crammed for final exams, completed the finishing touches on their final papers, and turned in unfinished assignments. A buzz of energy intoxicated every inch of the campus's square mile. While the collegiate pressure was in full swing, the Midwest weather had finally turned a corner, and no student could deny the pull to the outdoors to enjoy the warm, sunny afternoon, even with their future grades on the line. The winter had been cold and brutal with record-low temperatures so when Mother Nature decided to bless the patient residents of Iowa with sunshine, mild temperatures, and millions of signs of spring, no one could contain their appreciation.

While the sun hung high in the clear blue sky, I relaxed alone under the shade of a beautiful, blooming crabapple tree. The gorgeous pink buds exuded a gloriously fresh, sweet floral scent that announced the long-awaited arrival of spring. Hours before, a strong breeze had blown through campus and caused many of the delicate petals to abandon the safety of the tree and coat the green grass below. That was where I chose to sit, among the blush pink petals.

Birds chirped their sing-song greetings to one another on the tree branches above me. When they fluttered off to their next stop, another bloom would loosen from its bud, and I'd watch it aimlessly float down to the ground. I imagined I was trapped in a snow globe, and instead of white snowflakes, delicate pink flowers stirred all around me. As I watched random flakes slowly drift down from the branches, I breathed in a deep breath of the fresh, floral scent and savored the beauty that Mother Nature had provided. It was a slice of heaven.

From my people-watching perch, activity zoomed around me. Twenty-something men and women walked up and down the sidewalks with their bookbags draped over their shoulders. Small groups discussed summer plans, pending exams, and future celebrations. Individuals strolling alone were either rehearsing their study guides in their heads or contemplating their next task.

Indicating that he was late, a male student dressed in weather-optimistic shorts sprinted toward a building. His face wrinkled with concern as he frequently regarded his wristwatch. When he reached the top of the cement stairs that led into the building, a female student who was exiting the same building held open the door for the rushed male. The grin on her face indicated that she was pleased with her accomplishment, and she bounced down the steps, ready to celebrate the end of the semester.

Laying on a picnic blanket, absorbing the sun's rays, a man and woman listened to the Bee Gees from a bulky, black boombox. Even though I was at least twenty yards away, I could make out every word of the song, "To Love Somebody." I could only imagine how loud the music was to the couple's ears, only inches from the boombox's speakers. The young woman lay flat on her back, her face tilted to the sun, and her lover stretched out on his side facing her. From where I watched, it was unclear if he was singing the love song to her or mouthing the words, but either way, he yearned for her attention.

With the tip of his long index finger, the man slowly traced his girl-friend's curves. Beginning on the end of her nose, his finger lined her plump lips, causing a small smile to develop on her face. He leaned in and whispered something in her ear. His magic finger continued down her long neck and in between her small, apple-sized breasts. She didn't even flinch. Never losing steam, the appendage moved down to her flat stomach and circled her belly button, which was exposed after she'd pulled up her shirt so the sun would warm her flawless skin. After he finished his rotation, I noticed the man had decreased the speed of his taunting. His finger wasn't going uphill, but the intensity of its travel was increasing. Surprisingly, I noticed that my nostrils were widening to breathe in fresh air as I watched the two lovers from afar. Not only was the girlfriend experiencing the pleasure of his intimate touch, but so was I.

When his extremity reached the brim of her jean shorts, it paused, and suddenly his hand tip-toed under the denim material. Her head rolled to the side to face him, but she didn't move an inch or even squirm under his touch. As his entire hand disappeared under her shorts, moisture filled *my* lower region. While I was completely appalled by their public foreplay, I didn't want him to stop. I was invested in his teasing touches from the safety of my spot yards away and forgot about the pending exam I was supposed to be studying for. My throat became dry, and my chest rose and fell with considerable movement.

My head whipped around the rest of the yard to see if anyone else noticed them. I appeared to be the only one. Enveloped by friends, everyone else busied themselves with their immediate surroundings. There was a group of students to the right of the lovers sitting in a circle, directing their attention at one man sitting on a park bench. To the left, three friends played frisbee. They laughed as they dove for their tosses. Everyone else was oblivious to the passionate couple but me. I returned my attention to them.

With her right arm, she reached up and pulled his head down onto her wide-open mouth, kissing him hard. Their mouths mimicked their animalistic desire for each other. His hand moved in a rhythmic pattern under the denim material. Their passion for each other was undeniable, and I envied their disinhibited desire for one another. I'd never even had a boyfriend before, let alone been touched below or *above* the belt. My knowledge of sex had been obtained from juicy romance novels.

Abruptly, he broke from her kiss and removed his hand from inside her shorts. Neither she nor I were prepared for the abrupt development. She shook her head at his teasing, sat up on their shared blanket, and began to gather their belongings. The woman had made a choice—their intimacy required a more private location. The man's grin indicated that he'd won the challenge.

Even though part of me was appalled by their public display of physical intimacy, I realized that I was extremely turned on and felt teased by this man. Disappointment clouded my vision as I narrowed my eyes at the departing couple.

Needing to distract myself from my sexual unfulfillment, my attention shifted back to the group of friends sitting in a circle. One man squatted on the back side of a park bench that, thank goodness, was cemented to the ground or he would've tumbled ass-over-teakettle with the wrong distribution of his weight. His shiny, brown dress shoes were planted on the seat portion of the bench. Around the bench in the bright afternoon sun sat his dozen admirers, gazing adoringly up at him. Men and women of various cultures hung on his every word. Sometimes, they would nod in agreement or clap their hands in approval. A few times, I witnessed him throw back his head in laughter at something they'd said to him.

As I studied this group, I noticed that the man who held everyone's admiration was quite attractive and captivating. With his sandy brown hair, sparkling green eyes, and chiseled jawline, he resembled a movie star. Maybe a young Robert Redford, with his full head of wavy hair and long, dark sideburns. When he smiled, his voluptuous, pink lips surrounded a row of straight white teeth. My heart skipped a beat when, suddenly, his gaze found mine under the tree. I'd been staring at him. I quickly returned my attention to the book resting on my lap.

Geez, Lisa, you're all horned up. I smiled at my internal dialogue.

The intimate touching that I witnessed ignited my stale hormones that had been lying dormant my entire life. The way the Robert Redford look-alike held himself, his confidence, and his ease *were* attractive. I was not the only one who noticed because his circle of friends was mesmerized by his every word.

Because the group was seated too far away, I couldn't hear what they were discussing. That was for the best, I told myself because I needed to study and not be distracted by a bunch of hoodlums who didn't take college seriously. Not one of them had a book or bookbag in their immediate possession.

Maybe they're on a study break. I argued with my sad lonely self.

Part of me yearned for friends—to be accepted by any group of people. I'd always felt like I didn't belong. Maybe it was my childhood and the constant feeling that I was unwanted. Making friends did not come naturally to me. The part of me that normally won the arguments inside my brain convinced me that I was better off alone. *People are bound to disappoint you and leave you feeling unwanted and unloved.* Therefore, I avoided rejection at all costs by simply not participating.

I returned my focus to the thick book on my lap, *Psychology of Adoles-cents*, my last exam. If I aced this test, I'd secure my four-point grade point average.

Focus, Lisa.

Suddenly, the group who were gathered around the handsome, young man broke out in obnoxious laughter. Every one of them looked so happy and carefree as they let down their defenses and enjoyed an unbridled moment of happiness. I envied their spirit, wishing I could release a sliver of my pent-up anxiety. I felt so much pressure to prove myself so that no one questioned my right to be here. I wanted to make a name for myself. Prove Lisa Darling was someone special—someone who was trustworthy and honorable. I didn't have time to let down my guard and have a little fun. My reputation was at stake, and I couldn't allow anyone to stand in my way.

Let them have their afternoon party on the lawn.

I shook my head. Under this blooming crabapple tree, I was comfortable and content. Sure, it would've been great to share the floral-scented shade with a friend, but I wasn't interested in depending on anyone else for happiness. I was a loner and happy that way. I've spent too many years in the past worrying about other people's feelings. I tried to earn their love. I tried to be amiable, but like any dependable doormat, I only got stepped on and shoved to the side when I wasn't needed anymore. For too many years, I wasted youthful birthday wishes and innocent prayers trying to change people. I made excuses for how they treated me. No more. My current prayers were to thank God for helping me escape and giving me a chance to start over. I prayed for strength and courage. If I was stronger inside, I was sure that I'd never let someone use me again.

I'd worked too hard to get where I was to waste my time on a friendship or an intimate relationship that could stand in the way of my goals. I wanted to graduate at the top of my class and secure a teaching job at the school of my choice. I didn't plan on letting anyone stand in my way.

Chapter 2

Lisa - 1978

The next time I saw Tony, he strutted into the local coffee shop where I worked as a barista. The job allowed me a flexible work schedule. At five in the morning, I completed the opening tasks that included baking the food items, grounding fresh coffee for the early morning rush, and opening the doors at six for the first bunch of commuters. Until a half hour before my first-morning class, I worked. Many afternoons between classes, I'd plop down at one of the vacant tables to work on my homework, which also allowed me to jump in and help if the coffee shop was ever in a bind. It was a win-win; my two favorite things were coffee and books.

During my first year of college, over four years ago, I started working at Buzzed. Searching for a quiet place to study had been my goal that day. My roommate, who didn't believe in regularly attending her classes, used our tiny, cramped dorm room as the gathering space for her ever-growing social group. The college library was out of the question because it was known mainly for the random hookups in the periodical section on the second floor. I wanted to find a place to make my very own learning zone.

I stumbled into Buzzed during my first Midwest blizzard. I had not been prepared for the brutal wind that slapped my face and chapped my cheeks. Like anyone who has never experienced true winter, my first snowfall excited me, and I was eager to partake in outdoor activities like ice skating, sledding, and snowshoeing. I hadn't realized that by just walking down the sidewalk, my breath would catch in my throat and my nose hairs would freeze from the chill.

When I opened the door to the little coffee shop, a gust of wind grabbed hold of the door and threw it open, causing a small drift of snow to accumulate in the doorway. I pushed the door shut with all my strength. After I managed that small but mighty task, I rested my back against the door to catch my breath.

"You must be a transplant," said the woman standing behind the counter with her arms crossed over her chest. It was obvious from her sarcastic greeting and defensive body language that she wasn't thrilled by my arrival or the fact that I tracked snow in.

"Sorry about that. Do you have a broom?" My instinct was always to be a people-pleaser, but this time I also feared being tossed back into the blizzard.

"You're gonna *sweep* out the snow drift?" Before I could answer, she closed her eyes and shook her head. "Transplant. I was right," she muttered under her breath and then asked, "How about I make you a vanilla latte to warm you up?"

"That would be amazing. Thank you." As I took off my wool coat and scarf, I shook off the snow that had landed on me during my blizzard adventure and instantly felt like a child, wondering if the lady behind the counter would scold me again. I glanced up to see if she was watching me. Thankfully, her back was to me as she worked on my drink. While I listened to the coffee grinder and the espresso machines come to life, I hung my coat and scarf on the coat rack near the front door and settled in a big corner booth with a great view of the blizzard outside. Watching a raging snowfall from a safe, warm spot and trying to move against it were completely different experiences.

The snowflakes measured the size of a quarter and tumbled from the gray sky at a rapid pace. As I gazed out the floor-to-ceiling window, I noticed the road and sidewalks that I'd escaped were covered in white. My footprints, which were created only a minute ago, were no longer visible. I wasn't going anywhere for a while.

As I looked around at the quaint coffee shop, I was tickled with my discovery but hoped the absence of customers didn't correlate with the quality of the drinks. On the back wall, a beautiful hand-painted mural drew my attention. Each section of the painting contained elaborate details to make an eye-catching mural surrounded by a hodgepodge of brick. In the center of the image, the words 'Be the Change,' were painted.

At each small table, chairs of various styles and colors surrounded the mismatched table tops. The diverse furniture created a homey vibe. The differences made everything flow and created a feeling of comfort. I found my zen.

Making her way to my table was the woman who called me a transplant. Her black hair hung loose and framed her face. Even though my initial impression of her wasn't a pleasant one, she appeared harmless.

In front of me, she set down a steaming coffee cup and a saucer. The aroma of freshly ground beans permeated my nostrils. On another small plate sat a plump, warm blueberry muffin with sprinkled chunks of sugar melted on top. Both items smelled amazing, and my mouth watered.

"I'm Linda," she announced as she pulled out the chair opposite me. "I own Buzzed; therefore, I *had* to be here. I'm wondering where you're from because natives of Iowa would never leave their warm houses on a day like today. If I had to guess, I'd say this is your first blizzard."

"Yes, my first snowfall, actually. When I left my flat, I imagined frolicking in the snow like the actors do in the movies. But that *wind*. I wasn't at all prepared for that. I'm from Virginia."

"Well, Virginia, here in the Midwest we call it an apartment, not a flat, and if you're going to live here, you need to invest in a thick, sturdy pair of boots. Tennis shoes won't stop your toes from falling off. Frostbite is a real thing. And no one frolics in Iowa." She nodded toward my Nike runners that were soaked through now that the warmth of the little coffee shop had caused the layers of snow on my shoes and the bottoms of my jeans to melt.

By the end of our conversation fifteen minutes later, Linda offered me a job, and on my first day of work, she gave me my apron with 'Virginia' embroidered on it. The nickname stuck. Buzzed became my second home, and Linda was the mom I'd always wished I'd had. I was thankful for the afternoon that I stumbled into this cozy coffee shop.

Four years later, I settled into the same corner booth where I'd watched my first blizzard. Through the big picture window, the springtime sun warmed my skin without allowing the crisp wind to blow my papers around. My research, which included loose-leaf papers and several text-books, was scattered across the tabletop. I planned on finishing my final paper for my Creative Writing course that afternoon. It was my senior year of college, and I couldn't wait to hold my teaching certificate in my hand.

When the front door of the coffee shop opened, a little bell announced the entrance of a new customer. My barista ears were trained to listen for the chirp, and automatically, my eyes traveled to the door even though I wasn't working. As he effortlessly pulled open the heavy, solid glass door, TSH—tall, smoldering hunk, my nickname for an attractive man—sauntered through the opening. The afternoon sun beamed down on his sandy brown hair, causing a halo-like effect around his head. The spring breeze tousled his wavy hair, prompting his large fingers to reach up to his head and finger-comb his hair back into place. As his eyes adjusted to the indoor lighting, I watched him glance around the room. He was looking for someone. His gaze never settled on anyone for long as he moved forward in line to place his order.

I recognized him right away as the guy who had his friends hanging on his every word from that beautiful afternoon on the lawn a few days before. He was the one sitting on the top of the park bench. Maybe he was looking for someone from that group.

Even though I hated myself for thinking about him or giving this handsome stranger any of my spare time, I had to admit there was something about him that drew a person in. Even from my spot under the tree, where I couldn't hear what he was saying, some unseen force grabbed my attention. Maybe it was the confident way he carried himself, but that didn't seem enough because there were plenty of overconfident college boys on any given campus. Maybe it was the fact that his chiseled smile was mesmerizing. Maybe it was the fact he was the complete package: good-looking, charming, and engaging. I wasn't sure, but I'd be lying if I said I hadn't daydreamed about TSH, and here he was only twenty feet away from me.

Now's your chance, dared my subconscious. My subconscious was riskier than I'd ever be. It suggested outrageous dares that it knew I'd never give more than a thought to. I shook my head slightly and dismissed the taunt. Confident and daring were *not* two adjectives that described me. I'd always been more comfortable in the background, watching the action unfold around me. I would never be the one to approach someone, whether it be to befriend them or ask them out. I wasn't a leader. I was a follower and very content in my position.

I couldn't help but stare. A large section of my eager, lonely heart yearned to be embraced by someone like him, with his sculpted arm muscles ready to bust through the cotton of his shirt sleeve. I imagined his strong hands tilting my chin up so that he could plant his full, moist lips on mine. The kiss would start gentle but would grow intense as our bodies pushed against one another. His long fingers would comb through my hair and grab onto the back of my head, pressing me into him.

Wow, Lisa. I'm impressed. Didn't think you had it in you. My internal voice teased me.

From the back pocket of his jeans, his hands pulled out his wallet to pay for his order. He flipped through it, looking for the correct amount. I imagined he'd be one of those men who knew what he wanted and wouldn't be afraid to ask for it. I memorized every detail so I could replay it in my daydream later on after I completed this final paper.

Crap. Control yourself.

I didn't need this distraction. I had work to do. The type A personality of my brain tore my curious eyes off his wavy brown hair, lush lips, and boyish smile. As I closed my eyes in an attempt to change my focus, I again shook my head. None of my daydreaming would lead to any good. With my eyes pressed shut, I practiced breathing techniques to return my focus to my schoolwork.

Inhale. Exhale. Inhale. Exhale.

"Excuse me."

The deep male voice interrupted my inner dialogue and caused me to slightly jump. My eyelids cracked open in slow motion.

Holy crap. TSH.

"Sorry. I didn't mean to startle you. I noticed you looking at me, so I figured you must be Anastacia."

There he was. All of him—gorgeous, muscular, and mouth-watering—standing directly in front of me. His wavy brown hair—*that I want to run my fingers through*—sparkling green eyes—*that I want to gaze into for hours*—and big white grin—*that I want to surround with my mouth*—focused on me, sitting in a large corner booth all alone. I was too stunned to speak.

"You *are* Anastacia from the Madison Globe, right?" He held out his hand for a handshake. "I'm Anthony Shade."

My hesitation and lack of being able to form a sentence were causing his eyebrows to crease together. My silence made him uncomfortable.

Say something! Say anything!

Before by-the-book Lisa could answer, my daring subconscious spit out, "Yep. That's me, Anastacia. Sorry. I was completely engrossed in my research, and I lost track of time."

What the hell! And who the hell is Anastacia?

"Black coffee and a blueberry muffin," Linda announced as she placed his order on the edge of the counter. Her eyes scanned the room, and she noticed that 'black coffee and blueberry muffin' was standing near my table and talking to me. Her eyes widened, and a small smirk rose on her lips. Linda's sass was legendary, along with her ability to tell it like it was. I could almost imagine the lively conversation that we'd have after this encounter.

"That's my order. I'll be right back. Do you need anything?" He took back the hand that I hadn't accepted yet.

"No. I'm good, but thanks."

As he turned his back to me and walked to the counter, I frantically started to pick up my scattered papers and stack them into a pile.

What the hell did I just do?

I finger-combed my hair like I'd seen him do a minute ago and prayed that my breath wasn't too sour. After he deposited three sugar cubes in his coffee cup, he picked up his order and walked toward me. Now, his smile was aimed in my direction, and I wasn't regretting my lie about my name, at least for the time being.

When he sat down and placed his cup and plate on the table, I watched him adjust the angles of the cup and saucer. As soon as he realized I was watching him, he glanced up with a worried look on his face. "Sorry about that. I'm kind of particular about things, and I've discovered that I won't be comfortable until they're all in place. Must be some type of control issue." He laughed.

"Thanks for agreeing to meet today and not tomorrow. Thrilled doesn't begin to describe how I felt when asked to do this interview. My paper on religion in schools earned me deep respect from my theology professor, and well, now, I have your attention too. This is all part of His plan. I can feel it." He paused to take a sip of his steaming coffee, and then he flashed me one of his million-dollar smiles. I melted under his gaze. "Not only do I feel strongly that teaching religion in schools helps the students create healthy boundaries and coping skills, but it has also been proven to reduce stress and anxiety in the students and teachers."

He was uncomfortable whenever there was a lull in the conversation. If his hands weren't moving, his mouth was. Years ago, I learned that if I remained quiet, these types of people would divulge more than I wanted to know. Since I had no idea who Anastacia was, I figured my ability to keep my mouth shut would pay off. He was bursting with energy.

As he talked, his deep passion for the topic oozed from his pores. Through his excited chatter, I understood that a woman named Anastacia from the Madison Globe had scheduled an interview with him regarding his senior paper about why schools should incorporate religion into their curriculum.

Aren't you glad I said something? I wonder if the real Anastacia knows that her interviewee is a total hunk. Hubba Hubba.

Stop! Pay attention so you can ask relatable questions.

During my internal dialogue, I noticed his mouth stopped moving. He looked concerned. "Shouldn't you be taking notes or something? You aren't recording this interview, are you? Aren't you supposed to ask for my permission first?" He looked around the table and at the chairs around us to see if he could see a tape recorder hidden on the seat next to me.

I tapped my forehead with my index finger. "Steel trap." Anastacia exuded confidence. I winked at him. "Continue."

What am I doing?

He accepted my witty excuse and weak attempt to flirt, and he continued with his story and our interview. "Since I was a teenager, I've felt this invisible pull toward religion. Discovering everything about God and Heaven became an obsession for me, I guess. I didn't grow up in a religious household. In fact, when I first became interested in Him, I had to beg my father to attend church. He took me to a shrink first to confirm that I wasn't crazy." He chuckled at his childhood memory. "Even though my dad, Gus, had a heart of gold, he wasn't the smartest man. He was often influenced by the pressure below his belt, if you get my drift." He paused for a minute to make sure that I followed his joke.

I simply nodded. Even though I'd come off as witty and confident, butterflies bounced around in my stomach. Worse than butterflies, more like grasshoppers performing gymnastics on the inside of my gut. This gorgeous human was talking to me and confiding in me. I never in a million years dreamed I'd be talking to him, let alone sitting intimately in a booth in a cozy coffee shop. Okay, maybe not intimately, but still, his face was only a few feet away from me. I smelled his musky cologne.

"Anyway, religion and the lessons of the Bible have always interested me. I feel inspired by the gospel stories and how one man has influenced people for thousands of years. That control is impressive. Huge."

"Control?" Even though I wasn't an active Christian, I did believe in God, but I'd never heard anyone refer to what Jesus did as controlling, more influential.

"Yes, Jesus' leadership was powerful. If He told someone to jump off a cliff, they would've done it."

"But that isn't what He wanted. He didn't ask people to kill themselves for Him. He asked people to believe in Him, trust in Him, and tell others about Him." This was turning out to be an interesting conversation.

"No. Sorry, Anastacia, that isn't what I meant. He was persuasive like Hitler was in the 1900s. Hitler told intelligent, prominent men that Jews were poisoning society, and they all believed him. Their education and upbringing told them to know better, but power and inspiration erased their common sense and academic learning. How does one man have control over people without hard facts?" He caught himself and corrected his word choice: "I mean, power. It was His word. That is power. Words are power."

"Did you just compare Jesus to Hitler?" I was shocked. Part of me—the half below my waistline—was so attracted to him, but the other part—my brain—was appalled by what he said.

"No. No." He chuckled his little, nervous laugh and beamed that mesmerizing smile at me. "That came out wrong. Can I strike that from the record?" Abandoning his coffee cup, his thick, long fingers reached toward my hands, folded on the tabletop, as a gesture of sincerity. "Please. I'm sorry. I'm nervous. I don't know for sure what I'm saying."

"This isn't a courtroom, and I'm not a judge. I'm here to listen."

Chapter 3

Lisa - 1978

Like most young girls, I dreamed about the man who would play the role of Prince Charming in my love life–the guy to sweep me off my feet with his tender touch, the promise of a bright future, and his charismatic personality. Since horses scared the crap out of me, I had not pictured my Prince Charming dressed in a white tuxedo on the top of a white stallion because that was too impractical. No, in my dreams, he strolled into my life when I least expected a romance. He taunted and teased me until I reluctantly agreed to go out with him. When he leaned in to kiss me, I'd turn, forcing his lips to land on my cheek.

"No lip service on the first date." I'd play hard to get, and he'd wait at my beck and call until I was good and ready. I had it all planned out.

However, life doesn't always follow the rules created in my head. There was no white horse, no tuxedo, and no romantic gestures. I didn't even play hard to get.

During our fake interview, the conversation became more flirtatious. Immediately, I realized that I'd been right about his charisma. He was the whole package–a wonderful listener, an engaging storyteller, and a well-rounded man. Before that day, I'd been attracted to him physically, but after an hour of conversation with him, I became emotionally invested as well.

I wasn't prepared for a relationship. My intent that day was to prepare for my final college exams. I wasn't sure why I initially lied about who I was, and I didn't know how to take it back. I could never have predicted that one little fib would alter the course of my life, but it did.

In my quiet daydreams, I wondered how my life would've turned out if I hadn't lied about who I was that day—the day Tony mistook me for a reporter named Anastacia. If I had told the truth about my identity from the beginning and dove back into my homework, he would've moved on and waited at an empty table for the real Anastacia's arrival.

But the real Anastacia never showed up that day.

Instead, Tony and I raced hand in hand back to his nearby apartment, where we ripped each other's clothes off. The chemistry that I was feeling was mutual, and I'd never felt anything like it. It was animalistic and consuming. The daring voice in my head told me I deserved this. *Go for it.* She was pleased with the results of her dare.

A half-hour later after sprinting to his place, we were lying in his bed, trying to catch our breath. I felt so lucky and grateful for this encounter. Tony was way out of my league. I was a mousy, quiet book nerd who tried to blend in with every crowd, but I was wise enough to realize I was a fraud. As he started to trace my profile with his index finger, his home phone rang.

"Aren't you going to answer that?" I asked after the phone rang twice and he still hadn't moved.

"No. Nothing can be as important as this moment with you, Anastacia."

After five rings, his answering machine picked up, and I heard his seductive, warm voice echo from the living room. "Anthony and Monroe are busy. You know what to do."

Even his voicemail message ignited sparks inside of me. He was so confident and effortless like he didn't *actually* care if the person calling left a message because he was too busy being cool. Whenever my apartment phone rang, the ringing startled me so much that normally I jumped right out of my chair to discover who was calling me.

"Oh, hey, Anthony. It's Anastacia from the Globe. Sorry, I didn't make our appointment today. Someone rear-ended me across town, and I ended up having to get checked out at the hospital. Everything's fine. No worries, but I'd like to reschedule with you. Give me a call. You have my card." Click.

Oh my god! What are the chances? What do I do now? What the hell!

My eyes bulged out of my face, and my throat dried up. I was butt-ass naked in a strange man's bed, pretending to be someone else. And that *someone else* had just telephoned him. I had the absolute worst luck.

This is why lying is a sin!

The moment between when she announced her name and when I took a breath lasted an eternity. It reminded me of that scene in a movie when the tension becomes so thick that you can't even imagine what will happen next. My body produced an insane amount of sweat and ejected it out of my pores, causing sweat beads to slide down my forehead, shimmy down my cheeks, and land on my upper lip. Everything was in slow motion. Tony's finger had paused on the tip of my nose.

During these few seconds, my heart began beating triple time, causing my blood pressure to soar and my vision to blur. I was so hypervigilant that there was a naked man next to me with only a thin sheet separating us that the hairs on my arms stood straight up. My nostrils opened and closed, breathing in the tense, heavy air. I felt like a deer in the headlights of a car—too scared to move.

I couldn't bring myself to look at his face to witness his anger and disappointment. I was beyond terrified to discover what his reaction would be, but I did notice that his manhood had become erect again and was now throbbing under the thin, white sheet.

That's a good sign, right? At least he doesn't know your real name, so he can't hunt you down later or tell his friends about you. The voice whispered in my head. Are all daredevils optimists?

Shut up, Anastacia. My temptress subconscious earned a nickname.

Questions bounced off the walls of my brain like a silver, weighted ball in a pinball machine when it gets tossed around by the knockers.

Is he going to kick me out of his bed? Ding.

Will he toss my clothes down the flight of stairs in the apartment hallway for me to retrieve in the nude? Ding.

The most epic walk of shame in the history of hookups! Ding.

Will he sell this story to the real Anastacia to run on the front page of the paper? Ding.

Will a picture of my face be plastered around the tri-state area to be laughed at and told to young children about what type of woman to avoid becoming? Ding.

All my years of hard work to make something of myself would be thrown away for one lust-filled afternoon. Did I think that poorly of myself? Did I have no morals? Ding. Ding. Ding.

I was preparing myself for something dramatic because I deserved to be punished. I'd been so caught up in my flaming desire that I didn't even pause to consider how Tony would feel if he found out I wasn't Anastacia.

Now, I was caught red-handed. I deserved this humiliation.

In hindsight, I wanted to slap my young, naive self. Why was humiliation the only thing I'd been worried about? Tony could've been a rapist or a murderer. I could've been beaten and killed, even chopped into little pieces to only be discovered in a shallow grave years later. During my teenage years, stories of the serial killer, Ted Bundy, were told to scare young women into realizing that just because he looked like a nice guy didn't mean he was. Ted was charming and incredibly good-looking. Like

Ted, Tony was educated and well-spoken, and both men were always sur-rounded by a flock of admirers.

Where were the warning bells? Possibly. Locked deep inside me, over-powered by my lust.

But rather than listening to my common sense, my lust led me astray. I convinced myself that he saw something special in me since he could've been with any number of women, but he chose me. This hunky, charis-matic man was attracted to little old me. I needed to believe that this was a regular occurrence for him.

When my eyes finally reached his face, I didn't see surprise or disdain like I'd assumed I'd see. I recognized pure amazement like the Irish phrase suggested; *Tony's eyes were smiling.*

"Well, this is sure a pickle." As he situated himself to an upright position, his hand rubbed his five o'clock shadow. "I'm not sure quite what to say, and I'm *never* at a loss for words. I rushed to a scheduled interview with a local reporter, whom you led me to believe was you." With his free hand, palm facing upward, he gestured to me as I was still lying on my stomach, naked, under the same sheet. "Then I spilled my guts to an attentive, attractive woman who I thought was named Anastacia. In fact, when I replay our coffee shop conversation in my head, you realize that you didn't ask me any actual, detailed questions. You just allowed me to talk and talk."

Still, I didn't move. I was a wild rabbit who was humping–I mean hopping–along when suddenly a possible predator spotted me, and I froze, pretending to be invisible. Only the little tip of my nose wiggled back and forth to indicate that I was alive. Like a bunny, I didn't plan on moving again until the immediate threat of danger subsided.

"Interesting." Tony was still perplexed by the plot twist. "The Bible talks about pride and how it's a major sin. I see it now. Loud and clear. I was floating on air, basking in my success because a paper that I'd written had caught the eye of a local newspaper. I let my arrogance and pride trump my common sense." Even though he shook his head, he was still grinning from ear to ear. "This is amazing. God tested me, and I completely failed."

His words admitted that he had failed God, but he didn't seem too disappointed. The smile never left his lips. Listening to Tony rationalize what happened between us made me feel less guilty–like I had less control of the situation because God had used me to tempt Tony.

Yes, it is God's fault that I let lust control my sense of right and wrong.

His monologue with himself turned my attention back onto him. "You're Eve." He pointed at me. "And I'm Adam. Even though Eve was the one who initially sinned–which was you lying–Adam stood by her and tried to condone what she did." Suddenly, as if all the overthinking had worn him out, he plopped back down onto his pillow and threw his hands up in defeat. "And then you seduced me."

"Wait. What? I don't think so." This was my first time having sex, and I was positive that I had no idea what I was doing, let alone having the ability to seduce an educated, very attractive, smooth talker. The confidence that I'd shown at the beginning evaporated.

A hearty laugh that developed deep in his body shook the bed. That sound encouraged laughter. An awkward giggle escaped my lips, but it felt inappropriate, as though I was laughing during a horror movie instead of screaming.

"Well, now that I know you *aren't* Anastacia, I'm wondering who you are. Who is this mystery woman who hypnotized me with her charm and bewitching looks and lured me back to my apartment, where she blew my mind?"

Chapter 4

Lisa – 1978

Tony proposed to me on a hot summer night along the river in Yankton, South Dakota, where we were camping for the weekend. The end of summer was only weeks away, and I'd accepted a teaching job in Des Moines, Iowa. Both of us were struggling with what that meant for our future. When he suggested this camping trip, I'd secretly hoped that promises of a future together would be discussed.

After making hot dogs over the campfire, we strolled hand in hand along the river's shoreline. The sun would be setting soon, and we planned on laying on a picnic blanket on the beach while taking in the beautiful colors. In the meantime, we searched for flat-skipping rocks so that Tony could teach me to skip rocks—something I should've learned as a child, he claimed.

"Lisa?"

Like any good seeker, I was engrossed in my search for the perfect stone, so I didn't look up when I answered, "Yeah?"

"Lisa." He sharply addressed me again.

When I turned to understand what had upset him, I witnessed him kneeling in the sand. While I was sidetracked by my search, Tony drew a huge heart in the sand with a piece of driftwood he'd collected. On one knee, he knelt in the middle of the heart, holding a small, black velvet box. His eyes searched mine for confirmation that this was what I wanted too.

Tony didn't enjoy feeling vulnerable. He liked control and knowing all the answers so I knew that his proposal was a big step for him. Before he could even speak, I squealed, "Yes!"

As I wrapped my arms around him, Tony whispered in my ear, "I love you, doll, with all of my heart. Together forever and never to part."

The next week, we were married by the Justice of the Peace at our local courthouse. Neither of us wanted a big to-do, and I had no family to worry about disappointing. It was perfect. We were delighted.

Unfortunately, after the honeymoon phase of our marriage ended, so did the facade of my fairytale. Crazy Tony unleashed all his pent-up desires. As his devoted wife, I'd promised for better or worse, but I'd assumed that vow referred to the worst health conditions, not emotional, physical, and sexual abuse.

I had no idea what I promised.

At first, his requests didn't seem outlandish. After a long day of teaching for me and counseling at a children's home for Tony, we cuddled on the couch. Tony snapped his Bible shut and looked at me.

"Do you know what I wish you'd do?" Tony asked.

We'd only been married for a few months at the time of this conversation, and I assumed he was referring to a sexual desire he had. I'd been a virgin when I met him; he'd been my first lover. When he discovered that he was my first, he was overwhelmingly pleased. He'd assumed, since I played my Anastacia role so well, that I'd bedded many men before him. During those four months, Tony enjoyed being my guide and molding me into the wife and lover he'd dreamed of. Because Tony's sexual preferences were like his mood swings, I wasn't sure what I was going to be dealing with. I learned to adapt.

I raised an eyebrow and formed a seductive smile. "Can't wait to find out."

Even though sex was new to me, I was a quick learner, and Tony wanted nothing more than to teach me *everything*. Sometimes, he asked me to play the innocent, naive wife that I truly was only a few short months ago, and sometimes, he preferred I play the part of the dominatrix. I wasn't an expert on his mood swings, but I got better over time and switched gears accordingly.

He shifted in his seat on the couch to face me. In his lime green eyes, I observed the tenderness that I fell in love with. "Every day when I come home from work, would you greet me at the door and plant a kiss on my cheek?"

I was surprised by his simple, sweet request. I set down the novel that I was reading, gently leaned over, and kissed him on his freshly shaven cheek. "I can do that."

This show of vulnerability and tenderness was the man who had stolen my heart, the man who showed me respect and love. Even though our courtship may have been considered too short by some people, those last four months have been filled with sweet, tender moments like this one. I'd only read about true love in books, so I was beyond thrilled that it existed in real life and that I was lucky enough to be experiencing it.

"Thank you, Lisa. That simple gesture would mean the world to me." His Adam's apple protruded outward to suggest that he swallowed a large lump that had formed in his throat. "When I was a teenager, my dad married a woman that he was completely crazy about. I think I told you about their messed-up relationship and how he loved her more than he loved me."

"I remember. Your stepmother had a daughter near your age."

"Yes. Her name was Katherine, but I called her Kitty. Anyway, whenever my dad arrived home from work, his new wife would stop whatever she was doing and rush to greet him at the front door. She'd plant a kiss on his cheek and help him bring in his briefcase, coffee mug, or whatever he was carrying. She'd ask him about his day, and they'd walk with each other into the kitchen, where she'd start cooking dinner, oblivious to anyone else around them."

"What a sweet memory of your father." Tony didn't talk much about his father after his second marriage fell apart and they moved away. What I did remember was the cloud that passed over Tony's face when I inquired further about his past.

"Yeah, if I'm honest, I was a bit jealous of their relationship. They got married not too long after my mom died, and he yanked me out of a school that I'd attended my whole life. He ripped me from everything I knew so that he could start a new family with this new woman and her kid. He explained it to me like it was going to be a huge adventure for the two of us. We'd become thick as thieves. He made it sound like we were in it together and that it would be the best life ever. He convinced me that we'd be happier. Instead, he married Tammy, and we moved thousands of miles away from the only place I'd ever known so he could start a new life with a new family. He tried to replace my mother with his new wife, and, heck, he showed Kitty more attention than he did me. I think he wanted a whole new family."

"I'm sorry, honey. That must've been so hard."

The greeting and sweet kiss on the cheek were examples of one of his simple requests that took a dark turn.

A week later, between the water running and my off-key singing, I didn't hear the front door as I scrubbed the shower. Tony wasn't due home for another hour. As I finished cracking out the chorus to "Don't Go Breaking My Heart," I stood up to direct my attention to the bathroom sink when I caught a glimpse of Tony's reflection in the mirror. Not only had I not been expecting anyone, but the look on his face also made my insides flip. His thick, dark eyebrows were pressing down on the top of his eyes, which were dilated to dark black saucers, like a cat's eyes, seconds before it pounced on its prey. His expression appeared blank and unreadable, with his lips tightly pinched.

My hand automatically reached for my chest as my disloyal lips let out a little yelp of surprise. "Tony! You scared the daylights right out of me. What are you doing home so early?"

In a very monotone, robotic voice, he replied, "You didn't meet me at the front door as I asked."

After I regained my composure, I began cleaning the sink again. I answered, "Sorry about that. I wasn't expecting you for another hour, so I haven't even started on supper. How does coconut shrimp with home-made mango salsa sound?"

Before I noticed his reflection behind me move in the big bathroom mirror, he yanked down my pants and began ripping my underwear from my lower half. As I tried to turn around and defend myself, I cried out, "What are you doing?"

"Don't *ever* disobey me again, Lisa. Do. You. Hear. Me?" His words escaped his clenched jaw. With one hand, he freed himself from his pants and held me in position, with his other hand holding a large chunk of my hair.

Tears raced down my face even before I realized I was crying. My body understood what was about to happen before my mind did. He was forcing himself on me from behind, another first for me and our relationship. There was no tenderness, no kisses on my neck, or words of encouragement. This was painful and unwanted.

"Tony, you're hurting me."

My hands, which seconds before had been cleaning toothpaste splatters from the sink basin, were now grasping the sides of the counter to keep my body from breaking in half as he thrust into me so hard that each time my hips cracked when they hit the edge of the counter. Through my blurry eyes, I watched a monster's reflection in the mirror. He raped me because I had not greeted him with a peck on the cheek after his long, hard day of work. If I was able to walk after this encounter, I didn't plan on making that mistake again.

Chapter 5

Jolene - 1978

By looking at my mother, no one would've guessed what kind of immoral woman lived beneath her girl-next-door exterior. Isabella Just's natural wavy blonde hair landed about three inches past her shoulders, signaling that she was too young for a bob and that she cared enough about her appearance to keep it long. On her eyelids, she always brushed a faint layer of amber-colored eyeshadow and used a touch of mascara to accent her dark brown eyes. Lip gloss was applied even on the days we stayed home. When given a compliment, she claimed she was blessed with good genes. Her appearance screamed a natural beauty, a carefree personality, and a low-maintenance woman, but never judge a book by its cover.

Even though her outward appearance shouted, 'I'm easy-going and breezy,' she was anything but. Her mind worked nonstop, weighing every option before she arrived at a decision. Every moment she created and every word she spoke was calculated. Instinctively, she was always thinking ahead. If she had played chess, she would've been a master. I would've bet everything I owned on her ability to outsmart any opponent.

In my opinion, my mother's lies started small and were simple challenges to see what she could get away with. At first, she lied to my father about where the budgeted grocery money went after he returned home from work to find the cupboards still bare. Loud, angry words were exchanged until I finally heard soft moans of pleasure and muffled giggles from the living room downstairs.

That became a pattern in their relationship. When she was backed into a corner, she'd managed to crawl her way out with lies and sex. Sometimes, I wondered if my father didn't mind the craziness that was my mother because he got what he wanted in the end.

With time, her lies grew to match the crime. They got bigger and more bold.

From the outside, my childhood was ideal. We looked like the perfect family of four who were active members of our local church. My younger sister and I were well-mannered, above-average students who attended school clean and rested. We weren't neglected or unloved. I remember playing board games around the dinner table and camping in a tent along a nearby river. We laughed, we cried, we fought, and we forgave. We were the image of a typical family from the 1970s.

My father resembled Tom Selleck from the popular TV show, *Magnum PI*. His thick, brown mustache tickled the top of his lip, and his smoldering eyes showed his intensity. Both men were tall, but Mother said that Father was built more like a linebacker with his broad chest and thick, muscular legs. Tom's legs were slender, like a runner. Father didn't take offense. He knew he was a looker and would puff out his chest when the comparison was made.

Because my father worked in construction his whole adult life, his physique was at peak performance, and to tease our widowed, lonely neighbor lady, my father often mowed our lawn without a shirt on. My parents joked about it all the time. "I noticed Mrs. Koerner enjoyed an *extra* tall gin and tonic on her porch this afternoon." My mother teased him after he came into the house sweaty and smelling like fresh-cut grass.

After he took a large drink of ice water, a smile formed on my father's lips. "Yes, I noticed her out there. I hope she enjoyed the show."

"I think her drool was a bit thick today. Maybe you need to tone it down next weekend. You're gonna cause that poor, old woman to have a heart attack." Mother swatted the kitchen towel in Father's direction. During their good stretches, they teased each other and got along well.

Mother enjoyed running, which helped her maintain a lean, athletic figure. On Saturday mornings, she participated in local road races for the sheer joy of jogging. Eventually, through dedication and lots of practice, she started winning her age division. What began as a simple hobby to relieve stress and get in shape turned into an obsession. After each medal was earned and hung on her wall of accomplishments, she'd sign up for her next race. As the awards grew, so did her amount of time away. Rather than being gone on a Saturday morning, she started traveling farther away, making her absences longer.

No one complained. We all adjusted. First, it was donuts with Dad at the nearby gas station when Mother wasn't around to join us for breakfast. Then, when she was gone most of the day, Saturday became cartoon mornings with cold cereal followed by peanut butter toast picnic lunches on the living room floor. My sister and I fended for ourselves when the races took Mother away from home for an entire day. Father chose to sleep in until noon and then excused himself for the afternoon. He filled his thermos full of whiskey and Coke and walked down to the neighbor's house to watch 'the game.' We didn't mind. We colored. We played with our dolls and ate junk food. We enjoyed our endless freedom. We were well-behaved children and followed the rule that 'children should be seen, not heard.'

As an adult looking back on these memories, it was obvious that my parents were having problems, but adjustments were made to keep the peace. The space between them was gradual.

My mother loved to tell the story of how they originally met. "The first time I saw him, he was casually leaning on his little red convertible, smoking a pipe. He was dressed in jeans, a white shirt, and a brown corduroy jacket. When he laughed at something his friend said, his smile reached up to the twinkle in his eyes, and at that moment I had to make him mine."

"Mother, that is the corniest story ever. Are you sure you didn't see that in some movie?" My sister and I laughed because we couldn't imagine our father being that cool.

"Nope, it's a true story. Every girl at that party wanted to date him, but he didn't show any of us the time of day." She looked off into the distance, as if telling that story could bring her back in time. "I didn't see him again for six months. But when I did, he noticed me."

I never doubted that. Mother possessed a gift for getting people to do what she wanted. It was as if she could peer into their souls to see what made them tick. She could smell a weakness a mile away.

For my father, his weakness was her. He loved everything about her; thought she walked on water and could do no wrong. Even when she spit on their marriage vows, he thought he was somehow to blame. It crushed me to watch him internalize how he could make her happier so she wouldn't stray. She wasn't sneaky like a cat who hunted for mice in the dark of the night. Mother snuck around in plain sight after she received my father's blessing to 'run' off.

Chapter 6

Jolene - 1978

One Friday night in Mother's absence, Father decided that we would surprise her by being at the finish line of the race. We'd be there to congratulate her on her speed and celebrate her achievement. The rest of that evening, Ivy and I colored and decorated giant posters to hold up to encourage her during the last leg of the race. Mine read, 'We are proud of you, Mother!' and my younger sister's read, 'Kick it in, Mommy!'

"Your mom is going to love this!" Father beamed.

Mother left earlier in the day to make sure she was on time for the runner's early morning check-in. She booked a hotel to get a good night's rest before the race. Because it was only two hours away, Father assured us that we could drive there if we left bright and early on Saturday morning.

It was going to be an adventure. We packed a picnic lunch, a cooler filled with beverages, and our homemade signs. During the two-hour car ride, the three of us sang songs, all of which were Father's favorites because he claimed, "Only the classic cowboys are allowed in my car." Johnny Cash, Merle Haggard, and Kenny Rogers. I remember sitting in the middle of our Buick between my father, who smelled like Old Spice, and my little sister, who smelled like maple syrup, thinking that that was the best day of my life. I felt truly happy.

When we pulled into the small town of Hartford and located the race's finish line, I made a suggestion. "How about we each stand a block apart so that we can cheer her on for three blocks rather than standing on the same street corner? More effective, right, Father?"

Right away, my father shook his head and said, "I don't want to be split up from you two. It isn't safe."

"We'll stay on the race route. I'll take the furthest block away, dropping off Ivy on the corner of the block in between us. After Mother runs past me, I will run back to Ivy." I used my best impression of my mother trying to convince my father to do something against his better judgment.

"I don't know, Jolene..." We didn't have a lot of time to discuss this new strategy. The quickest racers were due to arrive in the next couple of minutes. We'd already missed the shotgun start.

"Please, Daddy," Ivy begged. "I bet it'll help Mommy run faster. She'll be so happy." Her wide smile spread across her tiny face as she tugged on Father's arm.

"Okay. Let's do it. Yell really, really loud. Jolene, go two blocks that way and no further. Hurry!" He gave us one final thumbs-up before jogging to the finish line.

I firmly grabbed Ivy's arm and pulled her alongside me. As soon as we reached her assigned block, I told her, "Don't go anywhere. Do you hear me? As soon as Mother runs by me, I'll come back to you. Then we will run to Daddy's block. Okay?"

She jerked her arm free. "I'm ten. I'm not a baby. I'll be fine." Then, in her whiny voice that always helped her get her way, she asked, "Can I keep the stick of chap in *my* pocket?"

If holding onto a tube of lip balm would keep Ivy planted in her assigned spot, I was more than happy to oblige. In Ivy's adolescent mind, Chapstick was kid lipstick, and possessing a tube in her pocket was a simple way to make her feel important. My kid sister was easy to please.

"Here you go, Ivy. Don't lose this stick of chap. It's the last one I have."

Ivy's grin beamed up at me. "I won't." She applied a thick layer to her lips before jamming it in her pocket.

I turned and jogged to the corner of the next block. My poster swished against my leg as it fought against the brisk movement. I hurried because the first group of men were sprinting by. It was the last leg of the race, and this was the time Mother needed our encouragement so she could muster that last bit of energy to kick it into high gear and make record time.

As I ran down the sidewalk to the end of my assigned block, I held my head high and pretended I was Mother. While the wind whipped through my hair, I could hear it whispering in my ears, encouraging me to move even faster. The adrenaline pumped through my veins. I couldn't help but smile. It felt good.

When I reached the end of my block, I raised my hands straight up as I imagined breaking through the tape that signaled the first runner to cross the finish line. I stopped and bent at my waist, trying to catch my breath. My heart was beating over time as tiny little stars clouded my vision. I was out of shape.

Then I heard her unique giggle. Only my mother could giggle near the end of a race. I grinned at her mischievous nature. I wondered if she was laughing because she saw me and thought how ridiculous I looked running a sidewalk race. Since I was still bent over taking deep breaths and trying to regulate my breathing, I was concealed by a parked car. Goosebumps suddenly pricked my spine–something that later in life I'd recognize as a premonition that I'd often received before my life was about to be shaken.

As I started to straighten up, through the cars' windows, I caught a glimpse of my mother running down the street toward my assigned block. A huge, flirtatious smile covered her face. Running by her side was a lean, fit man who tried to grab her butt as she darted out of his reach, giggling.

Quickly, I kneeled back down next to the parked car so she wouldn't see me.

"Stop it!" I heard her teasingly tell her race partner in between her heavy breathing.

"Time to...kick it in, Fuck Buddy. The sooner we... finish, the sooner... I get you naked," nudged the sweaty man, whom I instantly hated.

My stomach bubbled with nerves and anguish.

Mother's brow creased as she concentrated on finding more fuel to sprint the last leg. She stretched out her stride and steadied her breathing. There were only three blocks until the end of the race.

Oh no. Ivy!

While I was still processing what my innocent eyes were seeing, my protective instinct for my little sister rose to the surface. As my mother and her friend raced past me, crouched next to a stranger's car, I realized that I wouldn't be able to make it back to Ivy in time to shield her from this shocking turn of events, but I still wanted to try. I dropped my handmade sign next to the parked car and ran back toward Ivy. She would be standing there holding her homemade sign written in her messy handwriting, jumping up and down to earn Mother's attention.

Another block past Ivy, my father, who'd combed and trimmed his thick, dark mustache, would be standing proudly in his 'Trophy Husband' shirt, cheering on his wife of fifteen years. During the car ride over, his perma grin proved how happy he was. He was as excited about surprising his wife as we'd been.

How could I reach them both in time to save them from learning what I did? I could only pray that Mother would be too focused on finishing the race to touch, flirt, or tease her 'friend.' Surprise tears started to moisten my cheeks as I ran. If I was unable to shield Ivy from this discovery, at least I could be there to console her.

As soon as I was close enough to see Ivy, I noticed her jumping up and down like I knew she would, screaming at the top of her lungs, "Momma, go! You can do it!"

I looked toward the street where I could only see the backside of Mother, and I noticed that she had recognized Ivy's sweet high-pitched voice. Mother's friend had not slowed his pace to observe the small cheerleader. The finish line was in sight, and he stretched out his long legs and sprinted toward it.

During the ten seconds that it took me to reach Ivy, I matured an entire decade. Only I knew. Only I had witnessed their bond. Ivy had been spared, and her innocence remained intact. During those ten seconds, I quickly decided to keep my newly gained knowledge to myself, at least for the time being. Hopefully, after recognizing Ivy, Mother would ditch her friend and realize Father and I were also among the crowd.

"Did you see Momma, Jolene? She was lightning fast. I wanna be like her someday–"

"No!" I couldn't stop myself. The betrayal to our family was brutally fresh. Ivy looked at me oddly when I interrupted her, so I forced out a little smile and tousled her hair. "Ivy, be you. Don't ever change." As the oldest, protection topped my list of sisterly duties. She'd grow up soon enough, and she didn't need to know how disappointing reality could be. "Come on. Let's go find Daddy." I nudged her along. I couldn't stand to hear another word about how wonderful Mother was, how great she did, and how fast she was.

By the time we reached the finish line, a crowd of supporters was congratulating the participants for a job well done. I held Ivy's hand as we waited on the sidewalk for Father to retrieve us. It wasn't long before we spotted his beaming smile bouncing our way. By the reflection of love and pride on his face, I knew he'd been spared what I saw as well.

"She got first place in her age division and a record time. You were right, Ivy!" He picked her up and spun her around. She screamed with excitement. I was a terrible actress. I stood frozen, trying to correctly label my feelings.

When he set her down, Father looked at me. "Jolene, are you okay? You don't look so good. Kinda pale. Maybe you need some water. I saw water at a table near the finish line. I'll go grab you one."

"I'll come with you, Daddy." Ivy grabbed onto his hand and pranced alongside him.

I did feel sick. I was burning up. However, it was not from the summer sun but from anger that I was trying to bottle up because minutes before, the stability of my family had been crushed. While my brain and heart were trying to process the knowledge, my stomach reacted instantly. Bile burned in the back of my throat. I looked around for a small spot of shade and plopped down. I rested my head between my knees.

About a minute later, I felt a gentle, familiar hand on my shoulder. "Jolene, are you okay?"

It was *her*.

She was touching me. Touching me with her cheating hands. Touching me with her lies and deceit.

I shook her hand off my shoulder and mumbled that I was fine without lifting my head. I wasn't ready to deal with her. I needed to wait until my stomach wasn't doing flip-flops. Although the thought of vomiting on her fancy running shoes did make me feel slightly better.

"I got her some water. Maybe she got a little overheated." Father and Ivy returned with a cup of cold water in a clear plastic cup. "Drink this, Jo. It'll help you feel better." I accepted his gift and chugged it down immediately while hoping it would magically erase the last ten minutes of my life.

"Nice race, Isabella. The girls knew that by surprising you and cheering for you the last three blocks, you'd find a little something extra. And it worked." My father pulled Mother into a side hug. She was sweaty and still trying to catch her breath. Her cheeks were flushed from the excursion.

"Yes, that was quite the surprise." She turned to my little sister and said, "Ivy, I love your sign. It made me smile."

"Jolene, show Momma your sign. It's the bestest."

"You made a sign too, Jolene? Where is it? I didn't see you. From the way you're acting, I thought maybe you ran the race too." Mother didn't appreciate that the focus was stolen from her, and I imagined after breaking a personal record, she was even more pissed.

Before I could think of an appropriate, yet sarcastic comment, Ivy chirped in again. "She was a block before me, Momma. When you turned and you could see the finish line, that's where Jo cheered from."

My mother's eyes clouded with questions and worry. She remembered what had happened at that turn. She'd received some inappropriate encouragement from a male runner, and now she knew that her oldest daughter had witnessed it.

I lifted my head from between my knees, and with some unknown authority, I asked, "Where did your running partner go? You were neck and neck at the corner just before the finish line."

I never mentioned a man or woman. I wanted to hold the information over her head. Make her sweat. I glared at her to pressure her into responding. With that one look, she understood. She read between the lines that my stare provided her. In the little information that I offered, she understood that I watched her with another man. She didn't know how much I witnessed, but she grasped that from what I did see, I could tell he was more than her running partner. Finally, she realized that I held the power to crush her in Father's eyes or keep quiet while she got her act together. Either way, I held the power.

Father had not read between the lines. In his defense, he didn't know there were any lines to read between. "And here, we thought you earned your best time ever because we were your good luck charms." He elbowed her in a teasing way. "Glad you found a friend who shares your love for running."

Chapter 7

Lisa - 1978

Abuse doesn't always leave visible physical marks on the body. As a child, I didn't understand what emotional damage meant or looked like. When I witnessed a fight on the school playground with fists flying and words shouted, the unhappy, crying child who walked away with the purple-blue shiner was labeled the loser of the scuffle. The one hailed as the winner may have earned a few scratches on his knuckles, but clearly, the fact that he was smiling proved his victory. That was how I defined a fight–one winner and one loser.

Unfortunately, as an adult, I learned that abuse can be inflicted through words and actions without any physical bruising. Emotional abuse entails using manipulation that can penetrate right to the heart. Furthermore, in my situation, abuse didn't turn on like a light switch. The abuse that I suffered grew like a thistle on a beautiful, healthy lawn.

After purchasing his first home, a homeowner educated himself on how to maintain a beautifully manicured yard. He fertilized. He watered. He mowed and repeated the process many times. He did everything right. He was prepared, educated, and diligent. Yet, one day, a light breeze carrying a small thistle seed blew into his yard and landed among thousands of grass blades. The gardener never noticed. The thistle seed grew roots that stretched out its large arms and intertwined with the grassroots, creating a very stable and firm settlement. Following supportive weather conditions, the thistle poked its colorful flower through the thick green grass reaching its sharp fingers toward the sun. The man noticed the purple oddity in his green yard and immediately focused his efforts on removing the pesky weed. He stormed over to the sharp, prickly weed and plucked it out of the soil. He breathed a sigh of relief. It was gone. He would not let it happen again. His yard was completely green again.

But the roots were already there, lying under his feet and winding their way into another section of the lawn. It laughed at his naivety, knowing that plucking its head only caused its roots to focus their attention on growing in a different direction. Its hidden strength increased daily. When the time was right, it would sprout two purple flowers toward the sun. He couldn't see them. He didn't know. He didn't know that plucking the head would only cause the roots to grow stronger and spread. If he had, would he have removed it? Was he supposed to claim defeat at the first sign of an obstacle? There were thistles in every yard. He convinced himself that he needed to better prepare himself. He could handle the random thistle.

I understood the plight of the gardener. Thistles multiplied and festered in my marriage, but the part that I didn't grasp was that the roots were out of my control. Deep down inside my husband laid a strong, thick thistle root that had taken years to grow and become secure. If I had a crystal ball to see what the next few years would involve, I would've run, changed my name, and never looked back, but I was young and naive. I thought I could change him. I thought if I was a better wife, he wouldn't *have* to punish me. If I was everything he wanted me to be, we would live happily ever after. I'd pluck the thistle and breathe a sigh of relief, not understanding that the monster continued to grow and fester inside Tony.

While Tony and I were dating, he swooned me with an abundance of love and affection. At times, the affection was overwhelming. I never doubted for a minute that he wasn't devoted to me. He doted on me and strived to make me happy. If he did something thoughtful and I thanked him, he also sought additional confirmation that he'd pleased me.

"You like the roses, right?"

"Yes, I love them. Thank you, Tony. They're gorgeous."

"They had red and yellow bouquets too, but you always wear pink nail polish, so I figured that that must be your favorite color." He rushed through his explanation.

"You did wonderfully." I leaned over and kissed him hard on the lips to reassure him.

"Or would you prefer daisies?"

I interpreted his neediness as part of his enduring charm. He projected himself as a confident, knowledgeable man, but as my boyfriend and lover, he yearned for affirmation. After sex, he inquired if he'd pleased me. Like any female, sometimes I made sounds of pleasure to appease him, but even my moans didn't always suffice. I perceived his continuous questioning as normal, and I petted his ego. Sometimes, I moaned a little too loudly or dug my fingernails into his back to emphasize my appreciation.

Another trait that surprised me during our courtship was his jealousy. For a man who earned people's respect and attention easily, Tony was needy and unsure of himself in our relationship. He raged if I shared more than four sentences with another man. It didn't matter if the man was our waiter at the restaurant, the dentist who cleaned my teeth, or the cashier at the gas station. Every man who I encountered was scrutinized.

One night in particular was etched in my memory. We'd met his friends at a local pub for cocktails and darts. As I did every time we went out in public, I stood close to Tony, usually within arm's reach. My eyes and lips flirted with him to remind him that I was his date, not anyone else's. I did all the things he liked; however, I only had control over myself and no one else. After returning home from a night out with friends, Tony's jealousy reared its ugly head. When we walked into the apartment that he shared with a friend, he slammed the front door and began pacing the kitchen floor, slapping his hand on the counter every five seconds.

"Tony! What's going on?" I'd never witnessed him so strung out.

My question jarred him from his trance-like pacing. Suddenly, he stopped and jerked his head in my direction, as if realizing for the first time I was in the room with him.

"What did Monroe say that was so amusing?"

Monroe was his roommate, who hadn't returned from the bar yet. Most of the friends we'd been socializing with headed to get breakfast. Tony and I opted for an hour alone at his apartment.

"What are you talking about?" I said as I draped my coat over the back of the couch.

"When you were talking to Monroe at the bar, you threw your head back and laughed at something he'd said. What was it? Were you two laughing at me?" Tony asked through clenched teeth.

His line of questioning amused me, but I knew better than to laugh or smile at him. I'd never seen him so agitated.

"Of course not. Tony, I'd never laugh at you. I wasn't sure what Monroe said because the music was so loud. So, I just laughed, pretending he said something funny. I don't know what he said, but it wasn't about you." I tried to assure him that he had nothing to be concerned about.

However, I lied. I heard *and* remembered what Monroe said as the two of us were collecting another round of drinks for our group. He told me that I was out of Tony's league and that I was too good for him, and awkwardly, in response, I laughed and told him that he was ridiculous. But I would *never* tell Tony that. Monroe was one of his closest friends, and I knew that telling him would only lead him down a rabbit hole. No good would come of it, and Monroe was known for his wild tongue after drinking too much.

Tony didn't fully accept my excuse, so I attempted to affirm my love and desire for him by performing several sexual acts that I'd been refusing to do. What better way to say, 'I have eyes only for you,' than by screwing your man in three compromising positions while on top of his roommate's bed?

When we were finished, Tony rolled off of me, and I scurried to get dressed. In the heat of the moment, I thought it was exciting to sneak into Monroe's room to have sex, but afterward, I wanted nothing more than to crawl into Tony's bed and put closure on this strange evening. With an exhausted, half-dazed smile, Tony removed the condom he'd been wearing and smeared the contents onto Monroe's pillow.

"Tony, what are you doing?" I was appalled.

"Serves him right for hitting on my girl." When he was finished, he tossed the condom under Monroe's bed and gathered his clothes. He didn't bother putting them on.

"But he wasn't hitting on me, and rubbing your jizz on his pillow is more than disgusting. Monroe is going to come home soon and lay right on it."

"Exactly." To prove that was his point, he grabbed my arm before I was able to put my pants on. He pulled me out of Monroe's room and down the hall to his. He laughed while I struggled to regain my composure. I planned on letting Tony fall asleep first, and then I'd replace Monroe's pillowcase with a clean one.

While we were brushing our teeth and getting ready to go to bed, Tony grabbed Monroe's toothbrush and wiped his buttcrack with it.

My eyes widened at the completely childish and repulsive act, but Tony laughed and said, "It's what men do, so we don't stay mad at each other." He shut the bathroom light off. "Don't worry. Monroe hardly ever brushes his teeth anyway."

Later, when I tried to bring up the argument, Tony brushed off my concerns by explaining that he loved me so much that he worried about losing me. "I'm sorry, Lisa. My love for you is all-consuming, and sometimes I can't control my worry."

Before we were married, these were the types of red flags that I noticed. Most of the time, he was an easy-going people-pleaser. I had no idea that saying, 'I do' would morph my new husband into a monster.

The abuse that I suffered at the hands of my husband wasn't visible to people around me, quite similar to the sneaky acts he did to other people who defied him. No one noticed that I withdrew from conversations or tended to avoid answering questions because none of the people we met after we were married knew the 'before me.' My limited family and friends from before were stricken from my life after we were married. Because Tony listened to my childhood stories of my neglect, he banned me from contacting my parents or grandparents.

"They had a chance to love and take care of you, Lisa, and they chose not to. I will protect you from them, and you won't waste your time gaining their unneeded approval." The lack of a relationship with my parents was a raw, gaping wound, and Tony knew this because I'd shared that I felt unloved, unseen, and unappreciated by my parents. When I moved away to college, it wasn't on good terms.

Tony's reasoning filled my heart with pleasure and love. He convinced me that he had my best interests in mind. I wanted to believe him. My whole life, I'd yearned for someone to be devoted to me like Tony was. I believed that God had a hand in bringing us together. I'd been independent and driven for so many years, and it felt good to be taken care of, loved, and cherished.

I was unable to recognize that I was being abused until the first time Tony locked me in our small, empty hallway closet. I knew that sounded ridiculous, but his excuses and explanations for everything that happened somehow made sense. Self-doubt and a lack of confidence in my judgment made it easy to believe him. I thought everything he did for me was out of protection and love. He told me exactly that, and I believed him.

The closet was thirty by twenty-two inches, and I knew this because I measured it after I was released twenty-four hours later.

Chapter 8

Lisa – 1978

The first time Tony locked me in the closet, panic consumed every inch of my body. Every hair stood on end. Every muscle tightened. My jaw clenched. My heart beat double time. To keep myself from hyperventilating, I started silently counting. As I took a deep breath, I would say a number in my head.

One.

As I exhaled a deep breath, I'd say the next number.

Two.

However, when I reached six thousand and twenty-two, I lost my shit. I'd been locked in a closet for one hundred minutes and twenty-one seconds. Too long. My legs started to cramp. I pounded on the inside of the closet door, screaming his name. I needed to pee, and my stomach was growling. Where did he go?

During the next few minutes of my imprisonment, I imagined Tony unlocking the door with the little iron skeleton key and throwing his arms around me. He'd beg for my forgiveness and vow to never lose his temper again. Tears would roll out of his green eyes and land on the top of my head as he wrapped a blanket around my shivering body. We'd rationally talk about how he needed professional help to better understand his anger. As a couple, we'd be better off after experiencing this horrible situation.

I clung to my imagination with every fiber of my being until my legs ached from standing for hours in one position.

I dropped to the hard, cold floor and pulled my knees up to my chest for warmth and protection. Plus, there wasn't enough room to straighten them. As my mind raced, questions bounced around in my head like a bee after its hive was shaken.

How long is he going to lock me in here?

Is he insane? Am I?

How long can I go without food and water?

My bladder is full. I need to pee.

Where is he?

As the thoughts raced and jumbled my brain, my ears picked up the sound of a door closing.

Is he going somewhere, or is he just getting home?

Without being able to see anything, I relied on my ears to interpret what was happening outside of my confinement.

Inhale. *Six thousand and twenty-three.*

Exhale. *Six thousand and twenty-four.*

Trying to control my breathing would help me to concentrate. Getting upset wouldn't help my situation. Hyperventilating had the opposite effect.

You're smart, Lisa. Think. Relax. Calm down.

Inhale. *Six thousand and twenty-five*

Exhale. *Six thousand and twenty-six.*

Breathing techniques were effective; however, it was hard to remember when your emotions reacted as if you were riding a ten-speed bike down a steep hill and your brakes weren't working.

As soon as my chest pushed the large puffs of air out of my nostrils and smaller amounts were sucked in, I detected random noises occurring around our house. Another door slammed closed, and then I heard footsteps. It had to be Tony. The heels of his dress shoes always clicked and echoed down the hallway, announcing his return. The footsteps grew louder as I squeezed my eyes shut and concentrated on what I was hearing.

Is he humming? Yes, it sounded like the chorus to "Cold as Ice" by Foreigner.

How could he be humming a little tune after he locked me in a closet bare-ass naked? Did I marry a monster?

I lost control of my breathing again as a river of angry tears moistened my chest and knees.

Six thousand and twenty-seven.

Panic filled my chest because I knew the answer to that brutal, harsh question, and it broke my heart. Following every one of his abusive acts, I waited for an apology over breakfast the next morning. One never came. I couldn't understand how he didn't feel any guilt after causing me such pain.

By locking me in the closet, Tony orchestrated a mind game. He couldn't physically touch me, but he still caused me pain. He controlled me without laying a finger on me. Normally, forcing himself on me was my punishment for whatever Tony decided I'd done wrong. Then he blamed me for requiring him to punish me like that, but I recognized the lust and excitement in his eyes. He enjoyed hearing me beg for him to stop. Just last week, he pressed down harder between my thighs when I tried to squeeze them shut. My tears proved to him that he hurt me, and the power to hurt me fueled him.

After my tears dried up, my dry, bloodshot eyes stared straight up at the ceiling above our bed. The alarm next to his side of the bed alerted him that it was time to start his day. Out of routine, his arm rose, he pushed the button back down, and he rolled over and dropped his heavy arm across me.

"Good morning, darling. I appreciate you lying here next to me in your birthday suit, but your man requires a hearty breakfast to start his day." He grabbed my left breast and pinched it to earn my attention. "Time to get up, sleepy head."

"Ouch!" His grasp squeezed so hard that a yelp escaped my lips before I could filter my response.

There was no apology. He let go, sprung out of bed, and headed to the shower, humming another song. Tears pricked the corners of my eyes, and I rose tenderly out of bed and wrapped my cotton robe around my sore body. The only bruises that Tony left were located on the parts of me never seen by anyone else.

Why do I stay? The logical section of my brain knew I wasn't safe. I should run. I recognized that I needed to get out, but the fear of the unknown, the fear of Tony, and the fear of admitting failure kept me from refusing to listen to my good sense. And of course, Tony had seen to it that I had nowhere to go and no one to turn to for help. All of our friends were people that Tony allowed into our lives. No one would believe me even if I were brave enough to ask for help.

As I crouched on the hard, cold floor of the closet, I silently cried for my innocence. I cried for all the flags that were there, but I chose not to see them. Tears ran down my cheeks and landed on my bare knees.

Tony had shoved me into this closet right after we had sex because he claimed that I'd faked my orgasm. When he finished, he rolled to his side, and in between his heavy breathing, he asked me, "Was that as good for you as it was for me?"

Honestly, I moaned and yelped because I knew that it would help Tony reach his climax quickly. So, I seductively smiled at him and answered, "Yes."

"Liar!" It wasn't a teasing accusation. He was enraged. He yanked me out of bed and dragged me to the closet.

As he shoved me in, he yelled, "You will stay in here until you're sorry for lying to me." He slammed the door shut, and I heard a key turn the lock.

"Tony? Don't leave me in here. I'm naked. Tony?" I heard him stomping out of the room.

***

I was married to a monster, but I didn't see a way out. I didn't think anyone would believe me if I told them what Tony was like behind closed doors. I could hardly believe it myself. This charming, good-looking, successful pastor locked up his wife in a closet if she glanced at another man incorrectly.

Another true story.

I pleaded with him, "He only said hello to me. I thought it would be rude if I didn't acknowledge him."

For a split second, he considered my explanation. "True, but I saw your lust-filled eyes. In those ten seconds, you were imagining him naked. I could tell. Now, get it in the closet, Lisa. Don't make me shove you in there."

The closet had become my time-out location for things I didn't understand that I did wrong.

"I'm sorry, Tony. I never meant to give him more than five seconds of my time." I knew from experience that it was better for the length of my punishment to agree with what he accused me of rather than argue.

"Get. In." He held the closet door open for me, and I tentatively stepped in. I was still dressed in my Sunday best—a cream, silk blouse and navy pencil skirt with short-heeled, black pumps. It was not the most comfortable choice for my imprisonment, but it was much better than the first time when I was locked in the closet naked for twenty-four hours.

I heard the key click the lock into place.

The closet belonged to the guest bedroom, which was located at the back of the house. Tony kept a bed in this room, but it was bare, and the mattress on it appeared stained. I referred to this room as my punishment room. If Tony could hold his temper long enough, he would drag me down here, where the walls were extra insulated and my screams would not be heard.

It was in this room, in the small closet, that I brainstormed how to survive. Sure, initially my brainstorming involved escaping Tony and our marriage, but after trying to run away from him, I learned quite quickly that when he found me, my punishment would not be worth the trial. So, my thoughts focused on survival. I needed to be better, to follow the rules, and to be one step ahead of Tony to avoid any punishment.

Chapter 9

Jolene - 1980

Learning that my picture-perfect family of four was a fraud at the age of twelve skyrocketed my maturity. Even though my mouth stayed shut, I kept a watchful eye on my mother's comings and goings, and I was pretty sure she knew that I was watching her. She treated our mother-daughter relationship with kid gloves, praying that I wouldn't share her secret. As far as I could tell, my mother stopped fooling around with her running partner. She even took a break from road races, claiming that her knee was bothering her. Happiness and relief flooded through my father, who was glad to have a partner in parenting and taking care of the house again. Mother's 'training' had taken up a lot of her free time.

The only one in our house who noticed or at least voiced her awareness of the change in me was Ivy.

"Jo, why won't you play with me anymore? You never smile or giggle like you used to. If this is what happens when a girl becomes a teenager, then count me out." She threw up her hands in defeat and dramatically fell onto her bed. We were in our shared bedroom, and I was propped up on some pillows on my bed reading *Flowers in the Attic*, which made my life seem like a fairytale in comparison.

"Don't be a diva, Ivy. This *is* what happens when you grow up. Your interests change." My words tumbled out with more of an edge than I'd intended, so I added, "I'll draw with you if you want."

Always the excitable and eager of the Just sisters, Ivy leaped from her bed and ran to the desk to retrieve a few blank pieces of paper. She snatched her box of ninety-four crayons and raced to my side. No one in our house could resist Ivy with her big, innocent eyes and puppy-dog playfulness. She handed me a sharpened pencil and a piece of paper.

My giggle echoed in our room as she climbed up next to me and snuggled in. "Will you draw our house and backyard, Jo? You do it so well. Put a carnival in the backyard this time."

"I'll do that, and you can color it in."

During a child's early teenage years, there are usually several years of rebellion and know-it-all phases. For a girl, this age often occurs at the age of thirteen or fourteen. Sassy comments like 'duh,' 'I know,' and 'whatever' naturally form on the lips. When deep into the throes of teenage sass, eye rolls often emphasize the comments.

However, in my case, I skipped that awkward age where I struggled to find my voice and assert my independence. Because in one eye-opening weekend, my fairytale life had been ripped from my grasp and spit back in my face. The woman I admired, looked up to, and loved unconditionally lied to our family for years. Anyone from the outside can judge this situation and claim that I overreacted; however, my heart and mind would beg to differ. I wanted with my entire being to forget what I'd witnessed that day on the side of the road. Everything would've been easier if I believed that the infidelity only affected the relationship between my mother and father, but that wasn't true. She'd been living a double life that I later discovered had lasted my entire childhood.

As soon as I discovered the fraud, I recalled days when I wondered if she'd been telling the truth when she had to work late, when she drove to the grocery store for an item she forgot, or when she punished me after I'd been caught eating strawberries from the neighbor's garden.

"Jolene, we taught you better than that. Mr. Brady trusted you when he showed you where he planted the strawberries. You told him that you found bunnies eating them. You lied. It was you who ate them all. Lying is a sin, and you'll be punished."

I questioned every childhood memory.

I couldn't understand how she could lie to my father every weekend and not feel any guilt for her deception. The only reason that it ended was that I caught her.

Lying is a sin, Mother. You'll be punished.

For months afterward, I wouldn't speak to her. Not one word. While at the dinner table, if I wanted the salt and pepper shaker but they were near her, I'd go without. If I needed her signature on a school document, I left it on the kitchen table with a note on it. I would not waste any words on her. I avoided all interaction because I feared my filter would tear into her and I wouldn't be able to stop. I wanted to scream and yell. Call her every bad name that I knew, but I was only twelve, and up until that pivotal weekend, I respected my parents and somewhat feared disappointing them. I was still sorting out how to handle the anger that raged inside.

Loyalty to my father also weighed heavily on my heart. The knowledge that his wife was unfaithful to him would break him. I believed that if I could make Mother change, I'd save my father from unnecessary heartache.

Fortunately for me, I never had to figure it out. One year later, fate did it for me.

During the summer months, my father often popped home for lunch to check on Ivy and me, and each time, Ivy begged to play 'restaurant.' We both enjoyed the one-on-one time with Father that these special summertime lunch dates provided us. After she grabbed her pen and pad of paper and instructed me to tie Mother's apron around her waist, she'd approach Father as he relaxed at our small round kitchen table reading the newspaper.

"Good afternoon, kind chap." Ivy tested out an English accent that she'd picked up while watching Mary Poppins.

Ivy's playfulness produced a big grin on Father's face. He folded up the paper and set it on his lap. "Well, bee's knees! This is a treat."

"What do you have a hankering for?" Ivy asked. From my station in the back of the kitchen as the cook and dishwasher, I laughed.

"Is that an English word?"

Keeping with her character, Ivy didn't crack a smile but replied firmly, "Chap, the kitchen closes in an hour. I hope you've made your selection."

"Well, in fact, I have, Miss. I'd like a peanut butter and dill pickle sandwich, apple slices, and a side of chips."

"Excellent choice. It's our chef's specialty. What can I bring you to wet your whistle?"

Since Ivy set the tone for the English setting, I cut the sandwiches into finger lengths for the three of us. We sat down and enjoyed each other's company for the next forty-five minutes before Father was due back to work. Father used this token of time to discuss worldly topics.

"I read in the paper that this Sunday the CNN station will be broadcasting its first twenty-four hours of news. News from around the world. What do you, young ladies, think of that?"

Ivy voiced her opinion, "Boring."

However, I wanted to hear what Father thought, so I engaged him. "What kind of news is so urgent that it can't wait until the next day's newspaper?"

After he finished chewing, he answered, "Good question, Jo. I guess it would have to be news that needs immediate attention, like a world war. How terrifying would it be to read about a nuclear bomb exploding the next day? If there'd been a warning to seek shelter, many lives would've been saved."

Ivy did not finish chewing before she piped in with her English accent. "That is what a blower is for."

"A blower?" An amused expression formed on Father's lips. "What the heck is a blower? We might need to get one in case of an emergency." Father had finished his lunch, so he relaxed in his chair to soak up the conversation with his children.

"It's a telephone, silly, and no more talking unless you use an English accent." Even though Ivy was the fun one in the family, her opinion was often voiced loudly. I think we all caved to it because it was hard not to. Ivy had an infectious influence.

When the 'blower' rang, I was washing the dishes while Ivy hauled out the trash to the bin. Father jumped up to answer it.

The majority of the time, he answered the phone, 'Just residence,' but if he was feeling silly, he'd crack a little joke with our family name. 'Hello. It's Just me.' or 'Just here... to answer your call.' But on that afternoon, Ivy set the English tone, so he picked up the receiver and said, "What can I do for ya, Chap?" I looked over in his direction, and we grinned at one another. I shook my head and returned to washing the dishes.

"Yes, this is Walter. Oh, hey, Justin, I didn't recognize your voice at first."

Justin was Father's A.A. sponsor and good friend. A few years ago, Father had stopped drinking. As the children of the home, Ivy and I were only supplied with simple answers. "Father quit drinking. There won't be any more yelling and screaming. Mommy and Daddy fought too much." Ivy and I hadn't been phased by the news. Our parents' loud fights were part of our lives. When you grow up in a household of yellers, you assume that was how people communicated. We had no idea that it wasn't healthy.

We also had no idea that many of the arguments were because of Father's drinking.

When Father paused to listen to Justin's reasoning for his phone call, his smile vanished and his skin turned an ash color. Justin wasn't delivering good news.

"How do you know?" He finally interjected. "How long?" He paused to hear the answer to his questions before blurting out his new one. "This happened today?"

As I set the last plate on the drying rack, I turned to watch my father bury his free hand in his face. Whatever news he'd been told wasn't good. My next thought was, *Where is Ivy?*

My eyes searched the backyard, where she carried the bag of trash to the bin. She deposited the bag and was skipping back toward the house. I tossed the washcloth in the sink and decided to give Father some privacy. I'd distracted Ivy by asking her to play hopscotch on the sidewalk. As the back screen door slapped shut behind me, I turned around to see my father slam the receiver down and collapse onto a kitchen chair. I wanted to comfort him, but I also strongly felt a desire to shield Ivy.

For ten minutes, we played hopscotch, pick-up sticks, and hangman with chalk on our front sidewalk. Normally, Father had an hour for his lunch break, and that time was about to end. I decided to check on him while Ivy was distracted by a ladybug.

As I peeked through the screen door, Father was still sitting in the same kitchen chair with his back facing me. He was on the phone again. Instead of fear in his questions, this time I recognized his anger.

"How could you do this *again*?" He paused to hear the other person's response. "So, he's your running *friend*? I thought Kelly was a girl's name." He sarcastically laughed at whatever the response was. "Seems like a pretty good friend. He's married too, Isabella, but I bet you knew that." He shook his head and combed his fingers through his hair.

The last thing he said before he slammed the receiver down broke my heart. "I quit drinking because you made me believe that my drinking was the reason you cheated on me. I can't believe you tricked me again. And all this time, I thought you loved me. You made me believe I was the problem."

Chapter 10

Lisa - 1980

"Lisa, you need to start dressing better. You look like a slob." As I scrubbed bits of meatloaf off our dinner dishes over our kitchen sink, I looked down at my outfit. I was wearing my usual: a pair of khaki dress pants and a V-neck shirt. No cover girl, but better than some. "People need to take notice of you, respect you. Old man Docker pants don't cut it."

I knew where this conversation was coming from. We watched two hours of the first twenty-four-hour news broadcast on CNN created by Ted Turner, someone whom Tony admired and respected because Ted never sugar-coated his opinion. The living room television was still broadcasting the show, and according to its proclamation, the news would never stop. As of June 1, 1980, we could tune into this station for twenty-four hours, seven days a week, to hear the latest news. Not only had Tony been enamored by Ted Turner, but his attention was also drawn to Lois Hart, the female anchor, who was dressed in a cream suit jacket with a turquoise blouse underneath. Blondes were Tony's type.

"I don't think by wearing certain clothes people will respect me, honey. Respect needs to be earned." I heard the words leave my mouth before I was able to edit them, so I added in a sweeter, gentler tone, "Plus, I don't want people to notice me. You're the star, Tony. I prefer being in the background supporting you." Over my shoulder from my position in front of the kitchen sink, I flashed him a big smile. I was petting his ego and prayed my words hadn't triggered him.

"It isn't about what *you* want. You and I have an image to maintain in this community. Your unkempt presentation reflects poorly on me and appears to others like you don't care." He cleared his throat to signal that his decision had been made. "You'll start wearing women's business suits. Women will envy you and want to be like you, while men will envision loosening the buttons of your tight suit jacket to see what will spill out."

The direction that this conversation was going traveled downhill very quickly. I couldn't help myself from speaking up. "I don't think that's a good idea, Tony. I don't want people picturing me naked."

As I washed the last supper dish and placed it carefully in the drying rack, two strong hands circled my neck. The sudden, threatening action would've made me physically jump if I'd been able to, but I couldn't move. While Tony's hands squeezed my fragile neck, I struggled to breathe.

His warm breath puffed near my earlobe. "Do not question me. I'm tired of you challenging my authority. You're just a whore doing my bidding. Do you understand? You are *nothing* without me."

Fat, heavy tears poured out of my eyes, betraying my mind. Showing Tony any sign of weakness would only lead to pain. Physical or sexual pain. I was angry with my mouth for betraying me when I knew no good would come of it. I was angry with my body's natural response to being harmed because it should know better. I willed myself not to panic. I tried to nod, but his hands tightened around my neck so much that I couldn't move my head up and down even slightly. My dishwater-pruned hands clawed at his strong grip, trying to free myself. Just as my eyes started fluttering and my body began slumping from lack of oxygen, he released me, and I crumbled to the kitchen floor.

His penny loafer soccer-kicked my rib cage as I struggled to suck air into my lungs. "Now, finish cleaning up this mess, so I can deliver your punishment in our bedroom."

My arms circled my chest and rib cage as I inhaled the fresh air that my body craved. I scrambled to stand so that I could finish the dishes because my punishment would last longer if I 'dilly-dallied.' Tony didn't appreciate waiting. My vision blurred as the oxygen entered my body, and tears streamed down my face. With Tony standing behind me, watching my every move, I struggled to regain my composure and put away the dishes as I dried them.

How did I get here? But more importantly, how will I ever get out?

***

The next morning, when I crawled out of bed and stumbled into our adjoining bathroom, I discovered a new emerald green suit hanging in the doorway. On the cheap wire hangers, it hung as a reminder of Tony's latest demand. I caught my reflection in the mirror, and I realized that the bruise growing over my ribs matched the color of my new green suit. Because my husband was cunning and devious, I wondered if he'd planned that.

In a hot shower, I tried to scrub the sin and guilt from my bruised skin. After I gently towel-dried my body, I dressed in the clothing my husband bought for me. Because my body ached in places normally only reached by bath water, I struggled to put one foot in front of the other as I walked down the stairs and into the kitchen in my heavily starched blazer and matching pencil skirt. Every step caused a sharp pain to shoot up and down my spine.

After I swallowed the small bit of pride that I still had, I entered the kitchen to greet my husband, only to be met with an empty room. He wasn't waiting for me like I'd expected him to be. No note lay on the counter explaining his absence like a normal husband would leave his wife if he left the house for the day. I assumed he went into the church office early.

Relief consumed my body, and ironically, I crumbled to the floor near where I lay last night when he kicked me. I tossed and turned the entire night after Tony served the punishment he deemed appropriate. Not only did every inch of my body ache, but emotionally I was also exhausted. I kicked off my high-heeled shoes and curled up into a ball on the kitchen floor.

I was a college-educated woman who knew right from wrong. I'd never been abused as a child, so I didn't perceive Tony's actions as acceptable or normal. However, it didn't happen overnight. I didn't go to bed one night with Prince Charming and wake up the next day married to the Devil. Were there plenty of warning signs indicating borderline abuse? Sometimes yes. At first, when he crossed the line, he'd been remorseful and sorry, but gradually those moments dissolved, and I questioned what a terrible wife I was. I started to believe that I deserved the punishments that he delivered. Even though I *knew* what Tony was doing to me was wrong, I believed that I deserved it. My educated brain knew better, but my tender heart, which only wanted to be loved and accepted, believed that I deserved it. I reasoned with myself and made ridiculous excuses for my husband's behavior.

He loves me.

He's only doing what he thinks is right.

The Bible tells me to obey my husband, so I should be held accountable for my actions when I don't.

He's a well-known and respected pastor, so obviously he would never do anything to truly cause me harm.

I believed that people were created good, and sometimes evil spread into their souls like weeds. As the groundskeeper of your garden—your soul—you had to constantly manage what grows in your garden. Because of pollination, gardens can come into contact with weeds that will want to populate and consume your land. As the groundskeeper, your job was to manage and maintain order by plucking the dandelions and fertilizing the good soil when needed.

For our souls, that means each weed—temptation—will cross our path. It's undeniable. However, as long as you pick yourself up after you stray and recognize your failure, you'll manage to have a beautiful, healthy garden. Unfortunately, often when we're led astray, we forget that our souls need to be regularly attended to, or weeds will prosper.

I believed Tony was born good, but after each weed entered his garden, he questioned the morals that he'd been taught. He found beauty in the weeds and let them multiply until he couldn't see right from wrong. To him, a dandelion looked like a miniature sunflower. He couldn't tell the difference anymore. Even though he knew better, Tony flourished by pushing the boundaries and felt victorious by deceiving people.

The definition of a weed is a plant growing where it is not wanted. To me, the evil that I saw in Tony was a weed, but I wondered if Tony saw them as flowers.

Chapter 11

Lisa - 1982

For the first few years of our marriage, Tony worked as a counselor at a behavioral facility. The children responded to him, his attention, and his encouragement. He helped them reach their potential. Because his employer was thrilled with his results, Tony earned the title of Employee of the Year, and his achievements were recognized in the local paper. His influence and good deeds were being rewarded. Yet Tony felt his calling was in a church.

"A gorilla could do my job. Molding young minds is rewarding, but it's *too* easy. Those little brats are sponges and so eager to please someone. They crave attention, and my influence is just what the doctor ordered." Over dinner one night, Tony tried to explain why he wasn't fulfilled at his job.

I swallowed my food before speaking because his biggest pet peeve was when people talked with food in their mouths. I learned that lesson early in my marriage. While we were dining at a nice restaurant, Tony asked me a random question, and I answered before swallowing my bite of steak. When we returned home, he used a thick piece of duct tape to tape my mouth shut, claiming that this punishment fit the crime. During the next twenty-four hours, he forced me to watch him eat and drink with my mouth taped shut. Lesson learned.

"I'm sorry, honey. I don't understand. You're amazing at your job. Everyone thinks so. Why aren't you happy?" I didn't intend to sound anything but curious; however, my questions offended him. I could read it on his face. He wasn't pleased by my comments and inquiry.

"Oh, Lisa, you're so much more simple-minded than I am. You're easily pleased. I need to feel challenged. I want to reach a larger audience. I want to make a bigger difference."

I heard the dig at me but chose to ignore it like I always did. "According to your boss, you're exceeding expectations. The kids adore you, and you're making an enormous difference in their lives. I'm proud of you, honey. That's all."

"Thank you, Lisa, but I already applied for a couple of pastoral positions in the area, so we will see if God knows better than you."

"Tony, that isn't what I meant."

"Sure," he replied condescendingly.

The following week, Tony started as an assistant pastor at a small local church. He enjoyed every minute of it, from preparing sermons to counseling the members of the church. He was living his dream. When he was giving his sermon, people hung on his every word. It was magical. If I hadn't seen it myself, I wouldn't have believed it. Even though it wasn't an appropriate response, the congregation often clapped at the end of his sermon. After a day in the office, he returned home with stories of how he helped turn someone's life around or helped someone better understand their faith. He was living his best life.

It was during those moments that my heart ached. My 'simple mind' couldn't fathom that this gifted pastor was also the man whose tongue caused my heart to crack in pain, the man who kicked me in places that were covered by my clothing, and the man who locked me in a closet when he didn't want to hear my questions. It didn't make sense that this amazing preacher was also the man who raped his wife, taped her mouth shut, and treated her worse than an animal.

When Tony announced that he received a head pastoral call to lead a small-town congregation in Iowa, immediately my gut instinct told me that our next church placement would somehow be even worse than what I was experiencing now. I wasn't sure if the feeling was a psychic premonition or a reaction to the excitement that I recognized in his dark eyes and behind his calculating smile. Maybe it was all of the above. No matter where the dread in my heart came from, I knew it wasn't good.

Tony explained that the following weekend he would be visiting the church in Normal alone. He'd attend church council meetings, coordinate the transfer, and meet lots of the congregation–his sheep. I welcomed the weekend off from pretending to be his perfect, obedient housewife. The only time Tony ever left me home alone was when he went to work, so I enjoyed the *entire* sixty hours. I did everything that he'd never allow me to do. In my pajamas, I watched old black-and-white movies, read three romance novels, and ate junk food–popcorn for breakfast and cereal for supper. I was a teenager disobeying her strict parents. It was glorious.

I don't know why I didn't run.

When he returned home, I heard the front door slam shut. Before I could rush to the front door to greet him, I heard him shout my name. His tone wasn't angry–thank goodness–but excited, which was almost as bad.

"Lisa? Where are you?"

I'd been preparing supper in the kitchen, which was located at the back of the house. I loved the view of our backyard from the small kitchen window above the sink. The back of our property line bordered Sinclair's yard. They had three beautiful young girls whom I fondly watched from my window. Each daughter looked like a mini version of their mother. Each one had long, dark, wavy brown hair and big, doe-brown eyes. For hours, they would play on their swingset, taking turns on the two swings and going down the slide. I marveled at how the older two doted on the youngest, always making sure she was happy and safe.

I yearned for children of my own, but because I feared for their safety, I'd never allow myself to become pregnant. I was married to a monster disguised as a good-looking, small-town pastor. No one knew the real Tony, and if I tried to tell them the truth, no one would believe me. He was a master manipulator and an accomplished actor. Sometimes, when he was laying on the charm, I even questioned myself and my memories from the night before, when he'd awaken me from my sleep to force himself on me. I'd almost choked when I awoke to his erect penis in my mouth.

So, that afternoon, as I watched the neighbor girls playing duck-duck-goose in their yard and Tony slammed the front door, the premonition that things were about to get worse almost tore my heart into two. I couldn't imagine how my life could get worse.

As I towel-dried my hands and reluctantly turned my attention to my husband as he stomped his way to the kitchen, I heard him again calling out to me. "Lisa, I have some wonderful news. There you are."

I rushed to his side, the ever-loyal and dutiful wife, and rose on my tip-toes to kiss his cheek as he'd instructed me to do whenever he returned home.

As he set down his traveling bag and his briefcase on the kitchen floor, he explained to me that he had put a down payment on a house.

"But I haven't even seen it." When I imagined his trip, I thought it would be all business, and in a few weeks, we'd visit Normal together to look at homes. We'd discuss the possibilities and make plans together, like a married couple.

"Why do *you* need to see it?"

"I'm your wife. I'll be the one making it into a home for us." I was slightly hurt that my opinion mattered so little to him. Would I ever learn?

He didn't even pretend to care that my feelings were hurt as he thumbed through the mail that had arrived while he was away. "I hired a decorator. You don't know the first thing about decorating. Obviously," he said as he gestured toward our modest but tasteful living room.

After that weekend, I recognized a shift in my husband. Crazy Tony appeared more and more, and the man who captivated my heart was all but a distant memory. Before the announcement of his new call, I enjoyed a few nights a week with the man who I fell in love with years ago. We'd watch a program together or sit on the back deck and discuss religion and education. During those sacred moments, I was always careful to not completely let my guard down because I learned that the second I did, he would unleash the crazy.

His demands weren't as surprising to me as they'd been at first. The things he asked me to do in the bedroom were still completely absurd and would be socially unacceptable to ninety-nine percent of women, but they didn't make my eyes pop out of my head or my throat dry up in distaste like they once did. Like most people in an abusive situation, I learned to compartmentalize my feelings and reactions to his sadistic requests. Since I was an avid reader who enjoyed escaping from my life with a good book, I often imagined that I was a character in one of my books instead of performing sexual circus acts for my sick and twisted husband.

However, it seemed that the stress of his new placement caused Crazy Tony to surface more often. Of course, in public, he was still the same charming, polite, and approachable pastor, but the second the front door lock clicked into place and the blinds were drawn shut, my husband morphed into Crazy Tony.

During our drive to Iowa, my stomach twisted in knots. I still couldn't shake the gut feeling that this move would be catastrophic. Maybe it was the change that I noticed in Tony's dilated eyes. Maybe it was the way he was so secretive about our new home. Maybe it was because I felt like a rat being used in a lab experiment. Something major was about to happen, and I was helpless to stop it.

Chapter 12

Lisa - 1982

I jarred awake to the feeling of being suffocated. In my dream, I'd been walking on a remote path through a densely wooded area when suddenly, from behind, a stranger jumped out of the trees and wrapped a plastic bag over my head. What an awful feeling.

When my eyes sprang open, I sat upright in my seat and gasped for air.

Tony's sadistic laugh echoed inside the walls of our car. "You should see your face. It's all blotchy and red."

"What happened?" Something startled me awake. I wiped drool from the side of my mouth. I looked in front of the car to see if he'd run over something.

"Nothing. Relax. I plugged your nose, so you couldn't breathe. I was trying to wake you up, and it worked." With his left arm on the wheel, he slugged my arm like a frat boy with the hand that had been restricting my air. His sense of humor was sadistic. "We're here."

I readjusted my cheap sunglasses to squint out the car window at my surroundings. As the sun hung in its late afternoon position, its rays sprinkled on the corn fields, making it appear as if the rows and rows of corn were made of gold. Perfectly aligned, parallel rows of corn glistened along the road. Straight ahead, the roofs of several short, stout buildings peeked on the horizon.

When we reached the end of the dusty, abandoned highway, our four-door sedan slowed, and I read the 'Welcome to Normal' sign at the entrance to the town. In small print under the welcome read a message: 'This is God's Country, so don't drive like you are going through Hell.' *Interesting and ominous.* It felt like a warning that the two distinctly different places co-existed in the same small town. I understood what that was like.

"This is it." Tony turned off the car's air conditioner, rolled down his window, and put his arm out the window.

The fresh country air flowed through the open window, and the sound of a ringing bell resonated inside the walls of our car. On the top of a tall building in the middle of the small town hung an old stone bell rocking back and forth, alerting the town that the six o'clock hour had arrived. Historically, the sound signaled significant periods of the day–time to wake up or time to eat either lunch or supper. I wondered if the bell ringing ever signaled a warning of something bad–a destructive tornado, a severe thunderstorm, or an evil man.

Starting at the southern tip of town, our car idled down the town's Main Street. Each of the three bars that lined the first block didn't contain any windows to showcase their patrons. One bar displayed its patriotic pride by using an American flag to cover the large exterior window. I guessed that this bar was the local VFW or American Legion. The handmade sign taped to the bottom of the window read, 'First cold beer is on the house for all Veterans.'

The next space contained another local establishment that served alcohol because a cracked Pabst Blue Ribbon beer sign hung above the dark, black door. Next to the north side of the building was a weak attempt at an outdoor patio with mismatched outdoor furniture and a small fire pit. The final bar, which was twice the size of the other two standing on the opposite side of the street, was named Rusty Nail. It appeared to be the most successful, nicest, and most well-kept bar with an actual lighted sign that read, 'Rusty Nail, must be 21.' I noticed a couple of men in business suits walking toward the bar's entrance. To my surprise, the men paused just before entering the bar and waved as we drove by. Tentatively, I waved back.

The next block contained a gravel parking lot and a few abandoned buildings. No forms of life were detected.

On the following block, several residents stood on the sidewalk surrounding a small post office. Most of them held their mail in their hands and were perhaps discussing the weekly weather forecast or how it affected their corn crops, which I read from the local newspapers that Tony brought home after his initial trip to Iowa, was taken very seriously in this area. But even though each cluster of people appeared to be engrossed in their conversation, they all turned to wave as we drove by.

Did they know we were coming? Their greeting appeared rehearsed or orchestrated. Again, I waved back. I looked at Tony, and he didn't appear phased.

Right next to the post office rested a gorgeous, old brick building. A beautiful wooden sign that hung on the outside of the building read 'Normal's Library.' At the top of the library steps, a gray-haired woman quickly turned to wave at us and just as quickly returned her attention to closing and locking the library's door.

On the left-hand side of the street, a locally owned grocery possessed the majority of the block. A man dressed in a long white apron over his dress clothes swept the sidewalk in front of the store and paused his housekeeping chore to raise his arm as we drove past.

What is going on?

As we crossed the small intersection, I read the big black stencil lettering, *Cafe*, on the large picture window. The open sign was turned off. It appeared tidy and welcoming, with red and white checkered curtains visible from the outside. A homemade sign leaned up against the glass said, 'Home of the famous Bet-Your-Ass BLT!'

"You will *never* step foot into that restaurant. Do you hear me?" Tony's demand startled me from my casual observation of our new hometown. I glanced at him and responded with a quick nod. I wasn't sure where that had come from, but I wasn't about to argue without knowing if it was worth it. It did strike me as odd since he didn't tell me I couldn't go into any of the bars, but maybe he figured I wouldn't anyway.

When we reached the end of the business section of Main Street, small, low-income homes claimed their residency. Most of the dwellings needed fresh paint and a little TLC. Front porches sagged, siding hung loose, and broken windows were common. Shoeless children shouted at each other as they ran freely from yard to yard. Neglected dogs barked at their owners. Discarded bikes and broken-down cars riddled the lawns. Under the mess, the grass was yellow and not maintained. If the lawns were mowed, the grass clippings were scattered on the sidewalk and in the street. It was obvious that the upkeep and repairs to these homes totaled more than the household incomes could manage.

After Tony turned left down a side road, the houses became more well-kept and loved. Only a few blocks away from the main drag, the income level of the tenants increased exponentially. We entered the side of the town where 'the other half lived.' Freshly mowed lawns, crisp white picket fences, and blooming flowers decorated these properties. No bikes, cars, or grass clippings rested on the green yards. The cars in the driveways—and not parked on the front lawn—were newer models that were washed and polished. Everything appeared perfect but almost staged.

A large, two-story house came into view. The value and grand style of the home made it stand out among its modest, middle-class neighbors that layered the edge of the town. Guarded by a black iron gate, the lawn was perfectly manicured and resembled more of a turf football field. Because this home was two stories tall, it loomed over the rest of the block with its black roof held up by tall, black pillars. A red brick chimney shot out from the top of the home. As we got closer, I squinted into the open drapes but didn't see any occupants.

Just as I noted that there wasn't a car in the long driveway that led to the back of the house, Tony pulled our car into the home's driveway. *I don't understand.* We couldn't afford this home on his pastoral salary, and I hadn't found a teaching job yet. In my profession, it was hard to transfer after a school year had already begun. I didn't understand. *Are we visiting a new friend of Tony's before we get to our house?*

"We're home," Tony announced as he shifted our car into park.

Even though normally I remained unemotional, I was surprised when a small, sharp intake of breath escaped from my lips after I heard his announcement. Unable to contain my surprise, I felt like a kid at Christmas time, staring at a wrapped gift and wondering what was inside. As I whipped my attention toward my husband, I imagined ripping away his skin like wrapping paper. The old Tony—the one I fell in love with—would've pranked me into thinking that the most expensive home in the town was ours, but the Tony that I married wasn't much of a jokester. I was confused.

"Is this a joke?" I asked.

Tony heard my tiny squeal of excitement. My confused reaction was what he wanted, and it thrilled him to be proven right.

After he turned off the engine, he readjusted his position behind the wheel to face me. He often reminded me, "You should always face your audience so they can visualize the sincerity of your words. Your tone of voice and body language are more important than your words. People will remember how you made them feel before they remember word-for-word what you said." If only he could comprehend his own advice.

In his expression, I recognized a wicked sparkle. Something more lay beneath his expression than he wanted me to know. I silently prayed that he hadn't stolen money from our previous congregation to finance this fancy new home. The lengths that he would go to achieve his goals were endless because he viewed obstacles as challenges that he would knock down and seize, even if the obstacles were living, breathing people. A shiver ran up my spine.

"Lisa, things are going to be very different here in Normal. You'll follow every rule that I set without question. Do you understand me?"

As an obedient pawn in his game, I moved my head up and down.

How can it get any worse? Patterns in my marriage should've taught me to never wonder because my life was about to nose-dive into the shallow end of a swimming pool.

Chapter 13

Lisa - 1982

In hindsight, being locked in a closet for a whole day without food, water, or a toilet would be a walk in the park compared to the nightmares that unfolded in our new hometown of Normal. My agreement to obey Tony's every rule of our new residency didn't seem ridiculous or out of character based on what my life had become. After years of abuse suffered at the hands of my husband, my naivety still surprised me. Before the nightmare fully became exposed to me, I glanced up at our new home and was intoxicated by its beauty and all the possibilities.

After we exited the car, Tony's excited chatter filled my ears as he led me to the front entrance. I wasn't sure if his excitement was based on the fact that he kept it all a secret from me or his eagerness to start a new adventure.

"Many of the very influential members of our new church have taken the liberty of preparing our new home for our arrival."

People *did* know we were driving into town at six o'clock. I knew it. Tony probably orchestrated our arrival by the minute so that the church bell would chime as we rode through town. Every move was calculated, and the depth of his influence always amazed me.

"They inform me that we have everything we need." Then he looked pointedly at me when he added, "We *are* grateful, Lisa."

"Of course," I answered obediently. I stood at the door to a palace that he claimed was ours. I *was* grateful yet a bit apprehensive.

When we were packing to move, I didn't understand why we left our possessions behind. From the mismatched furniture to our dinner dishes, Tony instructed me that I wasn't to pack any of it. Tony only packed his best suit. We donated everything else. Like a snake, we discarded our old, battered skin, grew a new, thicker one, and slithered away.

As Tony pulled open the heavy, black front door, I continued to be impressed with the grandeur of the home's interior. In the tall, open foyer above our heads hung a beautiful crystal chandelier casting rainbows of light onto white walls and the black and white checkerboard tile at our feet. It was mesmerizing. On the left side of the entryway, a beautiful, fully furnished sitting room was located. A formal floral couch built for two occupants faced two perfectly coordinating armchairs. Further into the room was a beautiful white stone fireplace where I imagined lighting a fire and enjoying its smokey scent.

Tony interrupted my daydreaming with his explanations. "The formal sitting room will be used to greet guests before welcoming them into the rest of our home. After you answer the door, you will invite them to wait in this room for me." My awe of the home diminished as I listened to Tony's new house rules. Tony's explanation and tour of our new home sounded like I was a newly hired servant and not his wife, his partner.

"That is my private office. Do not enter unless I invite you to do so."

Tony pointed to the right side of the foyer. That would be the room where he studied the Bible and created his jaw-dropping sermons. Even I could admit that he was a fabulous preacher. People hung on his every word, sucking up what he told them every Sunday. They saw him as God's speaker. Everyone recognized his passion and enthusiasm for his job and assumed it was because God had chosen him and blessed him. However, I knew the truth. As a lector, Tony manipulated the words he said and used each one to his advantage. He was a cult leader, but due to the infamous

Jonestown mass suicide orchestrated by their leader, Jim Jones, Tony was careful. Even though the massacre happened a few years before, the horrific details were fresh in people's minds. No one could make sense of the tragedy. I knew my husband, and he understood his power, a lot like Jim Jones. I didn't know what his plan was for it, but he was power-hungry. He thrived on control.

While Tony rambled on and on about the rules of his study, the top of the stairs grabbed my attention. Straight ahead above the entryway, a harsh, black iron railing enclosed the second level of the home. Like a cage at the zoo, the railing guarded the beast who slept on the upper level. The spindles were razor-sharp and screamed danger.

Under the grand catwalk and fifteen feet into the house, a beautiful black liquor cabinet with a glass top sat. Tony instructed that after I promptly answered our door to any visitor, I should always offer him a cocktail.

"Never offer a woman a drink from this bar unless she is accompanied by a man and he approves of her drinking. A woman should never drink unless she's in the presence of a man. That goes for you too, Lisa. It would look improper if the pastor's wife couldn't hold her liquor. One drink is social; two drinks release the stress of the day; and three drinks lower your morals. I will not have my wife become a spectacle at any social function." He raised an eyebrow to signal the importance of his words. "This week, you'll learn how to make some signature cocktails. I'll make you a list."

In college, if a superior—a professor—gave any detailed instructions, I relied heavily on my pen and paper. I didn't believe that my brain was capable of remembering every detail, so I scribbled detailed notes regarding all assignments. I always had a pen and paper handy in my purse for random thoughts I didn't want to forget. Years later, my college self would be impressed with my current memory recall, because my brain managed to remember *every* instruction Tony assigned me. Perhaps the difference in my memory capacity was the fear of punishment. My life depended on my memory.

My gut instinct begged my legs to run, but my eyes didn't see the bright flashing neon warning sign of the pending disaster. There was no siren piercing my eardrums. No tangible evidence alerted my common sense. The optimistic side of me yearned for this new home, new church, and new town to be a fresh beginning for us. A chance to be a normal husband and wife. No more cruel, demeaning insults, because those didn't belong inside a home as fancy as this one. As my eyes absorbed every detail of our new home, I prayed that these walls would come to know nothing but happiness from now on. I just needed to try harder to please Tony.

Chapter 14

Lisa - 1982

On the first morning that I woke up in our new home, a pounding headache threatened to ruin my day. I'd tossed and turned the whole night, begging for a few quality hours of sleep without reprieve. Tony's side of the bed was empty and hardly looked like it had been slept in. His half of the sheet and blanket lay smooth and stretched up to his pillow, which didn't contain one wrinkle to indicate where his head would've been lying. I knew that making the bed and fluffing his pillow was a morning ritual that he insisted I adopt as well. Tony liked everything 'just so,' and it was easier to oblige him than rock the boat.

While I tended to be a light sleeper because my head contained worries and stress, Tony never moved a muscle and snored like a freight train. Blessed with the ability to ignore his surroundings, Tony slept like a rock. Nothing caused him to worry, or at least enough for him to lose any sleep. I envied his sleeping ability. After his motionless slumber, he bounded out of bed to conquer his day. I, however, would've loved to pull the covers over my head and sleep for days, but lazy, nonproductive days weren't allowed in the Shade household.

Reluctantly, I crawled out of our new king-sized bed, shuffled my way into our attached master bathroom, and searched for some much-needed aspirin. I prayed that whoever stocked our home with such a magnificent, fancy poster bed didn't forget the simple toiletry necessities. I was in luck.

I found an unopened bottle of aspirin in the medicine cabinet behind the big mirror, scooped up a handful of water, and swallowed the two pills, hoping for a quick turnaround. It was our first day in our new home, and even though my initial gut instinct about the move to Normal had been filled with dread and worry, I couldn't help but be excited to explore my new surroundings. I was human, after all, and our new home was elegant and impressive. Something out of a magazine. I felt like a fraud. A curious and giddy fraud.

My bare feet made suction noises as I padded across the white tile floor. How was I going to keep this place clean? Everything was crisp white. As I descended the grand staircase, I shook my head at the luxuriousness. I traced my fingers along the black railing of the staircase. It felt cool to the touch. In the morning light, the railing didn't seem as ominous. I looked like a princess in this magnificent castle, but only I knew that inside I was a scared, abused woman.

If I had family or close friends, I would've loved to show off our fancy new home and invite everyone over for a memorable Thanksgiving feast. In my dream, Tony would've set the festive, cozy mood by building a small fire in the sitting room and welcoming our guests into our home. With the help of a local restaurant, I would've created an enormous spread of food that would be displayed in our formal dining room. A beautiful, mouth-watering thirty-pound turkey would be the centerpiece, surrounded by the traditional sides: mashed potatoes, green bean casserole, dried cranberries, homemade stuffing, and several cold salads. It was picturesque. The fictitious image in my head mirrored the happy family in the Norman Rockwell picture, which was also not real.

I rolled my eyes. I knew better than to dream about things that would never come true. Tony wasn't the type of husband to serve an expensive meal to a bunch of strangers; he'd alienated me from the few friends I did have and refused to meet my parents after I confessed some secrets about my painful childhood. He'd spend that kind of money if he saw it somehow as an investment in himself and his desires. Two of the things that initially attracted me to him–his ambition and his confidence–now made me fear and despise the man.

On the last step of the stairs, I slipped my 'mask' on. A fake smile rose on the corners of my lips as I removed my fingertips from the railing. I straightened my back and fluffed my bedhead.

"Tony? Tony-darling, are you down here?" I called out to find the true master of this home, but only my voice echoed through the hallways. I traced my fingertips along everything–a wall, a piece of furniture, the kitchen counter–as if I were verifying that it was all real. Even though Tony referred to it as our home, I felt like a guest. Nothing was familiar, and everything appeared brand new.

I didn't find Tony anywhere on the first floor–the living room, his study, the formal dining room, or the kitchen–but I did notice that the coffee pot was turned on, and the aroma of the fresh coffee beckoned me closer.

After I found a coffee cup in the fully stocked kitchen cupboards, I poured myself a cup and decided to explore. I pulled open the kitchen drawers to discover freshly washed silverware along with oven mitts and several pots and pans. Everything was neatly organized and ripped right out of a JCPenney's catalog. We had everything we'd ever need, as long as I could find it.

As I took stock of the room, I realized why Tony had insisted that we leave everything behind but a few clothes and toiletries. None of our belongings from the hand-me-down couch to the scratched kitchen table would've been suitable in our new home. Normal was a fresh start. Originally, I felt like a fugitive running off into the night when Tony instructed me to leave my unread stack of books, my household plants, my favorite coffee mug that said 'favorite teacher,' and my collection of vinyl records. The stack of books was already pre-approved by my husband, and the peace lily plant had been given as a going-away gift from the church members. I didn't understand why we couldn't bring them with us.

"We don't have room for every trivial thing that you've collected, Lisa." Tony dismissed my questioning.

Even though I knew I should be grateful to whoever purchased and unpacked our household essentials, I couldn't help but feel a bit violated. This person chose the style of the cutlery we would use, the color of the dishes I would serve our meals on, and then chose where each item would be stored. I'd always feel like a stranger in my own home. An instinctive chill ran up and down my spine.

In the formal dining room, a rich mahogany table rested in the center, surrounded by ten plum-colored padded chairs. In the shine of the table-top, I saw my reflection. It was a bit distorted, but it was me.

Ten chairs? I don't even have one friend to invite to dinner.

The space screamed elegance. Not my taste at all, but then again, as Tony liked to remind me, I had no taste. I shrugged. In my ideal home, this stuffy, formal room wouldn't be used much. In my dream, a big, round table would host family dinners and late-night board games. No need for coasters; water rings showed love and use. I grew up with very little, so wedding china and formal furniture that needed to be covered before usage seemed pointless.

Growing up in a trailer park on the edge of town, my parents didn't have disposable income. What little money they did earn was spent on bills and food. The bare nicotine-stained walls of our home were made of plywood boards and stood no more than an inch thick. Our kitchen was an arm-length away from the one worn-out sofa in the living room.

"Your parents probably thought Spam was an acceptable form of meat." Tony laughed at his slam regarding my childhood. I failed to mention to him that my mother might've been a drunk, but she could create amazing, tasty meals using very few ingredients, even Spam.

Above the shiny, polished table hung another enormous crystal chandelier. I'd never been in a house with one huge crystal chandelier, let alone two. The clear glass reflected the sunlight shining into the room and separated the white lights into a spectrum of colors that brightened up the plain, white walls. Even though I was impressed by the cascade of colors, I understood that whoever created such a beautiful light never took a second to imagine how hard all those little pieces would be to clean.

From my quick look into Tony's study, I noticed the bookshelves were stocked with a collection of books that I knew nothing about. Waiting to be used, an impressive, large wooden desk sat on the opposite side of the shelving. As I strolled by that room, I diverted my gaze. Tony's warning about the room rang in my ears.

In the living room, the fireplace beckoned me. I sat down on the stiff, floral couch and again felt like I was visiting someone else's home. I sipped my coffee and told myself to relax.

"It's only the first day. It'll get easier." Sometimes talking to myself helped to calm my nerves, and other times it made me realize how alone I truly was.

As I tilted my head back and closed my eyes, I remembered that day on the college campus lawn, studying and wishing I had a man to love, someone to call my own, someone, *anyone* who wanted to touch me down there so badly he did it in public. If only I knew then what I know now. I would've told my innocent virgin self, "Self, sex isn't the same as love, and you're better off alone. I've seen your future. Run. Learn to run like the wind."

None of these liberating thoughts would help me.

I forced myself up from the couch to continue exploring. One of my domestic responsibilities would be cooking and baking, so I returned to the kitchen. To familiarize myself with its contents, I opened every cupboard door and pulled open every drawer. I wanted to understand the organization, so then it would be easier for me to find the tools I needed. As I lifted my coffee cup to my lips and let the steam warm my face, I glanced around the kitchen.

"Silverware next to the sink. Glasses above the silverware. Both essentials are used the most often; therefore, they are washed and dried more often. Convenient to put away. Check." I smiled when I added the word 'check'. It was a word my mom used while grocery shopping. I remembered sitting very uncomfortably at the bottom of the shopping cart. She'd place the grocery items on top of me.

"What's next, Sugar?" She asked me because I insisted on holding the grocery list. I wanted to help.

"Bread."

Mom hated grocery shopping. She claimed she could survive on cereal and whiskey, but my father informed her otherwise. In a rather commanding voice, he shouted that she was a poor excuse for a wife and a mother. Then he threw forty dollars in cash at her and sent us out the door.

She detested this chore, but I enjoyed every second. During our solo trips to the local Piggly Wiggly, it was just the two of us, and that meant Mom would be sober for at least one more hour of the day. My mom loved me, but her alcoholism defined her, and she wasn't strong enough to stop on her own.

She threw a loaf of bread in the cart, landing at my feet when she said, "Check. Next?"

I pretended to look down at the grocery list and used my most confident voice. "Hershey's Bar."

She laughed, and before I was given fair warning, she started running and pushing the cart at full speed, barreling down the aisle. I squealed with delight. She jarred to a stop and said, "Check." She threw the candy bar into my lap and winked. "Next?"

Memories of my childhood never led to anything positive. Instead, it caused the crack in my heart to grow even wider. I pressed my eyelids tightly shut to reset my thinking. I leaned against the wall opposite the kitchen sink to memorize where everything was. After I walked around the room, slamming each drawer and door shut, I ended up at the wall with the refrigerator. When I pulled open the door, I wasn't surprised to find it fully stocked. Most of the items were normal essentials–milk, eggs, butter, cream, fresh vegetables, and an assortment of condiments–along with Tony's favorite dessert, lemon meringue pie.

As I pushed the refrigerator door shut, I opened the final tall cupboard door that was hidden when the fridge door was open. The cupboard door's size compared to a bedroom door. A little large for a broom closet, but then again, everything in this house screamed 'grand.' Maybe I'd discover a shiny new Kirby vacuum that would make my household chore of keeping our home spotless even easier. The TV commercials guaranteed my satisfaction or my money back. Or even better, what if there was a self-propelled broom stored in this little cupboard and I could fly away on it? I giggled at my unrealistic thoughts.

Being a witch would be the answer to my prayers!

Growing up, my favorite TV show was *Bewitched*. Samantha Stephens married an imperfect mortal and tried to fit in as the normal suburban housewife, except she often used her powers when she was in a jam. I twitched my nose back and forth, trying to conjure up a spell to open the cupboard door.

My efforts were futile.

I tugged open the door and peered into the opening. My snickering caught in my throat. There was a secret room behind the kitchen. It wasn't a closet. I discovered a hidden parlor jerked right out of the 1930s. In the center of the room rested a large red velvet couch with a high, stiff back. The arms were generously padded and reached the floor like a tiger about to pounce. Three gold armchairs were positioned opposite the roomy couch, and one large oval glass coffee table sat in the middle of the arrangement.

Thick-lined, dark-colored wallpaper lined the walls. Because the lighting was so poor, I couldn't tell if the walls were a dark burgundy, dried blood color, or gray. The walls were windowless, so three tall floor lamps cast the only light in the room and gave it a mysterious, scary vibe.

Tentatively, I tiptoed a few steps into the room.

"Oh!" My hand flew to my chest, and a tiny shriek escaped my lips as I caught a glimpse of a woman staring at me from the opposite side of the room. Her hazel eyes widened at the same time that mine did, and she dropped her hand from her chest. It wasn't a stranger. It was my reflection in the large mirror that hung the length of the wall just above the bar area. In the reflection, you could see every corner of this mysterious room.

What is this room?

Surely, Tony had no idea it was here. What a discovery I'd made. I wondered what he'd say.

Maybe I should let him discover it for himself; otherwise, he would think I'd overstepped my position. As my brain tried to catch up with my pounding heart, experience taught me that somehow I'd be punished for finding it. Best to appear clueless. Vowing to avoid closet time or any form of punishment, I decided to keep my mouth shut.

Before I disturbed anything, I slowly backed out of the strange room and quietly closed the door behind me.

Chapter 15

Lisa - 1982

I t's hard to believe what an emotional robot my marriage to Tony transformed me into. From the outside, everyone saw a polite, friendly, devoted wife to a thriving, successful pastor. I was the Stepford wife with perfectly styled hair and French tip nails in starched, coordinating business suits. I threw my head back and laughed at his corny jokes. I spoke only when spoken to, and I was never seen in public without having my face painted on, without my hair sprayed in place, and never without my wedding ring. We lived in a gorgeous, white, two-story house with a two-stall attached garage and immaculately manicured lawn. Not a thing was out of place. Every black shutter was hung with a fresh coat of paint.

I never found a teaching job after we moved to Normal. My rehearsed response was, "We moved after the school year had already started, so I'll see what's available next school year after we've adjusted to our new home." But in truth, it had been a topic that I didn't bring up again after my last concern.

I'd been anxious about finding a job. We couldn't afford this magnificent home on a pastoral salary, so nightly I scoured the local newspaper looking for possibilities. Tony brushed off concern for my employment.

"I could apply to be a substitute teacher."

"You don't need to work outside of the home. I like you waiting at my beck and call." As we relaxed next to each other in the formal sitting room, he was reading a black hardcover book that had no embossed title on the cover or spine. Strange.

"But Tony, we can't afford this gigantic, elegant house on your salary alone. I want to help. Maybe I could work at the library until school starts up next fall."

He slammed the book shut, which made me slightly jump. I avoided conversations that would cause us to argue.

"I'm finished with this discussion." He snatched the newspaper from my hands and ripped it into pieces. For dramatic closure, he stood up on top of the shredded mess. "You will no longer seek any employment outside of the home. You will become a full-time housewife, and I'll hear no more about this drama. Do you understand me?"

His eyes. The eyes are said to be the window to a person's soul. Tony's eyes were completely black. Hollow. Empty.

***

When we moved to Normal, Tony changed. The moments that allowed me a glimpse into the man I fell in love with years ago disappeared. He was a monster before we moved there, but Normal fertilized the monster inside of him. Normal appeared to be a typical small town with friendly neighbors, strict values, and active community members. Harmless. But after peeling back a few layers like an onion, the monsters reeked, and the odor stained everything it contacted. It was those monsters who crowned Tony the ringmaster.

The stress of our move and Tony's new congregation became a major trigger for his odd sexual desires. Weekly, he created new fantasies that we fulfilled in our home. More often than not, the following day my body would be tender and sore, but not wanting to complain for fear that my weakness would be read as displeasure, I kept my mouth shut. I feared Tony would interpret my complaint as a reason to escalate his fantasies. Over the years, I learned a lot about avoidance and triggers. Sometimes I pushed my luck. It was self-destructive, and I was miserable. But eventually, I learned to keep my opinions and questions to myself. From an outsider's perspective, I appeared complacent or stoic, but in honesty, I was simply trying to survive.

Since Tony had mandated that he would not allow me to work outside of the home, household chores became my priority when Tony was working. Daily, I scrubbed the kitchen floor on my hands and knees. Our silver always had a beautiful shine to it. Because our windows were streak-free from my constant cleaning, birds often crashed into them, seeking a passageway through our home. Since my marriage was toxic, the only thing I could control was my reactions to him and the appearances of myself and our home. I prided myself in keeping our home neat and tidy, while Tony made sure my image mirrored his idea of perfection.

One afternoon, while my focus was on tackling our laundry, I discovered a red book of matches in Tony's pants pocket. Black words embossed on the cover read 'Rusty Nail.' Normal was a very small town, so everyone knew that Rusty Nail was a strip club that was often the location of many illegal activities. The women of the congregation whispered about that bar while we were setting up for a funeral last week.

One of the perks of being a pastor's wife was the automatic invitations from the women of the church to participate in activities like Bible studies, church committees, lunches, fundraising events, and, of course, what I fondly referred to as the ACGM—After Church Gossip Mill. As the pastor's wife, I was accepted into their friend group without much effort. In the far corners of the narthex, the group gathered each Sunday after the service. Each one of these five women was married to a man who served on the church council. While the men discussed church politics, the women, who liked to bake as much as they liked to gossip, discussed the *real* news.

"Margie from the clinic told me that Dr. Opland found crabs in Ernie's eyebrows. That'll teach him to sit in the sniffer's row." A native of Chicago, Susan always led with the juiciest gossip and never beat around the bush. With her sparkling blue eyes and teased, sandy blonde hair, Susan's big smile seized up the bottom half of her face and put everyone at ease. People wanted Susan as their friend because she was loyal, honest, and would do anything for them. She was the first person to make me feel welcome in Normal.

Her blunt and visual comment caused Karen to giggle and cover her mouth with her hand. As soon as she recovered, she added, "Denise's cousin's husband said he watched the mayor from Sioux Center walk into the Rusty Nail last week. A bunch of suits sat in the back of the bar, pretending not to be interested in the naked women."

My ears grew hot listening to these women talk about scandalous behavior.

Tony insisted that husbands visited strip clubs to seek other women's attention because their wives wouldn't perform anything more than vanilla sex. The sex that I had with Tony was anything but vanilla, more like a swirl of chocolate, vanilla, and strawberry topped with colorful sprinkles, a cherry, and a pound of chocolate syrup. Discovering the matchbook in Tony's pocket didn't make sense to me. Whatever Tony asked of me sexually, I did. Often, I did not have a choice which only meant that Tony's visit to the local strip club was trouble.

Chapter 16

Lisa – 1982

Many things occurred during my marriage to Tony that I regret, obviously, but preventing myself from getting pregnant was not one of them. Ever since I was a young girl, I dreamed of becoming a mother to a busload of kids who ran around my feet, causing me grief and gray hair, while I silently loved every minute of it. However, in my dreams, I hadn't been married to a monster. Tony's outward appearance resembled the classy gentleman from my dreams. However, what lay beneath this exterior was much scarier than any nightmare could've prepared me for.

I could never willingly bring a child into this world with Tony as their father. Period.

I noticed how his gaze lingered longer than appropriate on teenage girls, and I heard his flirtatious comments to the girls in the church's youth group when no one but me was around. I never wanted to worry about a child under our roof. If we had a girl, I feared incest. If we had a boy, I feared that my son would be raised to believe that his father's way of thinking was acceptable.

Finally, after a scare had awakened my fear, I scheduled an appointment with a doctor in a nearby town. The doctor was not a member of our church, and I prayed that he wouldn't ask too many questions about why a married woman wanted birth control.

"If I were a mechanic, this is when I'd slam the hood of the car down and tell you that your engine looks good and all the parts are running properly." Dr. Opland wheeled his stool away from my exposed vagina and removed his gloves. Dr. Opland was a good-looking man with a gentle, kind bedside manner. With his car joke, he intended to calm my nerves and make me feel at ease, so I awarded him a small, courteous smile. It was all I could do, considering the circumstances. As I struggled to push my butt up the table with my feet still in the stirrups, a small squeak was created when my bare butt rubbed on the hard plastic examination table.

No! I did not fart. God, I hope he knows that wasn't a fart.

"Thank you, Jenny. That'll be all for now." As he tossed his latex gloves into the garbage, Dr. Opland dismissed his nurse so that we could have a private consultation. This was what I'd counted on. The fewer ears in the room, the more comfortable I'd be considering what I wanted to discuss.

When the door clicked behind Nurse Jenny, Dr. Opland and I both cleared our throats and started to talk at the same time.

"Mrs. Shade – "

"Dr. Opland – "

"Sorry." He chuckled. "You go first."

"I wanted... I wondered... I'd like to talk to you about birth control."

"Oh, I see."

"The problem is... I need... I don't..." The words that I wanted to say wouldn't form on my tongue. My brain wouldn't cooperate with my mouth. I inhaled a deep breath and pushed the words out. "I don't want my husband to know." As soon as the words rushed out, I wanted to reach out, grab them, and shove them back in where they'd be safe and trapped. Big, large tears pooled in my eyes. I squeezed my eyes shut and prayed that I wouldn't regret my confession.

I counted to five and opened my eyes. Dr. Opland's blue eyes showed his concern and empathy. Relief flooded my anxious heart.

"I won't pretend that I'm a marriage counselor. I don't know you personally, your marriage, or your husband. My job is to keep you healthy. My policy is to not ask unnecessary personal questions unless it's regarding your safety."

"Thank you." I quietly sniffled.

"I'm not sure if you are aware or not, but you were recently pregnant. Your hCG blood level was elevated, which indicates a recent pregnancy. However, you're no longer pregnant." He paused to let his words sink in and gauged how I received the news.

A few weeks ago, my body had become a foreign vessel that disobeyed me at every turn. First, the smell of cooking meat made me gag, which only progressively worsened every day. Running to the bathroom to throw up became a common occurrence during meal preparations. After the meat aversion, my sense of hearing intensified. I heard a car door shut from blocks away. If a neighbor's cat hissed at a wild rabbit, I knew about it. If Tony dropped a pen in his office, I wanted to pick it up. My breasts were so sore as if I'd slept on a cement slab, and I laid down to rest every second I could.

Then all of a sudden, those symptoms disappeared as quickly as they appeared, and I realized what had happened. The blood in my underwear confirmed what I suspected was happening to my body. Even though I always considered a baby a blessing, I felt an overwhelming sense of relief. As soon as I acknowledged that emotion, guilt surfaced.

I only blinked in response to Dr. Opland's observation.

"By your response or lack thereof, I will assume that you knew about the miscarriage. Some women miscarry even before they know there is or was a baby. Have you been feeling okay?"

"Yes and yes." I've always had a hard time lying, so I looked down at my feet.

"It's my job to ask these questions, but I don't particularly enjoy them. But Mrs. Shade, I noticed some bruising on your wrists when I took your pulse, as well as a few older bruises on your back when I listened to your breathing. Are you safe? Is there anything I can do to help?"

His concern was genuine, and it caused me to weaken my guard. "Thank you, Dr. Opland, for your concern. I'm fine; truly, I am. I'm just not ready to be a mother." I swallowed a large lump that had formed in my throat. It wasn't a complete lie. "The miscarriage was God's way of proving me right."

"I'm sure you know more about God than I do, being married to a pastor and all, but I don't believe God works that way, Mrs. Shade. Your miscarriage wasn't a punishment from God." When Dr. Opland revealed my secret, my heart rate instantly increased by twenty. He knew who I was.

Before he could continue, I stopped him by shaking my head. "No, the pregnancy was God's warning, and the miscarriage was God's way of correcting the situation. God knew what He was doing, and I'm grateful that my prayers were answered."

If Dr. Opland disagreed, he didn't argue his point again. He seemed to understand that I'd accepted the miscarriage and, honestly, didn't want to be in that situation again anytime soon. Dr. Opland prescribed me birth control pills that he'd call into the pharmacy each month under a false name so that I could keep my identity hidden from anyone in Normal, and then I'd pick them up, telling the pharmacist it was for a church member.

No matter how badly I wanted a child of my own, mentally, I could not be a vessel for Tony's offspring. I already worried about everything Tony did or said to me; I didn't think I could worry about protecting someone else from him. What kind of father would he be? I could never subject any innocent child to what he might be capable of. I knew all too well that appearances are not always what they seem.

My sacrifice was never being a mother because shielding the innocent from my husband was more important. I was only one tiny woman, but I'd do my part. My part was to never let Tony become a father, to wonder and worry if the monster inside of him was created or genetic. I didn't want to take that chance.

The fact that we didn't have any children of our own made us appear more human and approachable. In the eyes of the community, we were the perfect couple to raise children; however, God had other ideas for our role in society. Tony, of course, found a way to use our inability to procreate as part of many sermons that fed on the sympathy of the congregation. He stressed the fact that God had His plan, even if we didn't always agree with it or see what He had envisioned for our journey.

"The Bible tells us, 'For I know the plans I have for you,' declares the Lord, 'plans to prosper you and not to harm you, plans to give you hope and a future.' Even though these words don't give us the answer we want to hear, we must believe God will provide for us. He has a plan.

"Lisa and I have been married for five years, and during those wonderful years together," he always managed to look at me in the front pew and shine one of his famous, loving smiles at me, "God has blessed us in so many other ways. Lisa and I trust that He has a plan for us. We are mere humans here on Earth to serve Him. We're patient and believe He'll take care of us."

When he brought up our infertility issues in church, I forced a tight smile onto my face and pretended to feel the stress. I smiled back. I nodded in all the right places. I knew what was expected of me in these types of situations. I'd been groomed and trained by Tony.

It was all an act. I knew that it wasn't due to a lack of trying, praying, or planning. I was sabotaging it, and for once in our marriage, I was in control.

Chapter 17

Jolene - 1982

In 1980, when Father discovered Mother's affair with her running partner, I overheard Father suggesting that her infidelity had been an issue before. Father's drinking had caused her to seek another man's arms. She claimed she felt abandoned and hurt that Father preferred drinking to spending time with her. In response, Father quit drinking. Cold turkey.

I wondered what excuse she gave him about her running partner affair. It must have been believable because Father stayed, and they worked on stabilizing their marriage.

Father may have trusted her, but I didn't.

Mother tamed her wild ways, or at least it appeared that way to me. She preferred to stay home, snuggling Father on the couch and creating family night adventures. Each event included a theme, which I think helped her stay busy. Since she wasn't sneaking around and cheating on our family, she conjured up new tasks to keep herself occupied. Ivy basked in the extra attention and looked forward to every one of these invented celebrations.

One afternoon, as Ivy and I were completing our homework on the kitchen table, Mother arrived home from work with bags of groceries in her arms and made an announcement. "Tonight, we're watching *Laverne and Shirley* with Pepsi Milks, which is Laverne's favorite, and extra buttery popcorn, which is your daddy's favorite."

Ivy squealed in excitement while I refused to show any emotion. Even though, as she unpacked the groceries–bottles of Pepsi, kernels of popcorn, and real butter–my mouth watered, I would not give her the satisfaction of any positive reaction. I participated in each family night because Ivy's happiness was my main priority and because, secretly, I didn't mind. However, my teenage rebellion didn't allow me to react with pleasure.

For years, after Mother's wild oats were sowed, she pretended to be content and happy with the life she picked, and Father was elated when she hung up her running shoes and chose to spend her free time with the three of us. Being a naive and optimistic person, he believed that Mother had learned from her experience and didn't want to lose her family. He assumed that she chose him. He chose to believe she was a better person than she actually was.

When I turned sixteen and realized that the drama between my parents had flatlined, I relaxed my watchful eye and dropped my guard. I recognized her attempt to make her family her priority. The realization floated in with the fall breeze as the four of us were sitting around a small campfire in our backyard. Mother brushed a lock of hair that had fallen over Father's eyes. Admiration defined that tender touch. As he rotated his hotdog over the top of the campfire, Father continued to talk and talk about a baseball game without taking a moment to notice, but my heart fluttered and I felt my body relax. I took a deep breath and consciously advised myself that everything was good. I didn't need to keep worrying. *Time to put away the watchdog and enjoy my teenage years.* Plus, Father was a grown man. He could take care of himself, or he'd at least be able to lean on Ivy and me if something major did happen.

Sixteen brought other changes for me. While puberty was grabbing a hold of my body, I started noticing that the boys at school weren't as bad as I'd believed in middle school, and those same boys were noticing the changes in me. When I walked down the hallway to my locker or across the classroom to sharpen my pencil, male eyes followed my steps. It was a powerful feeling to realize that my changing body was being gawked at by others.

That family campfire was a pivotal point in taking back my life. As the amber flames reached out to the sky, I decided to join the school's debate team, coached by my English teacher. While I listened to the crackle of the fire, I pretended to throw in my worries and reservations about Mother and watched them burn to ash.

The next day at school, I signed up for the debate team. The first assignment was to choose a topic on which I'd be interested in debating both sides of the issue. I spent hours in the library researching topics. Finally, the one that piqued my interest was abortion. While my heart broke for the unborn babies and how vulnerable they were in this situation, I had to admit that I understood how incredibly painful it would be to carry a baby under certain circumstances. I could discuss this topic at great lengths.

Quickly, I returned the encyclopedia to the designated shelf. I glanced at my watch and saw that it was almost five o'clock. Mr. Knight might still be in his classroom since he held study sessions after school until five o'clock. I gathered up my notebook and pencils and threw everything in my bookbag.

"Where are you going in such a rush, Jolene?" Mrs. Welch, the school librarian, asked as I darted for the door.

"Gonna try to catch Coach Knight before he heads home. I think I found my topic for debate." I forced a smile on my lips as I continued my exit. "Thanks, Mrs. Welch."

"Kids. Always in a rush." She commented more to herself than to me. She shook her head and returned her focus to the book that she was reading.

I bound up the cement stairs two at a time, trying to reach his classroom before he locked his door. Every debate member had to choose a unique subject. Two of us could not choose the same topic, so I wanted to lay my claim on it before anyone else did. Abortion has been a hot matter ever since Roe vs. Wade Supreme Court case ten years ago. Everyone had an opinion about how to handle an unwanted pregnancy.

About fifty feet before his door, I stopped jogging and started walking to catch my breath. I needed to be able to speak. As I took a deep breath in, I heard it.

Her giggle.

Her high-pitched hyena laugh.

It echoed off the cement walls in his classroom.

It was the same flirtatious giggle that I'd heard on the side of the road as I waited for her to run by years ago when I was a kid. It felt like deja vu. Goosebumps created a gravel road of bumps on my arms.

My feet halted as if stuck in fresh tar. *What is she doing here? And why is she giggling uncontrollably like a schoolgirl?*

My nostrils flared wide open so they would get as much air in my lungs as possible as I silenced my breathing. In my head, I knew what was going on, but in my heart, which for some crazy reason, still held out hope. I just couldn't believe it.

"This is such a nice surprise–you stopping by unannounced with home-made cookies. Seriously, just so you know, there is no contest to be the favorite parent." Under his deep, husky breath, he added, "You're already my favorite."

Mother softly giggled in response. "I know. I guess I just wanted to see you..."

The inside of my stomach contents started to churn.

"The cookies are a bit of a bribe for you to take Jolene under your wing."

"I'll take good care of her. She's a very bright kid, and I'm sure she'll fit right in. No need to bribe me. Just doing my job."

"Well, thank you. I'm sure the girls in your class have a hard time paying attention since you're one of the most attractive men in Normal."

"Did you just call me *hot*?" Coach Knight teased her.

Another soft giggle—not her hyena cackle—escaped her lying lips. "Hot? I didn't say, *hot*."

The bile that I'd been able to shove down into the pit of my stomach began to force its way out. My hands automatically slapped my mouth shut as I turned and ran back in the direction I came, but before I descended the stairs, I threw up all over the painted cement floor on my new white tennis shoes.

Tears sprang from my eyes as I tripped over my own two feet and started moving again. I needed to get as far away from this building as I could. But no matter how far I ran, their flirting words burned in my ears. Their physical affair may not have started yet, but both parties seemed more than willing.

How could she?

How could he?

Chapter 18

Jolene - 1982

When faced with a difficult situation, the majority of people retreat. They surrender with silence and avoidance. I knew this because I did it for years when I first learned of Mother's infidelity. But this time, I wasn't going to sit back and watch. Rather than seal my lips and let my silence cause her to wonder what I was thinking, I decided revenge might feel pretty good.

At first, I remained silent for my plan to work. Unlike when she had an affair with her running partner, this time she didn't know that I knew. She had no idea, and I planned on working it to my advantage.

Like a television network does following the announcement of a dramatic event, I returned to my regular scheduled programming. The next morning, before school, I dropped by Coach Knight's classroom to claim my debate topic.

"Jolene, are you sure? That's a pretty heavy topic for your first debate. Maybe we could find you a less sensitive issue for your first one. How about something like, 'Should school be year-round' or 'Should school uniforms be mandatory'?"

"No, thank you. I would rather speak about something I feel passionate about than some issue that doesn't matter." I placed my hand on my heart, which was adorned with one of Ivy's silk blouses that was at least one size too small for me, and unbuttoned four buttons from my neck, revealing the cleavage that had earned me new attention. "Don't worry about me, Coach Knight; I can handle myself." I winked at him before turning on my heel and strutting out of his room. I peeked over my shoulder to verify that he was still watching me. And he was.

***

Seducing Coach Knight hadn't been the most difficult task I've ever accomplished, but it was one of the first goals for which, at its completion, I didn't feel a great sense of pride. Instead of my heart feeling fulfilled and accomplished, it felt heavy and disappointed. Breaking the man and proving to my mother that her new love interest wasn't worth the trouble hadn't made me feel good like I thought it would.

To put my plan into motion, I started with my morning routine. Rather than taking a shower the night before and letting my hair dry while I slept so I could whip it up into a ponytail the next morning, I showered before school, dried, and curled my hair. Instead of wearing shirts that were three sizes too big, I wore my appropriate size or Ivy's clothes that were one size smaller. I coated my eyelashes with mascara and spread gloss over my lips. Because my previous appearance reflected no effort, my new and improved look was noticed by lots of different people.

"Jolene, you look nice." Father's eyes peered over his morning newspaper. "Got a date that I should know about? Should I polish my shotgun?" He winked to show that even though his tone was deep and serious, he trusted my judgment, plus we both knew he didn't own a gun. He sipped his steaming cup of coffee while he waited for my answer.

"Just looking nice for you, Father." I teased back as I pulled out a box of cereal from the cupboard.

He chuckled and raised his newspaper back up, indicating that he didn't believe me but knew he wouldn't get any more information.

My answer was partly true. My plan to seduce Coach Knight *was* partially for my father. If I could show my mother that her current love interest wasn't worth her time, she'd return her attention to my father, which would make him happy. I was helping by reducing my father's heartache, even if I didn't think my mother deserved him. And of course, seducing Coach Knight would break my mother, which was an added benefit to the plan.

As she finished packing Father's lunch pail, Mother turned in my direction to examine what the fuss was all about. Her nose wrinkled. She wasn't impressed. The best part of the attention I was receiving was that it bothered Mother. She'd always been the bombshell, the woman who men stared at and women envied. However, people were noticing me and my 'developments,' and she wasn't interested in sharing the attention.

After paying close attention to Mother's comings and goings and becoming knowledgeable of Coach Knight's daily schedule, I was able to narrow down when their rendezvous occurred. I followed them down to the river, where they would go for a romantic walk into the trees. In one hand, Coach Knight held my mother's hand–that he would pull up to his lips to kiss–and in the other hand, he carried a wool blanket. Their river dates always happened after dusk and usually lasted twenty to thirty minutes.

When they returned from the riverbank, with the used picnic blanket thrown over his shoulder, Coach Knight would pick leaves and dried grass from Mother's hair. The moonlight flashed over my mother's white teeth as she smiled and giggled. Watching the two of them made my blood boil. I couldn't let her get away with this again. The last time I caught her, I was too young to do anything, and telling my father seemed like the worst-case scenario. She didn't deserve his love and devotion. He was too good for her. I didn't want to be the one to tell him something that I was sure would break his heart. No, punishing her sounded like much more fun.

I didn't know how or exactly what I was going to do, but I was prepared to be patient and let the plan happen naturally. For weeks, I focused on the little details. After his class, I made a point to always have a question for him. If I wasn't the last one to leave his room when class was dismissed, I'd accidentally leave something in his room that I'd retrieve after school to secure some alone time with him.

On the day of the English semester test, I contemplated the next level of my plan. With my hair hanging loose, I'd be able to whip it over my shoulder. My eyelashes were thick with mascara, and my lips were moistened with gloss. My outfit was chosen with care.

"Jolene, is that my old shirt? The same one you told me to throw away because the neck was all stretched out?" Ivy questioned me as she shoveled cold cereal into her mouth. The week before, I told her that the shirt was destined for the trash. The v-neck was so stretched out that it often fell to the side and off the shoulder. It was faded and worn across the breasts. It might have been a rag for Ivy, but it was perfect for me.

After the test had been administered and the quiet hush fell over the room, I pushed my pencil off the front of my desk. The sudden noise in the otherwise silent room earned the teacher's attention. Our eyes met, and a half-smirk rose on my lips as I leaned forward to retrieve my pencil. Under the stretched-out v-neck shirt, Ivy's size 32A bra, which was two cup sizes too small, made my breasts pop out of the top of my shirt. Because I'd practiced in front of a mirror at home, I knew Coach Knight received a perfect cleavage shot as I watched him watch me. He cleared his throat and adjusted his position in his chair behind his desk. As he quickly looked around the room to distract himself, his neck turned red, and I noticed the color move up to his cheeks.

Coach Knight was a boob man.

***

During family dinners, we discussed everyone's weekly activities and deadlines.

"The Steinbergs asked me to walk their dog, Boston, next week." Ivy declared as soon as we finished saying grace. "Lacy is having hip surgery. They offered me five bucks for the whole week."

"Good for you, honey. They probably asked you again because you did a good job last time." Mother patted the top of Ivy's head as if she were her pet.

"Yeah, I love Boston. He might have the worst dog breath, but I love his sloppy, wet kisses." Ivy brought her arms to her chest like she was hugging an imaginary dog.

My father turned to me, and with an almost empty mouth, asked, "Jolene, do you have a debate game tomorrow after school?"

As soon as he finished his question, he shoveled another spoonful of goulash into his mouth. He grinned back at me with a small noodle hanging from his smirk.

"It is not a game or a match," I said, shaking my head. Using athletic terms to talk about the debate was a standing joke between us. "I'm so glad you brought that up, Father. Are either of you able to attend? Coach Knight requested a headcount for the debate team's open house afterward."

At the mention of his name, I noticed Mother take a slight intake of breath while she waited for Father to answer.

With a mouthful of noodles and hamburger, he answered, "Shoot, Jolene, I'm meeting a potential client tomorrow at four, but maybe I can pop into the open house after I'm done."

"Father, please refrain from talking until *after* you swallow your food. Gross. Nah, that's okay. You can attend the next one." I gave him the out that he was looking for.

In a whiny, childlike voice, Ivy mumbled, "Please don't make me go, Daddy. I have a big test in Money Management that I need to study for."

Ivy didn't enjoy debate competitions. Arguing for fun was not in Ivy's DNA. "Didn't you use that excuse last time?" I teased her.

Father came to Ivy's rescue with a gentle reminder. "Ivy, I think you're on the do-not-allow-in-the-door list after spitting on Ella after her debate."

Ivy's mouth made a wide circle. "Daddy! Ella argued that animals should be used for advancing medical research." Ivy was mortified that Father would even joke about the debate that struck a chord in my big-hearted little sister. "I didn't spit on her. It's called gleeking. I didn't mean to do it, but I was so upset that spit came out of my mouth. How could she even research that topic?"

"That's what the debate team does," I explained. We already had this discussion after the debate the night of the famous spit.

"Is there really a list?" Ivy was mortified that she could be outlawed at an event that she didn't want to attend anyway.

"Jolene, I will be there," Mother added. Selfishly, I wondered if she waited to announce her attendance as soon as she knew no one else could be there.

"Great. Coach Knight asked me if you were coming." I took a drink from my glass of milk to give my statement a little extra punch. Silence settled in the room.

Ivy and Father were too busy chewing to notice the subtle change in Mother.

"He did?" She almost choked on her bite.

Casually, I added without looking up from my plate, "Yeah, he wanted to make sure you were coming and that Ivy wasn't."

Ivy covered her face with her hands and dropped her head on the table next to her plate. Her forehead hit the tabletop. "My flawless reputation is ruined."

Chapter 19

Jolene - 1982

There was no open house after our debate competition, but my family didn't know that.

When our school hosted the debate competition, we set up our tables and podiums in the school's choir room. After the risers were pushed to the outside wall of the room, two long tables were positioned in the front of the room. Two wooden podiums that were constructed by the shop teacher and last year's shop class were placed on the ends of each table. Since the choir room already had at least forty chairs set up for the daily classes, the rest of our set-up was minimal. Plus, Coach Knight appreciated the acoustics in this room.

The third benefit, that Coach Knight did not vocalize but every student knew about, supported his nicotine habit. In the back of the choir room was a small private room no bigger than a walk-in closet. Students believed it was a secret teacher's smoking lounge. While we were rehearsing, Coach Knight would disappear, and a few minutes later, he exited the little room reeking of smoke and wearing a relaxed smile.

The debate against Sioux Center's Warriors ended with a small victory, 3-2. They were known for their thorough research and well-versed students, so beating them for the first time in three years caused our normally introverted, calm group of nerds to yelp in approval. Even though our uncharacteristic show of emotion caused a small smile to form on Coach

Knight's face, he still shook his head to show the judge he didn't approve of our outburst.

As soon as the last of the crowd dispersed to the parking lot and our team made plans to celebrate at Kitty's Cafe, I noticed Coach Knight and my mother talking. My usual response to my mother's presence would be to ignore her, but instead, I turned on the charm. As I strutted my way over to them, their conversation halted.

"Thanks for coming, Mother. Wasn't that great? Griffin didn't even miss a beat with those questions about censorship."

"You're welcome, honey." She patted my shoulder, and it took everything in me to not cringe at her touch. "I thought you said there was an open house for your team afterward."

"Oh, yeah. Griffin made that up. Tricked me, too." I dismissed her as if it wasn't a big deal that plans had been altered.

"Jolene–"

"Whatever." I waved my hand in her direction and turned my attention to Coach Knight. "Everyone is going to Kitty's Cafe to celebrate. Can you join us, Coach?" I batted my lashes a bit too aggressively, so Mother would notice.

Coach Knight cleared his throat. "I'll try to stop by in a half hour. Need to finish some grading first." He excused himself with a nod and an eyebrow raised in my mother's direction and retreated to the secret teacher's lounge. "Nice to see you, Mrs. Just."

I watched Mother's eyes follow him as he walked away.

"Earth to Mother." I waved my hand in front of her face, pretending to break a trance. "Oh my God– "

"Jolene, don't use the Lord's name in vain." I knew how to get her attention.

"Shit–" My palm slapped my bare forehead.

"Jolene!"

"Sorry. I left my English paper at home in my bedroom. It's due today. Mrs. Newman said I could turn it in right after the debate, but I thought it was in my locker. It's not. I remember that I left it on my nightstand next to my bed. Mom, can you quickly drive home and get it? I'll see if I can catch Mrs. Newman. She's kind of a grump, but she said this one time she'd let it slide."

"Jolene, this is your responsibility. If you forget something like this, you need to pay the consequences." Mother's lectures fell short because she was a hypocrite.

"Mother, it's important. If I don't turn it in today, she will dock me ten points. That's the difference between an A and a B. You ran Ivy's gym shoes to her last week when she forgot them, and that had nothing to do with a final grade."

"That's different, Jolene."

"How? Because you love her more? You're always favoring her over me." I heard the whiny voice pouring out of my mouth, but now was the time to play this card. A month ago, I overheard my parents discussing this very issue. Father accused Mother of playing favorites when she assigned household chores. She denied that accusation and seemed hurt by his suggestion. But the facts don't lie. Every week, while Ivy was assigned emptying the garbage and dusting the woodwork, Mother determined that scrubbing toilets and floors were my chores. My nickname should've been Cinderella.

"That is not true, Jolene. I love you both equally." She shook her head to dismiss the notion. "Fine. I'll go get it and come right back. Where is it again?" Her hand reached into her purse in search of her car keys.

"On the top of my nightstand. I finished it right before I crawled under the covers." I forced an appreciative smile on my face. "Thanks, Mother. You're the best." I pulled her in for a quick hug.

"Are you wearing my perfume?" Mother's signature perfume was Obsession by Calvin Klein.

"Just a little. It was a big day. I thought it might bring me luck." I hadn't expected her to recognize that I'd coated my neck and wrists with her scent. A forced, full-body shiver overtook my body. "Could I borrow your sweater? I'm kind of chilly, plus you wore a coat too. I'll give it back as soon as we get home. I promise."

Her cashmere cardigan had been a generous gift from Father for her birthday. It was emerald and matched the color of her eyes. It was her favorite, and she wore it every week. If she didn't let me borrow it, she'd suggest that I wear her coat. Either one would work to my benefit.

"Here, take my coat." As she shrugged off her black trench coat that also smelled like her Obsession perfume, she added, "Next time, dress more appropriately, and you won't be cold." She nodded at my thin, white silk blouse.

"Thanks." I slipped on her coat, which was still warm from her body heat.

She dashed out of the gym's side door, giving me approximately ten to fifteen minutes before she would return. According to facts I'd gathered on Coach Knight, he only ever needed a half hour.

***

When I'd entered the room, Coach Knight exhaled a drag from his Marlboro. The butt of the cigarette provided the only light in the room.

"About time." He'd been expecting someone.

I simply murmured a response. I shut the door behind me and advanced toward the sound of his voice. Thank goodness the room was narrow and mainly empty except for the desk and chair where Coach was seated because I didn't have much time to feel my way around. Plus, I didn't want him to question who I was. When I reached the chair that he was sitting in, I dropped to my knees and forcefully unbuckled and unzipped his pants.

"Well, I'm not sure what brought on your domineering side, but I like it."

He shifted his weight so that I could tug down his pants and boxers. After its release, his erection flopped out and stood at attention. I moaned and gasped, making all the appropriate noises to indicate my arousal. When I growled, he chuckled a little.

As I took him in my mouth and tried my best not to gag, he stopped laughing and moaned as well.

"Shit, Izzy, you've never done this before. That feels good." The palm of his hand pressed down on the back of my head, causing his penis to push further down my throat. "Honey, you gotta join me at my friend Tony's house. You could teach his wife some pointers." He moaned and then added, "She's all teeth."

I had no idea what I was doing. Only recently I let Griffin, my debate teammate, go to second base. Otherwise, I had zero sexual experience. From Coach's appreciation, I understood I was a natural.

But the fact that Coach Knight was offering up my mother's services to another man and his wife almost caused me to bite down on the large extremity in my mouth. Fortunately, I kept my anger in check because I had a plan and it hadn't reached completion yet. I'd focus on this tidbit of information at a later date.

The foreplay, which consisted of licking, sucking, and stopping for fear that he would ejaculate before it was time, lasted about eight minutes but felt more like eighty. The corners of my mouth stretched out to maximum potential, and the back of my throat was raw from his penis trying to punch through it. I'd read that blowjobs were an enormous pleasure for a man, but as a woman, it seemed like a lot of work. When he was completely relaxed and begging to relieve himself, I sat down on his naked lap. I wiggled around.

He pressed his face into my hair and neck. "Obsession is the perfect perfume for you. You smell so good."

One point for me, proving that even the smallest detail was worth the effort.

"Izzy, I'm telling you that you have a gift, and I'm so fucking glad you share it with me." Aggressively, Coach Knight tried to push into me as I squirmed around his lap, giggling and taunting him.

"Fuckin' tease." He lifted me off his lap and bent me over the desk. As soon as he shoved himself into me, he sighed. "Ahhhh..."

Each forceful thrust caused my hips to slam into the desk, moving it a few inches forward and hitting the wall. As the four metal legs scraped the linoleum floor, a screech echoed through the small room, followed by a yelp that escaped my lips. I'd been in control of the teasing, but from this position, I was at a disadvantage.

"Bitch, this ain't nothing." In between his thrusts, he grunted with pleasure, and just before he was about to explode, the door to the secret teacher's lounge opened, and the bright fluorescent lights blinded us. "What the hell?"

Fifteen minutes later, after I had entered the room, and right on time, Mother opened the door to the teacher's secret smoking lounge, as I'd predicted. Standing in the doorway with her eyes as wide as saucers and her mouth hanging open, Mother was panting and empty-handed. The trench coat that I'd borrowed to encourage Coach into believing I was my mother bunched up around my waist as Coach Knight pounded me from behind. My black slacks and lacy thong underwear were wrapped around my ankles. Coach Knight was also naked from the waist down, but he still wore his navy polo.

Mission accomplished.

No homework assignment had been forgotten at home on my night-stand. Furthermore, Mrs. Newman didn't exist, or at least wasn't employed by the Normal School District. These little facts proved how little Mother knew or cared about my life. Planting that lie along with the debate open house was part of my plan to get Mother where and when I wanted her.

The look on her face when she caught Coach Knight and me doing it doggy style was worth losing my virginity for. Big, juicy tears sprang into her wide eyes, her forehead wrinkles creased with curiosity, and as soon as her brain reset and she gathered all the information that she needed with her eyes, she turned and ran out of the school.

Chapter 20

Jolene – 1982

The next afternoon, life returned to normal–cold cereal for breakfast, Ivy crawling out of bed at the last minute, and Father and Mother saying quick goodbyes as they headed to work. At school, I turned in my homework, chatted with my friends, and listened to endless boring lectures. The only thing that wasn't like the day before was that my bottom silently screamed in pain every time I sat down on a hard metal desk.

Seconds before the bell rang to conclude Coach Knight's English class, he cleared his throat and announced, "Cheryl Mulder and..." He paused, pretending to look down at a stack of papers. "And Jolene Just, please see me after class." I wondered how this period of my day was going to go. I planned on pretending nothing had happened in the private smoking lounge, but I'd secretly wondered how Coach Knight would treat me.

He wants to face the music. This will be interesting.

There was no way Cheryl, Miss Goody-Two-Shoes, and I were staying after class for the same reason. As the noisy bell echoed in the room, kids immediately started talking and scurrying to the next class. The purpose of a school bell was to notify everyone of the end of a class period, and it was always followed by immediate talking, the screeching of chairs being scraped across the floor, and a scurry of activity.

I slowly began packing up my belongings as my heart beat double time, wondering what Coach Knight would say. Cheryl, true to her kiss-ass nature, quickly raced up to his desk.

"You wanted to see me, Coach Knight?" Even though her eagerness to please was apparent, her apprehension at being surprisingly summoned was obvious in her shaky voice.

"Yes, Cheryl. I have a few students in the other class who are falling behind. I wondered if you'd be interested in a mini-tutoring job to get them up to speed."

"For sure." Her response reflected that her enthusiasm and self-confidence had returned.

"Great. After I confirm with the kids and their parents, I will give you their names so that you can schedule the sessions."

"Awesome sauce." Cheryl and her tight ponytail bounced out the door, leaving Coach Knight and me alone.

From my student desk in the middle of the room, I said, "I'm not interested in performing another 'job' for you, Coach." I used air quotes around the word job. "If you want the blow job finished from last night, maybe you should ask Izzy." No one called my mother Izzy. The nickname sent a shiver of disgusted goosebumps up and down my arms.

In a matter of a few seconds, Coach leaped from his chair and marched six long strides to shut his classroom door. Because the school had a strict policy against a teacher being alone in their classrooms with a student, Coach Knight kept his distance with his back pressed up against the closed door. However, the rectangular window in the door reflected the hustle and bustle of students passing between classes.

"Jolene, we need to talk."

As soon as my mother appeared in the doorway last night during our rough bang, Coach's manhood went limp, and like a slap in the face, he realized he wasn't banging my mother. He'd been screwing one of his students, an underaged minor, on school grounds. No matter what he said, I knew I had the upper hand and the bruises on my hips to prove it. Even though my goal had only been to hurt my mother, I realized I also had the power to ruin his career.

"Sure. Let's talk. We didn't get much of a chance last night." I settled myself in my chair and dropped my backpack onto the floor next to me. "Speaking of talking, what did my mother say when you finally caught up to her?"

After the shock had settled, Mother ran out of the school, and after muttering a few dozen curse words, Coach Knight managed to yank up his pants so he could chase after her. Following the tryst, I joined my fellow debate team members at Kitty's Cafe to celebrate. My slice of pie was in honor of our debate win as well as my conquest of Coach Knight. By the time I arrived home, Mother's car wasn't parked in the garage yet.

"You know that I had no idea it was you, right? I would've never done that if I'd known." His excuse sounded lame coming from his mouth as if that line was the only immoral one he'd crossed.

"What does your wife think of your extracurricular activity?"

"Jolene." Coach Knight used a less defensive stance when he looked down at his feet. "Let's be honest. You knew what you were doing, and I appreciated your skills." He shifted his weight to the opposite foot. "Your mother seemed more upset with me than with you. *That* surprised me a bit." When he looked up at me, I recognized a sliver of vulnerability that I hadn't been expecting. "I'm sorry if I was too..."

While he searched his vocabulary for the right adjective, I inserted, "Barbaric?"

A small smile rose on his lips. "Maybe? If my memory serves me correctly, you enjoyed it."

Is this man flirting with me? I thought I'd have conflicting feelings about losing my virginity just to prove a point to my mother, but having Coach Knight become attracted to me wasn't one of the responses I'd considered. My stomach flip-flopped.

"I wanted to invite you to..." Again, he searched for a word. *Why is he fumbling with words? Did I cause this nervousness?* "A group."

"Like another debate team?" I had no idea where this conversation was going, but I wasn't expecting this. I'd been prepared to whip out my teenage sass and scold him for taking advantage of me. I expected him to be taken aback by my abrasiveness, but I never once considered that he'd show anything but remorse. "I think I should quit the debate team considering..."

Coach Knight ignored my comment and continued with his thoughts. "This group might fit more of your skills. You'd meet some influential people and get paid well for your attendance and participation."

I knew he wasn't offering me a tutoring job like he had Cheryl, but I was eager to know more. I'd be lying if I said I wasn't interested.

***

Who else can say that their first job during high school was as a prostitute? How many teenagers would admit that they allowed their bodies to be used for sexual pleasure by several men in one night? My compensation didn't even compare to that of my classmates. Kathy, who always let me copy her Chemistry exam answers, earned $3.50 an hour working at the neighboring town's Taco John's. The only trademark that our jobs had in common was our desire to shower as soon as we were finished. After standing for eight hours, Kathy's feet ached, and fast food grease oozed from her pores. The hot shower rinsed away the grease that was caked on her body. In my situation, my body required a hot shower to scrub off the sin before it seeped into my blood and caused my heart to blacken. A shower also hid the cascade of tears caused by the humility and shame that I felt after letting a handful of strangers take advantage of my body. However, the wad of cash secured my continued participation.

But there wasn't enough soap or hot water that could wipe away their panting, aggressive, lust-hungry images from my memory. I hadn't expected to feel overwhelming disgust. I accepted Coach Knight's invitation and considered it a challenge. Mother had never made it to this point. Then I allowed these older men to remove my clothing and explore my body. Because I was the one who chose to participate in the games, I thought I was the one in control. I showed up. I sauntered into the hotel room, confident and sexy in a tight dress with four-inch heels. But sometime after the numbing drugs evaporated from my bloodstream, I felt empty and depressed. Everything happened so fast, and suddenly, there was no turning back.

When I knocked on the hotel room door after I'd been summoned to work, I'd hear a scurry of activity behind the door as the men positioned themselves for my entry. Some of them chose to partially cover their faces for fear of identification. Each man had different demands and fetishes. As we became a tangle of naked bodies, he would whisper in my ear what he wanted me to do while his friends patiently waited their turn.

Some evenings I would be the only female in the room, and other times I'd see another pair of scared eyes. The only advice that I had for the newcomers was to offer her a small pink tablet. "It's called a Special K, and it'll help you detach from this scene." Coach Knight had given me a bag of them when I first started.

The men and their faces blurred together in my mind. I couldn't definitively tell them apart. Their mustaches, beards, dimples, and whiskey-smelling breaths blended into one nightmare after another.

Like Kathy, I showered and scrubbed to remove the stench. My feet didn't suffer the same dull ache that hers did after an eight-hour shift on her feet. No, the pain was in my heart and caused my pride and innocence to be ripped from my chest. No soap or boiling water could erase that ache.

Chapter 21

Jolene – 1983

As Ivy and I were playing cards–King's Corner–in our bedroom, we overheard raised voices coming from the kitchen below. I was nursing a hangover, and Ivy, a natural caretaker, helped by bringing me water, aspirin, and a deck of cards, which was her cure for whatever ailed anyone. After taking the medicine and gulping down the glass of water, we sprawled out on the floor of our room. I appreciated the distraction from my pounding head and guilty conscience, which were both earned the night before. The bedroom that we shared sat directly above the kitchen. The obvious benefit of this location was the smell of bacon floating up through the ventilation on weekend mornings, waking us with smiles on our faces.

The negative part was that often we'd be woken up by late-night snacking, pots and pans banging around, or arguments that my parents thought would take place more beneficially at a kitchen table at the back of the house than anywhere else. Maybe they assumed their voices could only carry up the stairs like their feet. They didn't realize that if we lay on the floor near the vent in our bedroom, we could make out almost every word, at least the ones spoken loudly and in a harsh, direct tone. The sad and mournful feelings that occurred in that room traveled up through the vents in a mumbled tone. Those words were harder to make out, which was fine with us. We were more interested in the fighting words–the arguments that caused Father or Mother to say the f-word all the time. On our wooden floorboards, Ivy used her pocket knife to carve little tally marks for every f-word she overheard. I feared that before we graduated high school, the marks would be carved all around the room.

As the beginning of the argument heated up, with her pocket knife in hand, Ivy raced to the vent to press her ear to it. I reluctantly stayed on the floor near my bed, trying to appear uninterested so that she'd become bored with their drama as well. After I discovered that my mother wasn't faithful to my father, I wanted to protect Ivy from that knowledge for as long as I could.

Beckoning me with her arm, Ivy whispered to me, "Come on, Jo. It just started. Get over here." With her left ear pressed to the vent, she quietly interpreted her discovery for me. "Daddy said he couldn't keep the money. He doesn't feel right about it."

What money? Our father worked for a local construction company and often picked up side jobs as well. He'd been working a lot of nights and weekends to finish a remodel on a house before the owners moved in. He told us all the overtime would mean a family trip this summer. Ivy had dreamed up all sorts of location possibilities: Disney World, Japan, Italy, or South America.

"While I appreciate your enthusiasm for larger-than-life adventures and your zealousness for my superhuman abilities, I was thinking more like a week-long camping trip." Over dinner, Father announced that he would be busier than usual for a few months, so Ivy and I needed to be extra well-behaved for Mother.

Whispering again, Ivy added, "It's sinful. Hush money." She looked confused. "Is that a foreign currency or something? Hush money?" She was asking me for clarification, but I had nothing to give her. I knew what it meant from reading my mystery books, but I had no idea how it applied to Father.

"Momma told him to keep his mouth shut. It can't be *that* bad. She says we need the money, and the work is done. Told Daddy to get off his f-ing high horse." Ivy pulled out the pocket knife from her pocket and scooted to the section where she needed to add her next tally mark. Before she scooted back to her listening perch—the vent—a spark flickered in her eye. "Do you think he's really on a horse down there in our kitchen? A horse would never fit through our kitchen door."

I threw a pillow at her as she giggled.

"Hey, I thought you said there are no dumb questions, only stupid answers." Ivy grabbed the pillow that I tossed at her and used it to get comfortable on our hard floor. She held up the palm of her hand toward me. "Wait! I just heard it—the horse. It asked if we liked our *neigh*-bors."

"Bad joke, Ivy. Stop while you're ahead."

Ivy loved making up jokes. She laughed harder than anyone else. As her grin grew from ear to ear and her laugh reached a high octave, I feared I was going to hear more bad horse jokes.

She sat up from her place on the hard floor, abandoning her eavesdropping for now, which had been my goal. I didn't want her to overhear an argument that might erase her innocence. To achieve my goal, I decided a few more made-up jokes would be better than the alternative.

"What sort of horses come out after dark, Jo?"

"I'm sure you'll tell me."

"Night-*mares*. Get it?" She giggled so much that she bent over at her waist, trying to gasp for air. I grinned at the scene, not at the joke.

Ivy's reenactment of our parent's fight interested me, so reluctantly, I crawled my way over to the vent so she'd stop messing up the argument and adding bad jokes to her story. She pressed her finger to her mouth to shush me, and we waited until this discussion resumed.

It was Mother's voice that broke the silence. "Walter, the job is done. You didn't know. You'll probably never know the whole truth."

"Yeah, but I suspected something. What kind of person would want a soundproof room behind a hidden door?" Because his words were smushed together, his breath became labored. He must've been pacing the room because sometimes his voice seemed farther away. "What if he's a murderer?"

A nervous laugh escaped from my mother's throat. "Don't be ridiculous. This is Normal, Iowa. Things like that don't happen here."

"Until they do." My father sounded defeated. "Do you know how guilty I'd feel if something bad happened in that room that I built with my own two hands, and I never said anything?"

Mother's tone softened as she realized that my father's concern was genuine and the guilt was eating away at him. "Walter, you did the work, so keep the money, and if you think you need to tell someone about your concerns, who would you tell?"

I looked at Ivy to see if she understood the gravity of the discussion happening below us. She did not. Her interest was lost when the f-word stopped being thrown around like candy during a hometown parade. The red chipped nail polish on her fingernails had earned her attention as she crawled back to her bed, where she intended to peel it all off.

In a hushed voice, my father mumbled, "I don't know." As he paused for a moment to search for his answer, I imagined him running his fingers through his hair like he did when he was processing information. It was one of his endearing traits that filled my heart with love.

Mother cleared her throat, one of *her* nervous traits that made my skin crawl. "I know you want to do the right thing, Walter, but sometimes the right thing is staying quiet. The construction is complete. Right now, everything that you're thinking about is speculation. You don't know the purpose of the room. Maybe this new pastor is a musician, and he wants a room in which he can practice his music at all hours."

Father mumbled her a 'not likely' comment under his breath.

"You don't know, honey. That scenario sounds more likely than what you're suggesting."

"You mean a torture room?"

"Yes, a torture room. Listen to how ridiculous that sounds—a man of God built a hidden room—"

"Soundproof. Don't forget soundproof."

"—a hidden, soundproof room in his own home so that no one could hear the screams of his victims."

"I know it sounds crazy, but I'm pretty sure he isn't in a band. And when Lenny and Kelvin hired me for the job, they told me it was a secret project and no one, *no one*, could know about it. If I kept my mouth shut, they'd pay me double. What if they are in on it too?"

I glanced over at Ivy. From her spot on her bed, she couldn't hear the conversation. She waited for me to tell her about any swear words. While she'd lost interest, my interest spiked. What money were my parents referring to? How much was it?

A few Sundays ago, I'd heard about the new pastor who'd been hired by our church.

"Our Savior congregation, I'm thrilled to announce that your permanent clergy call has been filled." The transition pastor's grin filled the bottom half of his face, and excitement filled his voice, which wasn't a good sound. His voice wasn't soothing or calming like most good preachers were blessed with. This interim pastor's sermons never held my attention because each time he opened his mouth, I tried to distract my brain so I wouldn't hear his squeaky voice. Have you ever met someone who didn't fit their voice? Have you ever seen a singer for the first time after hearing their song on the radio a million times, and the voice didn't match what your brain had envisioned? Pastor Palmer's voice belonged to a circus clown, the one who sucked helium from a party balloon. "Your prayers have been answered. He has heard you."

The last four words left his mouth with a shriek, and several parishioners looked at each other for an interpretation of what he said.

Afterward, as my family mingled in the crowded narthex like we did every Sunday after worship, I overheard several older women talking a bit too loudly about the new pastor.

"I heard he was a fox." The one woman who I remembered as Karen said to her overly perfumed friends.

"You think everyone is attractive, Karen. You're a walking hormone. Have you gotten laid since Aaron died?" Karen's group of friends laughed at her expense.

"Ladies, we aren't even ten feet away from where we just listened to the Word of God."

"Oh, shut up, Carrie. We all know Sparky satisfies you more than once a week."

Karen's trio of friends looked from Karen to Carrie with their mouths formed in the letter 'O.' They waited to see Carrie's reaction before they mumbled another word. Even though I was appalled about hearing older people talk about sex, I had to admit that their conversation had heated up, and I wanted to hear Carrie's response.

Carrie blushed a little but didn't deny the allegation. "Maybe we should put together a welcoming committee. Let's make sure he sticks around and makes Normal his home."

Karen piped up before the other had a chance to comment, "I've got some ideas on how to make him feel welcome." Her eyebrows moved up and down.

Finally, Karen's friends gestured her out of the church before other people overheard her comments by promising her breakfast. I heard her ask, "Will there be sausage?"

***

While I'd heard about the hiring of the 'foxy' new pastor, I could not have cared less. I doubted that my and Karen's ideas of attractiveness would be similar. However, the arrival of an attractive pastor who had a hidden, sound-proof room in his house piqued my interest.

Even though it was Ivy who encouraged me to join her near our secret-revealing vent, and it was Ivy who'd abandoned her post, I continued to lay with my ear over the floor vent to hear how my father and the new pastor's room intertwined. This discussion wasn't as heated as their normal arguments, so I strained to hear their low voices.

"Do you think you can wait until you get to know Pastor Shade? Then flat out ask him or tell him that you were the one who built the room. See if he elaborates." Mother's voice was slow and deliberate as she tried to calm Father down.

"Yeah, maybe." Father's words barely crawled up the vents. He didn't seem convinced, but Mother had managed to calm his worry.

After a few minutes of silence, I recognized some shuffling from the floor beneath me, and then I heard the TV turn on. They retreated to the living room to relax. I rose from my spot on the floor and strolled to my twin bed.

"Do I need to make any f-marks on the baseboard?" Ivy peeked over the top of her Nancy Drew mystery book.

"Nope. Sorry, Ivy."

She quickly returned her attention to her book as I situated myself under the covers. I loved a good mystery too, but I wasn't interested in a book when there was a real mystery to solve. My gut told me that I knew exactly what that room was going to be used for, and who would be using it. During my 'hotel shift' the night before, I heard whispers of a more private, secure location for future assignments. I assumed we were moving to a new hotel room, but now I understood the 'Room' they were referring to wasn't located in a hotel.

Chapter 22

Lisa – 1983

I'd been in the kitchen preparing one of Tony's favorite meals when I heard the squeak of the front door. I immediately washed my hands and scurried to greet him at the door with his requested peck on his cheek. I didn't make it in time. The door to his office slammed shut before I made it down the hallway.

Oh Lord, I hope I don't have to pay for that later.

During dinner, he took one bite of the garlic-crusted roasted rack of lamb and claimed he wasn't hungry. Being married to a man with an evil, abusive side kept me on my toes. When sleep blessed me, it was with one eye open. My shoulders tightened whenever I heard him enter a room, my jaw clenched as soon as a sound left his lips, and the hairs on my arm stood at attention in his presence. I can only imagine what a chiropractor would say about the knots in my back. By living through this unending stress, my heart suffered unusual duress.

My gut and woman's intuition recognized that something was going on. In response, my tongue tied up all disrespectful comments, my hands meticulously chopped and sauteed his favorite meals, and my stomach cooperated even though my nerves wanted to reject anything that my mouth consumed. Training and experience taught me to keep my mouth shut.

You can teach an old dog new tricks.

It was at times like that when I asked myself why I was fighting so hard to survive. As I completed my ritualistic daily chores that Tony insisted I accomplish, even though our house never had a speck of dust in it, the bleach bottle that I used to clean often tainted me.

Drink me.

Just a glass would do the trick, and then this nightmare would be over. But I couldn't do it. I wanted out of my marriage, but not out of my life. I needed to get organized and think strategically.

A few nights later, after the lamb dinner, when his thick sirloin steak was cooked to his preference, medium rare, I headed down the hall to his study, where I heard him talking on the phone. My heels clicked on the hardwood floor. As I approached the room, I inhaled a deep breath. Through the glass French doors, I viewed the phone receiver pressed to his left ear. He would not want to be interrupted.

"And I told *you* that I took care of it." He paused again before answering. "It means what you think it does. He *can't* say another word."

Tony's vision focused on the front yard with his back turned toward the doorway; therefore, he didn't realize that I was standing on the other side of the door, listening to his private conversation. While his solid red tie had been removed and draped over his office chair, he wore his starched white button-down shirt, which was still tucked tightly into the waist of his navy blue dress slacks. Through the reflection of the glass window, I could see several thin wrinkles lining his forehead as he concentrated on the voice from the other end. As his gaze followed something that was moving down the street in front of our house, the right side of his face became partially visible to me. A small smirk formed on his lips.

"No, it's not like in the movies. There's no gun for hire." He paused again, listening to the response. "Quit worrying, would you? I literally shut him up. We don't need to worry about him ever saying another word.

Ever. I even threw some empty liquor bottles in the back seat to assist the authorities in figuring out what might have caused the crash."

I hadn't realized that I was holding my breath until my lungs forced my body to gasp for air. Luckily, my brain clicked, and I raised my fist to signal my appearance in his doorway. I prayed that my gentle knock masked my gulp for air. I'd been trying diligently to be a good wife and avoid punishment.

He turned toward the doorway. I forced a weak smile onto my face and mouthed the words, "Supper is ready."

Luckily for me, Tony's attention was locked in on his phone conversation, and he didn't realize I heard any part of it. He turned his head in the direction of the door, where I stood like his obedient wife should—dressed in black pumps, a navy pencil skirt, and a white blouse protected by an apron. He blinked and tipped his chin upward in my direction to acknowledge my words.

As I spun on my heel and returned to the kitchen, the contents of my stomach felt unsettled. What was he talking about? It couldn't be as bad as it sounded. My overactive imagination was creating drama where there wasn't any. I shook my head to scatter the absurd ideas from my brain. Tony might have been an awful husband, but he was an amazing pastor. Surely, he wasn't capable of murder.

***

After the Sunday church service, Tony and I waited at the back of the sanctuary to thank and shake hands with the attendees. When the last congregation member exited, a polite wave motioned for me to join the group of ladies in a corner.

The ACGM group of five women stood in their usual spot in the narthex and left a small opening for me to complete the circle. With her helmet of blonde hair, Susan was the banker's wife and enjoyed gossiping about which farmers in the area were struggling. Even though she wasn't to be trusted with a secret, Susan was the storyteller of the group. If she had a tale to tell, everyone listened in. Her hands flew in exaggerated movements as she became fully engrossed in her story.

"His death is so tragic," whispered Susan to the group of friends. Her words sounded ominous, but last week she used the same word to explain that she didn't sleep for a week when she learned that honeybees die after they sting a human. "When a honeybee stings you, they can't pull out their stinger, so it self-amputates. How tragic is that?" She'd wiped away tears as they escaped her eyes. Her idea of tragedy and mine didn't match. However this time, she wasn't talking about an insect. "It's just awful. He was nice and very handy."

Carrie, the grocer's wife, never missed a beat in adding her opinion. "Yes, I heard he fixed a stranger's flat tire when they broke down at the edge of town. He could fix anything." She snapped her fingers in my direction. "He worked on your house before you moved in, Lisa."

All eyes turned to me.

"What? Who? I'm sorry, but I think I missed who we were talking about. Can we back up a smidge?" Even though these women spread town gossip faster than fleas can spread on a pack of stray dogs, I relished being included. They valued my opinion. This little group of overly perfumed and Aqua Net hairspray enthusiasts was the first set of friends I'd had since grade school.

"Oh, sorry." Susan reached out to grab a hold of my forearm as if I needed support to hear her next words. "Walter Just. He was the man who did some remodeling on your home before you moved to Normal.

He is—*was*—a local contractor. He was a member here but didn't attend regularly, I'm afraid."

"Oh…" I didn't know what to say or what the appropriate response was. As a pastor's wife, I expected to console them with the right words and to put their minds at ease, but this news caught me by complete surprise. I noticed the ladies within the little circle were all waiting for my response, and the longer it took me to respond, the more curious their stares became.

Before last week, his name wouldn't have meant a thing to me.

Walter Just—never heard of him. Never met him.

But last week, I met Walter Just. Walter delivered me a creepy warning about the man I was married to.

Chapter 23

Lisa – a week earlier

As I scrubbed the floors on my hands and knees, the doorbell rang its singsong tune. Making our floors shine was one of the many chores that Tony assigned me each week. Mondays included polishing all the woodwork throughout our home, while Tuesdays were for cleaning bathrooms from top to bottom. On Wednesdays, I washed all the first-floor walls, and on Thursdays, I tackled the second-floor walls. Fridays were reserved for cleaning floors and mowing the lawn. Besides keeping our home immaculate, I was also expected to prepare two meals daily, breakfast and dinner. The menu was pre-approved on Sundays and always consisted of three food groups. Since there wasn't a lot of free time during the day between my household chores and meal preparation, I often skipped eating lunch so my chores were completed before Tony arrived home from work. At least that fact helped eliminate one thing from my never ending to-do list.

Saturdays–like today–were the days I recleaned whatever Tony insisted I had not done a competent job the first time. This week, it was the floor. In the morning during breakfast, the kitchen floor did not reflect Tony's image properly, so he dumped a full glass of orange juice on the floor and advised me to scrub them again.

Someone might suggest that I could skip scrubbing walls each week to save myself some work because they truly didn't need it, but Tony tested me by wiping something small—a slimy booger, a piece of dirt from the bottom of his shoe, or the smushed body of a minuscule spider—on a random wall somewhere in our 4,000 square foot home before he left for work. "And you know what it means if I find you didn't get the cleaning done."

Punishment.

As the doorbell chimed again, I quickly hid the scrub bucket and rag in the cupboard. Because Tony hadn't informed me that he was expecting a guest, the doorbell chime surprised me. Tony would not appreciate having a guest witness his wife—not hired help—cleaning our home. I forcefully pressed the wrinkles out of my clothes and checked my hair in the hallway mirror. Appearances were important to Tony. Our home always appeared like a photo ripped right out of a magazine. Everything had a purpose, a function, and a place. As he explained to me, a man's wife and their home represented his worth. If his wife didn't appear put together or said something disrespectful, she would devalue the man. If his home didn't reflect good management, it also would devalue the man. I couldn't answer the door looking like I'd been washing the floors. I must appear unfazed by a surprise guest.

When I pulled the front door open, a very tall man with broad shoulders loomed on the step. Not only was his size quite intimidating, but the stern expression on his face also reflected a threatening presence. From his facial expression and body language, I gathered that he wasn't dropping by to welcome us to town. On the top of his head, he wore a dirty black hat with a mesh backing that covered most of his hair. Under the brim of his hat, his dark brown caterpillar eyebrows pressed down on his almost black eyes, causing them to be dark slits. His nose was as wide as it was long and rested above his light pink, thin lips that were covered by a thick mustache. The combination of his features made him quite attractive.

I forced a smile on my face and took a deep breath. Despite the warning signs and my gut instinct, I welcomed the giant of a man into our foyer like Tony advised me to do with any guest. As a pastor's wife, I did not judge and was always welcoming and open-minded.

"Please come in."

Even though he was the size of an ogre, his manners provided a contradiction. When he shuffled through the door and wiped his feet on the rug, he looked up at the grand staircase, sizing up the surroundings. After he took off his hat and tucked it under his arm, he finger-combed his wavy hair, trying to push it into place. As I gestured to our bar, I offered him a drink.

"Ma'am? It's one o'clock?" Even though it was a statement, his words formed a question. The expression on his face reflected pure bewilderment. At least the anger subsided.

I glanced at my wristwatch and confirmed the time of day. He was correct, but I didn't understand why he acted so confused. Most of the male visitors appreciated and accepted my offer of a stiff cocktail, no matter the time of day. I mastered the art of making a dry martini, a Manhattan, and a golden Cadillac. The fact that he declined the offer and seemed genuinely surprised by an afternoon cocktail should've been another red flag. However, on that afternoon, I hadn't noticed.

What did ring in my brain was that this visitor was unannounced, which Tony would not be thrilled by. Tony scheduled everything to the minute. He arrived at work by nine every morning, and dinner was to be served every evening at six o'clock sharp. Tony gave the impression that he was spontaneous, but every move and every conversation was calculated and had a purpose. Tony always informed me when he was expecting company.

"I'm sorry. You look very familiar, but I can't remember your name." I pretended to search my brain for his name. Tony taught me that this was the polite way to fish for the name of someone you should probably remember.

"Walter."

"Yes, Walter. I remember you. You're a member of Our Savior's." I had no idea if he attended our church, but the odds were in my favor. He nodded. "Is Tony expecting you?"

"He should be." His words were riddled with sarcasm. "But no, he didn't know I was coming over." His eyes darted back and forth, taking in his surroundings.

I ushered into our living room to have a seat.

"Walter, please have a seat while I retrieve Tony." I forced another polite smile as I backed out of the room.

"Are you his wife?" His eyebrows tilted inward as his curiosity increased.

"Of course, I'm so sorry. I should've introduced myself. How rude of me." I re-entered our living room and struck out my hand to shake his. I prayed that Walter wouldn't inform my husband what a poor hostess I'd been. "I'm Mrs. Tony Shade."

His big brown eyes stared at me and blinked rapidly. I didn't understand why he was acting so agitated.

Have we met before?

Out of common courtesy, Walter put out his right hand and shook mine. From his grip, his calluses rubbed my pruned hands. Dirt wedged under his fingernails. Walter was unlike the majority of the men who visited Tony. Their suits cost as much as a piece of furniture, and their hands were smooth as a baby's bottom. No signs of manual labor. Additionally, the congregation members visited Tony at his church office, so I tried to understand where Walter fit in. He attended our church, yet he dropped by without warning.

"Nice to see you, again, Walter." I cranked my neck up to meet his gaze. He was at least a foot taller than me.

"I'm sorry. I'm acting like a buffoon, but I thought maybe you were...were one of his servants."

Before I could filter my reaction to his words, a small, awkward giggle escaped, but as soon as it left my lips, I noticed the look in his eye. He wasn't joking. He truly thought I was Tony's housekeeper or butler. Even though most days I felt like it, no one else should suspect it. Tony would've been appalled if he heard that a guest in our home mistook me for a maid. He believed appearances spoke volumes, and he recently punished me for forgetting to wear lipstick to the grocery store.

I stared down at my outfit to verify I was dressed appropriately. I yanked my hand away from Walter's grasp and waved it over my hair to verify it wasn't a rat's nest. I pushed down some flyaway pieces and tucked a few loose strands behind my ears.

Walter noticed the fade in my self-confidence, and a small smile cracked his tough guy exterior.

"Sorry. I'm not so good with words. You don't *look* like a hired hand. That wasn't what I meant." His word-tumbling was enduring. "I was surprised that Tony was married, I guess."

"Oh..." I smoothed down the wrinkles in my clothing, still worried about my outward appearance. "Yes, I'm Lisa, his wife." This conversation was not going well.

When Walter refused a drink, I should've realized that the visit wasn't a social call. Walter marched up to our front door with a purpose, trying to catch Tony off guard. Furthermore, he acted too kind and considerate to be one of Tony's work associates who reminded me of starved, wild dogs as they eyed me like a juicy steak, patiently waiting for me to be unattended and discarded like scrap. Walter wasn't giving that vibe, but all the same,

I was on edge. I feared Tony's reaction to me being alone with a strange, good-looking man.

"I'll go get Tony. Wait here. I should only be a minute." Quickly, I turned away, fearing that any more time with this stranger would somehow lead to punishment.

"Wait!" His deep voice startled me. I turned to face him as I paused for a moment at the entrance to the room. Goosebumps rose on my arms, causing the hair on them to stand straight up. He dropped his voice to almost a whisper. "Listen. You seem like a nice, young woman, so I want to warn you..." He let his words linger in the air between us. "I'm not sure what is going on in this house, but I can't... no, I won't silently sit back and say nothing. You need to pack a bag and never look back."

His words struck a chord, and I felt seen for the first time in years. But how did he know? What did he know? Why was he here?

As my throat dried up, I fought back tears that were begging to be released. But my guard–the one that I'd built up and used to protect my heart–kept them at bay. This man was a stranger. There was no way he knew what was going on in my house or how Tony sexually assaulted me, abused me, and locked me up.

Is this a test? Tony recently spoke at great length during his Sunday sermon about Peter, one of Jesus' loyal disciples, who vowed to never leave His side. Jesus predicted that Peter would deny being one of His disciples three times. Peter laughed off this claim. He followed Jesus for hundreds of miles and loved this man. There was no way Peter would give up everything to follow Jesus and then deny ever knowing Him. Impossible.

I wasn't like Peter. I'd never betray Tony.

"Are you safe? Do you have somewhere you can go?" The concern was genuine, and he looked like he wanted to escort me right out of the house and into the safety of his truck.

However, according to Tony's preaching, the Devil will do whatever he can to earn your trust.

Tony's words echoed in the walls of my brain. *The Devil will say and do all the right things. He will test you, and if you are weak, you will fail.* I blinked back my tears and cleared my throat. "I'll be back shortly with Tony." And I backed out of the room.

Chapter 24

Jolene – 1983

To the citizens of Normal, Mother mimicked the image of the strong but grieving widow up until Father's funeral. Even though, while he was alive, Mother continuously sought out company from many other males, she appeared at a loss for how to function without the man who'd held our family together. Dressed from head to toe in black, Mother moped around the town, lost in her grief and overwhelmed with everyday life. Men opened doors for her when she stood clueless in front of a glass one, acting as if she didn't understand what to do next. Women prepared meals for our family because Mother insisted that buying groceries, paying bills, and washing clothes became huge tedious tasks that she couldn't focus on. She wore little makeup so that her pale skin better reflected her sorrow. Clumps of dry mascara flaked off her eyelashes and onto her high cheekbones. Ruby-red lipstick stained the outline of her lips. Mother was doing a hell of a good job at giving everyone the appearance of what they expected to see. Because I was aware of her acting ability from a young age, I recognized the real Mother only showed her true colors inside the walls of her bedroom, where she giggled for hours on the phone with callers. It was behind her closed bedroom door that I heard her favorite music being played as she danced around, celebrating her newfound freedom.

As we were piling into the family sedan and heading to the church to welcome other mourners, Mother informed Ivy that she'd prayed she could be as classy as Jackie O had been when her husband Jack Kennedy had been shot. She was acting, pretending to be someone else to appear like a woman in mourning. Her elegant, fitted black dress hugged every corner of her lean body, and the black veil that she insisted on wearing even though in small-town Iowa looked ridiculous and out of place masked her face. All of it was her costume for this 'role.'

"She's the pillar of class."

Under my breath, I muttered, "No one will ever mix you two up."

Ivy elbowed me in my side and shot me a dirty look. She was always Mother's protector.

Honestly, if Mother's grief didn't drip on and off like a rusty kitchen faucet and if I wasn't aware of her true colors, I would've felt bad for her, but I'd witnessed her act so many times before that I didn't rush to her side to comfort her. I'd seen her play this game before when she wanted something. And right now, she wanted attention and sympathy.

Move over, Meryl Streep. The Oscar goes to... Isabella Just.

We were the first to arrive at the church, and the beautiful, fragrant flowers surrounding the altar drew us in. Mother bee-lined her way to the coffin, where Father's body lay motionless. Mother had provided the funeral home with Father's only suit jacket and tie and complained when they requested a pair of shoes

"I'm already giving you the most expensive piece of clothing that the man owned. I could've gotten ten dollars for that jacket at a garage sale. He doesn't need shoes where he is going, plus no one will see his feet in his coffin. I'm selling those." Mother always loved a garage sale that was bursting at the seams, and she was already making plans for her next one, where she'd rake in a pile of money from Father's clothes... and shoes.

Even though it wasn't him lying there in the wooden box, morbid curiosity drew me to the casket. The outer shell of my father lay perfectly still, which in itself was odd. Even if Father fell asleep on the couch in the middle of a Sunday afternoon, he snored, and his body twitched. As young, mischievous girls, Ivy and I would tiptoe into the living room to poke and prod his body to witness what his body would do involuntarily. As I looked into his coffin, the urge to touch him was overwhelming, but my maturity level didn't agree. He wasn't going to sit up and chase Ivy and me around the room, pretending to be a tickle monster. He was gone. Tears ran down my cheeks.

When the guests arrived, we became barricaded at the front of the sanctuary. I hadn't attended a church service since the new pastor had been hired, so I felt like an imposter. The floral arrangements and cards drew people's attention, as did the body that lay cold and stiff in the coffin. The phrases people uttered as they peered at Father sounded absurd.

"He looks like he is sleeping."

"Walter was always smiling. Strange to see him without one now."

"His skin looks pale. He was always tan from working outdoors."

"He had great teeth. I wonder if you can donate your teeth when you die."

"Tragic that he couldn't fight the demons of alcohol. I heard his wife didn't know he was drinking again."

I wanted to respond to every one of those gossipy old ladies who attended the funeral for the free lunch and to fuel their rumors.

He isn't sleeping. Poke him and you'll see. But watch out because if he wakes up he will chase you around the room trying to tickle you.

And of course, he is pale. His body has been drained of blood. Are you idiots?

Father took great pride in his teeth since he said his father's yellowed from nicotine.

He wasn't drinking. He hasn't had a drop of alcohol in years. It was a tragic car accident. Get your facts straight, ladies.

I was still in the early stages of denial. My mind couldn't comprehend that he wasn't going to walk in the front door and kick off his heavy work boots after a long day, or that he wasn't going to call me 'Turd Muffin' again in front of my friends or ruffle my hair when he walked by me in the kitchen. The last few days felt like a nightmare. Our father was bigger than life, physically stronger than anyone else I knew, and the only man I'd ever loved. How could he be gone? It didn't seem real.

Finally, Mother insisted that we return to the narthex so we could proceed in as the music started. She excused us and pushed her way through the crowd of mourners. I would've preferred not to be the focus of everyone's attention and just slide into our immediate family's designated pew, but Mother didn't want to miss a second of having all eyes on her.

I had to admit that I was relieved to move away from the coffin. It wasn't Father in there. The parts that I loved about him—his passion, his generosity, and his playfulness—were gone. His soul had risen to Heaven. His body was only the shell of the man who was familiar to me.

Ivy, Mother, and I entered the sanctuary as the organist played "Amazing Grace." Mother turned on the faucet of tears and bowed her head as a devoted wife should do. I looked up and down the pews to see which friends and family filled the church waiting to 'celebrate his life.' In the back pews, our classmates from school attended with their parents. A few friends returned my gaze and looked pitifully at me with tear-stained eyes, while their parents locked their eyes on the book of hymns. The next set of pews contained adults that either Mother or Father knew. The women were dressed in simple floral dresses while their mates adorned a simple solid-colored tie. Their faces were familiar, but at the moment, not one name registered. Then, taking up a pew all their own, a group of five men stood one inch apart staring intently straight ahead. Each one wore a crisp black suit. Simply by their clothing alone, I recognized that they were not residents of Normal, Iowa. The men of our small town didn't have matching jackets and slacks, and most of them only owned one tie. We were a farming community that didn't have many occasions for suits. A simple tie and pair of Dockers would be more than acceptable for anything formal that they needed to attend.

Ask Mother who they are after the ceremony.

The rest of the pews were crammed full of distant relatives who felt the need for closure, even though we hadn't seen them in years. They were the group who had tears leaking from their eyes and regret in their hearts, wishing that they would've made Father and his family more of a priority.

I slid first into the front pew while Ivy sat down next to me. Her arm wrapped around Mother's shoulder as soon as we were seated.

I was sure that I looked cold and uncaring to the people who came to give their condolences, but unfortunately, I wasn't as good of an actress as my mother was. With me, what you saw was what you got. Games and pretending were not in my wheelhouse.

When the organ stopped playing the sorrowful tune, a good-looking, middle-aged man stood up and walked to the pulpit. His crisp, dark gray suit fit his physique and accented his athletic shape. His chiseled jawline framed his full lips. A chill ran up and down my spine when a small, timid smile appeared on his face.

He looks familiar. Who is that man?

I eyed him up and down and tried to understand where that chill and tummy flip had come from by the sudden appearance of the pastor. I do remember a fight that I'd heard my parents having about Father wanting to talk to him about some construction he had completed for him.

But it's his smile, those lips, and that defined jaw that I remember. Another intense shiver ran up my spine, causing Ivy to glance in my direction.

I shook my head to ensure that I was fine. *I was, wasn't I?* I tasted bile in the back of my throat.

"Welcome, friends and family of Walter James Just." He paused and looked around at the large group of wet eyes. "I'm Pastor Tony Shade, the head pastor at Our Savior's Church here in this wonderful town of Normal. Even though we're gathered here today to try to make sense of a tragedy, we must also remember to celebrate this talented, generous man. A life taken too soon from a family who loved and cherished him. We aren't supposed to understand. We're mere mortals who aren't able to fully grasp the bigger picture. That is why we must trust God to know what is best. We need to let him guide us through our heartache. Please bow your heads as we lift Walter's loved ones in prayer."

I watched everyone around me drop their chins to their chests and shut their eyes. Pastor Tony's eyes closed as his voice hypnotized the gathering with his words of comfort. "Dear God, bless those who mourn with the comfort of your love so that they may face each new day with hope and the certainty that nothing can destroy the good that has been given. May their memories become joyful, their days enriched with friendship, and their lives encircled with your love."

As I listened to his words of comfort fill the sanctuary, I tried to figure out why he looked familiar. I couldn't recall the last time I'd been in church, possibly when the last pastor was giving his farewell address. However, it wasn't his voice that triggered the recognition; it was his smile. Goosebumps traveled up my arms, and I rubbed them away. Before I could figure out the mystery of Pastor Tony, the service was coming to a close. I'd managed to daydream during the entire service. I glanced over at Mother, who had mascara running down her cheeks.

Not very Jackie O of her.

Ivy managed to push aside her grief to console our mother by rubbing her back and whispering that everything would be alright.

"Friends and family, please keep Walter's beloved wife and two beautiful daughters in your weekly prayers. We will keep his memory alive by sharing in fellowship in the church basement. Please join us if you'd like to pay your respects. God's mercy and grace onto you all. Amen." Following his closing, Pastor Tony bowed his head and turned toward the altar. He made the sign of the cross on his forehead and exited through the side door, which signaled our departure. Ivy pulled Mother from her hunched-over seated position, guiding her to walk down the aisle.

As soon as the three of us reached the back of the church, Mother dramatically broke down and fell to her knees in a perfectly timed act. Her weeping echoed through the church sanctuary, causing the mourners to turn and witness the drama. I turned my back as Ivy ran to her and pulled her into her arms. She petted the top of her head and said, "It'll be okay, Momma. I'm here."

Chapter 25

Jolene - 1983

I retreated to the church basement, where the luncheon would be held. Since the family was the first ones to exit the service, I was the first mourner to arrive in the musty-smelling basement. Approximately twenty round tables surrounded by folding chairs were covered with white table-cloths. In the center of each table, a small bouquet of artificial flowers had been dropped into a short, clear vase.

I dropped my purse and light jacket onto a table in the back of the room, hoping that my seclusion would scare off some people who wanted to share their grief with me. When a soft hand rested on the top of my shoulder, I jumped.

"Sorry. I didn't mean to scare you. Jolene, right?" questioned the familiar voice.

Behind me stood Pastor Tony. Another shiver enveloped my body. Even though his touch on my shoulder appeared innocent enough, it was in his dark eyes that I recognized mistrust. His move had been calculated, and his already large smile grew even more when he noticed that he startled me.

As I turned around to face him, his hand remained on my shoulder. An impressively white set of straight teeth grinned at me. His jawline was sharp and angled. On his head, not a hair was out of place. His suit screamed expensive, and every pleat was evenly pressed. I could've sworn that I saw my reflection in the shine of his shoes. Even though his appearance was flawless, I noticed that he missed a small clump of whiskers in the corner of his mouth, just above his top lip. Not perfect after all.

I eyed this man, who delivered a seemingly heartfelt eulogy about my father. He'd told stories about how they first met, about happy hour at a fellow member's home, and how much he'd miss Father's quick wit and craftsman skills.

A sparkle flickered in his eye as he realized that I was looking him over. A good-looking man like him was used to being gawked at, and he enjoyed it. I planned on erasing the smile and twinkle as soon as I could.

I cleared my throat and casually tried to shake his hand off my shoulder. "Thank you for the thoughtful eulogy. I wasn't aware that you and my father were such good friends. He never mentioned *you*." My statements were laced with sarcasm.

"We'd become more acquainted lately." The twinkle wasn't gone, but it had diminished some. I could tell that he wasn't used to being treated with anything but respect, and he didn't respond well to anything less. However, for some reason, I didn't trust him. "We met through the church council, and he worked on my house before my wife Lisa and I moved in. He was quite talented and handy, but you probably knew that since *you* were so close."

I remembered the fight I'd overheard weeks before when Ivy and I were in our bedroom eavesdropping. Father had mentioned wanting to confront someone about a soundproof room. Before I could control my natural responses to things that were bouncing around in my head, Tony noticed a slight shift in my regard for him.

Had I met him during one of my hotel 'jobs?' By the time I arrived at a hotel, I was usually very high or intoxicated. The rooms were dark, and many of the men preferred not to talk and some wore masks. I think they preferred it that way because they were harder to identify.

Run.

A strong feeling erupted from my gut, urging me to flee, but my stubbornness prevailed.

"Yes, he was an amazing, *honest* man, my father. I'm surprised you were friends. You don't seem to be his type, but thanks again for the eulogy. It seemed very heartfelt." Indicating that our conversation was finished, I turned to leave, but the hand that had been awkwardly resting on my shoulder slid down my arm and gripped my wrist, pulling my attention to him, and not allowing me to walk away.

"I'll never forget what your father did to help me." The sparkle that I saw in his eye was dilated like a cat's eyes do right before they attack their prey. They become black dots. Dropping his voice a few octaves, he added, "Walter was paid handsomely for his work, so I'd hate to have someone question the church's budget and realize where the money went. That kind of scandal would ruin his good name, his family's good name. I sure wouldn't want that to happen. Wouldn't you agree, Jolene?" His hand squeezed my wrist so hard that I was certain it would leave a bruise.

Before I could answer or rattle off a response, Mother strolled into the basement along with several other mourners.

"Pastor Tony, there you are." In record time, she managed to slither over to us, and her hand reached out to grab his bicep. Odd placement. He released my hand, and I rubbed my wrist to encourage the blood flow to return. "I see you've met my oldest daughter, Jolene."

"Yes, we were just talking about how resourceful and handy Walter was. Jolene couldn't believe that Walter and I were friends. You know that Jesus was a carpenter, right, Jolene? He worked with his hands just like your father, and I'm a man of God. So, we were more alike than you think."

Through my clenched teeth, I muttered, "You are nothing like him."

He turned his attention to my mother, and I felt the air in my immediate surroundings change. There was an intense energy. A charge. Their eyes locked on each other for a little too long to be considered necessary and appropriate. Instinctively, I peeled my eyes away. Their intensity made me uncomfortable. The part of me that was in charge of the filter on my mouth pulled my throat tight and wouldn't allow the words banging around in my head to escape.

This man, a pastor, threatened me, and now he was flirting with my mother at her husband's funeral in under five minutes. Is he nuts?

Maybe that was why he was threatening me—he wanted to make sure I kept my questions to myself while he made moves on my mother. *Or is it something else?*

Mother noticed me glaring in his direction. She knew I was perceptive. When she finally collected herself, her eyes fell to the floor like a flirty, shy teenager would do when she came face to face with her suitor, and she added, "I sure appreciate your sweet words on Walter's behalf. He would've been so pleased."

Pastor Tony's hand, which had recently squeezed my wrist too tightly, wiped away a silent tear that had fallen below my mother's eyes. "I'm glad I could help you during your time of need, Isabella. Please reach out," he emphasized the last two words. For some reason unknown to me, my mother's face flushed. He turned toward me and gave me a slight nod to acknowledge that he was aware that I'd been silently watching their exchange. "And Jolene, I hope to see you again soon."

With those words, he strolled toward the crowd of people who had gathered for the luncheon. I couldn't quite put my finger on it, but that man's physical presence demanded attention. Sure, his smile reached across his face, and every word that exited his mouth was polite and kind, but it was his eyes that sent goosebumps up and down my spine. In them, I detected danger. I feared what lay beyond them.

Mother cleared her throat to gain my attention. She glared at me and quietly muttered, "Do. Not. Make. A. Scene."

"Are you kidding me right now, Mother?"

"Jolene." Disdain filled her voice. Ever since I discovered her first affair, she tended to avoid using her motherly voice with me. I didn't respond fairly to her trying to reprimand me for not using phrases like 'please' and 'thank you' when morally she had no right. "You need to apologize. You were rude to that man. Pastor Tony was offering you his condolences and support."

A light bulb flashed in my brain.

"Are you sleeping with him?" My eyes burned with the possible realization of why this man was being overly kind and generous to our family. There must be something more going on. Plus, there was Pastor Tony's weird comment about stolen money.

In the deepest part of my heart, I was certain that my father would never have stolen money from our church. Honest and hard-working were adjectives that he lived by. Even if we were in a financial bind, Father would've found an additional job to supplement his income rather than asking anyone for help or, heaven forbid, stealing it.

Pastor Tony threatened me so I'd keep my mouth shut. There was something else going on. The section of my heart that had hardened when it came to Mother suggested that *she* was capable of stealing from a church. Morally, she didn't have a problem stepping over the line, but I doubted that she was smart enough to embezzle. It had to be something else.

I eyed her to see if there was any body language that would betray what lies came out of her mouth. Of course, she acted appalled and shocked by my question.

"Jolene, if I hadn't seen you pop out of my vagina all red and slimy, I'd swear you weren't my child." She waved her hand over me as if trying to make me disappear. She looked around the room to see if anyone had overheard our conversation. Then she added in a whisper, "You...you are a total disappointment." With that, she flipped her hair over her shoulder, spun on her heel, and dismissed my inquiry as guests began trickling into the church basement. She returned to doing what she did best: pretending. While she pretended to mourn my father, she pretended to appreciate everyone's concern and laughed away any awkward conversations.

I had my answer. She wasn't... yet, but that didn't mean that she wouldn't. Father's grave didn't even have dirt shoveled over it yet, but I thought to myself, *I doubted that would stop her.* By witnessing the two of them moments ago, I'd bet all my poker chips that he was attracted to her too. When she interrupted us, his eyes traveled up and down her body, and he looked like he wanted to devour her. The hunger faded as quickly as it appeared, making me question what I'd witnessed.

Pastor Tony began shaking hands and greeting guests a respectful distance away. I watched him. I understood how everyone who met him became hypnotized by his attention. His voice was smooth, and his words inspired them. He reminded me of a traditional Indian snake charmer. As the performer softly played his pungi, the wild, often poisonous snake appeared to be in a trance as it swayed back and forth to the relaxing music.

Pastor Tony, the snake charmer, recited passages from his personal, worn-out Bible and added words of wisdom for his herd. No one suspected anything horrible or untrustworthy from a man of God. Everyone followed his lead and embraced his words.

However, after my short encounter with him, my gut clenched and told me to proceed with caution. I had nothing else to go on, so I kept my mouth shut. For now. A full-body shiver radiated through my body as I tried to shake the uncomfortable feeling.

My stomach rumbled. It was time for a traditional funeral ham sandwich—fresh bakery buns with two slices of ham in the middle. If the church ladies who were in charge of the food had spare time, they usually slapped a thick coat of butter on one side of the bun. I prayed that was the case.

Before I gorged myself on free food, I glanced around the room for Ivy. She remained next to Mother in an awkward receiving line. Again, I didn't care if I looked like the older, difficult daughter of the deceased. Mother did enough pretending for all of us. I planned on leaving it to her.

There was no line yet for refreshments because people were still making their way down to the basement. I bee-lined for the kitchen counter, where a handful of older women stood eagerly waiting. I wasn't sure if they were waiting to feel useful, waiting for someone to thank them, or if they just didn't have anything better to do than stare at me as I scooped salads and chips onto my plate next to my three palm-sized ham sandwiches.

"Hey, I can carry over your dessert if you want to pick one," one of the church ladies offered.

"Thank you. That would be helpful. I'd love to try the pie."

"It's strawberry rhubarb. Delicious."

"Did you make it?

She chuckled. "No, but if you don't pick it, I'm going to grab it because I know it's amazing."

"Sold. Thank you for your help." In one hand, I balanced my heaping plate full of food on top of the wrapped silverware, and with the other, I carried a glass of lemonade. Even though a funeral would not be my first choice as a social gathering, at least the food was good.

I pulled out a chair from a nearby table and set down my food. Before I sat down to enjoy it, I made eye contact with the church lady who helped me. "Thanks."

She put down the small plate with pie at my place setting. "Anytime. I'm very sorry to hear about your dad. I met him once." Her eyes reflected genuine concern, and her words were heartfelt. "He was so tall and had such big, broad shoulders. He looked mean as hell." She giggled, and as she glanced up at the ceiling, she quietly whispered an apology for swearing in church. "But was he more of a gentle giant?"

I smiled. I'd never heard him described that way, but I could see how someone who didn't know him might have been intimidated by his stature. "Yeah, he was a big teddy bear. All growl but no bite."

I turned to sit down as she said, "If you need anything, let me know. I'm Lisa." And she walked back to her station in the church kitchen.

What a strange committee to volunteer for. Serving sandwiches and desserts at dead people's farewell parties. I can only imagine what those volunteers were like—their lives so perfect that they volunteered their time to gawk at a stranger's misery.

Chapter 26

Lisa – five days before the funeral

After learning that the stranger, who warned me a few days ago about the monster I was married to, had died, my gut suggested that it wasn't a coincidence. Something more was going on, but the invisible shield that protected my heart and retained my sanity couldn't deny the deafening alarm bells ringing in my head.

When we returned home after the Sunday service, we both were changing into our Sunday casual attire. As Tony slipped off his dress pants, he asked me, "Lisa, you're quiet. You mumbled every response to my comments about today's sermon. Do you want to share what's on your tiny mind?"

I hadn't realized that I'd been so distracted. After every Sunday service or any event where Tony talked publicly, he liked to discuss how his audience responded to what he said. Tony wanted every one of his words to affect his listeners. Out of habit on Sunday mornings, I usually glanced around the sanctuary to gauge the reaction of the listeners. I often reported what he wanted to hear. I exaggerated someone's reaction from a raised eyebrow to a surprised expression. I was careful. I never lied because he'd find out, and I'd be punished.

"Sorry, dear. I didn't sleep well, and I guess I'm a little tired." I slipped off my pantyhose and rolled them up to be washed.

I wanted to bombard him with questions about what I'd learned from the church ladies, but I held my tongue. I realized that in a normal marriage, a wife would simply ask her husband about what the ladies had said about Walter, but our marriage was far from typical. However, the old independent me–the one with a backbone who was curious about everything–had to know and to ask even though the new, wounded me–the one who suffered abuse at the hands of her husband–was scared. A battle raged inside my head.

As Tony removed his gold watch, the one that he'd yanked off his dead father's wrist, and placed it on the top of our dresser, I heard the words leave my mouth before I could censor them.

"Tony? Do you know a man named Walter?" My eyes searched for a reaction–any response to the man's name. Nothing. "After church, the ladies mentioned that he died. Do we know him?"

My husband, who could dial up any emotion without actually feeling it, took his time answering me and kept his expression blank. He rested on the footstool at the end of our bed to remove his black socks, and all the while I stood there patiently waiting for his response. The question itself was harmless, but Tony possessed the ability to create a mountain out of a molehill.

"Yes, Lisa, Walter was a member of our church. Very tragic, I'm afraid."

"What happened?"

"A car accident. He had too much to drink and then drove his rusty, old truck straight into a tree." As he cracked his knuckles for effect, he added, "Snapped his neck. He died instantly. Poor Walter." Tony's words sounded sympathetic but it was his tone that revealed the truth.

I gasped.

"I'm sure the ladies will be contacting you to help with his funeral."

"How do you know that he died instantly? Was he the man who visited you the other day?" I asked one too many questions. I seemed too eager.

He stopped unbuttoning his shirt and turned his black, dilated eyes at me. Whenever he was angry or about to lose it, his eyes reflected the initial sign that I should hide. My curiosity decided that I'd already crossed the line with my questioning, so I continued. "The church ladies said Walter quit drinking years ago, so they were surprised to hear about the discarded whiskey bottles. They suggested something major caused him to revert to the bottle again. The ladies also mentioned that he was the man who remodeled our home before we moved in."

Tony's jaw clenched, and his nostrils flared. He was calculating his response, and I knew at that moment that my punishment would be like no other that I'd experienced. However, my curiosity controlled my mouth at the moment and wouldn't let up. It gave no regard for what might happen to my body and soul, so I continued with my unwelcomed inquiries.

"Tony, I overheard you in your office on the phone the other day. You said something along the lines of 'he was taken care of.' Did that phone call have anything to do with this man's death?" My heart beat double time realizing that the words coming out of my mouth would land me in great danger.

My husband was abusive and controlling, but was he a murderer? I couldn't fathom that a man of God could take someone's life. He'd been called to serve and teach the lessons of the Bible, not to carelessly end another person's life. But I had to know.

"Lisa, are you suggesting that your generous husband, who provides for you, killed a man?" He waved his index finger at me as if he were scolding me for tracking mud into our house.

I didn't answer him, but the answer was obvious. That was exactly what I was wondering.

"Lisa, let's get changed, and we'll continue this tantalizing conversation downstairs. I have something to show you."

He was too calm, too controlled. This couldn't be good.

Chapter 27

Lisa - 1983

Being locked in a closet for twenty-four hours would've been a piece of cake as punishment for disrespecting my husband, compared to what I learned and experienced that Sunday afternoon. How naive it was for me to think solitude was the worst form of punishment that Tony was capable of.

I learned that my husband had been recruited by a sex cult to run a modern brothel out of his own home. While in Nevada–ironically the only state that legalized prostitution–attending a week-long pastoral conference, Tony claimed to have stumbled upon a bar where naked women were blindfolded and chained to beds in private rooms. For a hefty price, a man could 'visit' and spend time in these rooms to do as he pleased with the willing participants. Admittedly, Tony visited the brothel every night while he was away, and he became friends with a circle of powerful men who shared Tony's ambitious sexual drive. The men held jobs as politicians, law enforcement, and clergy. He claimed that it took him and his new friends only a few days to establish their business plan.

Every idea and every conversation excited the new friends so much that together they assured each other that they could pull it off, and the perfect cover would be a pastor's house in Normal, Iowa. No one would suspect a thing. Of course, my husband, always a savvy businessman, convinced the team that since he'd be the one most at risk, he should be paid handsomely.

Willing to do anything to see their plan succeed, the men agreed. Tony, as the headmaster of the room, controlled the finances, and the employment while his partners worked on bringing in business.

To safeguard his lifestyle, Tony formulated a plan: the men of power and influence who participated in the Room needed to pay a membership fee. This fee would protect their anonymity and allow them to participate whenever they desired. In exchange for a share of the profit and anonymity in the sex cult, the men protected their entertainment industry. They had thought of everything.

While Tony summarized what would be happening under our roof, I recognized an enormous amount of pride in his voice. His confidence oozed out of every word he said, and every one of the words created a shiver up my spine.

"With any successful plan, there are casualties." He tilted his head back and forth as if the casualty wasn't a person's life but more like a stubbed toe. "Unfortunately, Walter Just was in the wrong place at the wrong time. His death wasn't in the plan, but sometimes life throws you a curveball, and you can either swing the bat and hope to whack the shit out of the ball, or you can stand there like a dumbass, do nothing, and strike out. The game was only in the first inning, so I wasn't about to swing and miss."

I was utterly speechless. I couldn't make a sound. I just stared at him and wished with my entire being that I could go back in time and never have asked him anything. *Why couldn't I have kept my big mouth shut?* I was almost positive that I knew the answer before I asked the question, so why did I feel the need to open my mouth and push the limit?

I blamed myself. I was a slow learner. No good would ever come when I disobeyed Tony. *When will I learn?* It turned out that very soon after I asked myself that question, I would learn. I learned that things can get worse and that sometimes not knowing something is a blessing. Ignorance was bliss.

Walter Just was paid very well for the work he completed on constructing a soundproof, hidden room. Furthermore, he lied to all the right people about what kind of work he was doing at the pastor's house. As he was instructed to say, Walter initially claimed he completed some remodeling to the master suite and living room. At first, Walter wasn't interested in what he was building. The dollar signs that came with this side job affected his better judgment. However, his guilty conscience got the best of him, and he put two and two together and concluded that he had constructed something sinister.

When he visited our house that day, Walter arrived with questions that, like me, he knew the answers to. However, Walter wanted confirmation of his speculations, and part of him wanted to believe that there was a logical, healthy reasoning for the construction.

***

Tony unleashed a shock of information after he pushed open the secret door to his playroom and pulled me inside. He fixed himself a stiff cocktail behind the monstrous bar and invited me to sit on one of the red velvet couches. It was my first time in the Room *with* Tony. Of course, when he went to work, I'd open the door and venture into the Room a few times, but I was always careful not to disturb anything. I made flimsy excuses for the strange room, mostly so I could sleep at night. My avoidance of discovering the truth had been a way to protect myself. All of the answers were at my fingertips, but I never searched too hard. Once the truth was discovered, there would be no turning back.

When he was finished with the shocking details, he pulled me close to him. "Lisa, I fell in love with your adventurous nature. From day one, you proved to me that you would always keep me on my toes. At first, I liked that. I needed a challenge. Everything, especially women, came too easy for me." He planted a gentle kiss on my forehead. "But now, as my wife, you will not question me or my choices. I've grown tired of your curious nature and demand you to shut your trap." His tone of voice gradually escalated to his crazy level. He reached across the couch and forcefully shoved my jaw closed after it had dropped open in shock. "The time of your questioning my authority is over." His strong hand, which covered my chin, squeezed it. "Do you understand what I'm telling you?"

As a few disloyal tears sprang to my eyes, I nodded.

"If you do not understand what I'm asking of you, then I'll be forced to remind you. I will never kill you, Lisa, but I can promise you that you'll be begging me to end your life like I did to Walter and my father."

Did he just admit to killing Walter? And did he have something to do with his father's sudden death?

I'd never been so scared in all my life, and being married to Tony was pretty scary. I never wanted to believe that my husband could hurt, let alone kill, someone, but there was pride in his words. Taking someone's life had brought him a new sense of control that he hadn't felt before.

"Yes, you were right. I did take care of Walter. I'd meant to only scare him, but sometimes bad things happen. And my father, well, he was a miserable, unhealthy man anyway. He didn't have a pot to piss in. A respirator in a nursing home would've been the next logical step, and I wasn't about to foot the bill for a place where he was shitting himself in his bed." Tony shook his head. "Nah. I sped up the process. I bet he's thanking me now."

"No one would ever thank their killer." I couldn't keep the words from tumbling out of my mouth. They were quiet but powerful.

"Now, this is exactly what I'm talking about." He forcefully grabbed my wrist. "I will not allow this disrespect, Lisa. We're about to start a very lucrative business out of our home, and I can't have you questioning my authority." Tony stood up and started to unbutton his pants.

My eyes grew wide, but I kept my mouth shut. I knew what he planned as my punishment, and I almost begged to be locked alone in a closet.

He kneeled next to the couch and swiftly produced an ankle cuff that had been strategically secured under the couch out of sight. He clasped the cuff over my ankle.

"Tony? No..."

"Disrespect. I think I've been more than tolerant, but I'm done. Do not open your mouth to speak again unless it's to thank me." He ripped my blouse open, sending buttons flying across the room. As he leaned over me, he produced a set of handcuffs that were hanging behind the couch. Forcefully, he grabbed my wrists and locked them in the cuffs.

I couldn't stop the tears from falling down my cheeks. My curiosity for the truth had once again done more harm than good.

Chapter 28

Lisa – 1983

As a member of the funeral committee, I was expected to either provide bakery items or, if possible, assist at the funeral service. Most of the time, my schedule and Tony allowed me to do both. Baking became an outlet for me. Creating something from nuggets of ingredients was rewarding, and the noises of a little orgasmic moment in the mouth provided me with the pat on the back that I yearned for. Even though cooking and baking had been a chore assigned to me, I looked forward to witnessing the effect that it had on whoever consumed my creation.

Serving at a congregation member's funeral fulfilled a social need. Tony forbade me from making friends because he wanted to approve everything about my life, from relationships to the food I consumed. He encouraged my participation when it came to volunteering with the church. He assumed that the ladies of the church were harmless and good influences. He had no idea what well-respected, educated, high-class women talked about when the men weren't around; even I was shocked.

On the day of Walter Just's funeral, I looked forward to some much-needed giggles about silly trivial things with the ACGM ladies. I shoved the fact that my husband had something to do with Walter's death to the back of my mind. I had to.

Because it was a beautiful sunny afternoon, we were standing in the church parking lot waiting for the last member of the group to arrive.

As Rachael pulled in ten minutes after the designated time, we'd been discussing whether we thought we'd ever swallow Tylenol again. After the cyanide-laced Tylenol had killed people in Chicago, people were worried about tampering with over-the-counter medication.

Susan cleared her throat. "Ladies, don't be worried about what will cure your headache. Aspirin works, and no one has ever been poisoned by it. The Tylenol scandal will be old news in a week, but the news that I'm going to share will have you losing sleep for a long time." She paused to make sure she earned everyone's attention. "You need to be worried about who is sitting at your kitchen table."

Is it my imagination, or did Susan look directly at me? As my eyes bulged out of my head, I held my breath to see where this conversation was going. *Is she referring to my kitchen table? Does Susan know about what a monster my husband truly is?*

"I'm here to warn you that if you invite Rachael to your home for dinner, she *may* attend the dinner party commando," Susan announced to the group as she unlocked the church doors.

I released the breath I was holding as everyone giggled.

Rachael raised her hand to earn her friends' attention and clear up Susan's claim. "First of all, in my defense, we were on the boat all afternoon. Tubing, fishing, and swimming. But I made it to Susan's house right on time."

"First time *ever*." Susan chimed in. Rachael's tardiness was well-known among the group. She often arrived after the kitchen preparations were complete, but she was more than willing to help with clean up.

"I packed a change of clothes to bring with us to the lake— "

" —Incorrect." Susan chimed in again causing more laughter.

"Okay. I packed everything but a pair of underwear."

Carrie, the first to regain her composure, asked, "So, why didn't you keep your swimsuit bottoms on, or was this dinner party a panties-optional kind of night?"

Everyone snickered again.

"Again, in my defense, we'd been in the water all day, and they were wet. I didn't want them to soak through my skirt."

"You were commando in a skirt?" Carrie asked. More roars of laughter. "I'm not sure if we want to know how you discovered this fact, Susan."

More fits of laughter sprouted from the group.

We allowed ourselves one hour to set up before the crowd trickled in. We adorned the round tables with tablecloths and placed salt and pepper shakers, a pitcher of water, and a small fake floral arrangement depending on the season on each table as a centerpiece. If the funeral was a morning event, we arranged pastries on a serving platter and prepared pots and pots of coffee. If the function was scheduled over the lunch hour, we sliced and buttered buns for ham sandwiches. At afternoon services, cookies or bars were offered. All preparations were complete by the time the service was over and the family arrived in the basement. Because this group of ladies had been working together as a team for years, their process was a well-oiled machine. I stepped in and helped wherever needed.

The majority of the time, when I served on the funeral committee, the service was for an older member of the church. People said things like, "He led a good life" or "She died doing what she loved" and even "The illness changed him. He is much better off."

But the tragic and sudden deaths of a life taken too soon created a whole different atmosphere. Uncontrollable weeping, ten-minute embraces, and awkward silences often filled the church basement. Rather than smiles and a few chuckles behind the serving counter, my committee remained silent as family members picked through the offering of food. No one knew what to say that would remotely help. Silence was the best choice.

Because Walter's funeral was the latter, once we were inside the church, the giggling stopped, and we focused on the preparations.

Even though I looked forward to hanging with my only friends, I dreaded volunteering at Walter Just's funeral. The last week had been almost more than I could emotionally handle. After his unannounced visit, I felt an invisible tension surrounding Tony. He made several phone calls from his study, which wasn't unusual except that I could hear his raised voice from the kitchen. Something was not right. Then he claimed to have killed Walter. My head and heart were spinning.

Furthermore, the last conversation that I had with the deceased weighed heavily on my mind. When Walter appeared on our front steps, initially his physique scared me, but by the end of my interaction with him, his words frightened me more.

I'm not sure what is happening in this house, but I can't... no, I won't silently sit back and say nothing. You need to pack a bag and never look back.

At the time, I figured Walter knew about Tony abusing me. However, I found out later, with Tony's excited narration, that Walter must have been referring to the room that he constructed at the back of our house. And now, he was dead soon after he questioned and threatened Tony.

His warning bounced around in my head while I watched his daughters interact with people in the church basement. The white-blonde-haired daughter mourned alone and carried a weighted chip on her shoulder. That much was obvious from my observation of her before their guests followed them down the stairs. As soon as she dropped her purse onto her folding chair, my husband rested his hand on her shoulder. As I rolled silverware, I watched the interaction. From the church program, I learned that her name was Jolene, and she was Walter's oldest daughter.

Unlike most of Tony's followers–especially the female ones–Jolene didn't appear pleased that Tony approached her. His charm didn't break through the wall of grief that she was hiding behind. I wondered if her reaction was based on a permanent chip on her shoulder or something that Tony had done. Whatever the reason, I watched the exchange with keen interest.

After a few words, I witnessed Jolene shrugging Tony's hand from her shoulder as if she was repulsed by his touch, and just as swiftly, I watched Tony grab her by the wrist. Instantly, the hairs on the back of my neck stood at attention. Did she know something? Why was he being so forceful with someone? I'd never seen him act that way toward anyone but me.

As my brain fired questions back and forth, my hands dropped the silverware that I was wrapping in napkins, and the sudden noise alerted my friends.

"Everything okay, Lisa?" Susan rushed to my side, picking up the silverware from the floor.

"Yes, sorry about that. I'm so clumsy."

"No need to apologize, sweetheart. You did nothing wrong." Susan patted me on the back but leaned over to whisper in my ear. "Honey, you can stop. For the last twenty or so, you wrapped sugar packets instead of forks with only knives inside the napkins." With a slight nod, she indicated to the messy pile of napkins.

"Oh no. I'm so sorry."

"Stop apologizing. You're fine. No one noticed but me. I figured you must have something else on your mind." She pried the crumpled-up napkin from my fingers. "We can handle this one. Why don't you go home and get some rest?" Susan gave me her approval to take an afternoon off because she assumed that I needed a nap, but Tony wouldn't see it like that.

Before I took a break, I helped Walter's daughter carry food to her seat. My heart broke for her. She seemed lost and angry.

I followed part of Susan's advice and exited the kitchen's backdoor to get some fresh air. Susan wasn't completely wrong–I did need some rest, but I wasn't allowed naps. Since Tony would be busy for the next half an hour greeting friends and family of Walter, I chose that time to take a minute to gather my senses.

I squatted down on the cement steps outside the back of the church. The spot wasn't ideal with the smelly dumpster in the alley, but it did have a nice view of the side street appropriately named Faith Lane. Spring was beginning to show its coloring. Small green buds grew on the tree tops, and the golden hibernating grass sprinkled flecks of green on the yards. Rays of sunlight beamed down onto my little spot at the back of the building. As I closed my eyes and lifted my face toward the warmth, I took a deep breath of the fresh, crisp air.

A husky man's voice interrupted my moment of peace. "Well, I'll be the first to admit it; I didn't think he could pull it off." The speaking man chuckled a deep, throaty laugh. "That is one diabolical mother fu– "

A group of men dressed in dark suits exited the front door of the church. Without moving an inch and keeping my chin pointed to the sky, I peeked through one eye to watch them. I recognized the deep voice, but I couldn't conjure a face or name to match. My vision was still a bit blinded by the sun, so I struggled to focus on a group of men walking from the front doors of the church toward a window-tinted black sedan, but their conversation carried clearly through the calm spring-like air.

"Yeah, not only did he pull it off *himself*, but then he stood up in front of hundreds of people, offering his heartwarming condolences and telling everyone what a wonderful man the deceased had been." Another man with shiny auburn hair slapped the back of the first man who spoke.

The five men stood out like a sore thumb in our small-town farming community. Who were they and how did they know Walter? Their business suits were heavily pressed, and their shoes had been polished until they shone. Even though their bodies were strong and fit, it wasn't from hard, manual labor. I eyed them suspiciously.

"And how sorry he was that he passed too soon. Amazing. Why did that guy become a pastor? He would've made millions as a salesman," commented the first man.

"Shit. He'd be a better politician than you," said the red-head.

That tidbit of information helped me solve the mystery. The voice that I recognized belonged to Iowa's governor. I looked him up and down, dressed in a sharp, crisp black suit and dark sunglasses. As soon as he was elected, his movie-star-quality face was splashed on the front page of every newspaper. He was tall, good-looking, and Iowa's most eligible bachelor which caused young women throughout the state to become interested in politics. "Probably." He chuckled. "He almost had me convinced that he cared."

"Last night over the phone, he told me that he planned on bagging the widow within the week."

"Damn. That guy scares the shit out of me. I have a nickname for him; Super Shady," remarked the governor to his friends, who were laughing at the pun on my married name.

Chapter 29

Lisa - 1983

Before I married Tony and my life spiraled into this mess, I would have described myself as an intelligent, independent woman. Despite my family not playing an active role in my life, I felt worthy of love and admiration. I believed that I would achieve lofty goals of success and lead a productive life. Never had I imagined that one careless mistake, one white lie would drag me down into a sewer line connected to hell.

Part of the tour and introduction to the Room included Tony defining my responsibilities. "While I'm the Host, the Godfather, the President, and the King, you, Lisa, are the Madame, the supportive, obedient woman behind the visionary."

As his demands left his lips, his large, strong hands squeezed the back of my neck. I'd have to wear my hair down for the next week because his grip would leave a raw, finger imprint bruising.

"I'm not exaggerating, Lisa. I'll make your life hell if you choose to defy and disrespect me. I will not tolerate it. The men who are involved with this small business wanted to eliminate you from the start, but I promised them that you'd be an asset that I could control."

I doubted his words. My life was *already* a living hell, and Tony would've discarded anything if it didn't serve his purpose, me included. I wasn't sure why he wanted to keep me. I acted cooperatively, but my brain still operated at its full untrusting capacity. Abused women tend to appear impassive when, in fact, we have adopted this appearance as a form of survival. I was one hundred percent living in survival mode. Even though my heart seized in my chest and filled me with worry, my brain understood that the reason I was still alive was because Tony's marriage to a wholesome, picture-perfect woman helped cover up what devious acts were about to take place in our own home.

"Are you able to comprehend what your role in this venture is?" His grip tightened around my thin, fragile neck, which felt vulnerable under his strong, powerful hands. I nodded to show my compliance. There wasn't more I could do. I feared he could snap my neck if I'd chosen that moment to defy him.

Tony's pupils were dilated so much that I couldn't identify the color of his iris. It reminded me of a cat—not a cuddly house cat but a fierce, hungry tiger—just before it pounces on its prey. Ready to attack at the slightest movement.

My throat dried in panic.

"I defended you to my business partners. I'm the one who is keeping you alive, and I *expect* your gratitude and loyalty. The other men don't recognize your value, but I do." His hand released my neck and traveled onto my shoulder, down my arm, until he held my hand. "I want you to do this with me, Lisa, but if you defy me, you will leave us no choice." He gently squeezed my hand. "For better or worse, remember?"

I struggled to swallow the lump lodged in my throat. After what I'd overheard outside of the church today, my fear of my husband had grown. The men in suits were frightened by Tony and underestimated his ability to take whatever he wanted. I needed to keep my mouth shut. "I understand, Tony." The sound of my voice was weak and timid, one I'd come to adopt over the years of being beaten down and abused. "Can I ask who these men are? Do I already know them?"

"You'll meet them soon enough." The wicked smirk returned to his face. "But right now, I will provide you with a tour of our Room and explain the expectations."

One of my responsibilities was to lock the door, ensuring that no one left until the party was complete. Tony installed a combination lock that would be reprogrammed after every party to ensure the safety and privacy of our guests. Only Tony and I would know that combination.

I found it ironic that my husband was extremely proud of his venture but used words that downplayed its existence. I bet that internally bothered him. Party instead of orgy, Room instead of cage, and small business instead of a brothel.

"The men and I are aware that some ladies might change their minds once the party starts; however, their early departure is not allowed. No one—not you, me, the men, or the ladies—is permitted to leave after entering the Room. We realize that there might be some regret, tears, or acts of violence, but unfortunately, that rule isn't negotiable."

Acts of violence? Were we sex slaves? Who were these other women? Even though I didn't truly want to know what he was referring to, my head spun with possibilities: men forcing themselves on women, men slapping and choking women to show dominance, women clawing and kicking the rapists, and women pounding on the door to call for help. The images caused my stomach to create knots.

Tony explained that another part of my responsibility would be to record a list of everyone who attended a party.

"I bought a Polaroid camera that you'll use to photograph everyone who enters the room. Men and women. Write down their name on the white part of the film. It's our insurance. I'll be taking pictures with my camera as soon as the transaction is consummated." Again, he used these words instead of intercourse or rape. "It's all to protect us, Lisa."

Tony assumed that I was worried about the authorities bursting into our home and destroying Tony's dream and perfect life. I would've preferred jail time to the hell I was living in.

Tony showed me the log book where I'd keep a list of all the female and male attendee's names using a code. As soon as he handed me the little black book, I noticed that it wasn't brand new but a used black book. The first fifteen pages already included entries.

2.5.20.19.25.13.3

14.1.14.3.25 16.21.19.3.8

16.1.13 7

7.5.14.1.20.1.18.18.5.12.12

At the top of each page was a year, followed by a set of numbers and letters. The rest of the page was a sequence of number patterns.

"Nothing too mysterious, I'm afraid, but it's valuable to me." He pointed to the number at the top of the page. "That's the year."

The first page was labeled 1966.

"This is the geographic coordinate that signifies the exact location. See, this one is in San Rafael, California."

37.9735° N, 122.5311° W

My natural curiosity asked, "Is this a list of your sexual encounters starting when you were a boy?" The very first entry was in 1966, which would've been when Tony was only twelve years old.

A prideful smile spread on his face. "Yes, it is."

In my quick calculation that was based upon how many lines were on the pages, in 1972, when Tony was eighteen years old, he performed a sexual act with at least one hundred people. *How could he be proud of this fact?* A full-body shiver threatened to crawl up and down my spine. I didn't know how to process this information.

"I've taken the liberty of starting the next chapter." He quickly flipped through the little book until he came to a page with the current year on it. "I already figured out the longitude and latitude for you." He pointed to the collection of letters and numbers. "If you want to come up with a creative way to write the date, you go right ahead. Just tell me the code so I can decipher it too." He shot me a playful wink.

My husband was a stranger to me. When he winked at me, I saw a glimpse of the man I fell in love with in that small coffee shop. Back then, I thought I'd been pursuing him; I was seducing him, and I teased him. I thought I'd been in control of losing my virginity to a handsome, charming stranger. Tony was a master manipulator, and I'd fallen victim to his charm just like all of the pages and pages of women had. The difference with what happened in our situation was that I'd tricked him as well by claiming I was the reporter named Anastacia. He hadn't seen that coming, and he was in awe that he'd been duped.

After he licked his index finger, he paged backward and stopped on 1978.

1.14.1.19.20.1.3.9.1

This sequence of numbers was crossed out, and in red was written, '12.9.19.1 4.1.18.12.9.14.7.' My name. And even though I'd taken the wedding vows regarding staying faithful to my husband seriously, I saw pages and pages of number sequences after my entry.

"That's you, doll." After my numerical code, he'd drawn a red heart.

***

After the first night when he introduced me to his 'Room,' Tony scheduled a nightly ritual that included Tony performing unspeakable sex acts to my body–I can't say that he did it to *me* because that would imply I was a willing participant–and then he laid on the floor next to the couch where I was tortured and still cuffed. Deep, heavy pants escaped his mouth as he tried to catch his breath. On the other hand, my deep breathing was caused by my continuous sobbing and begging for him to stop. He'd only been fueled by my sign of weakness and rammed harder into my body. Every inch of my body ached from the ankle that was still cuffed to the side of the couch to the top of my head, where Tony yanked on my hair.

I'd never known such pain from the outside in. Physically, my body would heal; the bruises would fade; but emotionally, I would never be the same. And again, my naivety surprised me because I believed my life couldn't get any worse. Only days later, Tony proved me wrong.

Three days after my introduction to the Room, I made one of Tony's favorite meals, Beef Wellington. The words that fell from Tony's mouth in between bites burned my ears and broke my soul. If I had wanted to escape my life, I should've done it. It was too late. My official initiation was scheduled.

"Lisa, we're having company tomorrow night."

"Oh? What would you like me to cook for supper? How many are we expecting? I saw that the Piggly Wiggly is having a sale on pork tenderloin this week. Would you like me to make that?" In my head, I started to create a grocery list.

We'll need a starch and a vegetable too.

"They aren't coming over to enjoy your *cooking*."

"Oh. Okay. Would you like me to bake a dessert then?" I heard my robotic question. I was on auto-pilot, trying to please Tony and trying to anticipate his needs.

He placed his fork down on the side of his plate and wiped his mouth with his cloth napkin. "Our guests will be here to visit our Room." He let his words sink in before beginning again, and my heart rate quickened. "These men expect to be entertained by you and a few other women that I invited. You're the Madame; therefore, you're in charge of making sure everyone enjoys themselves."

My brain screamed silent questions. *What? What is he talking about? Entertain them how? This can't be real.*

As my eyes darted back and forth across his face, searching for an answer, it slowly became clear.

Sex.

My husband wanted me to have sex with strangers, men and women. If what Tony did to me alone in that Room wasn't bad enough, now perfect strangers were expecting the same demonic treatment. I hadn't understood that part when he informed me that I would log every attendee.

What has my life become? This can't be happening.

A squeak escaped my lips. "Why?"

I hadn't meant for the defiant word to be spoken out loud, and unfortunately, he heard me. When he answered me, his tone wasn't condescending like I'd expected it to be. It was almost as if he'd been waiting for me to ask that question all along.

"I don't know, Lisa. Some people like salty snacks instead of sugary snacks. Why? I don't know. Preferences are created by forks in the road. Why don't you tell me why you prefer chocolate ice cream to strawberry? Maybe as a kid, the indulgence of the strawberry ice cream cone was followed by a tragic experience that left you heartbroken and sad. Your family's dog was smashed by a speeding car. Since you witnessed the accident, throwing up the strawberry ice cream has always reminded you of that event. Or maybe your bare ass was harshly spanked by your father because you left a window open during a thunderstorm. I don't know.

"Some men will only bed blonde women because their first love, who made a great impact on their love life, was blonde. Some men fancy brunettes because they have an unhealthy attachment to their mothers. No one knows for sure what connections will be lifelong or will engrain permanent marks. I enjoy a handful of women at the same time. Perhaps a psychologist would suggest it's because I craved attention as a child and received nothing, especially from the opposite sex. Maybe it was because my first sexual experience was with two inquisitive college girls who explored my body like a road map. To me, the reasoning for why my sexual desires evolved this way isn't as important as how I feed that powerful urge."

***

The next morning, I heard Tony climb out of bed and start his daily morning ritual. He peed sitting down because his aim was worse from having a full bladder overnight; he made obnoxious yawns to wake himself up, and while brushing his teeth, he turned the shower on. Sleep avoided me while my mind raced with the knowledge of this information. When someone was nervous about something, they often described butterflies in their stomach. I understood what they meant, but butterflies weren't the insects that felt trapped. Grasshoppers bounced back and forth against the walls of my stomach.

I pretended to still be asleep when Tony leaned down and softly kissed my cheek before he left for work. As soon as I heard the bedroom door close behind him, my eyes opened, and my heart pounded. How was I going to survive the day, worrying about how I would survive the night? I rushed to the toilet and threw up the contents of my stomach.

When I stood up to get a drink of water from the sink, I saw a small jewelry box sitting next to my vanity. The box teased me as I tried to regain control. As soon as I drank enough water to rinse away the aftereffects of the vomit, I lifted the lid of the box to discover its contents. Right on top was a handwritten note from Tony.

"Every Madame needs an expensive piece of signature jewelry.
Lisa, my angel, you will wear pearls. Love, your Master."

Chapter 30

Lisa – 1983

The anxiety. The nerves. The fear of the unknown. I was a complete wreck. I was so worried about what was going to happen later that night that I couldn't concentrate. My head pounded from the stress. Clenching my teeth caused my jaw to ache. Because every fiber of my being was on high alert, I made simple blunders. After I dumped cereal into a bowl, I poured orange juice over the cornflakes without even realizing my mistake until I took a bite. I spit the spoonful back into the bowl.

Since it was garbage day, I dragged the bins out to the curb and walked back into the house. But when I turned the door handle, the door was locked. I twisted the knob back and forth until I finally realized that I was trying to open our neighbor's garage door. Thankfully, they were both at work. After I ran home, I slammed the door behind me and breathed a sigh of relief at not having to explain what had just happened to anyone.

The rest of the day was a mess of confusion as well. I'd forget why I entered a room or what was next on my to-do list. Tears of frustration poured down my face. Since the day had been a struggle, I decided something simple for dinner would be smart. No open flames or gas burners. I threw the ingredients for a roast into a crockpot.

While I completed my daily chores, my new pearl necklace felt tight around my neck. Of course, it was gorgeous, and any normal wife would be appreciative of an expensive, generous gift, but on my neck, the pearls weighed ten pounds and reminded me of a choker that a dog owner places around his pet's neck to mold into submission.

Oblivious to my debilitating dread, Tony arrived home early from work and bellowed out the lyrics to his favorite song. His excitement and anticipation were clear. He couldn't wait to show off the Room and to 'break it in.' Even though I was supposed to greet him with a kiss on the cheek, I remained in the kitchen, paying our monthly bills. While I feared what the evening would bring, I didn't care that my one act of defiance might cause more pain.

Tony accepted my silence and allowed me to brood, either because he recognized my crippling fear or because he was so wrapped up in his excitement that he didn't notice.

There was no doorbell chime to announce our visitors because they all entered through the back entrance of our home, which was located right next to the Room. Dressed in his usual business attire, Tony waited in the hallway to greet each guest. The first to arrive were the men, all strangers to me except the two of them that I recognized from Walter's funeral. With the Polaroid camera Tony had given me, I snapped their picture and wrote their names on the white tab of each photo. My hand shook with each stroke of the pen. They didn't bat an eye or put up a fuss. Afterward, they strolled into the Room as if it were just another night out with friends. They mixed themselves cocktails behind the bar and relaxed on the velvet furniture. Tony shut the door.

As soon as the eight men who had reserved their attendance had arrived, Tony welcomed three young females who appeared passive about the situation. I'd never met any of them before and had no idea who they were or where Tony had recruited them from. After they smiled seductively for the camera, Tony explained the rules of the night.

"Thank you, ladies, for attending our first party. As we've discussed, you'll be paid handsomely for your service at the conclusion of the evening. Don't forget that there are stiff repercussions if you mention *any* of this to anyone else. Trust me that I will not tolerate any break of the rules." Tony's voice was stern and unwavering. "Please turn around so that I can place these blindfolds on you."

"Hey. You never mentioned anything about blindfolds," said the shorter, more obviously bold woman.

"I did not. Unfortunately for you, Amanda, that comment will cost you one hundred dollars from your payment."

I noticed Amanda's face flush. She couldn't control the questions that popped out of her mouth. I prayed she was a quick learner, unlike me.

When the three women were blindfolded by Tony, he kindly ushered them into the Room where the eager men waited. I stood dumbfounded. My head urged me to follow Tony into the room, but my heart screamed and whimpered not to. My feet were cemented to the ground. Tony returned to my side.

"Lisa, you won't be wearing a blindfold tonight. I want you to see *everything*."

Even though I feared being blindfolded and forced to do things I couldn't see, now the thought of witnessing everything scared me even more. But Tony knew this. He knew the knowledge of what I would gain from watching would shut me into submission. My husband was diabolical.

The violent sexual scenes burned my eyes. The women's screams scarred my ears. Physically, every inch of my body ached from being forced into awkward positions. I *never* thought that my life could get any worse or that Tony could hurt me more than he had before. I learned that I should never use the word *never*.

Chapter 31

Jolene – 1983

As I stomped up the stairs to my bedroom, I mumbled under my breath, "What a bitch. I've had enough of her shit." With a quick jerk, I grabbed the doorknob and threw open the door, and then, with all my strength, I slammed it shut. Mother couldn't have cared less that I stormed off, so the slammed door only reinforced my rebellion.

With my back resting on the back of the door, I jumped when I realized I wasn't alone in our bedroom. Sitting cross-legged on our bedroom floor next to the secret-revealing vent, Ivy sat holding her pocket knife.

Crap.

"Ivy, I thought you were out with your friends." Her Friday night plans usually consisted of the high school baseball game and riding up and down Main Street with her friends until the town-enforced curfew of eleven.

How much did she hear of my argument with Mother? How am I going to find out what she knows? I planned to tread lightly to see what I could discover.

"Got my period, so I came home early." Her tone was flat and dry. A few tears raced down her cheeks. "Why are you so mean to Momma all the time? She's all we have left."

I hated that she defended her. Ivy possessed a fictitious image of our mother, which was partially my fault since I kept the darkest secrets to myself.

"We have each other, Ivy. Plus, how am I mean to her?" If we were going to discuss this, I wanted to know exactly what Ivy thought and why. Maybe it was time for her to learn the truth.

"You never look at her. When she tries to talk to you about anything–the weather, graduation, or heaven forbid, your attitude–you turn your back and walk away." With the palm of her hand, she wiped away the tears that had betrayed her.

As I started to remove my clothes and throw them in the hamper, I pulled out my pajamas from the dresser drawer and wiggled into them. "Ivy, you have no idea."

"Please enlighten me, holier-than-thou, Jo." Her words were laced with sarcasm and anger. She crossed her arms over her chest. She wasn't going to back down.

I didn't appreciate her shoving me into a defensive position already, but it would help me reveal the truth. "First of all, did you notice that Father's truck is gone? The one that *you* were going to drive as soon as we repaired the damage from the accident and you passed the driving test?" I could tell by her blank expression that she didn't notice the missing vehicle. I continued my attack on Mother. "The same woman that you're defending blew every cent of our family money at the casino; therefore, she can't pay our mortgage or the monthly bills. So, she sold Father's truck. It's gone, and so is your dream of making your own memories in his favorite truck. Bye-bye." I waved my hand to make a dramatic point. I wasn't sure if I should tell her that Mother also sold their wedding rings and their wedding china.

I'd never raised my voice at Ivy before. I'd always been her protector, shielding her from pain and heartache, so when tears fell out of her eyes and her mouth gaped open in shock from the words that I'd uttered, immediately my heart cracked. Those fat tears had been caused by me, her personal shield. She was only fifteen years old and had already lost her father, and even though she didn't realize it yet, her mother was worthless. As her protective older sister, I'd done a fabulous job at hiding our mother's failures and always distracted Ivy when trouble brewed.

Maybe that hadn't been a good thing, because now when I needed her to see our mother for her true colors, Ivy was blinded. As a person who'd been born with a huge heart, Ivy always believed in the best of everyone. The glass was always half full. Everyone deserved to be treated equally.

Had I done more harm than good by shielding her from the harsh truths of life? Did my paving her way toward happy, positive feelings result in her seeing life with blinders on? She defended our mother because she couldn't fathom disrespecting our parents. No one had disappointed her yet. She was a shiny new penny.

"Sorry, I didn't mean to yell, Ivy." Even though I wanted to shout from the rooftop what I knew to be true, I dialed down my honesty. For Ivy, I'd amend my tongue. Plus, I wasn't mad at Ivy; I was furious with our mother. "There are things you don't know. I tried to be civil. I tried to forgive her and move on, but she refused to change. She is making the same mistakes over and over again."

My apology didn't suffice with Ivy because she knew me better. She wiped away the tears that continued to leak from her eyes. "Jolene, you aren't always right, you know."

As my little sister, the person with whom I've shared a bedroom my whole life, the girl who knew what made me giggle with just one look, and the friend who brought me chicken noodle soup when my stomach ached, her knowledge of my flaws and fears was on point. She knew I didn't like to be wrong and that I tried, with every morsel of my soul, to be nothing like my mother.

"You're right. I'm not always right." I learned in my high school Psychology class that when disagreeing with someone, showing them that their opinion was valid–even if wrong–can be pivotal in making gains in the discussion. And allowing a slight pause also helped before changing courses. "However, Ivy, people follow patterns in life, behavioral patterns, whether they're beneficial to them or not. Some patterns, no matter how hard we fight them, always come back around. It's instinctive to react to stressors with the same method. Our mother has life patterns as well, and her pattern isn't a good one, Ivy. I've lost respect for her, so it's hard to treat her with kindness and grace."

"She's mourning, you know." Ivy pointed out the obvious. It had only been a few weeks since Father passed away. We were trying to discover our new normal.

"We all are. That's a fact, but it's not an excuse. Mourning doesn't give someone an 'out' for being a cheat and a liar. It doesn't give her a pass to lose thousands of dollars at a casino in one evening. Just because she mourns him doesn't make it okay to break promises. It's called being an adult and taking responsibility for your family. Actions speak louder than words. Plus, Mother has an elastic relationship with the truth."

"She's trying."

"But is she? I'm tired of her excuses. She's always trying to improve, but is she *actually* sorry for what she did, or is she sorry that she got caught? That is the most important question." I wanted to stress that point so I repeated it. "Ivy, pretend there is an invisible moral line. Step over it once or twice, and forgiveness can still be achieved by showing true regret. However, after a while, if that person still chooses to cross the line, the line doesn't matter anymore. Stepping over it *again* proves that there is no respect for the relationship that is being walked over. Everyone's line is different. Mother has trampled and spit on the invisible moral line. Since she shows no true remorse for her mistakes, I've built a wall instead of a line. The wall is my boundary. I'm not willing to negotiate anymore because she proved time and time again that she would not respect my boundaries." More than anything, I wanted Ivy to understand that I wasn't a cold-hearted bitch but that I tried to forgive and love our mother. However, those days were over.

The million-dollar question that Ivy needed to consider was if she felt that Mother was sorry and deserved forgiveness. I already knew the answer because I'd been watching our mother duck from the truth for six years. I heard how she bent the truth to suit her needs, and I listened to her vomit words that she didn't mean to appease her audience. Whenever I confronted or questioned her, she informed me that I was too young to understand or that it was how adults could sleep at night. Another lie.

"Just because you are leaving us and moving away to college doesn't mean—"

"—Is that what this is about? You're picking a fight with me because I'm leaving?"

"Not everything is about you, Jolene." Her sarcastic laughter bounced off the wall in our bedroom. "You know you're just like her. You're becoming Momma."

No words could've hurt me more, and she knew it. Before I knew what was happening, I stomped over to where she still sat next to the vent, raised my hand, and slapped my younger sister across the face.

Chapter 32
Jolene - 1983

What have I done?

Admittedly, my temper sometimes led me into trouble, but I'd never lashed out with anything more than my tongue. I looked down at my open palm as if the appendage betrayed me. Before my head could formulate a vocal response, my hand reacted to the heartache in my chest caused by Ivy's words. The inside of my palm stung.

I'm nothing like my mother, or am I?

As I watched my baby sister's eyes widen in shock and fill with tears, the hand that acted in violence flew to cover my gaping mouth.

"Ivy, I'm so sorry! I don't know what came over me." Even though it was my hand that completed the assault, I was as surprised as Ivy.

Instinctively, Ivy's hands reached up to cover her bright red cheek, and her round eyes dilated as she absorbed what happened. I could visibly see her internal struggle. The tears that swelled up in her eyes became trapped and pooled in her eyelids, causing her eyeballs to gloss over. Instead of a quivering chin, her jawline was clenched as she held back her emotions. As I waited for her response, the air in the room filled with tension, and the oxygen level decreased. I attempted to catch my breath.

My whole life, I'd fought hard to protect Ivy, and now I was the root cause of her pain. Perhaps that fact alone was why it was so much worse. She relied on me for protection and guidance. She trusted me to look out for her, and in a matter of a few seconds, I crushed that trust with the swing of my hand.

Part of why her words hurt me so much was because I feared they were true, and I wanted nothing more than the statement to be false. Ever since I caught Mother with another man, I saw–truly saw–the real Isabella Just. She tried hard to never let her guard down. She was a people-pleaser on the outside, always telling people what they wanted to hear, but on the inside, she was a selfish, manipulative liar. A chameleon that could blend into her surroundings, hiding in plain sight.

Since I was twelve, I vowed to always be truthful and not cater to others. Honesty became one of the most important traits I looked for in any relationship, and I didn't settle for anything less. Of course, being honest all the time, when little white lies were more acceptable, caused me to lose a lot of friendships, but being honest was essential to my character, and if I remained honest, I'd be nothing like Mother.

Patiently, I waited for Ivy's response, which could be either to wrap her hands tightly around my throat and choke me or to punish me with her words. I deserved both.

"Well, you made my point." She rubbed her red, swollen cheek. "You may despise her, Jolene, but I hate to tell you this: you *are* becoming her. It's true, and you know it. That's why you're so angry."

Ivy was referring to an identical slap that had ripped across my cheek after an argument that I'd had with Mother days after Father had died. I confronted her after a carload of men dropped her off at our house in the early morning hours. I'd stayed up and worried about her, pacing the living room floor all night, wondering if she had suffered the same fate as my father. Did she crash into a tree? Would Ivy and I be orphans? Would Ivy go into foster care if I left for college? My worry morphed into a full-on rage as I watched her tumble out of a car filled with obnoxious, drunk men.

"How low have your standards gotten? You're spitting on Father's memory before the grass has even had a chance to grow over his grave. Do you have no morals, Mother?" The words came out of my mouth in rushed anger as soon as she shut the front door.

"Don't be so dramatic, Jolene." She threw her purse on the couch and kicked off her high-heeled shoes.

I stood my ground in the hallway that led to the kitchen as she tried to stumble past me. Even though I knew I should wait until she was sober to have the conversation, my judgment was clouded with anger. My fury trumped my common sense.

"Mother, we need to talk."

She teetered back and forth. Because her balance was affected by consuming too much alcohol, I grabbed her shoulders so that she was forced to look me in the eye. Her breath reeked of cheap whiskey and cigarettes, and her bloodshot eyes stared blankly at me. Maybe my firm grip on her helped to stop her head from spinning, and she'd hear the words that were about to spew from my mouth.

"This has got to stop. Father died only days ago, and you're tramping around town like a two-bit whore."

Surprisingly, she mustered up enough strength and balance to slap me across the cheek just as Ivy was coming down the stairs to eat breakfast before school.

"Momma!" Ivy screamed a warning that was a little too late. She rushed to my side and asked, "Jo, are you okay?" She raised her hands to my swollen cheek. "Let me get some ice."

With a flip of an invisible switch, the stumbling drunk woman who moments ago managed to slap me with all her might returned to a weak, pathetic victim as she yanked Ivy's hands from my face and collapsed into Ivy's arms. Ivy's eyes searched mine as the scene turned from tension to drama in a matter of seconds. Struggling to balance her school backpack on her shoulder and her drunk mother, Ivy leaned against the wall to remain standing. Awkwardly, Ivy patted Mother's back as she wept into her shoulder.

"Oh, Ivy, what would I do without *you*?" Mother slurred.

That scene had happened a few weeks ago, and I attempted to shake the memory as a full-body shiver coursed through my body. Even though my heart insisted that I was nothing like my mother, my head recognized that I was created by half of her DNA. No matter what I wanted to be true, the facts didn't lie.

I decided to explain and defend my actions that led to the argument Ivy had overheard.

"Ivy, there are things that you don't know."

Through the slits of her narrowed eyes, Ivy responded, "Oh, please enlighten me with your knowledge, All Mighty One." She stood up from the floor and crawled into her bed.

"Our mother wasn't faithful to Father."

"In case you haven't noticed, Jolene, Daddy is gone, and that preacher is helping Momma. After he visits, she's relaxed and calm."

"Ivy, what are you talking about?"

"Same thing as you. It was hard at first to see her with someone else, but I know Daddy would want her to be happy."

It was my turn to pause and let the information sink in. Mother was already seeing someone? Daddy died only eight weeks ago.

"First of all, of course, Father would want us all to be happy. But normally, a widow doesn't find a replacement within weeks of her husband's body turning cold. And what do you mean by the preacher helping? The new pastor has been to our house? The one that delivered Father's eulogy?"

"Jolene, just keep your nose out of it. You've never been on Momma's team, so you'll never support any of her decisions."

"It's because I've seen her true colors, Ivy. And you, my sister, are blind to her flaws. Mother's core is rotten, and you *need* to understand that. I'm not mean to her for entertainment purposes. I treat her how she deserves to be treated." The blood in my veins boiled.

I walked over to sit on the side of my twin bed to gauge her reaction and hopefully stop the room from spinning. I wanted to be there for her if she needed me. I was about to burden her with some heavy information.

I inhaled a deep breath before continuing. "I'm not talking about what Mother has been up to since Daddy died—although it does prove my point about behavioral patterns—I'm referring to her affairs while Father was alive. She cheated on Father and lied about it for years. I caught her in lie after lie."

"Why are you bringing this up now?"

"You defend her without knowing the truth. I thought if you understood why I didn't respect her, you wouldn't be so quick to defend her."

"So, what you are saying is that you knew she cheated on Daddy, and you've known about it for a while?"

"Yes, I caught her years ago."

"You're mad because she never told Daddy the truth?"

"Correct."

"And now, you want me to hate her like you do because she never told the truth?" Ivy narrowed her eyes.

"Yes. I figured if you collected all the facts, you would understand why I treat her the way I do. Love and respect need to be earned. Neither one can be demanded."

"Isn't lying by omission the same as lying? Just for different reasons?"

I understood her point, but I didn't like it. I remained quiet.

Disappointment poured out of Ivy as she shook her head. "You're just like her, Jolene. Cover a pile of shit in chocolate, and it's still a pile of shit."

"Ivy, you don't understand. It's different."

"No, Jolene, *you* don't understand. You hate a woman who made a mistake, and you punish her every second of every day for it. She kept a secret, and *you* kept a secret. She didn't tell Daddy that she was unfaithful, yet you didn't tell anyone either. Recently, you confessed to me that you kissed Coach Knight but felt violated because he was our teacher and an authority figure. The tale you told me made it sound like he forced himself on you. You were devastated, bawling your eyes out. I held you in my arms, comforted you, and told you it would be okay. But you told me only a version of the truth, The version you wanted me to believe so that you would earn my sympathy. You used me." Her voice turned cold. "But you didn't just kiss him; you seduced and screwed him. You screwed a man to get back at our mother. Can you not see how twisted that is? Don't sit there and tell me that you value honesty because you only value it when it works in your favor. And you are right, Jolene, actions do speak louder than words. This is a perfect example."

In any good fight, even the loser goes down swinging, but in our case, there was no winner. Ivy threw the last punch, and this time, I didn't react because I wasn't surprised by her words. They were the truth.

Chapter 33

Jolene - 1983

I *have to get out of this house.*

I hadn't been able to sleep after my argument with Ivy. Our angry words burned a hole straight through my heart. Additionally, the fight that Mother and I had, which prompted my heated discussion with Ivy, barked in my ears as well.

Mother had been watching TV in the living room when I strolled into the house reeking of cigarettes and alcohol. My head was spinning. I wasn't sure about everything I ingested. In the shady hotel room, a bowl filled with pills floated around. I swallowed a rainbow.

I craved a giant glass of water and to lie down to stop the world from spinning, but Mother blocked the entryway to the kitchen and badgered me with her questions. *Where have you been? You smell like alcohol. You're not gonna graduate if you keep this up. Who were you with? What did you take?*

"Mother, I *am* graduating in a few days and moving far, far away from *you*. You won't be able to control me." The words came out of my mouth like cursive. "Plus, who are you to give me lectures about making poor choices?"

"Jolene, I'm the adult. I'm the parent; therefore, I make the rules." Mother barked her orders. "God only knows what you've been doing tonight, but from the looks of you, it wasn't good."

"Are you kidding me right now?" I rudely laughed and then hiccuped. I bulldozed past her and stomped into the kitchen. "Hi, Kettle. You're black."

"Jolene, you can't take the family car and not check in."

"Did you think I wouldn't notice Father's truck was missing? That's the real reason you're mad–I had the car–the only four wheels we have. Did you need it so you could meet your latest fuck?"

"Watch your mouth, young lady." Mother believed swear words would earn you a straight path into hell, but disobeying the Bible's seventh commandment of not committing adultery didn't seem to give her pause. "The people who you are choosing to spend time with are not the right sort of people. If you can't think about how this is affecting your life, consider Ivy's. For some reason, your sister admires you."

As I turned on the faucet to fill my water glass, I asked, "Do you hear the words that are spewing out of your mouth right now? This is comical." I paused for a moment and raised my hand to swat at her like a pesky fly.

"Jolene, are you acting this way to get back at me?" Her sadistic laugh bounced off the stained kitchen walls. Her motherly voice disappeared, and the real Isabella Just sprouted to the surface. "Do you think it bothers me that a dried-up, old football player chose you over me? You're more of an idiot than I thought. That just proves to me that Max Knight wasn't worth my time. Plus, when you seduced him, you were pretending to be me. How fucked up is that? He only slept with you because he thought you were me. You wore my perfume and my coat. How perverted is that?" With that, she turned a heel and retreated to her bedroom. Under her breath, I heard her mutter, "Loser."

I hated to admit it, but she was right. When I seduced Coach Knight, my primary goal was to hurt her and make her realize what a tramp she was. I wasn't sure if it worked, and months later, I still blamed her for my continued mistakes. I had sex with dirty, old men, drank their free alcohol, and swallowed their drugs. I convinced myself that I was punishing her, but I was trying to numb the pain of my continued bad choices. My choices didn't affect her, but they were ruining me.

The walls of my childhood were closing in with the heaviness of all the lies they heard and tried to contain. All the painful words shouted between me and my mother threatened to pull down the foundation. It was about to burst with the latest drama of Ivy and my argument. But maybe that was just me. I was about to burst because I couldn't take one more hurtful word, one more second with a mother whom I didn't respect, and one more painful memory of a man who was ripped from our lives. After last night, I'd lost the only person I cared about. Ivy.

When Ivy defended our immoral mother even after I disclosed how she'd defied our father, part of my soul broke. Something had to change, and I couldn't control Ivy. I could only control what I chose to do. I prayed time and time again that Ivy would recognize Mother's true nature. But after last night's argument, I concluded that it might never happen. Even if I told her everything–exploded all the lies that our mother told and lived–Ivy might not believe me or choose to accept them. I couldn't blame her for looking past them. It would be the easier choice. I witnessed Mother's infidelity firsthand, and Ivy heard it years later. It didn't have the same impact. A perspective is affected by time, previous experiences, and natural instinct. All the words in the world couldn't sway Ivy's opinion of our mother until she recognized it for herself. Without her willingness to look at our lives with an open mind, Ivy would never recognize our mother's true colors. The only way she'd learn that I was telling her the truth was through her own experiences.

An hour later, my head had stopped spinning, and my thoughts were clear. With a flood of tears running down my face, I made a decision. I quietly threw what few belongings I owned into my suitcase. As soon as I'd stuffed it to full capacity, I sat on the lid to zip it close. From my position on top of my suitcase, the shiny silver frame that always rested on the night-stand next to my bed caught my eye. The nightlight that was plugged in on Ivy's side of the bed made the silver frame shimmer as the light reflected its shiny surface. In the frame was my favorite childhood picture of Ivy and me. We wore matching plaid dresses with white knee-high stockings and black patent leather shoes with a big, shiny buckle on top. Over our eyes hung matching, badly cut bangs, while the rest of the hair fell down the middle of our backs. Even though I was two years older, by the time Ivy turned eight, we were the same height. Strangers asked my parents if we were twins. Ivy loved the idea of being a twin, so if she could, she'd answer before either of my parents had a chance to answer.

"Yes, we are, but Jolene is the smarter, prettier one." If my father was the one who was with us, he'd ruffle Ivy's hair and smile. If Mother was present, she'd correct the person and tenderly pinch Ivy's cheek, and say, "And if all children were like this one, I would've had a dozen."

I tip-toed over to my nightstand, grabbed the picture, and replaced it with a small token for Ivy—my last tube of chapstick. As I opened my stuffed suitcase and surveyed the overflowing pile, I pulled out a cable knit sweater and replaced it with the frame. I pushed the suitcase closed again and zipped up the sides. As I carefully folded the sweater, I placed it in our shared closet and left it on my bare shelf.

I took one more look around our room and listened to Ivy breathe deeply. In her bed, under her covers, I could make out the shape of her petite frame as she cooed and grunted. She slept on her right side, facing away from me, because she claimed she didn't want me to see her drool. Ivy didn't snore, but she often made peaceful noises while she slept. Those sweet noises can't be bottled up and snapped shut in my suitcase, but I'd hold tightly to the memory of how they sounded like home.

Ivy, I do love you.

After our fight, I hadn't been able to sleep. My head knew it was time to leave and save what was left of my soul, but my heart held me back. Ivy held me back. She was the only reason I hadn't left before. But after last night, I realized I disappointed her, and maybe giving our relationship some space would do it good.

With tears flowing from my tired, bloodshot eyes, I wrote her a short letter, giving hints as to where she could find me if and when she was ready. I couldn't force my opinion of our mother on her, but I wanted her to know that my love for her wouldn't change even if we didn't agree.

A few more tears fell down my cheeks as I turned away and reached for the doorknob to the front door. I prayed that someday she'd understand why I had to leave and that she'd forgive me.

As I backed out the front door, I glanced one last time around our family home. On the kitchen table, my letter to Ivy waited. Next to it, I laid the picnic blanket that Coach Knight and Mother used during their little hikes near the river. I stole it after school one day out of the back of his pickup truck that was parked in the school parking lot. On top of the crusty, dirty blanket, I laid a wad of cash to pay for the car that I planned on escaping in. The rest of the money I earned from the hotel room visits would be used for my get-away. I scribbled Mother a note as well. Her note was short and not-so-sweet.

Karma is a bitch. I hope she delivers everything you deserve. ~Jo

Chapter 34

Lisa - 1983

When Tony announced that he'd be supervising a youth camping trip with members of the church's youth group, a knot in the pit of my stomach tightened. I couldn't let him go alone. My woman's intuition screamed a warning.

"What a great idea, honey. I'd love to help. I'll be in charge of the meals and s'mores. How many children will be coming?" I pulled open our junk drawer and searched for a piece of paper and a pen to jot down the details.

"Sounds perfect, Lisa. How did I get so lucky?" He leaned over and kissed the top of my head. "I'm not sure how many we will have yet. The limit will depend on how many can fit comfortably in a tent. The church owns two larger tents, so we will put the girls in one and the boys in the other."

There were moments like this one that reminded me of the man I fell in love with. I wanted to shake the monster out of him and scream that this was the man I wanted to spend my life with. This was the man I believed could change the world. How could this man be the same man who caused me more pain than I thought humanly possible?

However, I recently noticed that the female participants who joined us in the Room seemed younger and younger. I wasn't sure where he was finding the women, and honestly, I never asked. Fear for my safety and punishment kept my mouth shut. Every time I pushed the boundaries, my life reached a new level of hell. Therefore, I learned to maintain a balance between sanity and reality. My abuse lessened after the opening of the Room. I assumed that Tony decided that the things he did to me in the Room were enough punishment for whatever imaginary line I crossed. Even though my mouth was sealed, my eyes witnessed the subtle changes. Tony's sexual adventures became more deviant, and his victims became younger.

"Some of the parents might not think it's appropriate for us to sleep in the same tent as the children. We'll have to buy a two-man tent." Selling my idea required a bit of creativity. I fed into what I knew he'd like. I turned around to face him and eyed him with flirtatious taunting. "Camping with you will be so much fun. I picture us becoming one with nature." I raised my eyebrows up and down several times. Keeping his sexual desires directed at me was a full-time job.

He laughed at my playfulness. "Oh, Lisa, you're a rare one. I'll have the church secretary purchase us a two-man tent so we can roll around together. Hopefully, we won't wake the children."

"They'll think that the noises are wild animals in the woods," I purred.

For months, the preparations for the trip occupied us both, and I welcomed the distraction. By the time the date of the camping trip arrived and I noticed how much fun everyone was having, our time and effort earned its reward. Not only did the children enjoy experiencing new adventures that we had planned, but I also enjoyed being out in the wild playing in nature. We were doing things a normal couple would do. Tony even had a spring in his step. If only I could've bottled this feeling up and taken it home with us.

The good feeling started during the road trip to Newton Hills. With the radio cranked up, we sang Bible songs. Not always in tune. While I looked around at everyone in our cramped car, I noticed Tony bellowing out the tunes as well. My heart swelled with happiness. We could be normal. This could be our life if only...

But I batted that thought from my head like swatting a fly. I couldn't allow myself to go there. Instead, I stayed present in the moment. Tony and I taught the children how to canoe, fish, and navigate directions by using the sun. We hiked, built a campfire, and talked about how God worked in our lives.

When Stella and Tarasue tipped over their canoe at least thirty yards from shore, my heart sank. I didn't want anything to ruin the fun we were all having. Thank goodness we already verified that every camper knew how to swim but still required life jackets to be worn when out on the water. I was worried that this accident would scar them and their memories of the weekend. When both of their heads popped out of the water, smiles erupted on their faces. Relief poured out of me as I released the breath I was holding.

"Lisa, you worry too much." Tony teased me, and he laughed along with the girls.

"They could've drowned on our watch, Tony." I shouted at the girls to come to shore. The urge to touch them, hug them, and check them over consumed me.

After at least fifteen minutes of attempting to flip the canoe and crawl back in, Stella and Tarasue paddled the canoe onto the sandy shoreline. They were giggling and grinning from ear to ear.

"Are you okay? You two had me so worried." I rushed to their side with two towels. I checked over their heads for bruising or scrapes.

"Mrs. Shade, we're fine. Really. It was hilarious." Water dripped off Stella, forming a small puddle at her feet.

"Yeah, Stella thought a shark swam by our canoe, so she leaned over to look in the water, and the next thing we knew, we'd capsized."

"I did not say that I saw a *shark*. I said I saw a fish *about the size* of a shark. Dude, everyone knows that sharks live in oceans," Stella defended.

"I know that. Duh. My mom is gonna get a kick out of this story though." Tarasue giggled.

"Yeah, Kitty finds humor in everything stupid I do."

Kitty.

Tarasue's mom was Kitty? Does Tony know this?

My head jerked around to see where Tony was located and if he heard his stepsister's name mentioned. He was fishing on a nearby bank with the male campers. The group was at least fifty yards away, so he couldn't have heard her name. I breathed a small sigh of relief.

As the girls used the towels to dry off, I wondered if Tony knew his ex-stepsister had a daughter. Without being too obvious, I looked Tarasue up and down. Her chestnut-colored hair was long and wavy, and matching brown freckles dotted her cheeks. She reminded me of an Indian princess, except for her lime-green eyes, which oddly reminded me of Tony's.

***

After a day of fresh air and vigorous activity, sleep overtook my body, and unlike my normal sleeping pattern, I slept six hours in a row. When I woke, I felt rested but alarmed that I'd let my guard down and slept so soundly. As soon as I opened my eyes, I noticed Tony crawling toward the door of the tent. When he slowly pulled on the zipper, its metal teeth unclicked, and he started to turn around to see if the noise had disturbed my slumber. I snapped my eyes shut. Why was he sneaking out of the tent? After he stepped out of the opening, he pulled the zipper closed. After counting to ten, I crept out of my sleeping bag toward the opening so I could see where he was going. My heart beat so hard that I feared he might hear it. I prayed that he hadn't planned on crawling into the girls' tent.

When I peeked through a small opening that I'd unzipped, I recognized the back of my husband jogging toward the restroom. *He must really have to pee.* I smiled. I was overreacting, just like he said I always do. As I started to zip the tent closed, I noticed the head of a woman wearing a red bandana sprinting toward Tony. With her arms stretched out before her, she picked up speed and jumped into Tony's awaiting arms. Her thighs wrapped around his waist, and her eager mouth covered his. Struggling to keep his balance, Tony carried her into the restroom building.

Tony's having an affair?

My heart, which was beating over time seconds ago, now cracked and broke into pieces. Of course, he had sex with other women in the Room, but that was different. Over time, I considered my Room participation more like a job, or a business. There were no feelings–no cuddling or kissing. When I worked in the Room, I pretended to be someone else, someone who didn't care that other men and women touched her. I stepped out of myself and became someone I didn't recognize or understand. I did it to survive.

To maintain my sanity, I compartmentalized my life. The woman who slept with multiple men in one night was not the real me. Before my wedding vows, I was a virgin in thought and deed. Never in my wildest imagination did I think that I would participate in such vile sexual acts with my husband, let alone strange men. That woman, who *only* wore pearls around her neck, had been created like Frankenstein in a lab.

I preferred to believe that my life was what people assumed it was when they met Tony and me in the church. We were a loving, devoted, and religious couple who worked hard in the community to help people in need. If I allowed myself to dwell too long about the Room, I feared I would not be able to live with myself.

But a woman leaping into my husband's arms threatened my survival. If he was emotionally invested in another woman, he'd replace me. He threatened my death before. Furthermore, if he snuck around to see this woman, he must have feelings for her. If it was a simple sexual attraction, he would've invited her to the Room. Who was she? How many others had there been?

I crawled back into my sleeping bag and cried. *What am I doing? Why don't I run? Why don't I leave Tony and never look back?*

I sobbed into my pillow, trying to muffle my cries. By the time I was able to collect myself, fifteen minutes had passed. I needed to calm down. I wiped my tears and listened to the chatter of the children's voices outside of the tent. Innocent and carefree, their morning discussion included music. A sad smile formed on my face. I needed to start protecting their innocence, one young girl at a time.

Stella softly sang the words to Air Supply's "All Out of Love." A lone tear escaped my eye.

I can't be too late; I know I was so wrong.

I crawled to the tent door, took a deep breath, and unzipped the opening. As if nothing had happened, Tony relaxed in a camping chair, sipping a steaming cup of coffee. His hair was slightly tousled, but nothing out of the ordinary for a morning look. Even though every fiber in my being ached, I slapped a smile on my face and greeted everyone. "Good morning, campers."

I acted like nothing changed in the last fifteen minutes. I pretended that I was a happily married pastor's wife and that my heart hadn't been broken. My feet shuffled in Tony's direction even though it was the last thing on Earth I wanted to do.

"Where is your red bandana? It looked nice in your hair," asked Lily, one of the female campers.

I looked at Lily and recognized that her question was completely innocent. She'd seen Tony with the other woman but thought it was me wearing the red bandana. I needed to cover this up. Act as if I had no idea what she was talking about.

"I'm sorry. What red bandanna?" I leaned over and kissed Tony. "Good morning, honey."

My husband's face had gone pale, which I interpreted as a good sign. He was nervous. I'd never seen him at a loss for words. Maybe stepping out of our marriage was something new. I'd use this new knowledge to my advantage. I could threaten divorce or say that I'd leave him unless he changed his ways.

I wasn't sure what I was going to do with my new knowledge, but my gut and heart told me that I'd finally reached my limit.

Chapter 35

Lisa – 1984

When Tony received the initial call from the synod informing him that we'd be moving to Normal, Iowa, my stomach dropped. It might have been women's intuition or a psychic premonition, but whatever it was, it wasn't good. Maybe it was the expression on his face or the storm in his eyes; either way, it made me nervous. His excitement was too deep for a simple transfer. I was afraid to pry or ask too many questions, both of which I knew would lead to pain on my end. I waited patiently for my husband to inform me why this call was so special.

And I didn't have to wait for long. Over dinner the next night, he told me.

"I know someone who lives in Normal."

I finished chewing my pork tenderloin before I was able to ask. "You do? Well, that's wonderful, honey."

After a long sip of his red wine, he added, "Not really, because she won't be excited to see me. Our relationship ended poorly, and I'm sure she still harbors ill feelings toward me."

An old girlfriend? He dated plenty of women before me, but it never occurred to me that someone else might know about how evil my husband was. Now, I was a little anxious to meet this mystery person.

"I'm sure that isn't true. You'll have to invite her over after we've settled in. I'm sure you can smooth things over. You're quite charming, Tony." I playfully winked at him.

"We'll see, but I doubt it. Years ago, when I knew her, Kitty was pretty headstrong and stubborn, so I'd be surprised if she mellowed out."

Kitty? Wasn't that the nickname of his ex-stepsister from his teenage years? *Should I ask him? Or should I pretend not to remember every detail of his life?* He hated it when I repeated word-for-word what he said. He thought it was haughty and accused me of using his words against him.

Before I was able to ask him anything, he excused himself from the table announcing that he needed to work on his weekend sermon.

I remember that night, as I washed the dishes and looked out our kitchen window, I wondered how he knew that Kitty lived in the same small town that we were moving to. Had he requested the transfer to Iowa to see her again? But why? What was going on?

***

The knowledge of my husband's infidelity didn't push me to pack my bags or confront him with the knowledge. Instead of putting my foot down and forcing a change, I broke one of his rules.

We'd been living in Normal for two years, and we'd never run into Tony's ex-stepsister, Kitty. I assumed, since Tony hadn't invited her to the house, that things *did* end badly between the two of them. Initially, I thought Tony might have requested the transfer to Normal to be near her and possibly patch up their relationship. My assumption was wrong. We lived within a mile of her, and he did not attempt to see her.

The only stories Tony shared with me were from his childhood and were clouded by nostalgia, so I wasn't sure what she looked like or who she'd become years later. Luckily for me, the ACGM church ladies mentioned her name during one of their gossip sessions. I interpreted it as a sign. We gathered together to stuff envelopes for the monthly church newsletter. While busy hands folded, creased, and stuffed the newsletter, big mouths flapped.

"If something ever happened to Sparky, I wouldn't be itching to find a replacement. Why in the world would I want to replace him with another man who is always either horny or hungry?" Carrie's announcement was met with uncontained giggles. "I used to think Cafe Kitty was a lesbian since she never married, but now I'm thinking she's brilliant. Life is much easier without a man."

Susan cleared her throat. "She isn't a lesbian. She has a child, you know."

"That doesn't mean anything. She probably switched teams after she got pregnant with Tarasue. She got knocked up by a stranger and then raised her little, curly-haired mini-me alone. That woman is a genius." Carrie's explanation earned snickers from the group.

"If you do the math, I think she had Tarasue when she was in high school. Doesn't seem to be a blessing, but more of an accident." Susan, the human filing cabinet filled with the town's trivia, licked her finger before she handed me a new pile of newsletters, and then she directed her attention toward me. "Kitty owns the little hometown restaurant here in town, so that's why we call her Cafe Kitty. She doesn't go to church or socialize much because she works long hours at that cafe. Have you been to her restaurant yet? Her pie melts in your mouth. Unfortunately, she doesn't share recipes, and I can't seem to duplicate them. Sparky prefers Kitty's pecan, strawberry, banana cream, and mountain medley pie to any pie Carrie makes."

"Do you know in the south they pronounce it pe-cahn? Everyone else says pee-can. Either way, you say it, it's still a nut." Carrie offered a token of trivia.

Sometimes, the conversation moved so quickly from one topic to the next that I wasn't able to answer or contribute much, but this time I yearned to remain on topic. I shoved the first words I could think of out of my mouth.

"I love pie. Pie is my favorite." *I sound like an idiot.* Everyone turned to look at me. "We haven't been to Kitty's yet. After a long day working at the church, Tony prefers to stay home. Plus, I love to cook. So, Kitty has never been married but has a daughter? What's the story?"

I phrased my question as one of the nosy ACGM would—like I was fishing for dirt. I was. I just didn't want them to know why.

As the leader of our pack, Susan explained, "Yeah, Tarasue is four-teen years old. Kitty appears to be a wonderful mother. Her daughter is well-rounded, smart, kind, and popular at school. I can't even begin to imagine how difficult it was to be a single parent. Obviously, I was joking when I said I'd prefer to parent alone." I looked around the room at the other women. Even though I was the only one who didn't know Kitty's story, they were all listening to Susan as their hands performed the task at hand. "People frequent the cafe for her pie, but Kitty is also like a free therapist. She is an exceptional listener and hands out free, spot-on advice. Sometimes, I wonder if she has a therapist license.

"Hank, my younger brother, has worked as the cook for like ten years. Kitty offered him a second chance when no one else in this town would." I didn't know Hank's story either, but a few of the other women seated around the table diverted their eyes. "He is fiercely loyal to her, so he doesn't divulge much about her. However, he did tell me that one night at closing time, Hank heard strange noises—like someone was being attacked.

Muffled cries and moans. He ran toward her office, threw open the office door, and found her curled up in a ball, crying hysterically. Since he didn't see an intruder, Hank kneeled and rested a gentle hand on her shoulder to ask what had happened. Kitty jumped and tried to gain her composure. He asked her who did this to her, and she mumbled, 'My stepbrother.' From what little Hank knew about his boss, he understood Kitty to be an only child. Hank told her that he'd catch him as he made a move for the door. Kitty explained that it had happened years ago, but that day was an anniversary that she wished she could forget."

Like any good storyteller, Susan's eyes dramatically widened when she finished the story. I struggled to keep my expression blank.

"Hank never had the nerve to bring up that evening to Kitty again. She pretended like it had never happened. Kitty is a bit of a mystery. No one knows what happened. Heck, no one remembers Kitty having a stepbrother."

Chapter 36

Lisa - 1984

"I wondered when we'd meet." She poured me a glass of ice water without even making eye contact with me. As she dropped a menu down in front of me, she asked, "Coffee?" Her calm demeanor did not indicate that this was our first conversation.

I nodded my head, too stunned to speak. As Kitty turned and walked away from my table, her braids whipped over her shoulder and slapped the back of her flowered blouse. Her long, flowing, colorful skirt swished in obedience as she strode away. Out of her pores oozed confidence and grace, two things I envied.

After her casual words and a quick visit to my table, she strolled by another table and filled their water cups with a polite nod while making her way to the counter. Another customer shouted from across the room, causing Kitty to glance in their direction. She simply nodded, and on her invisible to-do task list in her mind, she mentally added their request. Multi-tasking seemed second nature to her, and waiting on others didn't seem to phase her. Kitty didn't rush around; instead, she strolled effortlessly from station to station.

Since my idea to show up unannounced and watch from afar hadn't gone as planned, I observed her with my undivided attention. Even though her long, chestnut-colored hair was tamed into two long braids, a few curly strands escaped the sculptured twist and hung haphazardly around her face. Sprinkled across her nose and cheeks, brown freckles were visible because her face was absent of any makeup. Not one coat of mascara tickled her eyelashes, nor did one faint line of blush lay on her cheeks. Kitty was a natural beauty with a hippy-like aura. In her big brown eyes, her customers could see their reflection as she stared intently at them, listening to every word that fell from their mouths. It was obvious where Tarasue inherited her good looks.

Visiting Kitty's Cafe had been very spontaneous. That morning, Tony informed me that he'd be attending a conference in a neighboring town, so I shouldn't expect him home for supper. I welcomed the break from my normal daily routine, but fear shouted warning signals because my history with Tony cautioned me that it might be a test. On several occasions, early in our marriage, Tony returned home unexpectedly and caught me sitting down reading an unapproved novel or taking a forbidden nap. After I survived the punishment inflicted on those days, I tended to follow his rules, but like any rebel, when the bruises faded and the screams were mere whispers in the wind, I pushed the limit of his boundaries again.

I remembered that he warned me not to visit the cafe, but my curiosity, which caused me trouble so many times before, didn't care. I hadn't imagined that Kitty would be waiting for me this whole time or even know who I was. As far as I knew, Tony hadn't seen or talked to her since we moved to town, but then again, my husband was a man of secret layers.

I'd chosen my outfit with great care to make a good first impression. I didn't want to be threatening or closed off. Therefore, I avoided my Sunday morning church-coordinating outfits since they screamed prim and proper. My cleaning and gardening attire, which included an oversized tan sun hat, a pair of gray capris, and a pit-stained tank top, wasn't going to cut it either. I wanted to appear casual and approachable. As I sat in my khaki slacks, white button-down blouse, and a string of pearls, I was pleased that I'd taken the time to care about my outward appearance.

I stared at the laminated menu without actually comprehending the words. Before I could catch my breath and think of an appropriate response, Kitty returned with the hot, steaming coffee pot. She flipped over the white ceramic coffee cup and set it back down on its matching saucer.

The thick brown liquid fell into the cup underneath it, causing a cloud of steam to puff into the air. The fresh, bitter aroma teased me.

"Are you here to check me out, or are you going to eat something?" In one hand, she held the piping hot coffee pot while placing her other hand on her hip, indicating her patience level for this conversation.

Even though in my previous life–back in college before Tony–I would never have let another woman intimidate me like Kitty was doing now, that was exactly what was happening. I wanted to talk to her; I needed to talk to her, but I was scared for many reasons. First and foremost, if Tony found out that I disobeyed his rules of leaving the house and going out in public, he'd come unglued. Secondly, I had no clue what I had hoped to achieve by coming here to see her. Mainly, I was just curious about her and about what Tony was like as a teenager. Was he a monster back then? What did she think of him?

I tried to collect my thoughts while Kitty stared intently at me. I knew Tony's father married Kitty's mother and that they divorced not long after the ink dried on their marriage certificate. Tony claimed that Kitty was stubborn and probably held a grudge against him. But why would he think that if he hadn't talked to her in years? What did he do back then to make him think that? By her opening line, she indicated that she did know Tony–her ex-stepbrother–had moved to town. She knew he was married, and she recognized me. I guess there's a lot that I shouldn't have assumed about what was going on.

I cleared my throat, hoping to calm my nerves and sound more confident than I felt. But instead, my voice squeaked a one-word response: "Pie?"

"We do have pie. It's your lucky day because we have four to pick from blueberry, mountain medley, apple, and pecan."

"Mountain Medley, please."

As she removed the menu from my tabletop, she turned and walked to the counter, where she hung my order slip.

What are you doing, Lisa?

Innocently enough, I planned on coming in unnoticed, collecting some intel about her, and returning home to process. I planned to observe her from a safe distance before approaching her and explaining who I was. That plan had been a waste of time since she already knew who I was. I needed to think. My fingers tapped my forehead, willing my brain to work.

Less than five minutes later, Kitty strolled back to my table carrying a white, ceramic plate with a generous piece of pie and one scoop of vanilla ice cream. She set down the plate of deliciousness in front of me. Overtaking the bitter coffee smell was the sweet scent of fresh berry pie. Suddenly, I was ravished, and my mouth rudely started to water. As I licked my lips, excited to indulge in this delicious sweet treat that normally I was never allowed to enjoy, I couldn't wait to be alone to savor every bite.

To my surprise, Kitty dropped down in the booth across from me. With her arms crossed over her chest, she narrowed her eyes and looked me up and down suspiciously. I scanned the crowd in the small restaurant to see if anyone was paying attention to our table, but no one noticed. No one appeared phased by our encounter.

Every ounce of this stranger oozed confidence and ease, from her nonchalant attitude to her seventies apparel. I envied her, and we'd hardly spoken any words to each other, but she was everything I thought I'd grow up to be. Strong. Independent. Confident. With her long braids and hippy clothing, Kitty embraced her quirkiness and appeared comfortable in her skin. Her apron, tied around her waist, was filled with stains from the various meals she'd prepared for her customers.

But I knew from experience that outward appearances didn't reflect what was going on inside. The scars that spotted my heart were not visible to the naked eye. Kitty and my outside appearances were exact opposites, but I wondered how our insides compared.

While I sat stiffly in my starched clothes, I realized how much I stuck out at the small-town diner, even though I took great pains to blend in. Farmers in their bib-overalls lined the counter near the kitchen. A few gray-haired women settled in the back of the restaurant by the restroom sign and chuckled over their coffee cups. Every customer smiled and enjoyed each other's company. Only I sat with my back completely straight, my eyes darting to the door every time the chime announced a new entry. Was I the only one who purposefully sat with my back to a wall and a completely unobstructed view of the front door?

This was a bad idea. Not only would Tony find out, but I'd already made an enemy with a stranger who I thought might be my only source of comfort. Before I'd even been able to take a bite of the glorious-looking piece of pie, I fumbled to find my handbag resting on the seat next to me. I needed to pay for the untouched coffee and the pie so I could return to the safety of my home.

"This was a mistake," I mumbled as a weak attempt at an apology for wasting her time. Angry, hot tears threatened to pour out of my eyes as my vision became blurry. "I shouldn't have come."

As I laid down a five-dollar bill on top of the table, Kitty's warm hand rested on top of mine.

"You're here now, so enjoy the pie at least." She slowly removed her hand and finally, we looked each other in the eye.

She was right. I finally worked up the courage to find her, and I had the opportunity to find out more about my husband. I might as well make the best of it.

As I wiped the tears from my eyes, a deep sigh escaped my lips, and she flashed a smile at me that quickly faded as she began to talk.

"I picked those berries from my home garden, so you better not let them go to waste. It's my mother's recipe, and if I can say so myself, it's pretty fabulous. Hell, people from three counties away come to eat my pie. It's worth the trip." She gave me an encouraging nod with a set of instructions. "But before you take your first bite, close your eyes." She paused as she waited for me to follow her direction. After I blinked a couple of times, she nodded toward the pie.

Is she going to watch me eat with my eyes closed? This is not how I envisioned this conversation going.

As soon as I secured a bite onto my fork, I pinched my eyes closed, waiting for further instruction. "Go ahead."

I raised the fork to my mouth, keeping my eyes closed as I tried to relax and simply listened to her soothing voice. "Chew slowly. Savor the first bite. You can never redo a first. The first is always the best. Right away, you'll probably taste the blackberries because I picked them too early. They're a bit more tart than I would've liked. Then the sweet raspberries will tickle your taste buds."

Her words mimicked what was taking place—an explosion of flavors bursting in my mouth. I was positive that I wouldn't have noticed the perfect blend of sweetness if Kitty hadn't insisted that I close my eyes.

After I was done chewing, I opened my eyes to discover Kitty watching me.

"A little orgasm for your mouth, right?"

I choked on the last bit of crust still on my tongue.

"On the handwritten recipe card, my mother had written in perfect cursive, 'Orgasm Pie.' When I added it to my menu, I renamed it Mountain Medley because I didn't want to serve a slice of orgasm to the over-80 club that eats here regularly. Looks better on the menu, too. Because a person's sense of vision normally leads, if you eliminate it, your sense of taste becomes a more dominant guide. Just a little mind game," Kitty explained.

I could feel the blush on my cheeks. I gave her a small, embarrassed smile to acknowledge her personal story. Seconds later, an awkward apology poured out of my mouth, "I'm sorry that I showed up here unannounced."

"It's a restaurant. People do that all the time." She joked.

I flashed her another small smile at her attempt at humor.

"Well, we both know who each other is, so no formal introductions need to be made." The words stumbled out of my mouth. I wished I could be as relaxed as Kitty was, but sweat dripped down my back, and I felt my blood pressure rising.

"Correct. It's a small town."

"Do people know he was your stepbrother?" I'd lowered my voice because I wasn't sure if the information was public knowledge.

"No. They do not unless he's told people. I have no reason to. He was only my step-brother for a few years and that was a long time ago in California. I hoped never to see him again. And honestly, I'm shocked that you two moved here. Did he request to be transferred here? Did he know I lived here?" She giggled, but I didn't see what was funny. "Sorry. I guess I have a lot of questions for you, too."

"Don't be sorry. I'm glad I wasn't the only one." I swallowed my second bite of pie. "Unfortunately, I don't know the answers. I was very shocked when he announced we were moving here. I was a teacher, and I had to break my contract. I felt terrible, but he said it couldn't be helped."

"Well, I know the church was looking for a new pastor. Several of my regulars were part of the call committee, so I'd heard about the candidates over their morning coffee. And believe me, I about dumped coffee on their laps when I heard Pastor Anthony Shade had been hired. I wanted to believe that it was a whole different person. It's a fairly common name, but my gut told me differently.

"I grew up in California with my mom. She married Tony's father, and they moved in with us. When he lived across the hall in my childhood home back then, he became obsessed with the Bible and our family's pastor. Our parents supported his newfound admiration. Tony was no angel. He'd been kicked out of his school before he moved in with us. His dad and my mom thought their prayers had finally been answered. Even though I prayed that it was a different Tony Shade, I knew it was him, my ex-stepbrother." This was our quid pro quo moment; she shared something with me, and to gain her trust, I needed to do the same. Even though I would've rather taken another bite of the delicious pie, I inhaled deeply and exhaled word vomit.

"Tony's obsession with God's teaching has morphed to an unhealthy level. In college, he absorbed every word in his classes. It's almost like he injected the Bible into his veins. He was every professor's dream pupil. But somehow, somewhere, he began believing that not only was God speaking directly to him, but that he was some kind of God." Before I lost my nerve, I added, "He thinks he is untouchable and that he can do no wrong."

As I let my words resonate with her, I snuck a bite of pie and watched her choose her next words.

"Do you love him?" She asked.

"Tony is charismatic and personable. Years ago, when he noticed mousy ole me, I was ecstatic. I couldn't believe that a man so good-looking and prominent would be attracted to me. I latched on tightly before he could come to his senses. In hindsight, I did everything Tony dreamed someone would do–I worshiped him, I idolized him, and I did anything he asked. But somewhere along the way, he got power-hungry. He'll stop at nothing to get what he wants."

Kitty's eyes stared blankly at me. "I know all about that last part, but I don't believe that it's a new trait," she mumbled more to herself than to me.

"So, yes, to answer your question. I love the man I thought he was, but now I'm just..." I don't completely trust her or anyone with my feelings. I let my sentence trail off. Sometimes what's left unspoken speaks louder than what was said.

"Well, Lisa, I'm one of the few people in the state of Iowa who would agree with you. Tony has everyone fooled. The whole town raves about what an amazing preacher and healer he is, but he's a seasoned actor and knows all the right things to say." She looked around her cafe to make sure her attention wasn't needed elsewhere. "I'm not sure why you're here to see me."

"I'm not sure either," I admitted. "I was curious about you and wondered who you were. You're the only person Tony mentioned from his childhood. After his dad passed away, he erased everything from that era. He said it's too painful to talk about."

"I didn't know about Gus' passing." Her eyes softened at the mention of Gus. "He was a wonderful, caring man and treated my mom like a princess. Broke her heart when they divorced. I never straight-out asked, but I think they split up because of Tony."

Chapter 37

Lisa - 1984

I understood why Kitty was saddened by the knowledge of Gus' passing. Gus' generous heart and kindness left a positive mark on everyone he met. With a simple handshake and a genuine smile, Gus melted the thickest of barriers. I'd only met Tony's father twice before he died—once right after we got engaged, and the second time was the weekend he had passed away.

When Tony and I eloped, we extended our honeymoon a couple of days to visit Tony's father and share the good news. Gus lived in a small, one-bedroom apartment and offered to sleep on the couch if we slept in his bed. However, that was not how Tony had envisioned spending any part of our honeymoon, so he reserved a hotel room.

The night before he died, Gus invited us over to his apartment for a home-cooked meal. While I cleaned up the kitchen, Tony and Gus started arguing while they remained seated around the tiny folding table on the patio. Between the running water and my humming a happy tune, I hadn't heard their raised voices.

Tony stormed into the kitchen and announced that we were leaving. Tony spewed some harsh words in his father's direction and demanded that I collect my purse. I put down the dinner plate that I'd been drying and glanced at Gus in the doorway from the patio. His eyes reflected his shock, too. As Tony pulled me by my wrist and out the front door, Gus mouthed, "I'm sorry," when Tony wasn't looking. I didn't have a chance to say goodbye.

When we returned to our hotel room, I allowed Tony to take his anger out on my body. He ravaged my body over and over again, and as soon as I thought I might break in half, Tony fell on top of me, exhausted. Even though the sexual sprint should've worn out Tony, I heard him leave the hotel room shortly after midnight. I assumed he was either hungry or thirsty and dashed out to get something. I rolled over and fell back asleep. Hours later, I noticed him crawling back into bed. He smelled freshly showered and a bit like bleach.

When we initially made our weekend plans, we discussed a farewell breakfast on our last day in town to say our goodbyes to Gus. However, the next morning, Tony explained that we were leaving without a final meeting. Our curt departure was largely due to his argument with Gus, but I also knew he hadn't slept well the night before. Regrettably, I knew nothing I could say would change his mind. To keep my mouth closed, I'd adopted the nervous habit of twirling my wedding band on my ring finger.

Shit.

"Tony? We have to go back."

"Lisa." His tone was harsh and sharp. "I'm not interested in listening to you whine. I will not be explaining my decision in *any* simpler terms."

I hated when he talked to me as if I were beneath him, and normally, I would've accepted his insulting words, but this time I could not.

"I forgot my wedding band."

Tony had been stuffing his belongings into a suitcase when he whirled around to look at me. "What do you mean, you forgot it?"

"When I was washing dishes, I took it off and set it on the windowsill. In our rush out the door, I forgot it."

Under his breath, he mumbled a few swear words about how I was more trouble than I was worth. "Why couldn't I have married a woman with half a brain? Returning to the scene of the crime can't be good."

"What?"

"Quit asking questions and get your fat ass moving so we can run by his place."

When we arrived at his apartment complex, Tony pulled up alongside the curb and explained that I could retrieve my forgotten wedding band alone. His shifting eyes traveled up and down the street. When I looked over at him, his nerves were obvious. He didn't want to run into Gus after the awful words he'd shouted. I registered his regret as a positive sign.

As I advanced to Gus' apartment door, I silently prayed that he was home and the two of them would mend their relationship. I enjoyed Gus' company and craved a relationship with my father-in-law since neither of us had any other family ties. However, I understood that without Tony's blessing, there would be no relationship. I knocked repeatedly on his front door, but there was no answer.

"Gus? Hey, Gus, it's me, Lisa. Sorry to bother you. Can you answer the door? I forgot something in your apartment."

Suddenly, Tony was standing next to me, but he kept looking back at the street.

"Maybe he thought he was meeting us at the restaurant," I suggested. Without even a glance in my direction, Tony told me firmly no. As he pushed me to the side, he lifted the worn welcome mat and uncovered a spare key. "Oh..."

Before I could ask him how he knew that there was a hidden key, Tony inserted it into the lock and pushed the front door open. I called out to Gus as we entered his apartment. To Tony, he was family, but I felt we were barging in.

As I walked into the living room and kitchen, softly calling out his name, Tony marched straight back to his father's bedroom. Everything in the main living space looked like last night's family dinner was still occurring. The dishes that I'd almost finished cleaning were still sitting on the drying rack. The empty beer cans rested on the counter, and the burger condiments still sat on the table. The only thing that appeared distinctly different was that the smell of freshly grilled hamburgers had been replaced with a heavy chemical smell of bleach.

Hesitantly, I followed Tony to the back of the apartment. When I finally reached the entryway of Gus' bedroom, I gasped. Gus lay fully clothed, motionless, on top of his bed. His waxy eyes stared blankly up at the ceiling, and his mouth hung wide open. I'd never seen a dead body before, but it was obvious that Gus was dead. While I continued to take stock of the situation, I noticed my husband yanking off his dad's wristwatch and gold ring.

"Tony! What are you doing?"

"Go call 9-1-1." His voice wasn't heartbroken or scratchy, but firm and cold. When I hadn't moved or responded to his demand, he whipped his head around and glared at me. "Do. It. Now."

I stumbled over my own two feet as I raced to the kitchen, where the phone hung on the wall.

When the ambulance arrived, the paramedics informed us that Gus had suffered an asthma attack that caused him to stop breathing. He suffocated hours before we arrived. They estimated his time of death at around one in the morning.

"How do you know it was one in the morning? Miss...?" asked my curiosity. Tony glared at me again.

The first responder looked from Tony to me before responding. "You can call me Sergeant Lilianna. Rigor mortis has set in, but his core body temperature is still eighty-nine. It's just a rough estimate."

"How do you know he died from suffocation?" Another question burst from my mouth.

Tony piped in before the first responder could answer. "I'm sorry. My wife has a morbid curiosity, and she doesn't always understand when she has crossed the line." Tony's teeth clenched as the last few words escaped.

Lilianna smiled. "I get it. No harm in asking. Again, I'm not one hundred percent sure. The coroner will be able to answer both of those questions in a couple of days. However, I noticed his asthma inhaler on the nightstand. He also suffered a nosebleed, and his face appears slightly bluish, which suggests a lack of oxygen. It's a calculated guess."

A week later, Tony received the autopsy, and Lilianna had been correct. Gus had suffocated around twelve-fifty that morning.

I didn't tell Kitty the details of Gus' death but instead simply answered, "Yes."

"I'm so sorry."

"Tony seemed..." I searched for a word that wouldn't make my husband out to be a monster. "...detached when we found his father. At the time, I figured it was due to shock, but now when I think back, it's like he wasn't surprised, like he already knew."

That last sentence hung in the air like a day-old helium balloon does in a motionless, still room. Swaying a little, slightly bouncing, but able to move forward or backward. Just stuck. I didn't express that Tony also alluded to the fact that he had something to do with Walter *and* Gus' deaths. Until I could verify that information, I'd keep it to myself.

Finally, Kitty instructed, "Eat your pie. It tastes better warm."

As soon as I obliged her request, she rose from the table and headed to the counter. I wondered if my confession somehow offended her or upset her so much that she needed to excuse herself. I tried to choose my words carefully. Tony's reaction to Gus' death had always bothered me, but I'd never said those words out loud. Once random thoughts or concerns are given a voice, there was no taking them back.

What if she tells someone that I said that? What if she tells Tony?

How awful and disrespectful of me to think that of my husband! A husband who was a respected pastor. My entire body shuddered at the thought of the wicked punishment I'd suffer at the hands of my husband.

Why did I trust a perfect stranger with my deepest, darkest thoughts? When will I ever learn?

As my worried thoughts banged around in my brain, I shoveled the pie into my mouth. It could be my last meal. As I inhaled the last bite, Kitty slid back into the booth across from me. I'd been so engrossed in my worries that I hadn't seen her making her way back to my booth. She ripped off the top receipt of her guest checkbook; earlier, I'd watched her write down my order for pie and coffee. After she folded it in half and placed it under the palm of her hand, she slid it across the table in my direction. As I reached for the bill, she didn't raise her hand to surrender it but instead trapped mine underneath hers.

"The coffee and pie are on the house." She held eye contact with me for another ten seconds before she rose again from the table, turned, and walked away from me. She strolled past the counter filled with farmers and pushed open the swinging doors to the kitchen. I looked back at my hand, still warm from her touch, covering the piece of paper she had left. I picked it up, unfolded it, and saw flawless cursive handwriting.

Kitty #279-1229. Call me when you need me, not if.

Chapter 38

Lisa - 1985-8

Under the oddest circumstances, Kitty and I became friends, at least that was the label I slapped on our relationship. I wasn't sure how Kitty described it. Sometimes, when I would drop by the cafe, she'd be open and receptive, and other times, she'd be short and blunt with her advice. I couldn't completely blame her. Every visit was the same story–I'd tell her how awful my life was, and she'd advised me to pack a bag. Even I was tired of the redundancy.

During my conversations with Kitty, I never mentioned the Room. I only disclosed portions of the abuse that I suffered at my husband's hands. My stories contained tales of his physical, sexual, and emotional abuse. My mind wouldn't allow me to admit that by keeping my mouth shut about the Room, I was just as guilty as the men who frequented it. To keep my sanity, I kept the Room and my daily life separate. Both were beyond nightmarish, and I could only handle one nightmare at a time.

For months and months, I'd show up and expect her to listen and understand. She'd deliver her advice, and I'd listen with conviction to change the course of my life. Every time I exited the cafe, I felt determined to stand up to Tony, demand he stop what was happening under our roof, and force him into closing the Room. However, I never followed through on any of her advice.

That afternoon in 1985 was no exception. I'd stopped by Kitty's Cafe after running errands for Tony. I ordered my usual: a slice of pie and a cup of coffee. When Kitty found time to take a break, she dropped down in the seat across from me. After the first year of visits, we created a unique greeting in which we would acknowledge each other with a slam.

"Good afternoon, Lisa, looks like you were in a bit of a rush today. Do you need to borrow a hairbrush?"

I smiled and instinctively raised a hand to my hair. The wind had picked up this afternoon, and I was sure I looked a fright.

"Very kind of you to offer, Kitty; however, if I were you, I wouldn't offer up beauty tips since you aren't willing to take your own advice."

I'd gotten better at the slams over the past couple of years. At first, I couldn't think of anything to retort. My mouth would hang open in shock, and Kitty would laugh and tell me to lighten up. I was so appreciative of her friendship that I only wanted to compliment and thank her. But honestly, I looked forward to our quick-witted banter.

"Touché."

By the time our coffee date ended, Kitty played the role of my life coach once again, advising me that today was the day I'd muster up the courage to leave Tony. Her encouragement radiated out of her pores and landed on me. Her words energized me. I felt motivated to do what was right for my well-being. I was finished accepting that this was my life.

"The aura around you is different today. A change is happening. Lisa, I know you want to believe that if you stand up to him, he'll beg you not to leave, that he'll change, that he'll do better, but you've been married to him for long enough to know that won't happen. Those things happen only in fairytales, and honey, you aren't Cinder-fucking-ella. I hate to be the one to tell you this, but he won't change. He may tell you that he will, but he won't. The percentage of evil in that man has surpassed the point of return. You have to leave him. Run as far as you can. I have money. I can help you."

I assured her that I'd come to her for help after I faced him.

"Confronting him isn't for his closure. It's for me. He took our marriage vows lightly, but I did not. I need to say goodbye and end our marriage to his face. If I just run, I'll always be looking over my shoulder." The pride swelled in my chest as I formulated a plan. Being with Kitty helped me remind myself of the old, independent Lisa Darling. "Today is the day, Kitty. If I need a place to stay tonight, I'll knock on your front door."

A small smile tickled her lips. "Virginia, I wish you luck."

I liked it when she used the nickname I'd been given years ago when I worked at the coffee shop. It was another reminder of the old me. As we rose from our table, I leaned in to hug her.

I whispered, "Thank you, friend."

After I returned home, I was energized and inspired to make a change. I completed my daily chores like it wasn't my last day in Normal. I folded the laundry, put supper in the oven, and fixed Tony's evening cocktail. My bag was packed and sitting in my closet.

The front door slammed announcing his arrival. Tony stormed through the door and marched straight into his office. I inhaled a deep breath, gave myself a silent pep talk, and walked toward the front of our home. The clicking of my heels echoed down the hallway. To not startle him, I softly knocked on the frame of the open door.

"Tony, I need to talk to you."

"*Now* is not the time, Lisa. Go pack our shit. We're moving," he barked.

Three cardboard boxes sat open on his desk, and he began tossing files from his desk into them. His actions were frantic and crazed. I had no idea what was going on. He made no sense. *We aren't moving, I was moving.*

"What? When?" I was so shocked by his words and his behavior.

"Tonight. We've been transferred to a church in Nebraska." I recognized a trace of fear in his voice.

His words were rehearsed and only touched the surface of what had transpired this sudden move. No pastoral job was ever so in demand that a family had to leave in a 24-hour timeframe. Something was going on, and I was sure it had to do with the Room.

"Don't stand there like an idiot; go pack our closets." He stopped for one second to glare and shout his command at me before returning to the contents of his office.

My plans for freedom and venturing out on my own were forgotten as I worried about what had happened. Earlier that afternoon, I packed only the things that I needed for a new life, a solo adventure. I planned on leaving behind the two-piece skirt and blazer sets that Tony insisted I wear and only packing my favorite clothing. The pearls that Tony gave me to wear in the Room would've been pawned for money that I'd need for my escape. Even though they were the most expensive thing I owned, they were tainted.

Just hours ago, I planned on abandoning my husband for greener pastures, and now, suddenly, I worried that I'd never see a green pasture again.

As I threw our toiletries into a bag, the necklace tightened around my neck, causing the cry that I trapped in my heart to break free and cause a small squeal. Tears raced down my cheeks. I'd been so close.

We packed whatever we could fit in our cars and pulled out of our driveway at midnight. One last time, I looked up at the enormous house that had seemed impressive and full of potential when we arrived years earlier. A white, colonial-style house with tall black pillars accented its grandness. I wondered what would become of it. What its next resident would think of the hidden room.

I never said goodbye to my ACGM friends or Kitty. I knew our departure would be the talk of the town until something better came along. I wondered if they'd miss me. I wondered if Kitty would be worried about me. Would any of them look for me?

During the years in Nebraska, our marriage returned to the pre-Normal stage. There was no more room or strange, uptight men visiting our home. On rare occasions, I'd catch a glimpse of the man I fell in love with back in college. He picked a handful of wildflowers while out on a walk or wanted to cuddle and watch old black-and-white movies. But most of the time, he cursed, threatened, or sexually assaulted me. For the most part, we kept to ourselves and didn't venture far from home. Our life resembled a couple running from something, but I never asked questions.

In 1988, Tony and I moved to Canby, Minnesota, where he served as the head pastor at Holy Cross. With each move, I prayed that our new hometown would lead to a fresh start. My prayers went unanswered because each move produced new scars and heartache.

A downward spiral is clearly visible when viewed in hindsight. Each red flag chalks up to the decline. Each ominous feeling adds up to an ulcer. But in plain sight, the pivot feels more like a mosquito bite—a sharp pinch followed by a slap of the hand—or a pothole on a forgotten highway. Each bump reminds you not to take advantage of the smooth road and the times when life was carefree. Slow down, or you'll miss it.

If life is measured by the moments that take your breath away, then I counted the moment Tony strolled in the front door of our home in Canby with a pregnant teenager as one of those moments.

Chapter 39

Lisa - 1989

Life in Canby, Minnesota started on a gentler note than our transfer from Iowa to Nebraska. First of all, we didn't move out like criminals in the middle of the night. After saying our goodbyes to the small Nebraska congregation, we drove out of town two weeks later. When we pulled into Canby, I noticed it was the largest town we'd been assigned. The brick buildings scattered in the valley were three times as tall as our previous hometowns, and the city streets were twice as wide. Seven stoplights littered the town's main drag, and the number of residents was three times the size of Normal. I wondered what events would shape our lives in this picturesque town.

After living in Canby for almost one year and creating a new normal, Tony brought home a teenager. A very pregnant teenager.

I'd been in the kitchen cooking dinner when I heard the front door open, and like I'd been taught, I dropped everything and rushed to greet my husband at the front door. I heard Tony's voice explaining the layout of our home.

"Upstairs is the master bedroom and a smaller guest room, but we'll set you up in the guest room on the main floor so you don't have to mess with the stairs. I don't want you to overdo it."

As I rounded the corner, I observed Tony and a very young woman standing in the foyer. Immediately, bile rose in the back of my throat. *This can't be good.* When we lived in Normal, Tony invited young women to our house all the time to work in the Room, but those women always entered through the back door, never the front.

Tony carried two suitcases, and the teenager lugged a small bag and her purse. With her jet-black hair, she had the palest skin that I'd ever seen. Dark circles of exhaustion rounded her sunken eyes. Strapped to her waist, a large basketball rested under her oversized t-shirt. Her faded blue jeans needed to be washed, as did her white Kmart lace-up tennis shoes. Even though her appearance indicated that she was a normal, perhaps rebellious teenager, I didn't get the sense that she was neglected or came from an underprivileged family. Even though her appearance in our house couldn't mean anything good, my heart went out to her. Her shifty eyes and uncertain smile indicated that she questioned her presence in our house as much as I did. She was scared.

"Ah, Lisa, I'd like you to meet Lucy. You might recognize her from church." Tony looked down at Lucy with loving, gentle eyes. "Lucy, this is my wife, Lisa. She'll show you to your room, and after you freshen up, we'll have dinner."

Because I was caught off guard, an uncensored comment leaped from my lips: "Tony, you didn't tell me we would be having a guest. I didn't make enough food for dinner." The night's dinner had been marinated and grilled to perfection because I'd noticed that Tony had been more stressed this week. I'd chosen all of his favorites in hopes of pleasing him. Hours and hours of preparation dissolved as soon as I opened my mouth.

"Well, shoot, honey. I hope you ate a big lunch because Lucy will be eating yours." His tone was teasing, but his eyes reflected that he spoke the truth. He didn't like me questioning him, and hunger was the night's punishment. "Be sure to prepare more for dinner from now on because Lucy is moving in, and if you are done complaining, Lucy needs to rest.

She's cooking a precious baby in there." Tony reached down and lovingly rubbed the girl's growing stomach. "I have a few calls to make before dinner. Lisa, can you help her with her things and show her to the guest room?"

Lucy looked up at Tony with love and adoration. I forcefully swallowed the bile that had shot up my throat.

"Hi, Lucy. Welcome to our home. Let me show you to the guest room." Thank goodness, after years of marriage to Tony, I learned to mask my true feelings. I'd become a seasoned actress.

I picked up the suitcases that Tony left by the front door. Before he shut his office door, I announced, "Your drink is poured and waiting on your desk, Tony." Often, when my husband arrived home from work, he'd deposit his briefcase in his office, so I liked to have a drink ready for him. If he had a few phone calls to return, he could hold a cool drink in his hand. Plus, the calming effects of alcohol helped to relax him, which was one of my top priorities.

***

Following a very uncomfortable dinner where I sipped water and watched Tony and Lucy lick their lips over the meal I'd prepared, Tony tucked Lucy into the guest room's bed, and I slumped up to our bedroom. So many questions bounced around in my brain. *Who is she? What is she doing here? How far along is she? Where are her parents? Is she as young as she looks?* And the worst question that I wasn't sure if I wanted an answer to was, *Is she carrying Tony's baby?*

After I performed my nightly bedtime routine that Tony insisted on—washing and moisturizing my face, waxing every hair below my waist, and brushing my hair one hundred times–I crawled into our bed. I wondered what Kitty would say now. During the years I visited Kitty as her cafe, she never once said, 'I told you so,' but she could've, and I wouldn't have blamed her. She predicted that my life as Tony's wife would get worse. She was right.

As I reached to switch off my bedside lamp, Tony entered our room. He was smiling and humming to himself, which, for me, always signaled trouble. I retracted my arm and waited for him to explain what was going on. I couldn't ask. I knew that. When I belted out questions, Tony interpreted my inquiries as disrespectful. I needed to be patient, so I picked up my pre-approved novel and pretended to be interested in the words in front of me.

When he exited the bathroom ten minutes later, his smile still hung on his lips. "First of all, Lucy is going to be living with us. At this time, I'm not sure for how long. Her doctor ordered her to bed rest for the final weeks of her pregnancy, which means that she needs to stay off her feet. That's where you come in. I expect you to care for her daily needs. She'll need three nutritious meals a day. You'll need to drive her to her doctor's appointments." Tony threw his clothes in the hamper and crawled into the bed. "I know you have questions. You're allowed two."

This alteration was new. He'd never before welcomed my inquiry. I needed to choose my questions carefully, but the first one was obvious.

"Do you know who the father of her baby is?"

"Yes, and you're smart enough to know who that is too. However, I've persuaded one of her classmates to claim responsibility."

What does that mean? Claim responsibility? An innocent young man was going to tell everyone he was the father of Lucy's baby, even though he wasn't? Why would he do that? My husband knew me well. By supplying me with that information, my head swam with more inquiries. However, asking him more questions would be playing with fire.

I settled on asking a question that would be Tony-approved. "Is she allergic to anything?"

Chapter 40

Lisa - 1989

When Lucy first arrived at our house, conflicting emotions arose in me. Tony dreamed of having a family, and so far I failed to provide him with any children. I wondered if he planned on using Lucy as my replacement. I fantasized about pretending to be upset that Tony wanted to start a life with Lucy. I'd wail and scream that he should love me, not her. But inside, a giant ball of hope blossomed as I dreamed of escaping Tony and our marriage. I'd leave with my tail tucked between my legs and nothing more than the clothes on my back. As soon as I rounded a corner and was out of his eyesight, I'd run. I'd run so fast that my legs would burn.

However, while Lucy was on bed rest, I cared for her, came to trust her, and enjoyed her company. She was a bright, intelligent girl who thought she loved my husband and that he loved her. She wasn't a vindictive, evil woman who'd seduced and stolen my husband's affections. She was a young, naive girl who wanted to believe Tony's promises of love, security, and a life together. I wasn't sure how she imagined it happening since he was already married, but I assumed Tony told her not to worry about it, and like I had, she trusted him.

Our relationship was built on an odd foundation, and maybe my requirements for a friendship were low. Even though our circumstances were far from ideal, I was glad to have her in my life. Selfishly, I hoped she never left.

As soon as the baby arrived, instant love consumed my heart. Camille was born with a full head of dark brown hair, the cutest little button nose, and perfectly shaped pink lips that rested in an adorable pout. Not only was I enamored with Camille, but Tony also couldn't contain his excitement. He fussed over the baby every time she made a peep. He purchased every baby gadget to entertain her. If this baby hadn't been born to an underage teenager and been impregnated by her authority figure, I would've thought Tony's attention was adorable.

While Tony and I answered every wail and jumped at every noise, Lucy retreated inward. Every new mother feels exhausted physically, but in Lucy's case, she checked out emotionally too. Her eyes would stare blankly out the window when I'd sing Bible songs to Camille as I changed her diaper. She wanted nothing to do with breastfeeding and soaked in long baths alone while I rocked and cuddled Camille.

Her demeanor startled and scared me. Even though she was technically my husband's mistress, she was still a child. I was concerned. After a nice, warm bath, Camille fell asleep, and I started to tidy up Lucy's room. She was lying on her side, looking out the window. I took a break from my chores and sat down at the edge of her bed. I rested my hand on her leg, which was under the covers.

"Lucy, honey, is there something bothering you?" She shook her head. "Are you in pain?" This question gave her pause, but she shook her head again. "Talk to me. I might be able to help."

She turned to look at me when she answered, "I miss my mom."

Tears streamed down her face, and her eyes searched mine for a solution.

"That's perfectly normal. You've created a little human, and you want to share her with everyone." I didn't know the whole story of why Lucy was staying with us besides the fact that he was the father of her baby. Tony provided details as he deemed me worthy.

"Tony told me that I can't call her. I'm living here now, and I've made my choice. He also said that no one would believe me if I told anyone about him because he was a respected pastor and a powerful member of our community. Plus, Robby had already said he was the father of my baby. If I told anyone the truth, I'd look like a teenager with a ridiculous crush on her pastor." Lucy shared a lot with me, probably too much. Sometimes, she failed to recognize that I was Tony's wife and that she was the mistress. It didn't bother me. My love for Tony evaporated years ago.

"I broke my parents' hearts." She shook her head as if she couldn't fathom who she'd become. "They stopped going to church because they couldn't listen to Tony preaching the Word of God, but they both stopped by the house last week while you took Camille on a walk. My dad was bawling his eyes out, begging me to come home. Do you know what I did? I gave him the bird and slammed the door in his face. You should've seen his face. He was broken. I don't deserve their love."

"Love from a parent isn't like that, Lucy. You'd love Camille no matter what she did, right?" Her nod was tentative and questioning. "They love you unconditionally, Lucy. You can stomp on their heart one minute, and they'll hug you the next. Give them a chance."

After sniffling and wiping her nose with her sleeve, she asked, "Why don't you leave? You tell me all the time that I deserve better, that I'm missing out by growing up too fast, and that you don't love him anymore, so why do you stay here? Why do you stay with him?"

"It's complicated."

"That's a lame excuse, Lisa, and you know it. I'm your husband's girl-friend. I had his baby. He moved me into your home, and still, you stayed. I don't understand." As I listened to Lucy, it was hard to believe she was still a child. So wise beyond her years.

I slumped down into the chair next to Lucy and sighed. "I don't either."

Lucy reached out to touch my forearm. "Lisa, I'm not the only woman Tony has cheated on you with."

"I know."

"I don't think you do. She said no one knew. She didn't tell anyone but her best friend, my dad, and me. The only reason Tony chose me was to get back at her."

I didn't understand, and I wasn't sure if I wanted to.

"Tony had an affair with my mom, Molly, and when she broke it off with him, he vowed to make her pay for her rejection. She told me, and I didn't believe her. How could I? I thought Tony loved me. He told me that he'd do anything for me. He promised that we'd leave Canby someday and start a new life as a family. I figured my mom was jealous and saying anything to make me doubt his love, but it turned out she was right. Tony admitted it. She told me that Tony could go to jail for what he did to me."

My throat turned dry. I could see it in her eyes: fear and regret. Lucy was me years ago, alienated from her loved ones. Tony said all the right things to make her believe he was the only one she could count on. Even though her eyes were puffy from crying, they recognized the truth. She'd become me if she didn't do something to change the course of her life. As she stared into my eyes, she saw her future. A lonely, sad future.

***

As I made biscuits and gravy the following morning, I was surprised that I woke up before Camille and Lucy. Camille's feeding schedule was like clockwork, but it was an hour past when she normally wailed for her feeding. After everything was ready, I strolled down the hall to Lucy's room to check on them. When I gently pushed open the door, I peeked into the room and noticed that the bed was empty as well as the crib. I blinked several times to make sure my eyes were working properly. What was going on?

I pushed the door open completely. Her bed was made with all the throw pillows resting on top of the bed. The nightstand next to the bed was void of any personal effects. With the closet slightly ajar, I saw empty wire hangers hanging on the road. The bassinet was empty. The room felt like a tomb of silence.

I fell to my knees and cried. She wasn't like me after all. She was stronger.

Chapter 41

Lisa – five years later

During the summer of 1994, a beautiful, blonde woman's face splashed the headlines of every newspaper in the country. Her big brown eyes bore into the hearts of viewers, but unfortunately, she wasn't getting noticed for her beauty or brains. No, Nicole Brown Simpson became a household name because she'd been stabbed twelve times, her throat was slashed, and all the evidence pointed at her ex-husband, O.J. Simpson, a famous pro football player. The authorities had a list of emergency phone calls from Nicole claiming spousal abuse, but nothing was ever done. She'd been married and abused by her husband for seventeen years before finally divorcing him in 1992. However, the abuse didn't stop when the divorce was final, instead, her ex-husband's abuse took on a new form of terror. He stalked her, followed her multiple times a week, and threatened her. She never felt safe.

When her death and the famous white Bronco chase dominated the news, the big metal bars to the jail closed around me. I'd just started my jail sentence for my part in the brothel. My sentence was greatly reduced due to my testifying and supplying documentation against Tony. I'd never heard of Nicole Brown Simpson before that summer, but I'd never forget how relieved I felt because I'd survived similar abuse. I helped put my abuser behind bars. Unfortunately, Nicole's story didn't have a happy ending.

She'd been stabbed and left for dead, but then again, was my story a happy ending since I ended up in jail? Would I ever be free from Tony?

In 1993, Tony was arrested for soliciting sex from a minor. The charges continued to pile up as they uncovered his secrets. The local police were shocked to discover that the man they knew as a man of God owned and previously ran a brothel in a small town.

For me to avoid a hefty prison sentence, I agreed to provide evidence to seal Tony's fate. I told them everything, feeling relieved to release the heavy burden. Spending time behind bars was evident for my future, and I embraced it as a freedom from the lies. It wasn't a hard decision, and I'd collected plenty of physical evidence–the pictures of the attendees and a log book listing Tony's business associates.

When I handed over the pictures that documented all the guests in the Room, jaws dropped to the floor, and tears were shed. It was beyond shocking to see who had participated in the criminal activities. Some attendants participated willingly, and others did not. I'd lived it, but watching a law enforcement officer break down and cry at the sight of his niece in the Room reminded me how awful my life was. Witnessing that uncle's reaction, I realized that by remaining silent I was just as guilty. I was as awful as Tony because I kept my mouth shut and didn't stop him. I said nothing. After years of living it, it became normal–not acceptable. I didn't know any different. I became numb to it. I didn't see a way out, so I went through the motions without feeling.

Lucy and her mother, Molly, submitted statements about their affairs with Tony. Because Lucy was a minor, her statement would seal Tony's fate of life behind bars.

After getting used to my new stoic surroundings behind solid, metal bars and moving past wanting to kill myself, I slept better than I had while I was married to Tony. For three hundred sixty-four days, one day short of a year, I slept without worrying about my safety. While I was married, I slept with one eye open, worrying that I'd find Tony naked on top of me or if I'd physically and mentally survive another day. On a one-inch foam mattress in a six-by-eight-foot cement cell, I slept like a rock. I felt rested, healthy, and relieved. How many of my fellow inmates can say that?

Most inmates go through a stage of huge adjustment when they lose their freedom and worldly possessions. Many feel claustrophobic and anxious being constrained to a small cell. My closet time abuse helped me overcome that fear. My lack of misery caused the women to whisper about me. Some assumed I didn't show signs of stir-craziness because it wasn't my first time behind bars. Some guessed that it was because I wasn't a lifer. Only a few women who probably lived in a similar sort of hell recognized a kinship with me. They understood that prison was welcomed after what I'd endured before arriving.

During my incarceration, Kitty visited me at least once a month. Our conversations were usually light and only touched the surface of what was reality. She was proud that I finally did what was right, even if it took a stranger to force my hand.

"Lisa, I have a bit of advice for you as you're about to reenter the world."

"I can only imagine what advice you have. I hope it isn't beauty tips."

She smiled at my teasing. "Make friends with a cardiologist and an urologist."

I giggled even before I heard the punch line "I'm afraid to ask why."

"One keeps you alive, and the other keeps you pissing and screwing."

Thank goodness for Kitty and her regular visits. She was a bright spot in my drab world. I never told her about Lucy and what finally sent my life crashing down, but Normal was a small town, so I was sure that she heard some version of the truth. However, she never asked.

***

As soon as the tall, metal gates that surrounded the facility closed and I stood alone on the outside of them, the anxiety boulder that sat in the pit of my stomach weighed heavily. I had no one to call for a ride. Over the past seventeen years, while married to Tony, he alienated me from past relationships, and everyone with whom I formed a friendship was preapproved by Tony.

As my lip quivered and tears pooled in my eyes, I quietly told myself, "After all you've survived, don't lose it right now." A deep, purposeful breath entered my lungs, attempting to calm my emotions. "You can make amends as soon as you start getting your life back. One step at a time."

Suddenly, a white Chrysler Cirrus that had been parked forty feet away lurched forward and moved slowly in my direction. I froze. Tony was locked up in a men's prison hundreds of miles away, but at the moment, my heart controlled my feet, and I was paralyzed with fear. *Why is that car coming straight toward me? Is it someone I know? Did Tony send someone?* Illogically, I looked back at the gates and wondered if the guard would let me back in. I wasn't ready to face this world.

The clean, four-door car meandered toward me until it jerked to a stop alongside the curb. The young, blonde woman behind the steering wheel rolled down the window and asked, "Lisa?"

I blankly stared at her, unable to answer for fear of what my acknowledgment might mean.

After a few seconds, she glanced down at a piece of paper that was lying on the seat next to her. Even though she appeared harmless with her hair tied up in a tight bun and dressed in her waitress uniform, I was skeptical.

The baby blue shirt dress fit her like a glove, and the nametag pinned to the chest read, 'Jo.'

"Lisa Marie Shade? Born in Norfolk, Virginia. Age 38. Married and now divorced. No children." She tossed the paper on the dashboard of the car. "Listen, lady, I haven't gotten all day. Is that you or not?"

I nodded.

Who is this strange woman? How does she know all that about me?

"Get in." She gestured to the passenger side front seat. When I didn't move, she looked around the empty parking lot and added with a hint of sarcasm, "Doesn't look like you have a lot of other options, Lisa Marie. I'll count to fifteen. If you don't get in by then, I'll drive away, and you can wait for a better offer."

Jo was right. I didn't have any other options besides walking. And where would I walk to? I decided to get in and discover who she was and how she knew so much about me.

As I pulled up the handle of the car door, Jo informed me that she was from the halfway house that I'd been accepted to. When she noticed that I had no idea what she was talking about, she shook her head. "Those guards can't even help a bitch out and tell her what to expect. They love the control of spitting you onto the street and watching you sweat. They were probably watching our interaction and taking bets on whether you'd get in the car or not. Assholes." She aimed her middle finger toward the guard tower.

As soon as the car door was shut, she explained that upon leaving prison, inmates are assigned lodging to help them deal with the stress of their new life back on the outside of the barbed wire. The home was located in the roughest part of town next to the railroad tracks and the grain bins because "Nothing says welcome back to the real world like a freaking train screeching its wheels on an old rusty track to wake you up two or three times a night."

Twelve women were allowed to live there at a time. "Everyone is an addict like me or an ex-con like you. Because of our poor choices, we're at a crossroads, halfway between Heaven and Hell."

We each were assigned our own small, simple bedroom, but we shared two bathrooms. Everything had a tight schedule, and according to Jo, the rules were posted everywhere as reminders.

"You need to sign up to take a shower because there are only two showers. And don't try to pull one over on Christine. She's as smart as a whip." Jo spat out her last bit of advice.

"Who's Christine?"

Jo took a deep breath. "She's either God or the Devil. Depends on what you believe. She's all-knowing and all-seeing."

Jo reached for the car stereo and turned up the radio, signaling that our conversation was over.

As she drove through the town, I watched the town and its residents through the car window. Sitting on an outdoor patio, a woman in a red baggy sweatshirt threw her head back and laughed at whatever her bib-overall adorned friend had said. A few men dressed in untucked flannels walked past the women, shaking their heads. When we stopped at a red light, the driver of the car next to us glanced over, and I caught his eye. A pleasant smile formed on my lips out of pure manners, but he didn't return my grin. Instead, his eyes narrowed, and he glared at me.

For the next few blocks, every stranger's eyes judged me. People knew who I was because my marriage and the ruin of my life became a featured cover story, airing for months on the five o'clock news in our tri-state area. My face was splashed across the front page of several local newspapers labeled as the woman behind the monster. Radio DJs poked fun at my lack of a backbone, calling me 'a live blow-up doll.' Tony was characterized as the puppet master, and I was his cowardly hallow puppet who silently stood by his side. He pulled the strings, and I never spoke up. I never ran. I was guilty by association.

The whole town knew who I was. I had nowhere to hide.

***

After so many left and right turns that I lost track of my sense of direction, Jo pulled up along the curb of a two-story house that was in desperate need of repair. Although it had once been painted white, the paint that hadn't peeled off was now an antique color. The front steps sagged under the weight of the house. There were eight small windows on the front, each with its own different printed curtain, vaguely visible.

"Home sweet home," Jo announced as she turned off the car. "This is Christine's place. Don't forget it. And that's her."

Standing on the front step of my temporary residence was a stout woman with graying hair. She stood over six feet tall and wore an oversized flannel, baggy jeans, and a pair of black cowboy boots, even though it was summer. Not one bead of sweat ran down her face as she glared at us in between taking puffs of her cigarette. Cool as a cucumber.

Christine was the house facilitator. Her main responsibility was to ensure that everyone followed the rules, so she nagged the tenants twenty-four-seven. Because we were already on probation for breaking society's rules, she had every right to not trust us and expect the worst, and she told us just that. I wondered what kind of interview questions the state asked to weed through the applicants for her position. Unlike other job interviews, they wanted the answers to be the opposite of a regular interview.

"Are you a 'the-glass-is-half-empty' or the-glass-is-half-full' person? How would you handle an unhappy tenant?"

After she took a long drag of a cigarette and puffed the smoke in the direction of the man asking the questions, Christine squint-ed her eyes at him and answered, "Who cares? It's refillable. And do you want me to answer that or just take care of the problem myself?"

She was probably hired right on the spot. Christine's wide shoulders, flat chest, and solid stature also qualified her as the halfway house bouncer. Her graying hair was cut into a blunt bob and required no styling. The deep wrinkles around her lips and eyes suggested that she'd passed the prime of her life. Her nicotine habit colored her skin to a grayish tint, suggesting two packs a day had been a long-time addiction. Love and life hadn't been kind to Christine so her hardened exterior was built to protect what had been broken. No one dared to ask her any personal questions, so we were left to guess the basic facts of her past.

Her raspy voice called out her greeting, "This ain't no five-star hotel. In fact, it ain't even three stars. Obey my rules, do as you are told, shut your trap, don't make any trouble, and we'll get along just fine."

I appreciated her candor, but Christine and her house rules didn't scare me. I'd already lived in Hell.

Chapter 42

Jolene – twelve years later

After fleeing Normal in 1983, I didn't attend college like I previously planned; instead, I aimed my car southwest and didn't stop until I saw clear blue waters. I ended up in Huntington Beach, California. With the windows rolled down to allow the ocean breeze to blow through, I slept in my car parked on the beach. I fell asleep to the ocean's lullaby of calming waves crashing on the sandy shore, and in the morning, I'd awakened to a stronger, nudging crash of waves. The fresh, salty air smelled like freedom and adventure.

The first few weeks were tranquil. A perma-grin tickled my lips as I walked up and down the beach, collecting shells and sand dollars. I was living on the money I'd earned from my hotel room jobs, but it would run out soon. One morning, when I looked up from the sand, I noticed a restaurant constructed right on the beach. Instead of a grassy lawn and flat parking lot surrounding the building, sand crept up to its foundation, giving it the appearance of a massive sandcastle. *Is it a mirage?*

On the west side, a long patio hugged the building. Wooden tables and chairs were organized throughout the space for maximum seating. Twinkling lights draped from the roof of the restaurant to palm trees planted next to the edge of the patio. I faintly heard the sweet words of a Beach Boys song flowing from hidden stereo speakers.

Let's go surfing now. Everybody's learning how. Come on and safari with me.

Determined to make this area my new home, I applied for and landed a job as a waitress at Sandy's Beach Shack, where I was able to eat free while I worked; therefore, I picked up as many shifts as I could. While working at Sandy's Beach Shack, I socialized with several co-workers; however, they were not the kind of friends who were great influences. They were the type of people I could call for a good time, but not the kind of friends I could lean on when I needed a shoulder to cry on. After a few weeks of partying with this crew, cocaine and heroin were introduced at a party. After ingesting it and acting like a complete fool, they laughed when I hallucinated and cried about missing my sister.

The pattern of working enough to eat and party became my routine for several years. I crashed on co-workers' couches or slept in my car. I was barely getting by, and as soon as I numbed the pain, nothing else mattered.

Because my co-workers were far from quality influences, I didn't make any real friends for a few years. My first true friend was one of my regular customers, Howard Bass, and he became a father figure to me. Whenever he dined at Sandy's, which was quite often, he refused to have anyone else wait on him. The other wait staff thought it was creepy, but they were envious. None of them had a regular who was also a great tipper. Plus, I enjoyed his company. Howard was a witty fellow Midwesterner. Often, he liked to sit up at the counter and order his supper while sipping his Merlot.

"Jolene, what's a nice girl like you doing in a place like this?"

"Howard, if Sandy's is such a dive, why are you here almost every night for supper?" In his eyes, a twinkle sparkled. He claimed to be a forever bachelor, but I noticed his ring finger had an indentation where a wedding band left its mark.

"To see you, my dear. Howard's day is never complete without a little Jo and a glass of Merlot." He loved to talk about himself in the third person, and I found it entertaining. "Howard is a poet."

I shook my head at him. "Always the charmer, Howard. If you would settle down with *one* lucky lady, I'm sure she'd cook you dinner and pour you a glass of Merlot every night. You just need to pick *one*."

"Nah. Howard loves his life. Howard Bass will never settle."

"Getting married isn't *settling*, Howard. It's called settling *down*. You know, becoming an adult."

"Big words coming from Miss Too-Good-For-Anyone. I don't see you settling down either. Plus, Howard was married years ago. A lot of heartache for Howard."

"Howard, I'm twenty-five. You're like eighty–"

"Ouch. Correction, Forty-nine." He pretended to be offended as he sipped his wine. A small drop of his red wine landed on his pink, palm-tree-decorated shirt. He noticed that I was watching him. I pointed to the same area on my shirt to indicate that he should blot it out.

"Got a little hole in your lip, young fella?" I winked. "Sorry, my bad. I was taking a wild guess. I'm too young, and I have no prospects."

"Isn't that your fault? Maybe you should give one of these California boys a shot. What about that one?" Howard head-nodded toward the bartender.

"Chad?" I wrinkled my nose.

Chad's regular vocabulary contained phrases like 'Dude, surf's up' and 'No duh.' Even though he was a talented bartender and mirrored many of Tom Cruise's talents from the movie, *Cocktail* as Brian Flanagan, I wasn't interested in ordering an Orgasm or Ding-a-Ling from him anytime soon. "Very funny, Howard."

"Must be someone back home in Iowa that you're still pining for." Howard knew part of my story—where I was from, that I had a family that I left behind. Sometimes, it surprised me how much he remembered. I think he felt sorry for me and took a special interest in me because he recognized the same loneliness that he felt.

***

While the everyday weather in Huntington Beach was perfect—on a warm day, the high would be 80 degrees, and on a chilly day, the temperature dipped down to 60—the lifestyle that I led was killer. Waitressing every night at Sandy's Beach Shack had been lucrative, but the drugs my so-called friends introduced me to were expensive and addictive. For years, I'd been waiting tables from four in the afternoon until two in the morning, and after work, my co-workers and I partied on the beach until dawn. Even though a few times I crashed at a friend's house if our disorderly conduct earned us a boot off the beach, most nights I slept in the backseat of my car. It wasn't the life I'd pictured myself living after I abruptly left Normal, but I was too stubborn to return home to make amends with a woman I'd lost respect for a long time ago. I was determined to make this work. I convinced myself that I needed to catch a break. However, whenever I quit the party scene and vowed to save money to reach my goals, my sobriety would only last a few days before I'd find myself spending even more of my hard-earned money to get high. I was out of control.

One morning, not long after dawn, I found myself puking into a large metal garbage bin along the beach. Through the pounding of my headache, I heard the seagulls bragging to each other about their morning feast.

An early-morning street sweeper idled by and taunted, "But it was worth it, right?" He laughed at my expense.

I responded with a sarcastic thumbs-up but kept my head inside the stinky barrel. The bottom of the barrel was charred with crusty waste that I didn't want to consider its origin. The hot California sun had permanently melted its existence, and now, my vomit would blend in, stamping my presence forever along Huntington Beach, or until the city replaced the rusty trashcans with new ones.

As the dry heaves possessed my body, I faintly heard a car pull over to the side of the road and its engine shut off. Then a car door slammed shut, and I recognized footsteps becoming louder.

Great. The police. At least they didn't use their sirens this time.

Puking in the wee hours of the morning might earn me a trip to the drunk tank to sober up. Hopefully, they'd let me shower again before they kicked me out. The last time I was there, one of the officers took pity on me and washed my puke-stained clothes. I'd been so appreciative of her surprised kindness that I couldn't stop thanking her. She also gave me a toothbrush and a bit of advice.

"Jolene, don't thank me. Cleaning the outside is the easy part. The hard work is cleaning the inside, and that's totally up to you." Her words told the hard truth.

Suddenly, the palm of a large hand made comforting circles on the small of my back, and a familiar voice said, "Jolene."

Through my matted-down, sand-crusted hair, I peeked under my armpit to observe my only true friend, Howard Bass, standing next to me in a pair of tan cargo shorts and a Hawaiian shirt with neon pink flamingos. His hat, which was covering his balding head, read "Mitchell's Corn Palace." *What is he doing here?*

The small circles continued on my back until the dry heaves subsided, and I leaned my forearms over the top of the barrel. I greeted him, "I bet Howard Bass is impressed with his favorite waitress."

"Howard Bass wants to help Jolene. Will you let him?" His voice was low and filled with concern, not a trace of his normal teasing tone.

After we were sure the contents of my stomach had settled, Howard insisted that I lean on him, and he helped me to his car, which was parked along the curb. It wasn't any car–it was a 1965 silver, convertible Ford Mustang in mint condition.

"Howard is fancy," I hiccupped. My attempt at humor landed flat due to his concern for my well-being. As I crawled into the passenger seat of his very clean sports car, I noticed a large box of donuts in the backseat. "You must really like donuts."

"Old habit," replied Howard with a trace of sadness.

After falling asleep in his car, Howard claimed to have carried me into his house and laid me down in his guest bedroom. I woke up that evening and smelled the aroma of baked chicken. Nothing looked familiar, and I vaguely remembered Howard finding me at the beach. I tiptoed out of the room and followed my nose to the kitchen, where I found Howard talking on the phone.

"... yes, I'll keep you posted, Michael. I love you too." As soon as he hung up the receiver on the mount, he noticed me hovering in the entry of the kitchen.

"Howard loves someone? I must meet this mystery person." I shuffled into the unfamiliar kitchen and pulled out a chair.

"Howard loves many people. Howard sees the good in them, even if it's buried real deep."

It was obvious that he was referring to me. I slumped down in the hard, wooden chair. "I'm so sorry, Howard. Why are you helping me? I don't deserve it."

"That's where you are wrong, Jolene. You do deserve forgiveness and love. You're battling something wicked, and until you realize that, keep fighting. When the war is over, I'll be here."

"Just so you can say, I told you so?" I asked.

"Duh. Isn't that what you young kids say nowadays? Anyway, Howard enjoys being right."

Chapter 43

Jolene - 1995

For the next several years, I was in and out of treatment centers for my substance abuse. When I was sober and attending my meetings, I lived in Howard's guest bedroom. He opened his front door every time I showed up. He never asked questions and drove me to every therapy and rehab appointment. Howard was my guardian angel who supported me when I didn't deserve it.

My co-workers at Sandy's thought it was strange that I was living with an older man who was 'clearly obsessed' with me.

"When you wait on him, he hangs on your every word. He's like an infatuated little puppy. If you aren't working, he leaves. It's like he's only coming to see you and not enjoy the ocean view and the good eats," one of my co-workers complained.

"Maybe I'm just a really good waitress," I suggested.

"Witch, please. Howard is your sugar daddy. I know you're lying when you claim that he's never laid a hand on you."

They figured something sexual and inappropriate was going on. However, they couldn't have been more wrong. Howard was like a father to me, and he'd never been anything but kind and generous with me. I didn't understand how I deserved it, and I never asked.

If I wasn't living at Howard's and working at the restaurant, I wandered up and down the coast with whomever. It didn't matter where I was or who I was with, as long as I was high. Sober me always felt so remorseful that Howard cared about me unconditionally and helped me whenever I returned strung out, hungry, and broke. However, high me couldn't see past the next fix.

In 1994, while on a road trip with some so-called friends, I was arrested for possession of cocaine and spent time in jail in Kansas. After I sobered up, I was assigned to live in a halfway house since I had no permanent residence or family to return home to. Pride and shame kept me from reaching out to Howard for help.

I'd been living in the halfway house for a few months when Christine, the house's manager, CEO, and drill sergeant, asked me to pick up the newest tenant from the local prison. No one argued or denied a request from Christine. "You have the car today, so you will pick up a new tenant after your shift. Got it?" Sometimes, Christine allowed one of the tenants to borrow her car. The privilege was earned by respecting the house rules and not causing any unnecessary drama among the tenants. I nodded my acknowledgment and took the printout she handed me, on it was a mugshot of the woman and her basic information. "She'll be waiting outside of the gates. You know the rules. No questions. Tell her the essentials. Drive there and back."

After I finished my shift at the diner, I drove the house car to the edge of town to pick up the new guest. As I turned the corner, I noticed her standing outside of the tall, ominous, razor-wire gates, looking like a lost puppy with her tail between her legs. Her graying brunette hair was pulled to the back of her neck in a low, greasy ponytail. Her coordinating power suit fit her snuggly, hugging her curves. I wondered how long she'd been in prison. Normally, new tenants arrived malnourished and starving. This lady, who looked slightly familiar, had gained weight eating the prison food. The clothes that she wore into prison didn't fit when she checked out. *Interesting.* I pulled off to the side of the road to assess her. I picked up the printout that Christine had given me with her picture and details on it. Yep, it was her plus twenty-some pounds.

She looked up and down the street, looking for something. I took the car out of park and slowly drove toward her. As I pulled up beside her, I rolled down the car window. "Lisa?"

She bent down and peered into the car through the open passenger-side window. She stared blankly at me, trying to decide how she wanted to respond to a simple question.

I grabbed the printout again and read the information that was supplied. "Lisa Marie Shade? Born in Richmond, Virginia. Age 38. Married and now divorced. No children." When I glanced back up at her, she looked like she wanted to crawl back under the prison gates. I tossed the paper on the dashboard. "Listen, lady, I haven't got all day. Is that you or not?"

After she acknowledged her name, she reluctantly climbed into the passenger seat of Christine's car without saying a word, and as soon as she shut the passenger side door, I proceeded to explain how the house worked. I listed the rules and defined the consequences of breaking them. Christine ran a tight ship, but everyone respected her and appreciated the roof over our heads. When I was finished with the basics and Lisa's expression still seemed dumbfounded, I turned up the radio. Maybe she needed a minute to digest everything. Hearing the heavy, iron gates slam tended to stump even the hardened criminals. The sound signaled that we had survived our sentence but now had to figure out how to adapt to everyday life again.

During the ride to the house, I couldn't shake the peculiar feeling that she looked familiar, but I told myself that maybe I'd met her when I was high or intoxicated, or maybe I met her while we were both incarcerated. That possibility seemed unlikely since I socialized with the drunk tank inmates, and this chick appeared as uptight as they came. I was sure she'd never let her hair down, which also made the likelihood that we'd met before even more ridiculous.

Out of the corner of my eye, I peeked at her. Even though the car's seat had been slightly reclined by its previous occupant, my current passenger sat upright as if she were perched in the front of a church waiting for her soul to be saved. She was the pillar of a brown-noser who sat in the front of a classroom, raising her hand at every opportunity to answer the teacher's question. Even though her straight posture reflected someone from a strict, upper-class upbringing, her face revealed her internal fear. I imagined that her stomach was doing flip-flops with a ball of nerves. Her palms, as well as her armpits, were probably moist with apprehension.

My younger self would have reached out and tried to put her worries at ease, but my hardened, older self didn't have anything to give. I was functioning one day at a time. My Alcoholics Anonymous (A.A.) sponsor advised our group not to start a new romantic relationship during the first year of sobriety because we needed to make staying sober our number one priority. I took his advice one step further and threw in friendships as well.

She looks familiar, but she's also the epitome of every uptight, white person that I knew, with her arched back, nose to the sky, and stiff, name-brand clothing.

I didn't know anyone in Kansas, and after I'd been busted, my so-called friends let me take the rap as they hightailed it back to the beach. I decided that my gut instinct wasn't reliable because it hadn't served me well in the past, but the pink scars on my arms started to itch.

Chapter 44

Jolene - 1995

As an addict, I've experienced every kind of hallucination possible; therefore, I often doubted the information that my eyes supplied to my brain. Previous experiences proved that not everything my eyes told me was really there. For example, when giant, biting bugs crawled up and down my bare arms, I scratched at my raw skin until my sharp nails caused nasty claw marks on my forearms. The bugs weren't real, but the scars remained. Whenever something didn't seem right, the angry, dark pink scars itched.

When I read the name on the piece of paper that Christine handed me, the little voice in my mind whispered, *'Lisa Shade? That name sounds familiar.'* However, I didn't give that voice the time of day because it had tricked me so many times before. The paper included a picture of the lady's mugshot. The woman looked exhausted, worn out, and defeated. *I know that feeling.*

When I pulled up alongside the curb and told her to get in the car, I didn't care that the same little voice asked, 'Where have I seen her before?' I figured it didn't matter if she was someone from my past because, according to my counselor and sponsor, I needed to move on. *Let go of the past. Focus on your future.*

But a few weeks later, as I watched her out front of the house from my two-story bedroom window, I was again reminded of that initial gut instinct.

I returned to the house after working a double shift at the local diner. My feet ached from wearing cheap, uncomfortable shoes, and my clothes smelled like a greasy burger. I missed Sandy's Beach Shack. Even after working a long shift there, the ocean breeze and calming sounds of the waves relaxed me. Plus, the tips were better, and I had a favorite, regular customer, Howard. The diner had its own set of regulars, but the majority were uptight businessmen looking for a quick, greasy meal over their lunch hours or after work before they returned to their normally scheduled lives. The vibe on the beach didn't have the hustle and bustle of city life, and pleasure was taken in every experience. Waiting for your food at Sandy's meant more time to relax and enjoy your surroundings. Waiting for your food at the diner caused the men to become abrasive and rude as if their time were incredibly precious.

Daylight faded as I kicked off my shoes and collapsed on my double bed. While I massaged my sore feet, I grabbed my mail and started to open it. As soon as I tore into my letter, I heard faint crying. *Where is that coming from?* When I got up and walked to my window, I looked right and left, trying to locate the source of the sobbing. As my eyes searched up and down the sidewalk, I noticed Lisa rounding the corner at the end of our block. She was walking home from working at a local dentist's office. Concern filled her face. I followed where her gaze was landing. The crying child sat on the sidewalk in front of our house. I could only see the very top of her blonde head. A backpack that was stuffed full rested on her back while her head hung low as she continued to cry. I watched Lisa tentatively approach her. She kneeled next to her on the sidewalk, and I watched her lips move. I couldn't hear what she was saying.

For a few seconds, the loud crying stopped as the girl replied to her, and then she handed Lisa a piece of paper. Her hand flew to her chest, and I read as her lips formed the words, "For me?" Lisa stood up and looked up and down the street, perhaps for whoever caused the girl's misery. Even though Lisa still seemed very concerned, I noticed another emotion. Worry? Fear? I wasn't sure. She opened a piece of paper that the girl had handed her. Her eyes quickly scanned the note, and then her eyes widened.

Lisa looked confused and scared. Even from my second-floor window, I noticed her skin turn pasty white. Like she'd seen a ghost.

After letting the information settle for about thirty seconds, Lisa blinked several times, turned back to the girl, and held up the palm of her hand, telling her to stay where she was. The child's wails increased in volume, which caused Lisa to kneel next to her again. This time she put her arm around her shoulders and gave her a quick side hug. Then she rushed into the front door of the house, leaving the child on the sidewalk.

The little girl hadn't appreciated the open side of Lisa's palm or the fact that she abandoned her because her crying intensified. As I watched the child's shoulders shake, I questioned if I should go down and try to console her since Lisa did a poor job. After a few minutes of contemplation, the blond-headed girl turned toward the front door, looking for Lisa. While a steady stream of tears fell from her eyes, she used her sleeve to wipe her runny nose.

Oh my god.

I looked down at the letter and photograph I was still holding. It can't be. I held up the picture to the glass window so it was next to the little frightened girl on the sidewalk. Even though the boy in the photograph was a few years older and wore a smile from ear to ear, he looked oddly similar to the unhappy, scared girl just below my window. Same blonde, wavy hair. Same oval-shaped, hazel eyes. Same distinct jawline. Same sharp nose.

Warning bells rattled in my brain, telling me to listen, to calm down, to slow down, and to think. However, because the receptors that connected my brain to my vision were unreliable, I wasn't completely sure I believed what the bells were claiming. The pink scars on my arms started to itch again.

The child who stood outside waiting for Lisa–who my brain told me looked familiar–resembled my nephew. If my brain wasn't playing tricks on me, these children could be siblings.

Chapter 45

Dear Jolene,

I hope my letter finds you happy, healthy, and sober. I want you to know that I don't blame you for leaving. You had to get out. I see that now.

You were right about so many things that I wasn't able to recognize at the time. I was only fifteen years old when you left, and I had a lot of growing up to do. Unfortunately, life over the last ten years hasn't always been easy.

When you're ready, I'd love to hear from you. I have someone who I'd like you to meet. I've enclosed a recent school picture. His name is Cooper, and he is my whole world. I tell him stories about you and how great it was growing up with you as my sister. His favorite story is our bedtime toothbrush battle. We'd brush and brush our teeth. Our mouths would be burning from the fluoride. Finally, I'd give in and reach for the faucet to rinse, and you'd spit toothpaste on my hand. He's an only child, so hearing our childish pranks gives him such pleasure.

I have nothing to do with Isabella anymore. Let's just say you were right (I bet you love hearing that). She's a liar, a master manipulator, and has everyone fooled. I'm just sorry it took me so many years to figure it out. You knew at such an early age. I bet our perspectives on our childhood memories are very different.

Sisters forever, Ivy

P.S. This is my last stick of chap. I wanted you to have it.

Chapter 46

Lisa - 1995

This has to be some kind of joke.

My frantic eyes scanned the residential street up and down for a tinted-window, dark-colored sedan lurking nearby, idling on the side of the road, or perhaps a nosy camera crew with a large fuzzy microphone pointed at me, announcing that I was on a candid camera show. I looked for Lucy–sweet, tentative Lucy–with her cheaply colored, black hair. I held the damp, wrinkled note in my hand and silently prayed like I hadn't done in a very long time, before my faith was shaken to its core. I couldn't believe what I'd just read.

Lisa,

I know that none of this will make sense to you. It will seem sudden and tragic. It will make you question my sanity, but I want you to know that I've thought about this every day for the last six years. I regret that I didn't do it sooner.

I can't take care of her anymore. My parents have passed away. My sisters are tired of the drama that surrounds me. I've burned every bridge that I've ever crossed. I have nowhere else to turn.

Camille has done nothing wrong except to be born. She doesn't deserve a mother who doesn't love her like she should be loved; she doesn't deserve to be hated because she exists. She doesn't deserve to feel unwanted. She deserves so many things that I've failed to give her.

I want her to be loved, cared for, and cherished. I know you are capable of all these things because you're a good person. You showed me more kindness, love, and compassion than I deserved, considering the situation you were forced to live in. I'm so sorry for the pain that I caused you. If I could go back in time, there are so many things I would've done differently, like never getting involved with a much older, married man. I was young and naive, and I thought I knew everything.

Through the gossip mill that is quite alive and active in Canby, I've heard that Tony is in jail. That news makes me rest easier, knowing there is no chance he will ever meet his daughter. My hatred for Tony is so strong that it feels like I've swallowed a monster, and it's eating away at my soul. Every time I look at Camille, I'm reminded of this huge mistake that I made and the man who caused me so much pain.

She's a good kid. Hardly ever whines or throws tantrums. She likes the crust cut off her sandwiches, loves being outside, and sometimes sucks her thumb when she sleeps. Let her forget me so that she can live a normal, carefree life.

Thank you, Lucy

Chapter 47

Lisa - 1995

I hadn't been prepared when Lucy abandoned Camille on the front lawn of the halfway house, so I had to think quickly. Children and men were not allowed in the house, and there were no exceptions. I needed more time to think and allow the shock of the situation to sink in. Lucy might change her mind and come rushing back to claim Camille. In the meantime, I'd keep her safe. She was only an infant when she lived at our house, so obviously she didn't remember me, and I wasn't sure what her mom told her about me. I wondered if she read her mom's letter. I wasn't sure if I'd be able to get much out of her, so for the moment, I would plan on being physically there for her.

Running on gut instinct and fear, I dashed into the house to pack a bag in case I was unable to return. As I ran down the hallway, a few of the women threw me curious glances, but none showed any real concern or cared about my presence. The comings and goings of my fellow roommates were often hasty and dramatic; however, this was the first time I was the main character of the drama.

As I grabbed a few of my favorite articles of clothing, my toiletries, and some snacks that I'd kept hidden in my room, I thought back to the day about six years ago when Tony brought Lucy home and informed me that she was going to live with us. Immediately, my chest seized, and my protective instinct kicked into overdrive. A young, innocent teenager under the same roof as my husband, the sex maniac. How was I going to protect this child from his greedy hands, even though it appeared that he had already violated her? Keeping Tony satisfied was a full-time job. I didn't know if I had the energy to worry about another human being.

The conversation regarding a new house guest didn't take place at the dinner table like a normal couple. There wasn't a discussion between a husband and his wife. There were no preparations made to welcome our young guest. Instead, Tony showed up holding two suitcases, one in each hand, with a young Lucy following two steps behind.

Like the first time I met Lucy, her presence again rocked my world. She entered my life with a dramatic entrance and exit. Now, she did it again. I shook the memory from my brain and concentrated on the packing. Thankfully, I just received my paycheck. I verified that the money was tucked securely in the bottom of my purse before I rushed back out to Camille.

She was still standing on the sidewalk, crying uncontrollably, when I opened the door. I recognized a small bit of relief when she saw me. I wanted to be a person she could count on. The poor kid needed at least that.

I grabbed her grimy little hand and said, "Camille, I've had a long day. How about we buy some ice cream? Ice cream always makes me feel better. Do you like ice cream?" I peered into her tear-soaked eyes, and she nodded slightly. I ruffled her hair. "Great. My favorite is the vanilla and chocolate twist. What do you like?"

In between a few sniffles, she mumbled, "Strawberry."

"Good choice. Let's walk this way." I straightened up and guided her down the sidewalk.

"But what if my momma comes back?" She didn't know that she'd left her in my care. She didn't understand that Lucy hadn't planned on coming back.

"She'll know where to find us. Not to worry." My heart broke when I looked into her frightened, innocent face. Everything and everyone she knew and loved was gone, and she was left to trust a perfect stranger. I decided we could both use a little distraction, so I told her a story. I twisted the truth a bit, but every good storyteller does that.

"Camille, did you know that I knew you when you were a baby and wore a diaper?"

Her chest convulsed as she tried to regulate her breathing. Her tiny voice answered, "No."

"I did. Your mom lived with me for a while after you were born. You were such a good baby."

"Momma said I was a mistake. I wasn't supposed to *be*."

"God doesn't make mistakes, Camille. We're all born with a purpose; however, it's our choice to fulfill the purpose that He intended for us. God doesn't tell us what to do; He gives us lessons to learn. Like, if I pray for patience, God doesn't answer my prayer by giving me patience. Instead, He gives me *opportunities* to be patient so that patience becomes a natural response." I heard my own voice and noticed Camille staring at me with a completely blank expression. But my own words echoed inside my head. Was Camille sent to me now by God? Was she how I could rectify my past?

"Hey. Are we still getting ice cream?"

Without even realizing what I was doing, I stopped walking to have my internal conversation. "Yes, sorry. Call me Lisa. All my friends do."

As soon as our feet started moving again, Camille asked, "Lisa, can I have the biggest strawberry cone?"

I couldn't fathom what was going on in this child's mind. Not only had her grandparents died and her mother left her with a stranger, but she was also hungry. Even though a massive lump formed in my throat and my heart bled for her, my mind was certain about what needed to happen after we had our ice cream. It was at that moment that I knew I was going to run.

***

After I bought two tickets, Camille and I climbed on a Greyhound bus. Our tummies were full, and a food coma crept into our physically and mentally exhausted bodies. Camille chose seats in the middle of the bus and begged me to sit next to her. She was still worried that her mother wouldn't be able to find her. I held her small hand in mine as the bus jerked to a start and told her that I'd be sure to let her mother know where we were going.

"It'll be an adventure." I tried to make it sound fun. Maybe I was trying to convince myself as well.

As the bus rattled to a start and pulled out of town, the constant hum of the highway caused both of us to relax. After the adrenaline rush of the last few hours, every inch of my body ached. A twelve-hour bus ride would provide much-needed rest.

"My momma said you were the best cooker she'd ever met. She also said you'd take good care of me."

"She's right. Remember I was telling you that I knew you when you were a baby." She nodded as her eyes drooped, and she rested her head against the window. "You were the cutest baby I'd ever seen."

"Momma said I had baby charm because even the cranky lady named Charlotte who worked at the bank liked me." A big yawn caused her to pause her interjection into the story.

"Baby charm, huh? Yep, sounds about right." I noticed that she couldn't keep her eyes open, so I lowered my voice and talked monotonously. "A huge head of dark hair topped your head, but it's turned a beautiful blonde color now. And you were born with big, sparkling blue eyes that have turned hazel. Whenever you were hungry, wet, or tired, your attention-demanding howl echoed throughout the house. You cooed when you were happy. You loved to be rocked and sung to at bedtime." I noticed Camille's chest rising and falling as she dropped into a deep sleep. My words became a whisper. "I had every reason to hate you and drown you in the tub. But I loved you. I wanted to keep you, keep you safe from *him*. I imagined taking a trip." I looked around. "Kind of like this. I dreamed of stealing you and raising you as my own."

As the city lights passed outside of the bus window, I recognized that I was given a second chance. No Lucy. No Tony. Maybe God answered my prayers without a lesson first this time. If that was the case, I needed to thank Him.

Lucy had her chance for six years to be the best mom she could be, and by some insane miracle, she forfeited her rights and decided to give me a chance. I wasn't going to waste another minute questioning why. I would accept it and never look back.

As I watched Camille fall into a deep sleep next to me, my lips formed the first genuine smile in a long time. I had no idea how I was going to make this work, but I knew that I had someone worth fighting for. This little girl with hazel eyes and gorgeous blonde hair needed me. What she didn't know was how much I needed her.

I bowed my head, closed my eyes, and sent up a prayer of gratitude.

Chapter 48

Jolene - 1995

Call Ivy.

Reaching out to my sister felt like the hardest thing I've ever done. Slamming the door when I was eighteen and running as far as the gas in my car would take me had been an easy cop-out. Choosing to keep my mind numb on and off for ten years had also been easy once my body accepted the rollercoaster ride of my sobriety. Never making any real personal connections, besides Howard, protected my heart from ever feeling true love. However, picking up the phone meant I hadn't run away and created a fairy tale of a life on my own. When I shut Ivy out, I wasn't better off. I hadn't found happiness and fulfillment like I thought I was going to.

Instead, I ended up an addict who didn't respect my own body, just like my mother. She was the reason I left. I ran because I didn't want to be anything like her, and unfortunately, I became even worse. I couldn't even count the number of times that I'd accepted money for sexual favors. I wasn't proud of that fact and couldn't blame drugs or alcohol because, at the time of the agreement, I was sober. I proceeded to get high and drunk before the act itself. I needed the money, and in exchange, I traded a piece of my dignity and soul. This was my battle.

I'd been roaming the West Coast for the last ten years, and every few months, one of her letters would find me. Some letters talked about old memories that the two of us shared. "Remember our cranky old neighbor, Mr. Brady? He lived in that two-story, tan-colored house, three doors down. He paced the sidewalk around his yard like a junkyard dog. He scolded us if we even stepped foot on his beautifully manicured lawn. Well, I read that he died recently due to high blood pressure. Poor old guy."

Some of her letters mention funny stories that happened at work, or she'd write a book review about a thriller that she finished reading. Sometimes, when the letters arrived, the date on the letter would be months old, but every letter ended with the same salutation, 'Sisters forever, Ivy.' Her tone was light, only skimming the surface. I learned from her letters that she enjoyed her job as a secretary. Her return address label indicated that she was living in South Dakota with her husband.

"You'd like him, Jo. He's witty and smart." She wrote in one of her letters.

I met him when he pulled me over for speeding. Yep, you guessed it—he's a cop. The day that his flashing blue and red lights appeared in my rearview mirror, I cursed at myself for always running late. It was going to cost me this time. When I glanced in my rearview mirror after I put my car in park, I caught my first glimpse of him. He looked like Poncho from our favorite show, CHIPS. As he climbed out of the patrol car, the first thing that I noticed was his bicep bulging out of the sleeve of his uniform, and then the rest of his finely sculpted body. My breath seized in my throat. He was smoking hot, Jo! Sure, every chick digs a man in uniform, but this was something right out of a novel. I pinched myself to make sure that I wasn't dreaming.

Amid my daydream, a knock jilted my attention. I looked out my driver's side window, and the hunk was standing a few feet away from me. I slowly rolled down my window.

"License and registration, please." His voice matched his perfect body—deep and gravelly. My brain wasn't cooperating with my mouth. I didn't move or respond. "Miss?"

"Sorry. Yes, sorry about that. I was a little distracted." I fumbled to find my wallet in my purse.

Officer McHotty watched in fascination as I dumped the contents of my purse onto the passenger seat. A tampon, a huge grandma period pad, a generic bottle of gas relief pills, a tube of chapstick, and an expired condom. As my struggle continued, a small chuckle escape his lips. I glanced back at him to apologize for taking so long when I saw his beautiful, pearly white smile.

He cleared his throat, and I realized he was struggling to remain professional. Slowly, his genuine smile faded, and his cop persona asked, "Miss, do you know why I pulled you over?"

Was that a trick question? I decided to take a chance. What did I have to lose?

"Was it to spank me for speeding?" I raised my eyebrows up and down at him.

"What?" He cleared his throat again, which I know now, as his wife, is a nervous habit of his. Even though my comment was inappropriate, I made him smile again.

"I'll be honest, as cops, we hear a variety of excuses. Most of the justifications include diarrhea or a death in the family, but my favorite was when I pulled over this gray-haired guy. I asked him why he was driving so fast. He told me that he saw me sitting there on the side of the road, but his wife recently ran off with a police officer, and he was afraid I was bringing her back. That was my favorite excuse, at least until I heard yours."

He couldn't contain his smile, and if I thought he was a fox in my rearview mirror, up close standing right next to me only an arm-length away, he was stunning. My knees were weak. The physical attraction was instant and electrifying. Best of all, from his smile, I could tell the feeling was mutual.

I only received a warning that day, but when he took my driver's license back to his patrol car, he illegally jotted down my name so that he could look me up in the phone book when he got home. He called me that night, and we went on our first date that weekend.

Happiness and relief filled my heart the day that I read that letter. I was thrilled that my leaving hadn't caused Ivy any lasting harm, and the pressure that squeezed my heart decreased and sparked one of my sobriety kicks. Even though Ivy had no idea how her words affected my mental health, I appreciated that, for years, she continued to try to break through my stubborn wall. But before I could fulfill the ninth step of the twelve-step program—contacting those who have been hurt by you—I'd find myself in a downward spiral again. It was a vicious cycle.

***

The day I finally dialed the ten digits of her phone number, I wished I would've had the courage to do it sooner.

Before she announced her generic greeting on her end of the phone, I recognized her giggle as she communicated with whoever was in her home with her. "Hello?"

"Ivy..."

"Jolene? Is that you?" She asked in a slightly elevated voice. Not only did she seem surprised but also hopeful.

During the years that we'd been apart, I'd changed so much. I wasn't the big sister she used to look up to. I was damaged. I couldn't be that person she leaned on anymore. I wasn't strong, smart, or healthy enough to support someone else. I was afraid. Tears poured out of my eyes as I realized I'd finally initiated the ninth step of my program—making amends.

"Ivy." I couldn't seem to form any other words, but thankfully, Ivy was still a talker and realized my struggle to string a sentence together.

"Oh, Jo. It's so good to hear from you. I've missed you like crazy. You have no idea. I never knew if my letters were finding you or not, but one did because you dialed my phone number. We aren't listed in the phone book. With Michael being a cop, it's better to keep it unavailable to every Tom, Dick, and Harry. At least now, when the phone rings, it's someone I know and not someone trying to sell me something that I don't need. Because everyone knows what a sucker I am for a good deal." When she finally took a breath in the middle of her ramble, she giggled. "Sorry. I'm rambling. Where do you live, Jo? Or, more importantly, *how* are you?"

Since where I lived was easier to explain than how I was, I answered, "California. Huntington Beach. When I left Normal, I headed straight for the ocean." My voice squeaked as the answer came out of my phone. I cleared my throat and wiped my tears. My A.A. sponsor would be so proud of me. She warned me that this wasn't going to be easy. Baby steps.

"California, huh? Wow. That's amazing. I've never been there. I bet I'd love the ocean. Is it as amazing and beautiful as the TV shows make it look?" I appreciated her attempt at making this conversation easy on me.

"Yes, it's gorgeous. Sandy beaches line the whole coast. Sunsets are my favorite to watch. They never get old. It's like a big, bright orange ball sinking into a huge, beautiful turquoise pool. There is nothing like it." I wasn't lying.

A short silence rested between us. Ivy hadn't changed after all these years. She was still the bubbly, full-of-life kid that she was when I left so many years ago.

"Jo, it is so wonderful to hear your voice. I've missed you."

"I'm so sorry, Ivy." I broke down in a full-blown meltdown that lasted at least five minutes, which was going to cost me when the phone bill came, but I reminded myself that it was cheaper than therapy. The meltdown was long overdue. The tension I was feeling before I picked up the phone was released from my body through tears and sobbing.

When I was finally able to control my crying, I took deep breaths to regulate my breathing. I wondered if I was gripping a phone without a caller on the other end. She didn't say a word.

As if she heard my internal question, she softly said, "I'm here, Jolene. I'll always be here for you."

Chapter 49

Jolene - 1995

Because making that long overdue phone call was epic in itself, I didn't feel it was the right time to tell her I'd met the notorious Mrs. Shade from Normal, Iowa, or the fact that the little girl she was talking to outside on the sidewalk resembled the young boy in the picture that Ivy had mailed me of Cooper. I decided–or maybe a better way to describe it was that I chickened out–to wait until we saw each other in person. I wanted Ivy to focus on the fact that I missed her and wanted to mend our relationship.

I also avoided telling her that I wasn't in California but in a halfway house in Wichita, Kansas, fulfilling my probation. Some facts just weren't appropriate for a phone conversation. Mending our relationship was my main priority. I hadn't thought past that goal when I dialed her number.

However, before I knew it, Ivy insisted that she visit me in California.

"We need to make up for lost time, and I've never been to the West Coast. Shit! I've never seen the ocean, but it's on my bucket list. I'll make it a road trip! This will be amazing. I can't wait to see you, Jo." I could feel her excitement through the phone receiver, like static electricity that jolts you.

"Ivy, we have a couple of problems with that idea." I hated to say the words, but no bridge could be mended by lies. I clearly remember that conversation with my sister. Those were some of the last words we spoke. "I currently live in a halfway house... in Kansas, and you can't stay with me here. I can't even have visitors." I hated to dampen her excitement about a magical sister weekend, but I had to tell her.

"Oh... no biggie at all." Her tone didn't match the words that left her mouth. Through the phone lines, her disappointment was apparent, but she moved on to her next positive thought. "Kansas is closer. That will work great. I'll reserve a hotel near you so we can spend every second getting caught up." Her enthusiasm only took one second before returning to its cheerful level.

Then I explained to her that, as part of my probation, I had to maintain my job and attend biweekly A.A. meetings after work. "My free time is limited right now. Keeping busy helps with self-doubt."

"Jo, it's all good. I can find plenty of other activities. Plus, quality time is much more important than quantity." She jotted down the house's phone number so she could call me back with the details of her trip.

"Power twins activate!" She yelled before hanging up the receiver.

As I hung up the phone, I smiled. The phrase was from one of our favorite childhood cartoons. The superhero siblings would bang their wrists together to ignite their powers. Many afternoons in our backyard, Ivy begged me to reenact that scene.

With one phone call, I was able to mend a bridge that had been broken for a decade. 'I'm sorry' are powerful words. I picked up the receiver again and dialed another long-distance phone number. I needed to apologize and correct another more recent mistake. As soon as I heard his voice, I knew I'd made the right decision.

"Howard, it's Jolene."

***

Seeing Ivy after ten years felt like finding the missing puzzle piece that was lodged in the back of the game drawer. The piece belonged in the middle of the puzzle. It wasn't complete until that last piece snapped into place.

To make the most of her adventure, Ivy was driving from Mitchell, South Dakota, to Wichita, Kansas. There was so much of the country that she hadn't seen yet. "Remember Lily Armstrong from the good old days in Normal? She told me her dad, who was a truck driver, used to bring her state magnets from every state he visited. I'm starting a collection, beginning with all the states that I drive through to get to you.

"I've been so busy being a mom that I haven't taken much time for myself. It'll be good for the soul." She explained that her mother-in-law would help with her son while she was away. "Michael is an only child, and his mother–even though she means well–is always in our business. So, I bet taking care of Cooper is the highlight of her year. She relishes being needed. She is divorced and kind of lonely."

She pulled out of her driveway on Tuesday morning as soon as Cooper jumped on the school bus. She called me every couple hundred miles to give me an update on her arrival time. If I wasn't around, one of my housemates took a message. One of the notes left on the door of my room said it all.

> *Some super happy chick named after a bush called to tell you that she was sleeping in Nebraska tonight. She will be here tomorrow, and she said she wants her stick of chap back. (?) She is nuts. Good luck with that one.*

***

Our first sister weekend was everything we both needed. We shared stories, we laughed until we cried, we forgave each other, and we made promises to stay close. We never talked about Mother in the present tense. Our childhood memories referred to both of our parents, but I knew the topic would come up eventually. I needed to be prepared to not let it ruin our mending relationship.

As soon as I completed my probation and was allowed to travel, I sped to Mitchell, South Dakota, to meet my brother-in-law and nephew. Ivy talked so much about them that I felt I knew them already but couldn't wait to create my relationship with them. The immediate, deep love that I developed for Cooper shocked me. The stories that Ivy told about him were entertaining, so I wasn't surprised that I found this precocious ten-year-old amusing, but the intense affection that developed surprised me.

When I rolled into town, Cooper was still at school, and Michael was at work. Ivy ran out into the driveway with her arms spread as wide as they would go.

"I can't believe you're here. I'm so excited! I plan on spoiling you so much that you'll never want to leave." She yanked me into a big bear hug. I had every intention of returning to California to resume my life, but I didn't want to rain on Ivy's excitement, so I smiled and hugged her back.

As she ushered me into her small ranch-style home, I smelled a hint of Pine-Sol. She must have been cleaning before I arrived. Her decorating style was simple, with not a lot of miscellaneous items set out. The living room, which was located off the entryway, contained a large, cozy-looking brown couch. On each side of the couch, there were two reclining chairs. One appeared more worn than the other. An oval, wooden coffee table rested in the middle of the room. A stack of fashion magazines littered the top. On the living room wall hung a mounted fish with a golden plate under it labeled, 'Bass.' Next to the odd choice of decor were rectangle stains, where the sun must have discolored the paint on the walls. The shapes indicated that a few picture frames had been hanging there but were recently removed.

Ivy tossed her shoes on the rug in the entryway, and I followed her example. "Welcome to our home."

Even though Ivy's enthusiasm for my visit to meet her family was enormous, I noticed that her eyes were bloodshot, and puffy bags hung under them. Her bouncy, upbeat self was dialed down a few notches. Since we were still in the early stages of rebuilding our relationship, I decided to not focus on that and listen to the words pouring out of her excited mouth. I didn't want to pry. Maybe my visit was causing some unnecessary stress on her marriage. I wasn't sure, and her endless chatter didn't divulge any secrets.

"Let me show you to the guest room. The only people who stay with us are Michael's parents, so you might find traces of items that they left behind." I followed her to the back of the house, where I noticed a tire swing hanging from the giant willow tree. Ivy's life mirrored a storybook. "Throw your stuff in the closet, or you can even unpack and use the dresser. Whatever you are comfortable with."

I set my suitcase on the floor in the closet and shut the door.

Ivy smiled. "No fuss. No mess. Still the same, Jo." She turned back around and gestured to the kitchen. "Want a glass of wine? I know it's the middle of the day, but..."

"No thanks. A cup of coffee would be fabulous if you have it."

"Oh shit! I forgot. You don't drink." She smacked the palm of her hand into her forehead.

"It's no big deal, but yes, I don't drink. However, I never say no to caffeine." I shot her a little smirk. Being sober often stumped people. They didn't know if *they* were allowed to drink in my presence or if it would be a trigger for me. "Ivy, have a glass of wine. It doesn't bother me. I know my limitations, and one is never enough."

We relaxed on the back patio, sharing more stories from our childhood and getting to know each other. We laughed. We cried. It was wonderful.

Getting to know my nephew was the largest, sweetest cherry on top of this whole sloppy sundae. I never considered myself a fan of kids until Cooper surpassed all of my expectations. Who knew I'd adore a booger-picking know-it-all who still had to be reminded to brush his teeth? I didn't see it coming.

Michael lived up to all of Ivy's hype as well. He was charming and welcoming. I appreciated him not giving me the third degree about where I've been for the last ten years. He probably read my rap sheet and knew that I didn't deserve a second chance, but he granted me one anyway because his wife insisted.

Chapter 50

Jolene - 1995

The first night in Ivy's home was magical. Michael worked his magic on the grill. Ribeye steaks with twice-baked potatoes. Everything smelled fabulous and made my mouth water. On the back deck, Ivy had set up a little picnic for the four of us. On top of the red and white checked tablecloth that covered the wooden picnic table, Cooper set four place settings with the necessary condiments.

"We don't buy steak sauce because Michael is a master at seasoning his meat." Ivy complimented her husband with a small wink. It warmed my heart to see my sister so happy. After years of being together, they still flirted. I couldn't help but feel a little envious.

From behind the grill, Michael asked my permission to drink a beer, which indicated that he knew where I'd been for the last ten years. Then he asked if I missed alcohol. At first, it caught me off guard, but at least it was easier than having to explain my history myself.

I was already sitting at *my* spot at the table as Ivy was tossing a salad to add to our feast. "I don't have a problem with other people drinking. My only problem is that I know I can't stop at one. When I drank, it wasn't for the taste. It was the numbness that it gave."

Michael nodded and pinched his lips together, which made his mustache tickle his nose. "That makes sense."

In the small red and white cooler next to the picnic table, Michael pulled out a chilled Coors, cracked it open, and took a long pull. Trying not to be too obvious, I checked out my sister's husband. He was a good-looking guy with a muscular build. On the top of his head, a thick, dark mat of hair sat trimmed in a neat, short cut. His eyebrows reminded me of dark brown caterpillars that matched his dark brown mustache. I bet his chest and back were covered in the same dark hair. The man was part sasquatch. When he smiled, his eyes became little slits, and a dimple appeared on his left cheek. I understood Ivy's attraction to him, and from her stories, his inner beauty was just as amazing.

As the summertime cicadas sang their nightly tune, memories of my childhood growing up in Iowa surfaced. I remembered Ivy and me playing for hours outside and not wanting to return home when our mother called us in. We blamed the cicadas for being so noisy that we couldn't hear her yelling. That excuse was only part of the truth.

"Jolene, we are glad you're here. You're welcome to stay as long as you'd like." While I'd been distracted by the mating calls of the large bugs, Michael had given me the once-over as well. He was smiling when I glanced back at him.

"I appreciate your hospitality, Michael." Opening up his home to a stranger with a checkered past wasn't easy. In his line of work, Michael witnessed the vicious cycle of addiction so he didn't trust easily. I couldn't blame him. However, I hoped he looked at my whole past and noticed that, while growing up in Normal, I didn't have a record.

During dinner, Cooper was extremely polite and well-behaved, and both of his parents mentioned that they'd like me to move in if this would be how Cooper acted in my presence.

"Jolene, Ivy might have been the one to invite you to visit, but after seeing the magic your presence affects Cooper, I'd like to ask you to move in. Michael is impressed." When Michael referred to himself in the third person, I felt a small tug at my heart. Back in California, Howard Bass referred to himself in the third person all the time, and it made me giggle. It was a good reminder to reach out to him.

"You're being extreme, Dad." Even though he was a very mature ten-year-old, his adolescent rebellion wouldn't completely shut down when he felt he needed to defend himself.

Michael grinned when he responded by counting his fingers: "First, you didn't complain about joining us for dinner." The second finger rose. "Then you engaged in conversation with more than 'yeah' and 'nope' answers." Michael pointed at his third finger and said, "Michael saw your teeth, so that means you smiled at least once, and you used the words, 'please' and 'thank you', which Michael didn't realize were in your vocabulary. Michael owes Jolene." As his thumb popped out to indicate that he had a fifth point, Cooper interrupted him.

"I think we got the point, Dad." But there was a lilt in his voice. He was amused as well. He looked at me and smiled. "I guess that means you need to stick around Aunt Jolene because in a few years, I will be entering my teenage years, and we know that is going to be hell–"

"Cooper!" Ivy scolded.

"What? You say that word all the time." Typical kid excuse. We all smiled.

***

I'd only been in South Dakota for forty-eight hours when I realized that I felt a sense of belonging, a sense of family. I hadn't felt that sense of home since before Father passed away.

After Cooper hopped on the school bus and Michael backed out of the driveway in his patrol car, Ivy and I plopped down on her back porch to enjoy our morning coffee in our pajamas before we ventured out of the house on little excursions that Ivy planned to entice me to fall in love with South Dakota. One day, we toured the World's Only Corn Palace, which wasn't an actual palace but more of an old historic museum, and it wasn't made out of corn but *decorated* with twelve different shades of ears of corn. During the tour, we learned that it took 325,000 multicolored ears to cover the palace, and each year this task was completed to ensure the beauty of the landmark. The residents of Mitchell took great pride in agriculture, which was the main source of income for the area.

"I bet California doesn't have a palace like this." Ivy nudged with her arm and raised her eyebrows like I should be impressed.

"If it did, the kernels would make popcorn under the heat of the intense sun, but at least the salty air would give it a nice flavor."

Ivy snickered.

Another day, we hiked around Lake Mitchell. Between our heavy breathing, we listened to native songbirds sing their afternoon chatter to each other. The wind breezed through the trees, causing rustling in the leaves. Since I'd spent the majority of the last ten years in a big city, I was used to the hustle and bustle of the city–the honking of horns, the squeal of tires, and the whiz of traffic. The sounds of nature were calming. Our hike had gotten our heart rate up and filled an emptiness in my soul.

When we returned home and waited for the men in Ivy's life to return, we sank into her couch with our Cokes and shared narratives.

"Something strange happened that day right before I first called you." I sipped my Coke and told her about Lisa Shade staying at the halfway house and then witnessing her and a young girl outside of my window. "Right after I opened your letter–the one with a picture of Cooper in it–I heard crying. Not adult crying, more like whimpering. When I looked out my second-floor bedroom window, I saw Lisa talking to a very upset little girl. She was about five years old. I'd never seen her before. We weren't allowed to invite anyone into the halfway house, so I didn't know where she came from. And I'm no kid expert, but she looked familiar."

"Okay..." Ivy didn't understand where I was going with my story.

"Ever since I picked up Lisa from the jail, I had this weird sense of deja vu. Nothing you can tangibly hold in your hand. Just a gut feeling. Then that day, I saw her talking to a little girl. Even though she wasn't the same age, that kid looked a lot like Cooper."

Chapter 51

Jolene - 1995

An awkward silence fell between us, and I wasn't sure why, so I kept talking.

"I'm not sure if it was a subconscious sign telling me that it was time to call you or if she *actually* resembled Cooper. Whatever the reason, it prompted me to dial your number, and I'm eternally grateful. But how peculiar is it that Lisa Shade from Normal, our hometown, would be in Kansas in the same sober living house as me and then talking to a child who looked like my nephew? I couldn't get over the coincidences."

As I pulled down my sunglasses that were protecting my eyes from the warm summer day, I peeked at my sister, who was sitting quietly in the lounge chair next to me. Even though we were soaking up Vitamin D, her skin paled.

"Ivy? Are you okay?" Maybe she'd had too much sun. I sat up and leaned in closer to her. "Do you need some water?"

"No. I'm fine." Her words rushed out. Even though she claimed nothing was wrong, I leaned over and put my hand on her forehead to see if she had a temperature. "Jolene, who was the kid? Was she Lisa's daughter?"

I was surprised she still wanted to talk about it when she wasn't feeling well. "I don't think so. From what I remember her sharing in our group therapy sessions, she never had any children." Distracting Ivy wasn't helping her look any better, so I suggested that we go inside for a bit. "I don't want you to get heat stroke."

"Tell me why you think she looked like Cooper, Jolene."

"Well, like I said, I'd just opened your letter when I heard the crying. I don't know if I had the picture of Cooper in my head, and that is why I thought they looked like each other." Ivy gestured with a wave of her hand for me to continue. "When Lisa ran into the house, she left the kid standing on the sidewalk all alone. With tears streaming down her face, she turned and watched Lisa enter the house. That's when I saw her face and recognized a resemblance between the two. Same blond hair, same nose, same eye shape, same chiseled chin." I stared off into the backyard, trying to conjure up the memory. "I remember wondering if I should run outside and try to console the kid, but instead I took the whole encounter as a sign that I needed to finally call you. And that's what I did."

Ivy was listening intently to my story about a memory that didn't seem incredibly significant at the time. I wished I could give her more information, but that was all I had.

"Jo, I need to stop you there, and maybe I do need some water." Ivy retreated into the house while I replayed our conversation so I could figure out what had upset her.

When she returned to the back deck a few minutes later, she handed me a glass of ice water and sat down at the picnic table under a large table umbrella that provided shade. Not completely understanding what was happening, I got up and joined her. I sensed a seriousness in the change in our conversation.

"Jolene, what I'm about to tell you happened ten years ago, and I don't like to talk about it." Her introduction to the topic of conversation caused my stomach to flip. "I attended therapy, and it helped immensely, but I never wanted to be defined by *that* event."

I kept my mouth shut to allow Ivy to set her own pace for her story.

"Jo, Michael isn't Cooper's biological father. Michael and I met five years ago when Cooper was five years old." Ivy delivered the news as if somehow it would affect me, which made me not take her words with a grain of salt.

Math had never been my strong suit, but a third grader could have figured out this fact faster than me.

"Oh yeah, I guess that makes sense now when I stop and think about it. I guess I assumed Michael was Cooper's dad." I took a sip of my ice water, which was quickly warming in the afternoon sun.

"Wait. Cooper is ten?" Again, math hated me.

Ivy nodded as she watched patiently for my brain to catch up. I ran away from Normal eleven years ago, so that would mean Ivy had gotten pregnant soon after my departure. She was fifteen years old and still whined when she didn't get her way, complained that I never squeezed the toothpaste out of the tube correctly, and tattle-tailed to Mother if I didn't do my weekly chores. In my memories, Ivy was a child, not a woman with hormones and sexual desire. Imagining that the young girl who I left behind had been pregnant a few months later didn't fit. At the time I moved out, she hadn't even kissed a boy.

When the puzzle pieces aligned, I looked at her and noticed she'd been waiting for me to catch up. "I know you probably have a lot of questions, Jo, but let me answer a few right now." She cleared her throat, indicating that this was a difficult conversation for her.

"Ivy, you don't owe me anything. Your forgiveness and allowing me back into your life are more than enough. You don't need to tell me." This conversation had taken me by surprise. I wasn't sure how it got started. I'd simply been telling her what prompted me to finally reach out to her.

As if I hadn't said anything, her voice cracked when she continued, "Yes, I was still in high school when I had Cooper. I ended up dropping out and getting my GED a few years later. Things were..." She searched for a word to explain. "Traumatic."

"I'm so sorry, Ivy." If I had known that my leaving would've caused her life to tailspin out of control, I would never have left.

"None of this is your fault, Jo. Don't blame yourself." She reached across the table and squeezed my hand. Our relationship had switched roles, she was the protector and the strong one now. "I was raped, Jolene, by four different men. I don't know who Cooper's father is."

Our conversation kept getting worse and worse. My eyes widened, and I searched hers. She delivered that fact with great poise.

"I've had a lot of therapy. The last ten years have been a rollercoaster, and it isn't something I enjoy talking about. Of course, Michael knows part of the story, but since he's in law enforcement, I didn't tell him everything. I don't think he could listen to what happened without hunting down and beheading those men." An awkward giggle escaped when she mentioned Michael. "And even though I wouldn't mind seeing justice, I don't want to lose my husband. He's too pretty to go to jail." She smiled and locked eyes with me again.

Ivy was strong and resilient. I was amazed at what a sane, healthy, and vibrant woman she had become. I blamed my father's tragic death on my downward spiral. I took the easy way out and used drugs and alcohol to numb my pain. I didn't deal with it; I pushed it down deeper, where it grew and festered. But my sister suffered a tragedy and came out on top.

"Jolene, I don't want Cooper to ever know that he was a product of such a violent, vulgar act. It isn't something I'm proud of or like to discuss, so I'm hoping you can keep it between us. I thought you should know now that you're in his life."

"Ivy, I don't know what to say. I'm so sorry seems lame; but I am. I feel terrible that that happened to you in the first place, and then you were pregnant because of it. How scary." I tried to picture Ivy at that age trying to deal with a teenage pregnancy, a gang rape after her father had died and her older sister abandoned her. It was too much. I can't help but ask, "Did Mother know? How did Mother deal with it?"

Instantly, I saw a flash of something in Ivy's expression, but I wasn't quite sure what it was. When she answered, she looked me straight in the eye and nodded. "Yes. Mother knew, but I don't call her that anymore. Mother or Mom is an earned title. I refer to her as Isabella."

My gut warned me that there was something more to her answer as it flip-flopped in my stomach. "What aren't you telling me?"

After a deep breath and what felt like an eternity but was probably only ten seconds, Ivy answered, "Not only was she there, but she also brought me to the party. She knew what was going to happen before it happened and allowed it. It sounds horrible and too hard to believe, I know, but it's true."

Ivy's gaze focused on something off in the distance. Maybe it was a locked vault that stored the memories, and she was getting ready to close it after she revealed the contents. I was glad she wasn't able to look at me anymore as she told me this part of the story because I was unable to disguise my shock. Our mother, Isabella, was the devil. Huge tears swelled in my eyes. My baby sister had not only been raped by more than one man, but our mother had given her daughter's consent.

"Jolene, I know this is a lot to digest. I don't want you to feel sorry for me. I don't want you to fix anything. You've always been a fixer and protected me the best way you know how, but I'm fine now. This is my past. I've healed and let go of my anger. It was awful and it messed me up—no doubt about that, but if it hadn't happened, I wouldn't have Cooper, and he is my whole world. I've made a conscious decision to not let one night ruin my entire life. It will not shape or define the rest of my life. Those men have stolen enough." Ivy paused and looked at me as I blinked, and my tears fell from my eyes. Oddly enough, Ivy reached over and grabbed my hand to console me.

"Ivy... I don't know what to say." It was the truth. There were no words to help this situation.

"There is nothing to say except that you won't tell Cooper." As large droplets of tears fell from her eyes, she added, "One of the men who raped me was Lisa Shade's husband, Pastor Tony."

Chapter 52

Jolene - 1995

As I cleared the cobwebs in my brain, I recalled the last time I saw Pastor Tony. It was at my father's funeral. The man had given me creepy vibes. Something about the way he looked me up and down like I was a piece of meat made shivers travel up and down my spine. When he grabbed my arm, his touch felt familiar, but I didn't know why. Then, a few minutes after our conversation, Mother strolled into the room, and the two of them flirted with each other as if they had already consummated a love affair. The fact that my mother would flirt at her husband's funeral hadn't surprised me, but what surprised me was the way he immediately responded to her advances. Inappropriate, not only because of where we were but also because he was the pastor of the church. I shrugged off my intuition at the disgust I felt seeing the two of them together.

Ivy's confession that Pastor Tony raped her, along with multiple other men, made my blood boil. What kind of man rapes a young girl—a virgin—with a group of his friends? How could this man be the pastor of a church? It made no sense, but I believed Ivy's every word.

I didn't understand how our mother could be involved in this nightmare. I may have lost all respect for her, but I had a hard time imagining what kind of role she played in this horrific story.

"Ivy..." I couldn't find the right words to appropriately react to this information. How do I console her? It was ten years ago, but still, how does someone heal from being so tragically victimized?

"Jolene, it's okay."

"But it's not okay."

"Like I said before, I'm not letting that event shape my life. I chose to move forward. I've chosen to not let those men take away my happiness and my chance at a future. I just can't."

"I have so many questions. I don't understand. He was our pastor, and I swear that at Father's funeral, he was interested in Isabella."

"I'm not quite sure what Pastor Tony was interested in besides himself. I can't speculate on what drives anyone else. I can only control my reactions." Ivy flashed me a weak smile. "That sentence took me years and thousands of dollars in therapy to understand."

With her glossy eyes filled with tears, Ivy told me a story that broke my heart and fueled a black anger that caused my nostrils to flare like a Spanish fighting bull when it saw red. "Jo, I can't tell you why, but I can tell you *what* happened. After you left, my life and the choices I made—well, let's just say—aren't something I'm proud of. Looking back on it, I can see the beginning of the tidal wave, but when I was living in it, I couldn't see the bigger picture. With each crashing wave, I tried to stay afloat and catch my breath until the next wave came. Isabella and I didn't start attending church services again, but we were seeing a lot of Pastor Tony. So yes, you were right. He suddenly became obsessed with Isabella and helped her with her grief process, or at least that's what she told me was happening. I was naive and believed in the good in everyone.

"But unfortunately, I learned that isn't always the case. Evil is a seed, and if given the right circumstances and ingredients, evil will grow and prosper. I imagine evil growing in someone's soul. Depending on the encouragement, it can either learn right from wrong or it can fester and decide it doesn't matter. In Isabella's case, I imagine Daddy as her weed killer. With his love and support, the evil in Isabella's soul was tamed. However, once he was gone, the evil flourished under Pastor Tony's care. His influences were the water, soil, and sun. I wish I would've been stronger. I wish I dared to speak up. Tell her no. Tell him no, but I didn't have the tools or the strength at the time."

"Ivy, there are so many things I wish I could do over. One of them would be never leaving you. I shouldn't have written in that letter I left you. I should've woken you up and told you to your face."

"What letter?"

"I should've just dragged you with me instead of leaving clues in a note."

"Jo, what letter?"

"I wrote you an apology the night we got into that big fight and I slapped you." I glanced at her to gauge her reaction. "I left it on the kitchen table so you would find it in the morning."

"I didn't get your letter, Jo."

***

Dear Ivy,

I'm sorry. So sorry. I have no idea what came over me. I should never have raised my hand to you.

You're my little sister, and I've only tried to protect you from heartache. I thought I was doing that for the past several years, but maybe I was doing more harm than good by not telling you what was happening under our own roof. I know you think I've been hard on Mother, but believe me, Ivy, you don't know what that woman is capable of. She is a master manipulator who will do anything to get what she wants. She doesn't care if she hurts anyone else. Including her own children.

If you meet me at the city park, I will tell you everything, and we can decide what to do together. If you don't come, I will leave today and pray that someday you will forgive me for running away. I can't stay, Ivy. I wish I could, but she has already poisoned my heart more than I should've allowed. No mother should be capable of the deception she has already committed.

Sisters forever – Jo

P.S. I left you the last stick of chap on my nightstand.

Chapter 53

Jolene - 1995

For years, I assumed that Ivy had moved on and that she had decided she was better off without me in her life. I believed that she read my letter, and even though I begged her to find me before I left town, she chose to stay. She chose Mother. I wondered how different our lives would have turned out if I hadn't run, if I'd stayed, or if I'd been able to get Ivy to understand.

I realized that someone *had* read the letter I left Ivy on the kitchen table, but it wasn't Ivy. It was Mother.

"The morning after our fight, I remember hearing my alarm clock and reaching over to slap the snooze button. As I rolled over to get comfortable for nine more minutes, I peeked at your bed, waiting to hear you complain about me pressing the snooze button, but your bed was empty. When I rolled over, I was lying on the cheek that had been slapped, and as it pressed into the pillow, it started to throb." As Ivy recalled that painful moment, her hand reached up and touched her cheek. Tears pooled in both of our eyes. "In fifteen years of being siblings, that night was the first time physical violence ever occurred. We yelled and called each other names before, but nothing violent had ever happened."

Those were some of the same thoughts that filled my mind when I thought about our fight. I wished I could somehow go back in time and change that night.

Ivy kept talking. "I remember that not only did my swollen cheek ache but my heart, too. At the time, I wanted you so badly to see that Isabella was trying her best and that she was grieving just like us. She lost the man she married at twenty years old when they were both young and naive. They survived hard times, but they stayed together. Didn't that count for something? I didn't know. I'd never even had a boyfriend, so I had no idea what a twenty-year marriage felt like. What I did know was that I loved both of our parents with all my heart. Daddy and his corny jokes always tickled my funny bone. Isabella and her strength never ceased to amaze me. Even though you didn't recognize Isabella's good qualities, I knew they were there. Sometimes it was just hidden a bit. Even though I knew she wasn't perfect, I couldn't let those thoughts penetrate my soul. Where would I be then? Our father was dead, and our mother was all we had left. We all missed Father, and we were trying to figure out our new family norm."

I pictured Ivy that morning, shuffling into the kitchen to find something for breakfast. Her puffy eyes would've been glazed over and red from crying, with tear crust in the corners of her eyes. She slept in Father's old Iowa Hawkeyes t-shirt. Because Father was a huge man, the neck of the shirt would've been draped over Ivy's shoulder and hung down to her knees. Her hair would've been in a messy bun with lots of stray hairs hanging in her face.

"When I strolled into the kitchen that morning, an olive-green pea stain on the ceiling above the refrigerator caught my eye. Do you remember our canned pea fights that we'd have on the first day of every summer break?" Through her tears, Ivy managed to smile.

"Of course. Those were the best."

On the first day of our summer break, after our parents left for work and Ivy and I were alone to complete a list of chores and read our assigned library books, Ivy and I would simultaneously open a can of peas and, at the count of three, chuck slimy peas at each other. I don't remember how or why we started this tradition, but we looked forward to our small rebellious act every summer. After the war was over and our sides hurt from giggling nonstop, we would scrub the walls of the kitchen from top to bottom. We cleaned the cupboards and the sides of the refrigerator to remove any traces of green stains. As long as we removed all traces of our fun, the pea battle remained our little secret.

"The morning after our fight, I found Isabella in the kitchen with her hands wrapped around her coffee mug. She stared into the dark brown liquid. Her black eyeliner rested under the bottom eyelid, and her lips were stained with red lipstick. She looked rough, exhausted, and broken. She aged so much in the months after Father's death. Above her thin brown eyebrows, a worried crease formed on her forehead, and gray, wiry hair sprouted up through her dark hair. Maybe Isabella's grief was more external. She bottled up all her feelings so they cracked out in other ways.

"I decided not to ask her about your whereabouts. Instead, I offered to make her breakfast. She didn't notice that I entered the room. She forced a smile onto her wrinkled, tired face and looked up at me. Red veins cracked in the pupils of her eyes."

Ivy explained that she sat down in the chair next to our mother at the table, which had always been designated as Father's chair, hoping to channel some of his wisdom. Ivy told her that she understood why she was sad—that we all missed Father.

"Her glossy eyes met mine, and I recognized a surprised, intrigued expression. I told her that I still cried every time I heard a Johnny Cash song on the radio."

"We'll get through this together. I'm sad too, Momma."

"Ivy, you're amazing. You know that? Always so jovial and agreeable. When you were a baby, you smiled even when your diaper was full of crap. If all babies were like that, parents would want a hundred." A weak smile formed through her tears as the memories flooded in. Mother's beauty was richest when she smiled. Daddy had claimed that he couldn't resist her grin and the sparkle in her eyes. "Your sister, on the other hand, has caused me more stress and heartache than a schoolroom full of bratty children could."

Mother cleared her throat and earned my attention. "Ivy, she's gone."

"Who? Who's gone?" Because I'd been lost in my daydream, I missed who she was referring to.

She stared at me like I should've known. Since no answer had been given yet and I assumed she needed to talk about the friend she had lost, I stood up to pour myself a cup of coffee. I dropped in two sugar cubes and stirred my cup with a spoon. I turned around to find her glossy eyes searching mine.

*"Do you want me to make some eggs, Momma, while you talk?"
I figured I could listen while she talked. That was when I
noticed a pile of cash sitting next to her on the table. "Why is this
dirty picnic blanket on the table? What's up with the cash? Did
you get a job at Rusty Nail or something?" I joked. Normally, a
big pile of cash made a person happy and relieved, but instead,
I read hurt, anger, and resentment in her eyes. The two things
didn't match. "Mother?"*

*"She left us, Ivy. The little bitch abandoned us. Ran like a thief
in the night." She wiped a single tear from her cheek.*

"What do you mean? Who left us?"

*"Your selfish, good-for-nothing sister abandoned us, and she
stole our damn car." What she was saying didn't make sense.
Why would Jolene leave? "We're struggling financially, Ivy.
We're drowning in debt."*

*"Momma, we'll figure it out." Since nothing made sense, I tried
to console her. What she was claiming about Jolene running
away didn't sound right. I figured it was best to appease her
until I could sort through what was happening.*

"Ivy, with your father gone, we don't have his income. We can't afford this house. We're hardly getting by. Do you have any idea how expensive funerals are?" I didn't. I had no idea. It wasn't something I thought about. I was only fifteen.

"I'll get a job, Momma. I can help with our bills."

She paused for a moment before she responded. "Good idea. I'm glad you mentioned that. Pastor Tony has been incredibly supportive during this difficult time. Paying bills that I couldn't pay. Buying us groceries. I couldn't have done it without his help."

"I'm glad, Momma. Should I offer to clean the church or mow the grass for free?"

"I don't think that will be necessary. He has another idea in mind."

Ivy then explained in morbid detail how our mother convinced her to help. "With an odd, emotionless expression, Isabella explained that Pastor Tony generously offered to help us. He would pay monthly bills, including the mortgage if we attended a couple of parties at his house. Innocently, I agreed. I was fifteen. I imagined that we'd wear fancy dresses, pantyhose, and high heels while sipping champagne from real crystal goblets, and eating bite-size hors d'oeuvres served by waiters in tuxedos. I couldn't have been more wrong. After we polished off three bottles of wine, Isabella explained that the men wouldn't hurt me and that it was no big deal. I didn't understand. *Hurt me? What was no big deal?* Instead of a cocktail dress, I was stripped nude. Instead of sipping bubbly champagne, I was offered copper-colored bourbon to relax me. Instead of tiny appetizers, I was slapped on the ass and told that I needed to lay off meat and potatoes. Instead of attending a party, I attended an orgy."

Chapter 54

Jolene - 1995

I couldn't decide if I was more outraged or disturbed. Furious or sad.

My ears bled with Ivy's revelation. My heart broke into tiny dust particles. My mind couldn't wrap itself around her words. Tears swelled in my eyes. Our mother, Isabella Just, convinced her fifteen-year-old daughter that sleeping with multiple grown men would help them save the roof over their heads. Our mother placed a value on Ivy's innocence and assured her that losing her virginity to pay a debt wasn't too steep of a price to pay. She guilted her daughter into abandoning her morals to save our family home.

If I thought I'd hated our mother before, it was nothing compared to how I felt about her now that I knew what she'd done to Ivy's innocence. What kind of person—let alone a mother—could knowingly force her child into having sex with multiple men? All to save her ass for something she had done in the first place? She was worse than I'd ever imagined.

After a long silence, I struggled to stomach the fact that my sister had been violated by several men in one evening, which led to her wonderful, brilliant child. Would this have happened if I hadn't run away? Would I have been the one to attend the orgy instead of Ivy? Would Ivy have been spared?

Ivy giggled and then quickly covered her mouth with her hand. "Sorry. It's a completely inappropriate time to laugh, but I was thinking that in the last ten years, separately, we've both managed to royally fuck up our lives. Both of us have been through hell and back. In the silence just now, I swear that I heard Daddy's voice in my head. Do you remember that he used to tell us that as long as we were a team, nothing would ever be able to break us?"

I smiled at Ivy mentioning our father. He loved being a father, and we had him wrapped around our little fingers. "Yeah, I remember him saying that, and it was always after we'd gotten away with something–a second dessert or an hour tagged onto our bedtime, or what about that time he caught us laying on the roof to watch that lunar eclipse?"

"Yes. It was right after the Fourth of July. 1982, I think. It was a full-blood moon."

Over breakfast one morning, Father read the article out loud from the Sunday newspaper.

"'On Tuesday, July 6, 1982, a few minutes past midnight, a total eclipse of the moon will take place. The earth's shadow will move in front of the moon, and it will gradually darken. Onlookers who manage to stay up late will first see the moon as a perfect circle, followed by all the moon phases. As the earth's shadow moves across the face of the moon during this eclipse period, its surface gradually darkens.'

"That sounds amazing, right, girls?" Father directed his questions at Ivy and me as we scooped bites of cereal into our mouths. "But what chaps my ass is–"

"Walter, language."

" –how the heck can they determine what time the eclipse will happen when they can't even predict the weather? That tornado in Marion, Illinois, leveled the town. Why didn't someone predict that?" Father crinkled the newsletter as he folded it on his lap.

"Walter, an astronomer predicts moon patterns and solar eclipses, but it's a meteorologist who predicts the weather. Totally different set of scientists." Mother gently explained while she scrambled eggs.

"Well, they all attended the same university. University of BS. Bullshit–"

"Walter!" Mother detested the use of swear words.

"They get paid a crap ton of money to guess shit. Sorry, but I could do that job."

A couple of nights later, after getting tucked into bed, Ivy and I talked about random topics to keep each other awake. Hours later, I tip-toed to the floor vent to listen for our parents' voices in the basement. If they were still awake, I'd hear the TV. If the TV was off, then I'd know that they'd gone to bed. The coast was clear. We snuck out of our beds and crawled out onto the roof through our bedroom window.

The shingles were abrasive on our bare feet, but luckily I'd grabbed a blanket for Ivy and me to lay on. As soon as we were settled on our backs and looking up at the dark, black sky, Ivy commented that it felt like we were the only ones in the world. No cars moved up and down our quiet street, none of the neighborhood dogs were barking, and no human voices could be detected. The only creatures broadcasting their attendance were the crickets and owls. The night was still and peaceful. All our neighbors' houses were dark and quiet.

I remembered watching Ivy reach out to touch the moon because it looked so giant and bright hanging in the sky. She thought it looked like a balloon. I grabbed her hand and squeezed it tight. Everything felt complete with her by my side.

A few minutes later, our father's deep, husky voice broke the silence.

"Your mother is going to throw a fit." But he didn't sound mad. He sounded impressed.

Before we knew it, he managed to wiggle his gigantic body through our bedroom window and crawl out onto the roof to join us. He told us that he had gotten up to wake us but found our beds empty, and then he said, "Stick together, girls, and I'll never have to worry. You're unstoppable together as a team."

Ivy nodded her head with a big smile on her face as the memory enveloped her. "We begged him not to tell Mother because the next day was my birthday, and she'd threatened so many times to cancel my party if we didn't behave."

"Funny that even if *I* misbehaved, *your* birthday party would be canceled."

"Yep, that confirms what Daddy always said about us—we were a package." Tears raced down her face as she tried to unsuccessfully wipe them away. "Jolene, I never stopped loving you. I never blamed you for leaving. I never want to lose you again, so I need to tell you that for the last five years, I've been looking for you." She paused to let the news sink in. Her eyes, which were a constant flow of tears, searched mine before she added, "I knew you were in California. It was Michael's idea to send Howard."

"Howard Bass? My Howard?" The afternoon's conversations caused my head to spin. I was starting to question everything that I knew.

Chapter 55

Jolene - 1995

My trip to South Dakota, while wonderful and necessary to rebuild our relationship, revealed major hurdles. By sharing our darkest secrets, we were building bridges, trusting each other, and helping each other heal, but stretching to leap over that six-foot hurdle when your legs are only two to three feet long was proving to be a major stretch.

During my struggles with sobriety, I imagined that Ivy was safe, healthy, and happy back in Iowa. My imagination created the picture of a perfect life for her. Free of drama. Free of family squabbles between me and Mother. Ivy wouldn't need to play the referee anymore because I'd removed myself from that equation. I imagined an easy, simple life for her. No more overprotective, grumpy older sister bossing her around. She'd grow up to be a happy, healthy young adult.

I figured she and Mother fell into a new relaxed routine, bonding over movies and popcorn. Their relationship would thrive as a family of two. No one would buck Mother's authority and cause shouting matches. Maybe Ivy would try out to be a high school cheerleader. Her bubbly personality, big, wide smile, and natural rhythm would benefit her. This was the way I pictured her. She'd miss me at times, but I told myself that my departure was best for everyone. Mother and I'd never get along, and Ivy would always feel the pressure to smooth over the tension. I convinced myself that Ivy would be better off without me.

Never in my mind did I picture Ivy searching for me, let alone finding me and hiring someone to watch over me. I didn't understand.

"Yes, let me explain. It wasn't like he was working for us. Howard is a retired private detective and a retired police officer. He went searching for you at our request, but on his own accord, he decided to move to California. He loved it. The sun. The sand. And driving with his top down." A smile grew on her face as she talked about Howard. "He even made shirts that said, 'I prefer to be topless.' Howard is a character."

Remembering Howard wearing that shirt into the restaurant and getting a lot of strange looks made a smile form on my lips as well. "I've seen him wearing that shirt. He told me that he sold that phrase to Jeep after he drew up a design to go with it and made a shit ton of money." As the words left my mouth, I wondered if that story was even true.

"Yeah, that man oozes charisma. Howard could sell oceanfront property to an Arizona resident."

"But I don't understand." My brain shuffled my memories around to make sense of what Ivy was saying. "Why didn't you come to California yourself after you found me?"

"Believe me, it wasn't easy. There were several times that I told Howard I was coming down there myself. Shake some sense into you. I remember the time he called me and told me that he found you puking into a garbage can on the beach. He said he hadn't recognized you at first. He mistook you for a homeless person. You were a complete mess—by far the worst he'd ever seen you. He told us that he couldn't just watch you anymore. He took you home." She shook her head. "Broke my heart, Jo. I wanted to jump on the next plane and hold you, but Howard convinced me that while he helped you get sober, I needed to be patient because our reconciliation had to be *your* move. Plus, we were nervous about telling you what was going on because we didn't know what would push you over the edge. We were waiting for the perfect time. Unfortunately, we waited too long because Howard woke up one morning and you were gone."

I felt the need to explain, but I definitely couldn't defend my actions because they were selfish and self-destructive. "Not one of my proudest moments. Howard is amazing. He was always there for me. Picking up the pieces and encouraging me to be better. On the night that I left, I woke up in a complete sweat. Drenched from head to toe in sweat. I'd had a nightmare about being trapped in a cage. The urge to flee and run from my problems convinced me to leave. Everything that I worked so hard for–that Howard pushed me to achieve–was crushed by my fear of failing again. The voices in my head shouted that I didn't deserve to be happy, that I didn't deserve a friend like Howard who would do anything to help me, and that I didn't deserve to live. So, I crawled out of Howard's guest room window and ran right back to my friends, who provided me with more than enough drugs to numb my regret.

"Unfortunately, my friends–I use that word very loosely–informed me that we were going on a road trip. I didn't have the sense to say no. I hopped in the back seat of the car, happy to tag along for free lines of cocaine. And I think you know how that story ends." It hurt to say the words out loud, but maybe Ivy needed to hear them to realize how bad my past was.

Suddenly, a huge dollar sign flashed in my mind. "Ivy, I don't have any money to pay you back for all the months I lived with Howard, but I promise I will pay you back." While I lived with Howard, I believed that I was helping him out as much as he was helping me. Howard provided a roof over my head, and I provided him company. Now, I saw what a burden I was.

"Don't worry about that, Jo. Staying with family is free."

"But Howard isn't my family."

"He is now. He's Michael's dad, Cooper's grandfather." It dawned on me that I never asked what Ivy's married name was.

***

That afternoon, when Michael arrived home from work, Ivy and I were settled in the same spots on the couch that he had found us on every day since I came. This time we hadn't showered or prepped for dinner. Our eyes were bloodshot and puffy. After he dropped his travel coffee mug into the sink, I watched his thick caterpillar eyebrows arch when he looked at Ivy. Ivy smiled at me and closed her eyes as she nodded.

Michael knew the topic of today's conversations, and I realized that Cooper's slumber party at a school friend's house might have been planned on purpose. They figured that it was going to be an emotional discussion and might warrant a few extra hours. We'd covered a lot of ground in the last eight hours, with our hike around Lake Mitchell and our tongues. I was emotionally and physically exhausted.

As I watched Michael cross the room toward Ivy, I recognized the physical similarities between Michael and Howard. When Michael referred to himself in the third person, I instantly remembered loving that silly habit of Howard's. Now that I knew they were related, I realized that they both possessed bushy eyebrows and dark brown eyes that became little slits when they smiled. If my memory served me correctly, Howard also had a dimple on his left cheek.

Before he sat down, Michael planted a kiss on the top of Ivy's head. Once he slid in next to my sister, Ivy cuddled into the crook of his side as he draped his arm around her. She tilted her head at him and batted her eyelashes. In the silence, I recognized the love that I'd wished for Ivy.

"Jolene, let's stretch our legs. Fresh air and a little exercise will do us both some good." Ivy rose from the couch and walked a few steps toward me to offer her hand to pull me up.

"I took my bra off hours ago."

Michael cleared his throat. My lack of a filter caused him to blush.

"Sorry to break it to you, sister, but I totally can't tell. You're still as flat as a board."

"Ouch." I playfully batted her hand away. "Just because I'm a smidge older doesn't mean that I can't get off the couch by myself." But to my dismay, I struggled to stand. After sitting curled up on their fluffy couch, I did need assistance. I reached for Ivy's hand. Accepting help didn't make me weak. It made me human.

"Whatever you two do, please don't get called in for indecent exposure. I'm on call tonight, but I planned on whipping up some tasty burgers for my two favorite girls." He grinned.

Ivy glanced adoringly at her husband, who was still dressed in his uniform. Ivy told me that early in their relationship, she asked Michael if he'd leave his uniform on for at least thirty minutes after his shift.

Michael considered her request for a second before innocently asking, "Why?"

"Honey, men in uniform are sexy, and Michael, it's even more attractive that you don't know you're *smoking* hot."

"Really?" Ivy explained that Michael looked down at his chest in bewilderment. He had no idea. "This shirt is too tight with my vest under it, and the waist of my pants is one size too small, so I feel the need to adjust all the time."

"Exactly." Ivy hummed and licked her lips. "Keep talking."

"Okay." Michael was getting the idea. "What about these thick-soled, old man shoes?" He lifted a foot for inspection.

"Nope, not attractive, but usually I'm not checking out your feet."

When they stood in front of the Justice of the Peace on their wedding day, she was delighted when Michael added a personal vow. "I, Michael Bass, take you, Ivy Lynn Just, to be my wife, to have and to hold from this day forward, for better, for worse, for richer, for poorer, in my uniform and out, in sickness and in health, to love and to cherish, until parted by death."

They had nicknamed the half hour after he arrived home as *in-cop-nito*. Ivy explained, "Like incognito, but with cop instead of cog."

I laughed at her funny play on words, "Yes, Ivy, I get it."

As I watched the two of them flirt moments ago, my heart swelled. Even though imagining what usually occurs to get Michael out of his police uniform made me want to hurl, I couldn't help myself from acknowledging it.

"Listen, I need thirty—exactly thirty minutes to digest our conversation, so I think I'll take a walk alone during in-cop-nito time."

Michael's cheeks turned three shades of deep red while Ivy bellowed out a loud laugh.

"You told her that?" Michael looked to Ivy for an answer.

Unable to respond, Ivy bent over her waist in fits of laughter.

"So, this is what sisters are like. No secrets. Wow. This ought to be interesting." He wasn't mad about Ivy sharing a secret. He was amused. As he rose from the couch and headed toward the kitchen, he shook his head. "Over dinner, let's tell Jolene about the time you had too much to drink and called 9-1-1 to tell me that you loved me for the first time."

When she was able to collect herself, Ivy acted appalled. "True story, but in my defense, I couldn't remember your home phone number, so I called you at work. Some people would say that was sweet of me."

"That is what the whole police force thought, Ivy. Nice work."

While I was lacing up my tennis shoes, Ivy's voice cracked. "Jo?"

I looked up and smiled at her. A worry wrinkle creased across her forehead.

"I'll come back, Ivy. I promise. I'm not leaving you again."

Chapter 56

Jolene – 1995

Since the cat was out of the bag, and with my permission, Michael and Ivy invited Howard over for breakfast the following morning.

When the doorbell announced a visitor, Ivy rushed to open it. Her appreciation and love for her father-in-law gushed out of her. Her excitement to reunite her family was abundantly clear. This was the day Ivy had been dreaming about since they found me years ago in California; however, she hadn't been expecting it to take so long.

Standing on the front step dressed in a familiar pink Hawaiian shirt with palm trees and coconuts was Howard, the same Howard I remembered from Huntington Beach. It had been over six months since I last saw him, and instantly my heart swelled with love. When Ivy pulled him in for a hug, he leaned toward her, even though his arms were filled with donuts and orange juice. As soon as Ivy released him, our gazes locked. He was worried that I wouldn't be happy about our reunion. He was worried that I was angry with him for not telling me the truth. He knew I had a difficult time trusting people.

I rushed forward to wrap my arms around him. Before I reached him, he set down his bags so that he could hug me back. In all those years that I knew him as my loyal customer and protector, I had never hugged him. I used my words to thank him, but there was never any physical contact. I think he had been worried that I would interpret his actions wrong, and I feared that all of my so-called friends would be right and that he had other motives for helping me.

"So good to see you, old friend." I managed to utter.

Always quick with a witty comment, Howard softly responded, "Who are you calling old?"

"Cops really do like donuts, huh?" I winked at him.

Even though they lied to me, I really couldn't be mad otherwise our reunion wouldn't have been as effective. If the old me knew what their intention was, I would've run the other way. I'd built those walls up to protect myself from further pain, and I knew without a doubt we would not be embracing each other had I known what they were doing behind my back. This was the first time I understood the necessity of a lie. Ivy was looking out for me. A group of wonderful people cared about me even when I didn't care about myself. Their gentle love and unwavering support reminded me of bumper railings for beginner bowlers. The bumper railings created a clear path to victory. Strike.

***

After a wonderful morning of sharing stories, we said our goodbyes to Howard. After making the road trip to South Dakota, he decided to make a little vacation out of it. He was heading to the Black Hills to camp, fish, and relax.

After cleaning up the kitchen, Ivy and I settled on the back patio with our faces pointed up toward the sky, soaking up the rays. The weather forecasted an unseasonably cool day for summer in South Dakota, which simply meant that the humidity would be down and outdoor activities would be very pleasant. Ivy bent over and rolled her capri pants up to her knees.

"I saw her once. The wife," Ivy stated without inflection. Her statement was out of the blue, but I knew who she was talking about.

"Yeah, we probably saw her at a church function. That's where I figured I recognized her from."

"No. It was after that." Ivy explained that Michael came home from work one day and asked her if she'd ever attended Our Savior's Church when she lived in Normal. While she scrubbed potatoes for supper, she confirmed that, as a child, our family had been members of that church.

Michael asked, "Do you remember a pastor with the last name Shade?"

The simple mention of his name created a sinking feeling in my gut. The potato that I was washing tumbled out of my hands and onto the floor. Michael scurried to retrieve it. He didn't notice that my back had straightened, that my gaze contained a blank stare, or that my pulse had quickened. He set the potato next to the sink and proceeded to wash his hands and the potato. He explained why he'd asked that question.

"My buddy Ford from Canby called today to ask if you lived in Normal when this Pastor Shade presided over Our Savior's." He continued his story as he dried his hands on a towel. "Then Ford proceeded to tell me that this pastor had been arrested

in Canby for soliciting a prostitute. Not a big deal. Honestly, it happens all the time, but that was just the beginning of the stuff that they are charging this guy with. It turns out he ran a brothel out the back of his house in Normal. What the hell, right?"

Michael sometimes needed to vent about work. It was a stressful job, so it was normal that he sometimes rambled on for thirty minutes while I remained silent.

As he grabbed a beer from the refrigerator and cracked it open, he continued, "Ford said the creep made his wife participate in all the..." He searched for a more appropriate word that Ford must have used. "...activities. Supposedly, the guy is on trial right now in Canby, and it's been a circus. The courtroom is packed to the gills with reporters, nosy residents, and tons of his congregation members, past and present." He paused to take a long pull from his beer. I hadn't moved an inch from my spot at the kitchen sink. "I wonder if your parents knew him. They would've been around the same age."

Ivy said that the only reason Michael stopped talking was because she threw up in the sink. "Jo, that poor woman was brainwashed by that man. Can you imagine what her life must've been like living with that monster every day? I can't. It must've been hell."

"You cannot give that woman a free pass, Ivy. She was married to the man for a long time, so that means she had a million chances to run, to turn him in, or to do the right thing."

"I don't know, Jo. I hate to judge her or place blame on her because she was trapped in an abusive situation."

"How do you know she was trapped? Maybe the whole brothel was her idea, and she convinced Tony to do it. Or maybe she liked it?"

Ivy confessed that she attended part of Pastor Tony's trial, where Lisa testified against him. When Lisa appeared, it was obvious that she'd attempted to cover up the dark circles under her eyes with foundation and dusted blush on her cheeks to give color to her pale, defined cheekbones. A thin layer of mascara brushed her eyelashes, but they clumped together from tears that were shed before she entered the room. Covering her skeleton-like frame were a navy blazer and pencil skirt, both of which hung on her. Her high heels clicked on the hard floor, drawing every eye in the courtroom.

As Ivy explained it, Lisa Shade didn't bask in the attention. Her shoulders slumped as soon as she realized that conversations paused with her entrance into the room.

"Jo, I need to tell you something."

"Whenever you start a conversation with that statement, it can't be good. Ivy, I hate to admit it, but I think I've reached my limit on revelations and big family secrets. Nothing that will make me throw up, please." I teased her. I kept my face pointed up toward the sun, letting its rays penetrate my skin.

"I asked Howard to find Lisa."

"What? Why?"

"If what you say is true about the little girl with her, Cooper might have a sibling."

"Again, why? I don't see the point of adding more drama and pain to our lives." I couldn't look at her. I didn't agree, but I didn't want to start a fight, so I tried to keep my tone even. "Not every reunion is going to be as pleasant as ours, Ivy. Lisa may not want to be found. She left the halfway house and never came back, and I could be mistaken about the kid looking like Cooper. I told you that. I think this is a bad idea and will just lead down a road of more bad memories. You should look ahead, Ivy. Be grateful for what you do have. Be thankful for your family. Your husband is amazing. Cooper is a gem. And we already know I adore Howard. I don't see how this can be beneficial to anyone. What if Cooper asks questions?"

"I've thought about all that, too. Maybe I was wrong for never telling Cooper who his father is. I do know that right now, not telling him is best, but maybe someday he will understand. I don't know what will be best in five or ten years. I'm willing to figure that out as it happens."

After everything my little sister had been through, her drive to do what was best for others still amazed me. Ivy was willing to sacrifice her perfect, stable life to bring people together. I wondered if she ever considered what it would've been like if I'd never contacted her. Had she ever wondered if I even opened her letters? So, I decided to ask.

"Ivy, do you ever consider the worst might happen? Like I could've never reached out to you?"

"Nope. It's called faith, Jo. I have faith in God, and I have faith that things will always work out. I may not always agree with the results, but I have faith in God that it's part of His plan, not mine."

"You might call it faith, but some people call it being naive." I didn't know why I had to bring her down, to point out the obvious. I wish I could've bottled some of her optimism, or, as she called it, faith. However, I'd always been the realist and Ivy the dreamer.

"I understand that that is what it looks like to people with little faith."

"You're right. I have little faith. I've lived through hell and back, and somewhere along the way, my faith got stomped on. But, Ivy, you need to see it from my point of view. No good will come from this reunion. Lisa doesn't want to be found. She ran. She was on probation. If she is found, she might have to go back to jail for not obeying her parole guidelines." Anger and stress rushed from my gut and spilled out of my mouth. Our sister reunion had been going great. I moved past the fact that she and Howard had lied to me for years. Their intentions were honorable. I embraced Howard and our new relationship with open arms. *How much more am I supposed to take? When is enough enough?*

"I know you think you've reached your limit, Jo, and are wondering how much more you can take, but you have a support system now. You aren't going to battle this alone."

"I'm not interested in a battle, Ivy. That's what you don't understand. Why can't you leave well enough alone? You're stirring up the past and causing new drama. Leave her be, and let us all get on with our lives."

The new sober me wanted to reach a resolution with Ivy and this discussion, but the old me felt stressed and craved a drink or a pill. Instead, I decided a nap would be the best solution. I excused myself and retreated to my guest room.

Chapter 57

Lisa - 1996

For a year, I kept Camille safe and away from the drama that surrounded her heritage. At six years old, she wasn't able to comprehend what had happened. It was traumatic and confusing. When we found a place to call home in the Black Hills, I enrolled her in school, and we started functioning as a family of two. At first, she asked questions about her mom, but eventually, we didn't talk about her. It was too painful, and honestly, I wanted Camille to forget. As the memories from her first five years of life slowly faded, they were replaced by new ones of playdates with friends from school, soccer games, and piano lessons. Camille's curiosity about everything gave her a variety of pastimes. Her zest for life filled my heart with joy. When she was happy, I was happy. The stronger her foundation, the easier time she would have when she found out who her father was. I realized that was inevitable, but I was willing to push it off for as long as possible. And there was no way I'd be the one to bring that heartache to life.

While I tried to shield her from the drama of her creation, genetics wouldn't allow me to forget. Camille inherited Tony's crispy jawline and almond-shaped eyes. Even some of Camille's mannerisms reminded me of Tony—the way she'd shrug her shoulders when she didn't know an answer, the way she raised her eyebrows when she didn't agree with my response, or the way she fell asleep with one arm draped over her head.

These simple behaviors caused my heart to skip a beat. I reminded myself that just because they had things in common, it did not mean that Camille would turn into a monster like her biological father. That was my greatest fear.

Always the charmer, Tony could talk his way into and out of everything. Camille had that same effect on others, especially me. I chalked up my impairment to loving her unconditionally like every mother loves her daughter. However, I witnessed her ability several times with a perfect stranger on the street. A small compliment or a simple hello would blossom into a conversation with Camille being doted over and cherished.

After Camille had been living with me as my daughter for a year and a half, a large envelope arrived in the mail addressed to me. The return address label read Pearson Law Office. With trembling hands, I tore open the sealed envelope and discovered that Camille's biological mother, Lucy, had taken her own life. In her suicide note, she explained that I should receive sole custody of her only daughter, Camille. Also enclosed was the official adoption paperwork. All that was left to do was sign my signature, and Camille would legally be my daughter.

Never one to deny a gift horse, I grabbed the nearest pen and signed the document before even reading the fine print. Wanting to make it official as soon as possible, I loaded Camille into the car and headed to the local post office so I could return the official document in the mail. The sooner the lawyer received it, the sooner I'd be Camille's legal guardian.

Part of me ached learning the news that after all she'd been through Lucy took her own life, but the other part of me felt guilty that I was relieved. I wouldn't be looking over my shoulder, wondering if she was coming back for Camille. I wouldn't worry that she'd change her mind. That was over. Camille would be mine.

"Mommy, slow down. You're makin' my crackers spill."

"Sorry, pumpkin. Mommy has a bit of lead foot this afternoon."

"Lead foot? Is that like Mr. Harvey, who walks funny because he lost his real foot to the dabeets?"

I smiled at six-year-old Camille, trying to understand my terminology. "Diabetes. And no, it just means I was pushing the gas pedal because I wanted to arrive at our destination sooner."

"You must be pushin' too hard because you are happy. What are we celebratin', Mommy?"

"What do you mean, Camille?"

"We only have ice cream when we are celebratin'. Is it my birthday?"

She was right. A trip to our local ice cream parlor had become our destination when something positive happened—Camille was assigned the kindergarten line leader or I received a five-dollar credit on our phone bill.

While I was married to Tony, I was not allowed to eat sweets. I could bake but never indulge. Tony claimed that sugar was the Devil's candy. It still amazed me that I believed every word that came out of my ex-husband's mouth. Maybe believed was too strong of a word. I didn't resist his claims. As an adult who'd been denied sugar for ten years, I felt like a child who would do anything for sweets. Camille and I always celebrated with ice cream.

"Is Howard comin' too? I bet he'd like a turtle sundae with a big, bright-red cherry on top."

I met Howard two months earlier at a neighborhood block party. Because we were the only single ones in attendance, we gravitated toward each other and ended up talking about a book that we'd both read recently. We both loved to read, so we decided to meet the following week at the local library to inquire if they had a book club. When we discovered that they didn't, the librarian suggested that we start one and meet at the library every few weeks. Howard loved the idea, and his enthusiasm was something lacking in my life. In preparing for the first meeting, Howard and I met several times to create a list of books to discuss, our group goals, and how to reach other readers. We spent a lot of time together, and I looked forward to seeing him.

Talking with Howard was easy and refreshing, and even though I vowed never to fall in love again for fear of pain and heartache, I found my heart quickening whenever we shared a long stare or his arm brushed mine. I didn't plan on acting on any of those feelings. I figured they would disappear eventually. It had been a long time since I'd had any romantic feelings for a man, so I convinced myself it wasn't real. My heart and soul would always crave attention since, for years, I'd been given the wrong kind.

During our first meeting, twenty residents from our small community attended. We were surprised and very pleased. For our first book club discussion, we'd chosen to discuss Mitch Albom's *Tuesdays with Morrie*. Since the turnaround time for signing up and holding our first meeting wasn't very long, we chose a short but meaningful book.

During the group discussion, our eyes met across the room. In that one glance, I knew the attraction was mutual. Terrified doesn't describe how my heart felt. The difference this time was that my brain agreed with my heart. Howard was a good man. However, any man, good or bad, would run and never look back if they knew my story. How I worked in a brothel for years, standing loyally beside my messed-up husband. No good would come from this.

As the group broke up and chose a date for our next meeting, Howard approached me. But his flirtatious grin had been replaced by a somber expression. "Lisa, could you grab a cup of coffee?"

"Tonight?" He nodded. I looked down at my wristwatch. "Camille's babysitter said she'd be good until ten. So, sure. I have a little less than one hour."

As we ordered our decaf coffee, Howard's expression remained serious. I was concerned. We'd become friends in the last few weeks, and I was afraid that he had some grave news to tell me. Or maybe he was afraid of our growing attraction for one another, too.

"Howard, is everything alright?" I reached across the table and gently put my hand on one of his.

Before he responded, he looked down at my simple gesture. "I hope so. I need to tell you something. But you need to be patient and let me explain." He took a deep breath and explained how he knew who I was before we'd officially met at the potluck. "I'd been watching you."

"You'd been what?" Shivers ran up and down my spine.

"It's not as bad as it sounds." He chuckled a bit, trying to ease my concerns. "Let me explain. My daughter-in-law asked me to find you. She is from Normal."

My stomach sank. Bile rose in my throat. I felt sick. It had been over a year since I ran away from my past. I'd gotten comfortable in that time and let my guard down. I let someone 'in' only to discover that he knew everything about me and my poisoned past.

"But when I found you, I don't know how to explain it, but you were more than a quest." Finally, he looked me in the eye, and his eyes were wet. "You're an amazing person and a wonderful mother. What I'm saying is..." Howard stumbled for the right words, "I like you. I wanted you to know the truth. I feel our friendship growing, and before it gets any more..."

"Who sent you?"

"My daughter-in-law is Ivy. Ivy Just."

Walter Just. This wasn't good.

***

Because the heaviness of our conversation would not fit into one hour, my heart decided to invite Howard over to my house to continue our discussion. Even though my head screamed, *Run, run again, and never look back.*

The babysitter had already put Camille to bed before we got home. Camille met Howard during a few of our planning sessions, and they instantly hit it off. She'd be disappointed to know that she missed out on spending time with Howard.

I fixed us a couple of lemonades while Howard waited on the back patio for me. Thankfully, Howard was a gentleman and knew it would not be appropriate for me to invite him into our house.

I had no idea where this conversation was going to go, but dread seized my heart, because no matter where it led, it wasn't going to be good. And we'd never be able to go back and have things the way they were. No innocent friendship. Howard had dropped a fifty-pound weight on the chest of our relationship, and I felt exposed.

When I opened the screen door with my hip, Howard rose from the porch chair to help me carry in the serving tray. He set it down on the little table between the two chairs. After he returned to his seat and took one big, long gulp, he cleared his throat.

"Lisa, in my former life, I was a police officer and then a private investigator. Before I met you, I did some digging." His eyes reflected his concern. "I discovered facts about your life in Normal. You served time as part of your plea deal by testifying and supplying information against your ex-husband. I read the charges against Tony. I only know the facts, and hopefully, over time, you'll trust me enough to tell me your side of the story. " He paused to allow me to respond. Since I wasn't ready to speak, I focused on the ice in my glass.

Howard wanted to remain friends even though he knew where I'd come from. He learned the facts from the trial and arrest records, but thankfully, he also knew that there was more to the story. Howard was too good for me. I wasn't sure I deserved that wonderful of a friend. I didn't know what to say.

"My daughter-in-law did not ask me to find you for malicious reasons. I'm a grandfather now. Cooper is his name." The name of his grandson caused his voice to crack and pride filled his chest. "He's a great kid. I never knew being a grandparent would be so wonderful." He laughed at a memory. "That kid thinks Howard hung the moon."

I looked over at him, and tears had swelled in his eyes.

From his back pocket, he pulled out his wallet. "Let me show you a picture." He dug into a side pocket and pulled out a wrinkled school picture. As he smiled down at it, he handed it to me. "This is Cooper."

But it wasn't Cooper. The young boy looked like a male, older version of Camille.

Chapter 58

Lisa - 1996

Howard explained that Jolene, who recognized me during my short stay at the Kansas halfway house, saw me with Camille and recognized a resemblance between her nephew, Cooper, and Camille. Putting two and two together, Ivy figured that there might be more to the story, and of course, they didn't know the half of it.

After our conversation about how he found me, I explained to Howard that I needed time to digest everything. Not only did I need to comprehend the news that he'd been sent by Ivy, but I also needed time to register that our relationship could be more than friendship. I felt the same electricity when we were together, but I hadn't planned on acting on it.

Part of me wanted to run. Leave Miner City and never look back. This time I would change our names. My secret was exposed, and I wanted to protect the life I'd built with Camille. But the other part of me begged me to stay and see where this new fork in the road led.

He agreed that there was no rush. He didn't feel the need to tell Ivy right away that he'd found me. For the next few weeks, we spent time together as friends, even though there was electricity when we were near each other. We worked on our book club assignments, explored hiking trails with Camille, and enjoyed many meals together. Howard never pressured me into giving more and never crossed the friendship line. We simply enjoyed each other's company, like normal friends do.

One evening, after we cleaned up the dinner dishes, we retreated to the back patio to watch Camille play in the backyard. As I pulled the corded phone from the kitchen onto the patio, I asked Howard, "Can I have Michael and Ivy's phone number? I'd like to call her."

My question surprised Howard. "I do. Are you sure?"

"Yes. I've been thinking about it ever since you told me about what brought you to Miner City. I ran from my past because I wasn't proud of who I was and how I handled everything that happened in Normal, but I like to think that I'm a better person now."

"You are."

"Howard, I wasn't fishing for a compliment." I smiled at him. "I think this is what God wants me to do. For a long time, I didn't believe in happy endings. I figured that I didn't deserve love and happiness, but Camille has changed me. When she first arrived on my doorstep, I thought it was another punishment from God. How was I going to care for a little kid when I had so much to learn from my mistakes? I didn't have a home. Heck, I couldn't even let her in the front door of the halfway house. I was fresh out of jail. I had nothing to offer her." I looked out to where Camille was chasing a leaf that was blowing in the breeze. "She isn't a punishment. Camille was a blessing. I'm not sure I'd even be alive if it wasn't for her. I didn't have much to live for when I got out of jail."

I hadn't planned on disclosing my suicidal thoughts, but if I learned anything from this ordeal, it was that honesty brought healing. Through my prayers, God had seen a path that I couldn't. As Camille's mother, I could make my life worthwhile. I believed that Howard's finding me was also part of the plan.

Howard picked up the receiver and dialed the long-distance phone number. As soon as he heard the phone ringing, he handed the receiver to me and mouthed, "You can do this, Lisa. I'm proud of you."

Even though every nerve in my body stood at attention, Ivy calmed them as soon as she greeted me and responded, "Oh, Lisa, I'm so glad you called."

I wasn't sure if I expected a tongue-lashing or a jumble of swear words, but hearing that she was pleased to hear from me caused my anxiety to lessen.

After the first call, Howard and I had weekly phone conversations with Ivy and Jolene, but it was hard to discuss such a heavy, dark topic over the phone. Howard suggested that we make a road trip to visit them in Mitchell to build trust face-to-face.

"Ivy won't be the one you need to win over. My son married an angel. She's been through hell and back, like you, and came out a better person. It's Jo who carries a chip on her shoulder. She blames herself for everything bad that happened after their father died. She moved away not long after. She's a great gal, but she doesn't trust easily."

Howard had constructed independent relationships with both women, and it warmed my heart that he cared for each of them so much. The girls lost their father when they were young, and Howard supported them like a parent.

By the time we headed east across South Dakota, Howard and I had kissed... a lot. We were taking our relationship slow, and Camille didn't notice the difference. I appreciated that Howard understood that forming a relationship with me and Camille would be messy, and now the fact that my past intertwined with his daughter-in-law created even more pressure. Every kiss, every promise, and every step forward would affect not just us but three other females.

During our road trip as my gaze looked out onto the horizon, peace filled my soul. Yes, the conversations with Ivy and Jolene would be ugly and messy, but it was worth the heartache. I felt that in my heart. As I inhaled a deep breath, an invisible, faith-filled embrace from God warmed my body. My prayers hadn't gone unanswered; God had a plan.

"Howard, can I ask you a favor?"

He glanced in the rearview mirror to check on Camille. Her head rested on the car window as her mouth hung open. The rhythm of the interstate had lulled her to sleep.

"Howard likes favors." His eyebrows moved up and down.

"Not that kind of favor, silly." I shook my head. Even though he was teasing, physical intimacy was going to take an enormous amount of patience if he wanted to continue our relationship. "Since you're good at finding people, I wondered if you could do some digging on Camille's biological mom, Lucy. Camille has two aunts out there, maybe some cousins. Someday she might want to find them."

Howard's expression returned serious as he concentrated on the road. "Sure. I could do that. When we get home, I'll have you make a list of everything you know about her, and then I'll do my magic."

"Thanks, Howard."

"I know this is hard on you, Lisa, but you're doing an amazing job. I'm proud of you. It's hard to make decisions when you know the road isn't smooth."

***

Right after I pushed the doorbell to Ivy's home, Howard grabbed my hand. Our eyes met, and he nodded his head. Camille stood next to me, unwrapping a piece of gum. Thank goodness she hadn't asked many questions and was satisfied with the explanation that we were going to visit Howard's family.

"I don't think now is the time," I whispered.

"Lisa, no more secrets. This is family." He squeezed my hand as a younger version of himself pulled the door open.

Howard told stories of Michael playing defense on his high school and college football teams because it was an instinct for him to protect others. When Michael announced that he was going into law enforcement, Howard wasn't surprised. The kid was a chip off the old block. In Howard's pictures, Michael appeared to be a happy-go-lucky young linebacker with a grin that took up half his face.

Standing in the doorway, Howard's pride and joy grinned from ear to ear. In a matter of five seconds, he sized all three of us up and noticed our hand-holding. Michael's grin stretched even farther across his face.

"You ole horndog." With that comment, he pulled his father into an embrace, jerking me forward as well since Howard did not let go of my hand.

***

During the road trip across the plains of South Dakota, I decided that I was going to tell Ivy and Jolene that I suspected that Tony had something to do with their father's death. It wouldn't go over well, and I was worried about how it would affect our budding relationship, but I couldn't hold onto the secret anymore. To give us some much-needed privacy, Howard and Michael took Cooper and Camille to a nearby park to play frisbee.

I realized that had been a fabulous idea as soon as I heard Jolene's reaction to my news.

"Shit. You have to be fucking kidding me, right now. Your husband murdered our father?" Jolene jumped up from the couch.

"Ex-husband, and I didn't say murder. I said he had something to do with it. He knew about it before it was made public." Even though it sounded like it, I wasn't making excuses. I was stating facts. I had no proof.

"Why the hell would you keep that information to yourself all these years?" She yelled as she paced the living room.

"Jo, calm down," Ivy hushed.

"I'm not about to calm down."

"I have no proof. I overheard a phone conversation. I told my lawyer, but without any physical evidence linking him to the accident, it was hearsay. Plus, my lawyer said that Tony had enough sex offenses against him to lock him away for a long time."

"Oh! Well, then I guess it's okay that he murdered someone. One hundred rapes equals one murder. Good to know."

With those final words, Jolene stomped out of the living room and headed to her guest bedroom. The door slammed closed. I expected that type of reaction. It was normal, but it was Ivy's response that shocked me.

Ivy cleared her throat. "I'm so sorry, Lisa. My sister was born with a broken filter, and I do see it as a blessing. I always know exactly how she feels; therefore, I never wonder where I stand. Nothing will bring back my dad. Knowing why it happened or who played a role in his death doesn't change the fact that he is gone. Does it suck? Yeah, of course it does. It isn't fair, but knowing the details of his death will not change it. You amaze me, Lisa. It breaks my heart to think about how you suffered all those years. You're a true survivor. I'm very impressed by you."

Ivy's simple acceptance and instant forgiveness awed me. I didn't know what to say.

Chapter 59

Dear Members of the Parole Board,

As the parole board, you can't simply administer a true or false test to an inmate to decide his fate. Your job is much more difficult. Trying to measure regret and rehabilitation can't be accomplished through schoolroom processes. I don't envy you and your decision, but I do have some information that I'd like you to consider.

For over ten years of my life, I was manipulated and abused by inmate number JR5157201683, Anthony Stanley Shade, who is currently up for early release. He was my husband and a sworn man of God. I assumed those titles would include being my protector and best friend. All victims of abuse have complex feelings regarding their abusers. For years, I believed with my whole heart that my husband Tony had my best interests in mind. When I questioned his authority, my defiance only led to more punishment. Obedience became my survival strategy.

Unfortunately, the damage that Tony inflicted on so many lives can't be measured with a mathematical formula. In my experience, two plus two did not equal four. I can tell you for a fact that Tony owned and managed a brothel in Normal, Iowa. Over one hundred influential men were members of this underground club, and over one hundred women were sexually assaulted by this group.

I attached a list of men who were paid members of Tony's Room. As you can see, some of these men were government officials or successful businessmen with major influence. As the matriarch, I tracked the room's attendance. The main purpose of the list was insurance. Tony used the ledger to bribe judges, reduce fees, persuade local laws, and simply exert his power.

Biblical forgiveness requires repentance, which means turning away from our old life of sin and leading a faithful life serving Jesus Christ. Daily, I pray that Tony will feel remorse for the pain he inflicted on hundreds of women and will seek forgiveness for his sins. However, I don't believe he has reached that point, and perhaps he never will. He believes that what he did was necessary to establish his dominance in our community. I would urge you to cross-check his visitors with the names of the men I supplied. Tony has no friends who are concerned with his well-being. He views relationships as a tool to advance his *ambition. They visit to receive assurances that their anonymity remains solid and leave with assigned tasks to help build a new and improved brothel.*

I want to forgive my ex-husband and believe the best in him, but I also fear the solitude of living behind bars has only fueled the monster within him. From my experience, Tony is like a caged animal who once unleashed will cause great havoc. I don't believe my ex-husband has changed, and his release would be detrimental to society.

Sincerely, Lisa Darling Shade

***

Re: #JR5157201683

Anthony Stanley Shade

Dear Members of the Parole Board,

Because we're all busy people, I don't want to waste your time. I'll get right to the point. I've moved on from the evening that I was raped and tortured repeatedly by Pastor Tony and his friends. While I don't condone or think he should go unpunished for what he did to me and hundreds of other innocent women, I do not hate him or wish him ill will. I want Pastor Tony Shade to learn from his mistakes. God will judge him when it's his turn.

He robbed me of my innocence and stole my virginity, but he also blessed me with the one thing that I love and cherish the most, my son, Cooper. Cooper is my son, no one else's. Affectionate family titles are earned, not assigned. He will never be Cooper's father.

You've been assigned the difficult task of deciding if he is worthy of parole. I want you to consider all the chances that Tony had to change his ways. For over two years, or seven hundred and thirty days, or 17,531 hours, Tony could've chosen a different path. He could've stopped the pain he was causing all those women, but he didn't. Each year, more men participated in the Room than before, and each year, new women were recruited and abused. Those numbers don't lie, and they paint a pretty awful picture of a man who tortured women for selfish pleasure.

I wish you luck in making your decision, but no, I don't think he should ever get out of prison.

Thank you, Ivy Just Bass

***

To whom it may concern,

Lisa Darling Shade, the former wife of Pastor Tony Shade, asked me to mail this letter regarding the early release of JR5157201683, Anthony Stanley Shade's (short for ASS which I don't think is a coincidence).

Should Tony Shade be granted early parole? Hell no.

Should he be allowed to see the light of day? Hell no.

Should he be burned alive at the stake while the millions of women who suffered at his hands watch and cheer? Hell yes. I'll even host the barbecue.

Respectively, Jolene Just

Epilogue

Lisa

Howard had been right about not keeping secrets. Coming clean to Ivy and Jolene helped establish trust. Trust and respect were the foundation of healthy, solid relationships. Even though the conversation was nothing I imagined discussing, the guilt I would've carried around for the rest of my life would've caused me more stress and heartache. Our relationship required a clean slate to create something worth more than grudges and stress—family.

The adults promised each other that we'd prioritize our new relationships. I felt grateful for this opportunity to create a family, and even though I wanted to protect Camille and shield her from the evil that was her biological father, I also knew that these people were like me and Camille—innocent victims. No one deserved this heartache, and through my faith, I believed that while Tony poisoned our lives, he also brought us together. Ivy's philosophy of not letting one night affect the rest of her life resonated with me. Her unwavering strength impressed me. It was Tony's choices and influence that caused this tidal wave of pain, but it was my faith in God and the support of my 'family' that would give me the desire to love again.

The children embraced the new family dynamic much easier than any of the adults had expected. The questions Camille asked showed her innocence and how willing she was to adapt to the changes. "Why do I have to spend holidays with Cooper?"

"He's your half-brother."

"Why does he live so far away? Sam's brother sleeps in the same room as him. They even share the same toilet, which Sam says sucks."

"Camille, we don't say 'sucks' in our family. But, yes, some families live under the same roof, but some don't."

"So, Cooper will never ride the school bus with me?"

"No."

"Will Cooper ever share my bathroom?"

"Only if he comes to visit or we go to his house."

"Okay. Cooper smells better than Sam's brother does, and he doesn't pick on me."

I had my bad days–days that I didn't want to get out of bed and deal with the guilt. I blamed myself for not fighting back or saying something. I felt awful for not protecting the women that came into the room. I could still hear their screams. They begged me to unlock the Room's door, to free them from Tony's grasp. I looked the other way, ignored the cries, and pretended that their pain didn't bother me. I contributed to these women's torment by not stopping it.

Guilt settled in every corner, casting shadows on my life. Even hundreds of miles away, I still felt the weight of it resting on my shoulders. I couldn't forget.

On other days, I recognized the unconditional love in Camille's eyes, and I understood that the pain was worth *this* feeling. On those same days, gratitude filled my heart because I have a group of people whom I look forward to spending time with, whom I want to create memories with, and whom I love with my whole, cracked but stitched-together heart.

When I glance around my home, I see disarray. In the living room, wrapping paper liters the carpet, and big, genuine smiles rest on everyone's face. A half-eaten cake sits on the kitchen table while dirty dishes pile in the sink. Shoes and coats have been discarded in the entryway. The mess is a blessing that ten years ago I would never have imagined taking place under my roof. Laughter bounces off the walls of my modest home as my guests enjoy each other's company.

This group of people has chosen to create a family out of a jumble of strangers. We don't all share the same DNA. There isn't a hereditary gene that dominates all of us, like dark hair or pointed noses. We don't share the same last name or even know each other's middle names yet. We are a patchwork family, but our stitching is strong.

I don't see the hurt and anger that one man created years ago. I don't see him in their faces. I don't see him, lurking in the shadows trying to disrupt our family gatherings. I will only give that man credit for bringing us together. Without him, we wouldn't have each other.

I've had to accept my life, forgive the past, and move forward to enjoy the present, and it hasn't always been easy. But I'm learning.

After Camille blew out the seven candles on her heavily frosted birthday cake, Cooper asked her what she wished for.

"Last year, for my birthday, Mom baked me a bright red firetruck cake, and when I blew out my six candles, I wished for a brother or a sister." With complete innocence, Camille grinned at the group seated around the kitchen table. "And it came true. I got you, Coop. So this year, I wished for a daddy." Camille looked directly at Howard.

An awkward laugh escaped Howard's lips. Everyone looked at each other, wondering what the appropriate response was. My cheeks flashed to a scarlet-red color. Maybe I did believe in happy endings after all.

Dear Reader,

Thank you for taking the time to read my latest creation. If you prefer a happy *Hallmark* ending, stop at this page. Close the book, pour yourself a glass of wine, and leave me a glowing review on *Goodreads*.

or...

If you're naturally curious like Jamie Lee Curtis who plays Laurie Strode in *Friday the 13th* movies, turn the page. But remember that I warned you.

I knew it.

Epilogue – Part 2

Lisa

When I asked Camille what she wanted for her seventh birthday, her only response was a party. She insisted on inviting our new family. She dreamed of playing Pin the Tail on the Donkey and having a sleepover with her new big brother. Everyone would need to travel to the Black Hills so I needed to explain that to Camille.

"If we host a family party, we'll have to see when and if everyone can come. Can you wait to open your presents for a few weeks, Camille?"

"Mom, you underestimate me."

"Where did you learn that word?"

"School. Mrs. Wagner says that because we are short, adults underestimate how smart we are, so we need to prove it."

"I like this Mrs. Wagner. She's a good egg."

"She's not an egg. She's a teacher. Duh. Anyway, let's call everyone. I can wait."

Even though we phoned everyone, Camille insisted on sending out party invitations. I stamped and addressed four Barbie-themed birthday party invitations. After Howard received his card, he asked if I'd help him pick out the perfect doll for Camille. Ivy, Michael, and Cooper—the second invitation—picked up Jolene—the third invite—and made a road trip to the Black Hills. Only one invitation went unacknowledged.

Between my house and Howard's, every guest room was occupied. Camille begged Cooper to stay at our house so she could share a bathroom with him like her friend Sam did with his brother.

When we retreated to the living room to enjoy our cake and ice cream, the doorbell rang. Howard jumped up to answer the door. Since he spent so much time at our house, it was second nature for him to help.

"Are you expecting someone, Lisa?" Ivy looked at me for reassurance. She was the only one who acknowledged the announcement of a new arrival. Everyone else was too engrossed in watching Camille open her gifts on the living room floor.

"No." I half-mumbled. I wasn't *expecting* someone. Did I *invite* someone else? Yes. That was a different question.

"Lisa?" Howard called from the front door. "Someone is here for you." I recognized a question in his tone while he attempted to be polite to the unannounced guest looming in the doorway.

As I rose from the couch, my heart beat double time. I smoothed out the wrinkles in my coordinating jacket and slacks. I tucked the strands of hair behind my ears. Appearances were important. Quickly, I said a silent prayer that Ivy and Jolene would be receptive to our new, surprise guest considering all they've suffered.

The last of our patchwork family had arrived.

Acknowledgements

When you love something, it shows. Excitement and enthusiasm exude from every pore. I love story-telling. Every aspect of it thrills me, from the birth of a character to hearing from a reader. I enjoy it all!

When I created the fictional character, Pastor Tony Shade, I asked myself: Who is someone every community respects and admires? A pastor. One of my goals when writing a book is to make my fictional world believable, even with inconceivable ideas. It's what keeps the reader engaged and entertained.

Even though the protagonist is a pastor—a man of God—by no means does that imply I'm not a believer. In fact, the opposite is true. God has always been a part of my life. I can't recite a Bible verse on demand, but I believe in His teachings and know I'll meet Him someday in Heaven. I credit God for my blessings.

Next up on my long thank-you list are my readers. You fly through the pages in record time, even though it takes me over a year to write it. I appreciate your passion for reading, your support of my dream, and your referral to your family and friends. There is no bigger compliment.

To my beta team—Gena, Nancy, Betsy, and Pam—you're the first ones to read each creation. I can't thank you enough for reading past your bedtime to help me reach my deadlines. I value your input and suggestions. You guys are the absolute best.

To my ARC team–Katie, Denise, Jenny, Heidi, Mel, Nikki, Susan, Liz, Samantha, Michelle, JLo, KHo, Jammers, Bethany, JFlo, Lindsey, Krissy, Chris, Erika, Kari, Cindy, Farah, Sarah, Sarah J, Kristin, Monica, Stacy, Dawn, Beth, Nicelle, Danielle, and Rachel–you're my peep squad. Mighty, little cheerleaders with colorful pompoms and booming voices! Through Bookstagram, I found you–my kind of people. You guys make every step of this process so much fun.

Comma Caramie, you are my editor, friend, and soul sister. God had a plan when I randomly reached out to you years ago, and only He knew what an essential role you'd play in my life. Thank you for adding one million commas and answering my endless questions. You are an angel, and I couldn't do it without you!

The saying goes, *Don't judge a book by its cover*, but I want you to! I'm proud of my book covers, thanks to Sandy Fritz. After we finalized Sandy Fritz's creation for the cover of *Secrets Maple Keeps,* I knew we'd work together again. Thank you, Sandy, for hearing what I *don't* say. (Are you psychic?) You are beyond talented.

I wouldn't be able to pursue my dream without the unwavering support of my husband. The man deserves a medal for constantly listening to me ramble on and on about fictional characters who he could care less about. He believes in me and cheers me on, even when I'm frustrated. I hit the jackpot with this guy! I love you, honey!

Thank you to my two sons for letting Mom lock herself in her room or 'go to bed early' to write. You are my inspiration! I love you unconditionally and am so proud to be your mom.

Thankfully, my life has been blessed with a wonderful pack of women, whom I fondly refer to as my Witches. Because my sense of humor is slightly off, I filter their names and stories in my books. It's one of the perks of being a storyteller. While the storyline is fictional, I throw in a bit of nonfiction to make them giggle. Thanks, Witches, for bringing fun and adventure into my life. I'd be lost without your friendships.

Thank you for choosing my book over the million other possibilities. You keep reading, and I'll keep writing!

Cheers, Emersyn Park

Recipe

Beef Wellington

Preheat the oven to 400. Combine the first seven ingredients and then set aside:

  2 eggs beaten

  1 pd of hamburger

  4 Tbsp bread crumbs

  3 Tbsp dried parsley

  1 tsp of salt

  1/2 cup of Grey Poupon mustard

In a large saucepan, melt 3 Tbsp of butter. Add 1 small onion and 8 oz of baby bella mushrooms. When tender, turn down the heat and add 4 cloves of minced garlic, 1 tsp basil, and 1/2 cup of beef broth. Turn up the heat and cook until the liquid is reduced. Cool.

On a lightly greased cooking sheet, cut a package of puffed pastry into six sections. Spread mushroom mix and then cheese of your choice. Then roll the meat mixture into six balls to place on top.

Pull up the corners of the pastry and pinch the edges together. Place on the pan with seams down. Brush with 2 Tbsp of melted butter. Cut 4 slits onto the top of the pastry.

Bake for 30-40 minutes. Serve with gravy.

"I'm not a great cook. I just have fabulous recipes!" ~Emersyn Park